Fires of Deception

Book 3 in the Carnal Fever Trilogy

Riley Kade

Manifold Publishing LLC

Paperback: 978-1-957572-05-5

E-book: 978-1-957572-06-2

Book Cover Design by ebooklaunch.com

Internal design by J.W. Donley

Manifold Publishing LLC

315 Prospect St.

Unit 5206

Bellingham, WA 98227

Contents

1. The Fallout — 1
2. Friends of Arlington — 11
3. Strange Encounters — 21
4. Forces too great — 30
5. Bold Choices — 44
6. Side Effects — 52
7. Thin Walls — 60
8. Misconceptions and Breakthroughs — 66
9. Gloves Off — 79
10. Memories So Sweet — 87
11. Trouble in Paradise — 90
12. Secrets and Seduction — 102
13. An Explosive Revelation — 121
14. Running Hot and Heavy — 136
15. Under Pressure — 153
16. Heating Up — 165
17. Where Armies Clash — 177
18. A Reunion Old and New — 191
19. The Sweetest Scent — 206
20. A Perfect Day — 221
21. Things Found in the River — 230
22. A Gamble — 242
23. The Siphon Estate — 247
24. A Dual Interrogation — 250
25. In the Eye of the Hurricane — 272
26. From the Ruins — 281
27. The Little Things — 287

Acknowledgments — 299
About the Author — 301

I dedicate this book to the people who supported me the most. You know who you are.

Chapter 1

The Fallout

It struck Sadie that the biggest lessons life had to offer, no one ever seemed to mention. Like the way love exists as a physical presence in your body. The way it sits in your gut and beats in your heart. The way you notice it most when it's far away.

Were these things which some people secretly knew and the initiated were sworn to secrecy? And if she'd known ahead of time, would she have done anything differently?

Yes. She would have. If she could do it again, she sure as hell wouldn't have wasted so much of the last year forcing her and Jimmy to keep their distance. Not if she'd known they'd end up on opposite sides of the country, contributing in different ways to the United resistance against the fascist government. With Jimmy back on the east coast, absorbed into Amadi's make-shift army, he felt a million miles away from Arlington, Washington, and Sadie's little side mission.

Sadie rolled over in bed, her gaze landing on Patricia. Her friend looked younger in sleep – void of her stylish make-up and clothes. It gave her a soft quality which made Sadie want to curl up in her arms for comfort, but getting that close wasn't possible if there was any risk they might actually touch skin.

Patricia's lack of a sexual history or interest also made it possible for Sadie, with her succubus vision, to not become distracted every time she looked at her. Not that it was much of a struggle these days to suppress the onslaught of information she received about people's sex lives. She'd gotten better at such things over the months since her Becoming, when she'd transitioned from human to succubus.

Patricia blinked open sleep-filled eyes. "Is it morning?"

"Not sure. Couldn't sleep," Sadie said, and flinched at the rasp in her voice. Apparently, her throat was still sore from crying.

Patricia ran her fingers through Sadie's hair, taking care not to touch her skin. But Sadie rolled to her back, afraid the empathy in her friend's eyes would activate all the big emotions in her. It was a new day. And when she got out of bed, she was going to pull herself together and be ready to contribute something useful.

They'd rolled into Arlington late last night after a humiliating, long day of travel with Sadie sniffling pathetically to herself. She hated that Troy and Hetia had seen her like that. The fact that Jimmy wasn't with them made it perfectly clear what was causing the emotion, so there seemed no need to explain. Patricia had been doing her best to comfort her, while the other two mostly averted their eyes.

Hetia seemed the most embarrassed. Apparently, the skilled fighter and warrior for the underground resistance force squirmed at the sight of crying women. Troy, rather, kept throwing genuinely worried glances her way and merely seemed to be giving her space out of politeness.

At least they were a well-rounded team for this investigation. Afterall, they didn't have long to uncover the truth of what happened to the bomb the Coalition government commissioned fifteen years ago and what, if anything, it had to do with the death of Hetia's father the same day. Two weeks, Amadi had said, before he would need them back for the next battle. And given that The Coalition had been planning this war for decades – the powerful Siphon, Maddox, and Griffith families leading the efforts for feeder dominance – having weapons like Hetia would be essential if The United had any real hope of fighting back.

"I'm going to take a shower," Sadie said, kicking her way out of the covers.

A minute later, she stepped into the warm water, letting it run down her face as she imagined it washing away the past twenty-four hours. She wanted to go back to just before Jimmy had told her he wasn't coming with them and pause time. Back to their departing encounter. They'd stayed up most of the night and he had consumed her with an insatiable urgency, as if he were the succubus. Between that and what had happened with Troy just the night before, she probably wouldn't be hungry for days. Her sadness mixed with desire at the memories, leaving her as confused as she was overwhelmed.

Sadie cleaned between her legs, washing away the last scent of Jimmy before running her palms over the various markings on her flesh. As terrifying as it had been to be a captive of The Coalition, the moment it had created with Troy was still playing in her mind. And in her body. She traced the outline of his handprints on her hip and arm. He hadn't meant to bruise her, she was sure, but she liked the evidence of what had happened.

It was remarkable to think that just a few days ago she had been happily pretending to be a part of The Coalition – making friends with the Siphon family as she and Troy infiltrated their organization, Troy using his existing connections to bring her in as his alleged lover. And now, not only had their ruse been discovered, but the *his lover* part of their scheme was no longer a lie. At least not completely.

Sadie dried off and rubbed at the mirror until she could see her reflection. Her eyes finally looked clear and her face clean. Auburn curls hung in wet clumps around her shoulders, dripping tiny droplets over her generous curves. Despite a lifetime spent working her parents' farm, puberty had brought an outward softness to her body which she'd cherished ever since.

She froze as her own image of herself was abruptly overpowered by someone else's. Sadie knew immediately that it was coming from Troy. She could feel him from the room next door. He was awake and thinking about her intensely, which was the only thing that had made her aware of it. She saw her own features through his desire as she ran her hand over her breasts while he imagined doing the same.

The bathrooms must have had a shared wall, because she usually couldn't make out specific images unless someone was close by, and even then, she often had to be looking at them. But when someone was stroking himself as he fixated on her, walls didn't seem to matter. Sadie's breath hitched as she got swept up in Troy's desire, and suddenly she wasn't sure if all the feeding of the past few days would be enough to prevent her from wanting more. It seemed her little encounter with Troy was affecting her almost as much as it was him.

Sadie understood why Jimmy had decided not to come with them, though she hated his cool logic that the two of them needed time to develop as people. Even if he was right, she loathed the maturity of it. Why couldn't they just chase their desires? She slicked a finger between her legs as Troy stroked faster. Why did they have to do the right thing? It was just stupid. People were animals, after all. And who was getting hurt really if they had just stayed together and lost themselves in it?

Troy was getting close. She could feel his arousal sharpening.

It had been an awkward moment when they'd arrived and had to sort out the room situation. Patricia had wanted to stay with Troy, but Hetia hadn't wanted to stay with Sadie. Since Sadie had shut down the idea of Troy and her rooming together, that had left only Patricia as a safe choice for her. Which put Troy and Hetia together. Since they were decent friends, that decision didn't seem too uncomfortable.

Sadie rocked against her hand, chasing her own pleasure now. She clearly couldn't have roomed with Troy, though. Yes, Jimmy had been right that there was *something* between them, but as they'd only recently moved away from outright hostility towards each other, it wasn't like they could just cuddle up in bed together.

Especially since a part of her was irrationally annoyed with Troy. After all, would Jimmy have really wanted the time apart if he hadn't seen them talking? Hadn't known they'd slept together? Though such a thought made no sense given Sadie had been sexual with dozens of other people since she and Jimmy had gotten together – why was Troy any different?

The man in question bucked into his hand as his climax hit and Sadie sped up the circling of her own finger as she pictured him standing hard and wet under the shower a few feet away. Okay, she was more attracted to Troy than most of the other people she'd slept with, and yes, he'd definitely gotten under her skin. But how did Jimmy know all that, anyway?

It wasn't like Troy was all that special, with his clear charisma and ability to fill out a finely tailored suit in a way that caught everyone's attention. His thoughtfulness and skill as her partner during their time working as spies together. His stupid shaggy brown hair that clumped a little too perfectly around his face and a nice jaw and—*Fuck.* Sadie clamped her thighs around her hand and braced against the counter as her hips convulsed.

But really, Troy was just another guy she'd once fed from. And now they were back to being co-conspirators on a shared mission to uncover some hidden secrets of Hetia's father's death. Which would hopefully reveal something about those plans to build a bomb that they'd stolen from Siphon's office. They weren't here to kiss and make up for all the snark and mistrust they'd shared during their last pursuit.

Sadie washed her hands and cupped her sensitive nipples, trying to coax them to relax. It didn't work.

When a knock came on the door of their hotel room twenty minutes later, Patricia was taking her own shower, so Sadie pulled on her sweater and took a deep breath. She was going to have to face Troy sometime given they would be spending a lot of time together, so she wiped all emotion from her expression and opened the door.

Hetia was standing there with her feet spread wide and her hands behind her back. She looked like a soldier called to attention. A very pretty soldier in tight pants and a miniature-sized utility belt. Her light grey eyes flicked to Sadie's damp hair as an image of her wet in the shower bloomed in Hetia's mind.

How had her life become this complicated?

Sadie gave her a small smile. As expected, Hetia just bobbed her head and got right to business. "I remembered something," she said, and Sadie stepped aside to let her in.

Hetia handed her a bag. At first, she thought it had something to do with what Hetia was going to tell her, but then the sweet aroma of warm bread told her otherwise. Sadie made the bed and sat down in the middle. Hetia didn't join her, preferring to pace as Sadie started on breakfast.

"The day my dad left, before our visit to the Siphon estate, I asked where we were going," Hetia said without looking at her. "He said he had to go *open a door for a friend*." She enunciated each word of this slowly and with a note of uncertainty. Then she paused for a while before adding, "I was distracted at the time, and later I'd forgotten he'd told me anything at all about that trip."

"That goes with something from Mia Siphon's memory," Sadie began, but stopped as the front door opened. Troy stepped in and they paused. He nodded to her, and she returned a quick non-verbal greeting before hurriedly looking away.

Sadie cleared her throat. "Umm... I forgot what— Oh, right, in Mia's memory of the meeting between Congressman Siphon and your father: he said something about your dad having the keys. And he needed access to the inner city."

Hetia glared at her and Sadie froze uncertainly. The woman hadn't taken the news of Sadie's memory-reading abilities very well, and she was glad that Amadi had warned her off telling Hetia about her other skills. Sadie wasn't the best at reading Hetia's emotions, but she guessed she was probably unhappy about the fact that Sadie might have read *her* memories the night they'd met – the one time they'd slept together.

She hadn't, but Sadie couldn't come up with the right way to bring this up. *Hey, Hetia, remember that really great night we had together before you decided to leave without saying goodbye and shut me out completely, until that one time you kissed me in the middle of a battle – which I'm totally not thrilled, hurt or confused by – well, I just wanted to let you know that I didn't know how to memory dive back then and so didn't see a peep of your private history that you protect so much.*

"What?" Sadie asked Hetia, as she continued to stare at her.

"Is there anything else from that memory you haven't shared?" Hetia said, revealing the source of her mood had nothing to do with their personal history after all.

"Oh. Sorry." Sadie hadn't realized she hadn't told them everything. "You're right. I should have mentioned it sooner." Hetia's posture softened and Sadie was surprised to see the woman display her emotions so clearly. Investigating her father's death definitely had her on edge.

Troy kicked off his shoes and joined Sadie on the bed. She shifted to put some space between them and handed him some bread without making eye contact, while Hetia moved forward to grab some bread as well. She continued to look sullen over the fact her revelation hadn't been as helpful as she'd clearly hoped.

Now only a few feet away, Sadie couldn't help but look her up and down as Hetia stared at the comforter in thought. If only she could alleviate her stress in some way, but of course, any comforting would involve Hetia letting someone else in, which clearly wasn't going to happen.

"Your memory still helps," Sadie tried. "We weren't sure if your dad's, umm, disappearance, was for sure related to that meeting. But this confirms it is. If it was the last thing he said to you..."

Hetia just blinked at her, the brief moment of showing her emotions swept back under the surface. They turned as Patricia came out of the bathroom, fully dressed and with her hair slicked back in a classy updo. Elegant lines of brown eyeliner matched her hair and her fashionable dress was in line with her usual look, only shifted for the cooler weather. After the arduous trip to Arlington, she looked back to her old self.

Troy smiled at her and Patricia returned the expression. Sadie followed the lines of light flowing between them, taking in the way it had changed. Patricia and Troy had been friends when she'd met them, and the pulsing green line which indicated such was stronger than ever, but the tiny black love line was newer and growing stronger by the day.

"We should get to know the inner city today, if that's where Siphon showed interest," Troy said, drawing Sadie's gaze to him as he looked to her. They held eye contact for the first time since two nights ago. He'd dreamed of her all last night, and the carnal images stood out brightly. Sadie's lips parted and his gaze flicked to them. For a long moment, Sadie couldn't remember what he'd just said.

Patricia cleared her throat. Sitting next to Troy, she reached for the bag of bread. It was empty.

"Sorry. I took two pieces. I didn't think," Troy said and handed her a half-eaten slice. They smiled again at each other and Sadie noticed the tiny love line pulse. She knew something had been developing between them, but they weren't sleeping together. Her friend was uninterested in sex and it didn't look like that had changed. She seemed shy about sharing what was going on though, and they hadn't actually gotten to talk about it.

Sadie tried to be happy for her, but she felt a pang of jealousy at their sweet smiles. Partially because she wished she and Troy could be like that. And partly because she missed Jimmy.

"Yeah, the inner city," Sadie said. "Jimmy and I spent some time there when we were here before. Arlington has the largest concentration of nymphs out of anywhere in the U.S. and most of them are clumped in the middle. It's a beautiful place." Sadie smiled at the memory of all the concentrated nymph power that made the city what it was.

"It sounds like it's big," Troy said. "We'll need to talk to the right people if we're going to get anywhere fast. Who would know—"

"Oh!" Sadie cut in. "In the center there's like a little museum built around this catastrophe with a fire that happened years back. We met a woman who works there. I bet she could give us a rundown of local history."

"Perfect. We can start there." Patricia dusted some crumbs away and stood up, enthusiastic in a way Sadie hadn't seen since Seattle.

"We'll have to wait," Hetia said, putting a halt to Sadie and Troy moving to rise.

"Why?" Sadie asked as they all looked at the blond woman with the same question.

"Because it's 4 a.m."

Sadie glanced to the window, still dark behind the curtain.

"Oh," Patricia said, and they fell into awkward silence. Apparently, not one of them had slept well last night.

"We can meet back here in a few hours." Hetia was already moving toward the door as she spoke.

"Where are you headed?" Sadie asked.

"I'll take another walk. Get a layout before everyone wakes up." Hetia bobbed her head goodbye and opened the door.

"Wait," Patricia called as she slid on her heels. "Can you point me toward that bakery?" The two women disappeared together, leaving Sadie and Troy rather abruptly alone.

Sadie squirmed off the bed like it was lava, but Troy didn't budge, and so she couldn't avoid looking at him. "What about you?" she asked.

He didn't respond right away, just ran a hand through his hair in the attractive way he did. "Well... if we have a few hours to kill. I thought you might want to feed for the day." He swallowed, and then added in a less-certain voice, "Off me."

Sadie's lips parted as her whole body grew involuntarily hot. She hadn't expected him to directly proposition her. He'd been acting so shy. Though she had spent most of yesterday crying...

"I'm... not hungry yet," she said in a quiet voice.

Troy stood up, coming to stand in front of her. "We could do other things. Anything you want," he whispered. This was far from his usual playful snark. "If you just ask..." The image of her tied in front of him, her knees hiked up and legs spread, desperate for him to touch her, burned in his thoughts. He went hard, despite having just climaxed in the shower.

Sadie felt her face heat at the memory. If it had been Jimmy who'd found her like that, things would have been different. But being at the mercy of a man she'd been competing and arguing with for weeks made her feel just a little too vulnerable. And now he was offering himself up, so sure she would want him.

Which she did, but...

"That won't be necessary." She crossed her arms. "I can find someone later." Sadie stood up straighter, trying to ignore her red face.

Troy looked disbelieving for a second and then he, too, changed his posture. He adjusted himself, but the bulge in his pants wasn't something he could just tuck away. "Alright." He took a deep breath and when he spoke again, his tone had switched to match hers.

"Good. I—" He cleared his throat as he too flushed. "I won't have to waste time here then."

Sadie blanched at the words, already regretting her dispassionate response to his proposition. "Fine," she said and gave a shrug as she slid her hands in her pockets in an attempt to look casual.

"Fine," he repeated. Troy stepped around her slowly while she did everything she could not to react as he passed so close. A minute later, while Sadie was still panting and feeling guilty, she felt Troy back in the shower, thinking of her.

She'd known the intensity of them sleeping together when she'd been so hungry was going to have consequences. Consequences that affected them both. Though it seemed she'd made her bed. Sadie flopped back on the mattress with a groan, heavy with their shared arousal. And now she was going to lie in it.

Chapter 2

Friends of Arlington

They'd taken rooms near the train station, close to where Sadie and Jimmy had stayed shortly after they'd left home together, figuring it would help her get her bearings. The first time she'd been here, Sadie had been shocked and overwhelmed by the hustle and bustle of it all. Now, as they stepped out into the open-air marketplace that stretched the long expanse of a wide road which led from the train station deep into the heart of the city, Sadie had a very different emotion.

She was surrounded by the sounds of the place she'd been during one of the happiest times in her life. Jimmy and she had explored this city for weeks as they were falling in love, or at least into a new kind of love then they'd had growing up together. And the air smelled of that time. Hot spices of cinnamon and cloves poured out of steamy ovens and Sadie felt again as if there were a Jimmy-shaped hole in her heart.

"We'll head inward a bit and then go up," she told the group, blinking away the tears that were threatening to return.

"Up?" Troy asked.

"The city is very vertical, and all crossings into its core happen through the bridges on level four," she explained as she led them through the crowd, while the tall buildings towered on either side of them in one solid block.

"There aren't any buildings that aren't attached to the whole. And all the housing is on floors two and three throughout the entire city. These bridges," Sadie gestured above them, "turn the place into a connected web. You can see the buildings are partially nymph-grown, but they become actual trees as we go in deeper."

The architecture had a coherent theme, molded by tree nymphs to follow somewhat natural lines. It was a work of art, and Sadie was glad to have a reason to revisit it.

She took them to an elevator between two buildings. Patricia and Troy peered out the window with curiosity, but Hetia seemed even more withdrawn than usual. "Look at that view," Sadie said, trying to pull the woman from what were probably heavy thoughts.

Hetia stared at the tiny sliver of city they could see as the sun lit it up. She nodded in appreciation and then, in a rare move, smiled at Sadie. "It's lovely."

Sadie returned the smile, hoping that the secrets they were trying to uncover would bring the woman some closure, and not further pain. She hated seeing her like this.

Hetia's smile was gone by the time they emerged onto the fourth floor and into a dense and colorful garden. As they followed a path between buildings, it almost felt as if they were outside. Vines snaked up the pillars that supported the upper floors, and flowers coated nearly everything.

Several flower nymphs, marked by their colorful dress, looked at them as they passed. Every one of them smiled and waved. It was hard not to feel a lightness of spirit as they walked through the gardens, which were clearly imbued with a nymph presence. Sadie had felt this before, though perhaps not in the exact same way. When nymphs were wrapped fully in their element, the place just seemed to feel even more like what it was. And this place was a vibrant wonderland.

Even Hetia seemed noticeably giddy by the time they'd moved on. "I can't believe I've never been here," she said to the group. "This is a place worth visiting."

Hetia's engagement surprised Sadie, but she wasn't going to waste the opportunity. "Wait till you see what's next," she told her as they crossed one of the elaborately decorated sky bridges. "Have you ever been in a real nymph forest?"

Hetia glanced at her. "A few times," she said, and Sadie caught a quick glance of an old sexual memory. The faded image of a younger Hetia pinning a tiny woman against a tree momentarily dominated the more recent interactions with Sadie that had become Hetia's predominant feature whenever Sadie looked at her.

"Anything worth sharing?" Sadie asked.

To her shock, Hetia gave her a devilish grin and then began to talk about the time Amadi had taken her to visit his partner, Mae, for the summer, just outside the redwoods in California. Hetia's tale went on for miles while Troy and Patricia dropped back, lost in their own conversation.

"And they never noticed you were gone every night?" Sadie asked.

"Well... they probably did, but they were busy enough with their own adventures, I'm sure." Hetia held up her hands as if to say she didn't want to think about it. "The unspoken breakfast rule was for everyone to pretend they'd slept. And then to separate all afternoon to work on separate... *projects*. Meaning, take a five-hour nap."

Sadie laughed. "Sounds like a good time."

"It was." Hetia nodded. "It was the first time I'd ever just—" She paused, looking thoughtful as her smile slowly faded.

The break in conversation caused Sadie to look around. She'd been so distracted by Hetia's attention that she'd barely noticed the change in their surroundings. The hard corners of the buildings had morphed into soft, free-flowing shapes until they were walking through living, nymph-altered trees as tall as the buildings of the outer city. The effects of entering the heart of the forest consumed her senses in a rush, and the conversation died all around. There was a stillness that felt heavy, and a silence that drew the attention to the songs of various birds.

They crossed a bridge from one tree to the next and, as opposed to all the previous such connections, this arch was made up of the intricately woven branches of the two trees entwined with each other, as if holding hands.

Once on the other side, the heavy serenity of the place was accompanied by the creeping feeling that the stillness was teeming with life. Every tree was now filled with little, nest-like homes. Some nymphs smiled or nodded politely as they passed, the rest ignored them.

On the whole, it was a much more positive reaction than she'd had coming through here with Jimmy. These nymphs weren't too friendly with humans, after all, but as their group consisted of two human feeders and two nymphs, they apparently weren't going to receive the same glares humans did. Not every feeder could tell someone's species on sight, but as Sadie had learned last time, the inner city had elder nymphs at the entrances who spread the word when humans came in. How they managed this was just another mystery of the place.

"Are we getting close?" Patricia whispered from behind her as Sadie stopped for the fifth time to look around. She knew exactly where they were going, but she was less sure on where they were.

"Excuse me, ma'am?" Troy said. "We heard there was a museum nearby here, regarding the fire that—"

The passing woman turned her full attention to Troy. "The museum. Yes, it's around the old tree. You just go that way and hang a left. You can't miss it." She stepped forward until she was a mere foot from him and then boldly put a hand on Troy's chest. Sadie was surprised he didn't flinch at this invasion of a universally respected personal bubble. "It's the oldest and biggest tree in the whole city." The woman smiled. "Just go that way and hang a left. I promise you won't miss it," she repeated.

Troy just smiled warmly at her and took her hand in his, subtly removing it from his body. "Thank you," he said, and Sadie noticed the way he maneuvered himself away so it wouldn't appear rude to depart. She'd seen him sidestep female attention like this during their time spying on The Coalition. He seemed to have a knack with people, both in getting in and in getting out. She secretly admired this about him, but it did annoy her as he stepped into the lead. Her knowledge of the city was one of the main things she was contributing to their mission, and she was currently failing to be a good guide. Unfortunately, this place was a lot bigger than she'd realized.

Glaring at the back of Troy's head, she followed him to a giant spiral staircase wrapped around a tree large enough to enclose an entire house. Strings of yellow lights looped along the staircase railing, lighting their path as they circled the tree to the bottom.

Toward the base, the outer bark was peeled and carved in places, displaying the history of the city. Nymphs had grown and constructed the place hundreds of years ago, but for a while it had turned into a place in which humans and feeders lived together.

Sadie slowed to trace the pictures with her fingers as she read. The turn of the century had marked a high period for scientific advancement, in which nymphs and feeders had worked to mix their abilities, creating novel devices. The free-standing glowing lights were a remnant of that time. Sadie thought about the boxes only succubi could open, a product of a succubus and stone nymph working together. She'd also had another taste of a succubi and stone collaboration when a few days ago, someone had attached a vibrating flattened rock between her legs that somehow knew how to turn off when a person was close to orgasm.

She blushed at the memory of being strung up with it for so many hours, at her desperation for Troy to finish her when he'd arrived on his rescue mission. "What is it?" Troy asked, coming to look curiously at the script she was glaring at without actually reading.

"Nothing," she said, speeding up her pace to the bottom and ignoring the rest of the history.

She knew what came next, anyway. A group of humans had set a fire, intending to burn down the tree and a chunk of the inner city. They'd released a statement that nymphs were becoming too powerful. Sadie remembered *that* in particular, as she'd been shocked at such intentional violence and hate. She was less surprised these days by such things. Last summer felt like a lifetime ago.

Sadie looped around the base of the tree until she was looking at the final scene. Her heart stopped. How could she have forgotten? The last panel was a list of everyone who had helped rebuild the city after the fire. Including the handful of powerful human feeder families who'd swept in with their benevolent assistance. The Siphon,

Maddox, and Griffith families were listed with an extra special thank you and deemed as *Friends of Arlington* for all time.

Sadie kicked herself for forgetting she'd seen Siphon's name here. She recalled now the way she'd even remarked on it out loud at the time, since she had recognized the outspoken congressman even back then. And now, she knew that those three names together signaled something even more sinister. The three powerhouse families that had set this war in motion generations ago had provided assistance immediately following the fire. And if they'd had their fingers in the events surrounding that tragedy, it could mean nothing good.

She cleared her throat and looked around at Patricia and Troy, who were both nearby. "I – uh, found something." Maybe she wouldn't mention she'd already seen this part, but her stomach clenched in guilt at her clumsiness. It wasn't like they had all the time in the world, after all. Not if they wanted to get back to Amadi's army before the next battle began.

As the other two read, Sadie searched her memory for if there was anything else of importance that she'd forgotten. She was desperate to be as useful as she could.

"They were here?" Patricia said as Troy traced the outline of people holding hands around the tree in a symbol of their collective work.

"Yep," he said. "Smells like trouble."

Sadie wandered back up the stairwell a ways to find Hetia while Troy and Patricia talked through the important news. The woman was standing in front of one of the panels describing the fire, but her eyes weren't moving. "I have something down here. It seems the Coalition power families helped rebuild after the fire," Sadie told her. Hetia didn't budge.

Sadie stepped forward to look at the place Hetia was staring. Sadie read the text several times before noticing the date. "Fifteen years ago? The same week that—" Sadie stopped. Troy and Patricia stepped up next to them, and Sadie, dumbstruck, just pointed. "The date."

They all looked at it until Patricia said, "The fire – happened the week your father disappeared. The week Siphon asked for his help."

They were silent a minute. Sadie couldn't believe this. Well, if they'd come here to learn about a disappearance fifteen years ago, it seemed they'd come to the right place. It satisfied her that she'd suggested just the right person to interview first, but what the hell did the disappearance of Eirik Pierce, Hetia's father, have to do with that fire? She suddenly wasn't sure they wanted to know.

Sadie put a hand tentatively on Hetia's back, and her attention snapped to focus on the group.

"Smart. Offering help. It's perfectly in line with their attempt to ally nymphs with them in their war against humans," Hetia said, responding to Sadie's earlier news.

"Some vigilante humans attack. They offer assistance." Patricia waved a hand as if to say, *and voila.*

"It also says here that for ten years after, humans weren't even allowed in the inner city. Way to jump in when tensions were high," Troy pointed out.

Sadie had the horrible thought then that Hetia's father might have died in the fire, and she wondered if that was exactly what Hetia was thinking.

"First time visiting?" a woman asked from below. She wore the same brown colors that marked her as a local, only she was dressed more formally.

"No, we met last summer," Sadie said, nodding politely. "I came back to show my friends this beautiful museum."

The woman faltered in returning her smile. "The museum is the remnants of a tragedy."

"No. Of course. I just mean, I was—" Sadie tried to correct while Troy stepped in.

"She means that she's been enthralled by Arlington ever since she'd stepped foot in it. She's been raving about the beauty of the city for months but wanted to show us that creating it has had a history of struggle. No one who comes here should overlook that." Troy's words sounded genuine, even if they were not fully true. The woman relaxed.

"Well, we all lost something or someone in that fire, but none of it erases the power of what we've built over the years." She gestured for them to follow her and led the way over to a small plaque; one of many scattered around the base of the tree.

"This was put in five years ago," the woman said, taking them to a nearby slab with further history. "Baton Rouge has been using Arlington as a model, and they're growing bigger every day." She beamed.

Sadie and Troy nodded politely. Hetia just stared, and Patricia asked, "May I inquire, the men who started the fire, were they ever caught?"

"Oh." The woman seemed obviously disappointed they weren't asking more about Baton Rouge.

"It's just that, I'm wondering if they're still a threat?" Patricia added, realizing she'd fumbled.

"Yes, the men were caught. But that same night, they disappeared from their cells. Most people believe they are dead or fled the state. And nothing like the fire has happened since." She smiled at Patricia. "I wouldn't worry. That time is behind us."

"Are there any pictures of the men?" Sadie asked.

"Umm. No." The woman blinked in surprise.

"None were taken when they were arrested?" Sadie asked. She couldn't be sure that their identities were relevant in any way, but they had few leads to go on.

"There were pictures taken," the woman said slowly, her eyes narrowing with every word, "only they, too, disappeared."

"I'm sorry, I didn't catch your name?" Troy offered her his hand.

"Annie Black," she said, accepting the handshake.

"We weren't being totally honest before," Troy told her. "This woman lost her parents in a house fire some years ago. We're helping her investigate what she believes to be their murder." Sadie blinked at the fast lie, but tamed her expression quickly to play along. "The case was never investigated due to low evidence," Troy continued, "but she believes she might have seen one of the men."

The woman looked honestly pained at this story, and Sadie had to fight through another wave of guilt. "I'm sorry for your loss. I know what it's like to have fire take the things you love." She dropped her professional stance, sinking into one hip and biting at a fingernail. "I have a friend... a guy who thinks he saw them. He was working nearby when the first flames went up. I can give you his address." She thought a minute. "He's a bit reclusive, but I'm sure if you tell him your story, he would help."

Annie pulled a pen and paper out of her breast pocket and scribbled something before handing it to Troy. "Thank you," he said. "And I'd love to hear about the rest of the museum. I'll have to come back sometime."

She smiled and the group moved to depart, except for Hetia, who seemed to be thinking something over. "Anything else?" the woman prodded.

There was a pause as Hetia finished her thought. "Trees are more stable than buildings. And the city was built centuries ago, but... do you know if the inner city contracts earthquake nymphs before building new structures?"

"Not anymore. They did before choosing this location, of course. And the outer city does for any building repairs. But the last time we needed such an opinion here was during the fire. Are you... looking for work?"

"Yes, possibly. Do you know who I would talk to about it?" Hetia asked.

"Certainly. The office is just next to the inner city hall." Annie scribbled a note for Hetia and handed it over. "Anything else?"

"No. Thank you, Annie." Troy said before leading the way back up the stairs.

They reached the upper platform and formed a circle to face each other.

"I'm going to find out if my father was contracted by the city," Hetia said without preamble.

"The rest of us can go interview this guy about the attackers," Patricia suggested, and the others nodded in agreement.

Sadie was relieved their trip to the museum had proved to be more fruitful than she'd expected. She had a glimmer of hope that they might actually be able to uncover Siphon's secrets quickly and get back to the real fight. After all, this investigation hardly compared to the very present threat of the Coalition army just dying to make its next move. But if the disappearance of Eirik Pierce, Hetia's father, was connected to the bomb Siphon had constructed fifteen years ago, then they might just learn where that bomb was now and when he planned to use it.

Sadie watched Hetia depart with worry as the group split up. Though time was limited, and it was more efficient this way, she didn't want the other woman to be alone. Not when she was having to dig through what was probably the most painful part of her past. Not when Hetia knew that the answers to all their questions might lie in her own memory. And that letting Sadie in, something she was clearly unwilling to do, might be the only way to access it.

Chapter 3

Strange Encounters

"You're clearly lost, Troy. Will you let one of us look at the paper?" Sadie said after an hour of blindly following him.

"I just misinterpreted what the numbers mean. I've got it now."

"You said that last time," Sadie said, trying to snatch the paper in a rapid launch of her hand.

He pivoted his body, laughing, but didn't take his eyes off the paper at which he was frowning. Sadie switched tactics. Pressing into his side she put her chin on his shoulder and whispered, "Please."

It worked. He was immediately distracted.

She snatched the paper.

He snatched it back. Then with a sigh, handed it to Patricia.

The woman glared at the two of them. "This is the district number, not the tree number, dear. They're clearly naming it by the largest thing first. District, neighborhood, tree, home."

"How can you tell?" Troy asked, frowning over her shoulder.

"Because it makes sense," Patricia said. "This way."

Sadie shot a shit-eating grin at Troy as Patricia stepped in front. He just winked at Sadie before following their new leader. It was an action chosen to deliberately annoy her since it made no sense. She glared at the back of his head until Patricia finally pulled them to a stop at what felt like an hour later.

The man's home was as removed as it was possible to be in the inner city. It was suspended between three distant trees, each of which contributed branches to support the structure in their center. Only one of the trees had a decent pathway to reach the front door. Patricia kicked off her heels as the walkway was less of a bridge and more a haphazard mixture of entwined branches.

When they were about halfway across, Sadie made the horrible mistake of looking down. There was no railing. She immediately dropped to her hands and knees. Patricia gave her an envious look, like she wanted to do the same, but she remained standing.

Sadie watched her try to step forward, but her foot seemed caught. They all stared at the foot. It was buried in the branches in a way that was only possible if they had moved up around her ankle. "Shit," Patricia said, crouching down to tug at it.

"Excuse me," Troy called out. "Mr. Red? Lance Red?" he said, looking down at the paper as if confirming the name. Continuing to call out to the house some twenty feet ahead, Troy gave the same sap story he'd told Annie. There was a long pause, and then the side of the house moved.

No, it was the man. He'd been leaning up against the branches which encased his home, only Sadie hadn't noticed him until just now. Patricia's foot came free as the man stepped forward. Annie hadn't been lying about the man being a recluse, but she'd left out his paranoia.

"Come on then," came a deep, gravelly voice. Sadie couldn't see the man's torso from her crouched position, but she watched feet move as he assisted them across. Patricia and Troy looked back at her, and suddenly she didn't want to be the only one crouching down. She stood up accompanied by a wave of panic, but plastered a smile on her face all the same.

The man walked toward her without looking at his feet as if he knew the exact contour of the land. He held out a hand and she accepted. "Thank you... Lance?"

He nodded. They assessed each other as she introduced herself.

The man was definitely a loner, but he had a healthy sex life with himself. He eyed her gloves with interest, as if he knew it was a succubus feature. Sadie felt warmed as he looked at her, enjoying the attention as she admitted that she also found him interesting.

"I've got you," he said and pulled her up against him before pivoting them so she was in front. She held onto his arm like a rail as he shepherded her across. When they'd made it to firmer ground, she pivoted to face him.

"Thank you. I – uhh, appear to be afraid of heights," she said, tucking a curl behind her ear.

"And yet you came here," he said, opening his door and gesturing them inside. Despite his brusque tone, he wasn't turning them away. They followed him into a one room, oval-shaped dwelling. The table in the center had only two chairs, but he motioned for them to sit all the same, which Sadie and Patricia did.

Lance straightened out his bed and directed Troy to take a seat there. Then, still standing himself, he asked without preamble, "What is it you want?"

Patricia cleared her throat. "I know it's a bad memory, but we were wondering if you could tell us about the night of the fire? A friend of yours, Annie – uh, Black, said you saw the men?"

Lance grunted. "Oh, I saw them. Clear as day. I was about your age." He nodded to Sadie. "Working my first job."

He began bustling around making tea, handing them each a warm cup as he spoke. The story went on for an hour, and Sadie watched Patricia's face throughout it. As a hag, she fed off of life experience, and if the story was false, Patricia would know. Sadie noted that Troy was also watching the woman. Apparently, Sadie wasn't the only one in on her secret ability.

When it was done, Patricia gave a tiny nod. Sadie was glad to know Lance was telling the truth, but there weren't any details that gave them something useful. "Did you see anyone else that day? Anyone you didn't recognize?" Sadie asked.

"Yes, of course. There were hundreds of people running around trying to put out the fire or escape. Why?"

This wasn't getting them anywhere, but Sadie had an idea. "Well, thank you for your time. We should probably go. I still need to feed and the day is getting late." She looked at her two companions, trying to communicate. They just frowned at her. Sadie set down her tea and stood up.

"I could make you something. If you all want to stay a while," Lance said.

"No, thank you. Sadie's right," Patricia said. "We appreciate you sharing your story with us, though." It was clear she meant it. In fact, Patricia seemed relaxed the way Sadie was right after she'd fed.

As they moved to the door, Sadie stopped and looked back at Lance as if she'd just had an idea. His expression turned hopeful as she looked him up and down with an obviously approving assessment. By the time they found each other's eyes, it seemed that they were on the same page. "Actually, I wouldn't mind staying a little longer if you two don't mind?" she said, not looking away from the stranger.

Troy and Patricia stopped.

"Alright," Troy said after a minute, but they didn't move, and when Sadie glanced over, she found them staring at her in confusion.

"Perhaps you could go ahead and I'll *catch up*," Sadie said, trying to be more obvious.

Comprehension dawned at the same time on their faces. Patricia looked embarrassed as she bobbed her head in parting while Troy looked agitated. He hesitated before grudgingly following Patricia out the door.

Sadie turned back to Lance. He lifted his chin. "When you said feed…"

"I know it's very forward of me. But it's sort of how things work for my kind."

"Yes, I know. I—"

"But I can leave too if I misread," she added in a rush.

"No. Here." He offered to take her coat. The unheated place was chilly and she was reluctant to remove clothing, but she hadn't misread. She could see clearly that he was very much excited by this turn of events in his day. Though Sadie had learned that internal interest and outward choices to act on that interest were often two very different things.

He stepped closer to help her remove the coat and she assessed her own interest. He was nearly twice her age, and small age-lines creased the corners of his eyes, but his face was attractive in a hard sort of way. Though as a succubus, it wasn't a person's physical features that stood out the most to Sadie. In this man's case, it was his lonely life and keen interest in her attention that she found appealing.

His eyes flicked over her face in turn. "How old are you?"

"I'm twenty, but a succubus gains sexual experience fast," she said.

He gave a nervous chuckle. "I bet."

Sadie wrapped her arms around herself against the cool air as he hung the coat. "Sorry, I don't need it very warm. Give me a minute." Lance hurried about, lighting several lanterns around the room. The flames were big, clearly meant to heat, but they also turned the dark dwelling into a brightly lit sphere that glowed around them.

He gestured her to sit before taking the seat across from her, looking uncertain as to what to do. The man was clearly nervous, and Sadie knew this wasn't going to be a fast task. However, she was going to kill two birds with one stone: feed for the day and memory dive to get a good look at exactly what this man saw on the day of the fire. And since the information was valuable enough to be patient, she did her best not to push.

They talked for an hour, or mostly he talked. It was easy to keep the attention off her since he seemed to enjoy having someone to tell his life to. But none of the conversation was flirtatious, despite her efforts. And the unspoken reason for her staying hung in the air with increasing awkwardness.

Sadie had dealt with such situations before, however. When the conversation had gone on long enough, she decided to take matters into her own hands. Waiting for a brief moment of pause, she stood up and removed her gloves before Lance could rush on to fill the silence. He froze. Without speaking or hesitation, Sadie pulled off her shirt and bra in one swipe and tossed it on the table. The mood turned instantly.

Lance cleared his throat and leaned back in the chair.

"We can stop at any time. If you change your mind," she said.

"I—" He adjusted himself as he stared at her breasts. "I don't really like to be touched."

Now *that,* she couldn't see. His desire was clear and there were various images of him touching himself as he looked at her, but the things people didn't want weren't as easily identifiable in the images which made up their sexualities.

"Oh." Sadie sat back down. After thinking a moment, she asked, "What about holding my hand?"

His brows drew down sharply. "Is that enough for you?"

"It is." Sadie held out one hand across the table. She was worried he was about to take her up on her offer to change his mind, but instead he reached out, hesitantly, and ran his thumb along her palm.

He sucked in a sharp breath, and she intentionally kept the sensation mild. They stared at each other as he caressed her palm, his mouth slightly open.

After a minute she asked, "Do you like it?"

"Yes," he whispered, clasping his hand in hers and sinking down in the chair. His other hand disappeared under the table and she heard him unzip his pants.

Through the contact she could feel every cell in his body as though it were an extension of her own. His heart was pounding as if he were in the middle of a sprint, and the heavy thudding aroused her desire to feed. As he wrapped his hand around himself, she felt exactly what he was feeling. He was wet enough that his grip slicked easily up and down.

"This is strange," he said.

"Maybe," Sadie said, though she didn't think it was strange at all. "It's going to get pretty intense. You might want a towel if you don't want things to get messy."

He stroked himself a few more times, his gaze flicking from her breasts, to her hair, to her eyes, before he said, "I don't care."

Sadie smiled. This interview was turning out to be a lot more interesting than she'd thought it'd be. She felt some guilt, however, that he didn't know she was about to dig through his thoughts. When she'd covertly done such things while spying on The Coalition, she hadn't had such reservations. But this was a very different situation.

There didn't seem to be anything she could do about it, though. She wasn't going to tell a stranger her big secret. She would just have to make up for it by giving him an experience he could remember for years. Sadie sucked on her finger and then ran it from the hollow of her throat down between her breasts. She cupped them each and then began toying with her own nipples. His gaze grew heavy and she matched it with several bursts of pleasure.

Lance was stroking himself too quickly for her to align the rhythm of orgasmic waves to his motion, so she matched them to the squeezing of her own breasts. He ate it up feverishly, all awkwardness forgotten. He didn't make any noise as the climax began, but a flush spread up his neck and he slowed to pump his hips slowly into his grip.

This was her chance. Lance probably thought this was the end, but Sadie had developed her control significantly over the past few months. She was ready to show off her succubus skill as well as give herself enough time to go digging through his head.

"Keep breathing," she told him. "And hold on."

Sadie closed her eyes and – keeping the spasms of orgasm coming with increasing intensity – relaxed her mind. Memory diving began with desire, the natural domain of her species. She could locate memories only through finding moments in which the person had wanted something. It didn't have to be something sexual, but the points of wanting were her roadmap.

In this particular case, finding what she was looking for was incredibly easy. The memory of that day was the sharpest thing in his thoughts, competing only with the current sexual moment he was experiencing. A clear desire to get away from hot flames drew her onward until she was looking out at the world through his eyes fifteen years ago. Sadie knew from experience that these dives into the past tended to translate to only a second or so in the present world. It would all happen between one spasm and the next, and her thoughts would be back in time to focus on what was happening. He would never know it had happened.

She connected immediately to the fear of the moment, having recently had her own stint with fire. There were people screaming overhead, and somewhere in the distance came the distinct sound of a very large tree falling to earth.

Lance ignored it all. The office of scientific development had just caught fire and no one was rushing in to save it. It was up to him. He thought of those journals, centuries old, and all the prototypes. They couldn't burn. His own life wasn't nearly as important.

He tied his shirt over his nose and mouth and ran inside. Only one corner of the room had caught, and the flames were burning slowly. The wood had been polished to be fire resistant, but if you got anything hot enough it burned.

He scooped up whatever he could carry, shoving trinkets into pant pockets and clutching books in one arm, before running back outside. There was still plenty more to rescue.

"Help!" he yelled, but there was no one nearby. Or at least so he first thought. A shape moved just on the other side of some nearby flames. It looked almost as if it were in the fire.

"Hello?" Lance called.

The flames shifted direction and a man appeared from out behind them. He didn't seem to see Lance, and something about the man made Lance hesitate. Sadie registered that the man was wearing the flame-retardant body suit of human firefighters, but Lance's mind was focused on the man's expression – calm and calculating. As the man glanced around at the destruction with approval, two more men joined him. They patted each other on the back as they shared identical grins. Sadie thought one of the newcomers looked vaguely familiar, but she couldn't place him.

Were these firemen? Lance wondered, noticing their uniforms. If so, they were not fire nymphs, since they weren't wearing those flame-retardant shorts with most of their skin exposed. Which meant they weren't going to be as helpful in this situation if they didn't have water with them. Lance shrunk back in fear as the men continued to smile in satisfaction; clearly putting the fire out was not on their agenda.

He retreated back to the burning office. Just as he was considering rushing back inside for more, the treasure trove of knowledge went entirely up in flames. His heart pounded with sorrow as his mind went blank with the horror of losing so much history. A moment later a tree collapsed between him and the dangerous men and he took off in a sprint, clutching the pittance of scientific development he'd been able to save.

As he ran, Lance thought only of loss. He didn't notice what Sadie did. Gaining some autonomy within his memory, Sadie took in all she could of his surroundings. From the corner of his vision, three figures stepped freely through the flames and the fire grew bright and strong.

The *human-dressed fire nymphs* were continuing to spread destruction.

Sadie didn't have time to process that revelation as she opened her eyes in the present and took in the expression of agony on the man in front of her. For a brief second, she forgot that it was pleasure and not suffering that was causing it. The sounds and feel of flames still crackled in her mind as she released her hold on his climax. Lance jerked and convulsed in front of her, his eyes closed.

A moment later, she withdrew her hand.

They stared at each other, both panting heavily now, and Sadie waited for him to come down off the high before moving. A minute later, Lance said, "That was – I don't know. A very strange afternoon."

Sadie knew that only a year ago she would have completely agreed. But now, she just smiled and reached for her clothes. Standing at the door, dressed and ready to leave, she looked back at him. "It was a pleasure meeting you, Lance Red."

He nodded in silent agreement, still looking a little shocked. And then, as if she'd done nothing more than share tea with a stranger, she bobbed her head goodbye and went to catch up with the others.

Chapter 4

Forces too great

Sadie crossed the bridge with no help on the way back and was surprised to find her friends waiting for her just on the other side. Well, one friend and one... something or other. "I thought you'd just head back," Sadie said in a tone that suggested they really shouldn't have waited.

"We didn't think it would take that long," Patricia said, shooting a concerned look at Troy.

He looked quite agitated now. "What was going on in there? That took forever," he said.

Sadie shrugged. Grateful for an opportunity to bother him. "Well, I was stealing the man's memory, the least I could do was show him a really, *really* good time." Troy's jaw clenched and suddenly Sadie couldn't help herself. "I mean, he wanted me in so many different ways, I couldn't just rush through them all."

"Right. Let's go," Patricia said, stepping in between them to lead the way. Troy's thoughts were heavily fixated on imagining Sadie in a variety of sexual positions, and she smiled as he adjusted himself while glaring at her. Looking pointedly at his partial arousal, she turned to follow Patricia with a heavy dose of self-satisfaction.

Though a minute later she felt a little shame at her behavior. She didn't mean to be so mean. She never treated anyone else like that. Troy just seemed to bring it out in her. As they walked back in silence, Sadie resolved to be nicer to him. Next time she opened her mouth, it would be to say something sweet. Maybe. Well, only if he didn't do anything irritating or leave her feeling too vulnerable about their recent sexual interaction.

"Were you able to get anything?" Patricia called over her shoulder, making Sadie jump.

"Yes, but let's wait for Hetia," she replied with her mind still elsewhere.

They didn't speak again on the entire walk back, but Sadie could sense Troy waffling from successfully tamping down his arousal to staring at her ass as he remembered her naked and bound. The thoughts were as intoxicating as they were confusing, and she could feel his conflict mirrored in herself.

When they finally arrived back at their building, they found Hetia at a bar on the ground floor. They pulled up other stools and chairs as they crowded around her, Troy taking the spot across from Sadie. As they exchanged a glance for the first time after the long, lust-fueled walk, Sadie was surprised to find his expression soft. For a brief instant, he wore care and longing like an open book.

She swallowed, feeling guilty again for her taunting. After all, his current libido was an after-effect of her high-intensity feeding, probably mixing with their natural attraction.

Her face warmed though as she remembered her desperate need for him, and her self-defensiveness once again grew sharp. If only they could have slept together under different circumstances. She and Troy had been at odds up until just a week ago, and then with all that residual combativeness still sharp in her mind, she had been forced to ask him to fuck her. No, to *beg* him. And as much as he'd been happy to comply, Sadie didn't like that her desperate need for him in that moment had far outweighed his simple wanting of her.

"What'd you learn?" Troy asked, pulling his gaze from Sadie to look at Hetia.

Looking down at her drink, Hetia gently stirred the cocktail as she said, "My father was the senior contractor here during the five years before his disappearance."

"Oh my god, really?" Sadie said.

Hetia tapped the stick on the side of her glass, set it aside, and downed the glass in one swig. "He had a lot of odd jobs. Helping run an underground resistance organization doesn't exactly pay the bills, despite people's donations to the cause." Hetia looked up at Sadie and her expression appeared devoid of emotion. Even so, Sadie knew her better by now. This investigation was going to be an emotional roller coaster. Remembering the easy way Hetia had laughed just a few hours ago, Sadie had to fight down the instinct to reach out and touch her in comfort.

"And you?" Hetia asked.

Patricia waved away the waiter as they all turned their attention to Sadie. Lowering her voice, she said, "I took a peek into the man's past. He didn't see your father, or Siphon that night, but..." She looked around the table, anxious to finally share the big news. "I did get a look at the three men. And I'm fairly sure they were fire nymphs." She swept her hair behind her ear in a rush. "Also... one of them looked familiar."

"What?" Patricia asked. "How?"

"I've been trying to remember, but I just can't. It's like I saw him in a dream or something. The more I fixate on his face though, the more sure I am. I've seen him before."

They fell into thoughtful silence a while.

"At least it's clear something went on here that week. Beyond just the fire," Patricia said. "And knowing Siphon, it wasn't something benevolent like helping a community recover from tragedy."

"Do you think the men who started the fire were with The Coalition?"" Troy asked.

"It's possible, but we can't say for sure without more information." Patricia darted a quick glance at Hetia. They all fell silent. The knowledge that they might learn more if Hetia would let Sadie read her memories hung heavy in the sudden silence. Hetia swiveled a bit in her chair and stared down at her empty glass.

"Holy shit," a woman said from the other side of the room. She practically yelled the words and everyone turned to look at her. "Turn that up," she said, pointing at the tiny television behind the counter. The bartender complied and the entire room fell silent. Sadie squinted at the blurry image of the distant screen, gave up, and just listened to the words.

"The new laws will go into effect immediately. Every identification card must declare your species. To receive the code you will need to report to your local Species Oversight office which will be set up in every major city. You will keep your ID on you at all times. Failure to comply will be considered a serious crime. And I repeat, every city and town has two weeks to officially declare a side. The human government is hereby considered rogue and is called to disband promptly. If your city does not declare official support for the true government within the two-week grace period, swift action will be taken against all residents. Join or comply with The Coalition today and you will be part of a better future. I repeat, the new laws will go into effect immediately. Every identification—"

The bartender switched it off.

There was a long pause and then, almost all at once, the room erupted in noise.

"Holy shit is right," Sadie said. "The Coalition has officially declared war."

"We need to get back to the camp, be ready to fight. Amadi will be expecting it," Troy said in a rush.

"Hetia has a number she can call. If he left any urgent message for everyone, it will be there," Patricia told them.

"But... if The Coalition plans to punish any town that refuses to submit, that must mean their army must have grown significantly since I last saw it. How can The United stand up to that?" Sadie asked, cold fear hitting her as she thought of her hometown.

"Hopefully, our side has also drawn more recruits. Amadi's going to have to split up the main force in order to defend a lot of different places at once though," Patricia said.

"No," Hetia said quietly. "Dee – Amadi – thought this might be coming. He supposed it was months away, but I guess not. If they're doing this now, it means they had strong support after the fight last week."

"How is that possible? The Coalition attacked The United. Our side was just standing in their way," Sadie said.

"Not according to the well-crafted rumor mill. They were ready for the media spin. And they knew it." Patricia sighed.

Troy blew out a breath. "I bet that whole battle was just to build sympathy."

"And to see exactly what we had," Patricia added.

Sadie slumped back in her chair. "What do we do?"

They looked around at each other, but in the end they all turned to Hetia. She took a slow sip of her water. "We go back. Dee's going to need all hands on deck," she said, looking off into the distance.

And that was that. They'd just been starting to uncover something of Siphon's dirty secrets, and instead he was forcing them to call it short.

"But," Sadie shook her head, "what about the bomb? It can't be a coincidence those plans had a date that matched Mr. Pierce's disappearance. What if there's really something worth learning here?"

They chewed on that a minute.

"Even if that's the case, we don't have much choice in this. There's no more time to go picking through history, gathering information. It's time to prepare for the fight," Patricia said.

Sadie pulled her heels up to her butt and hugged her knees. "This is so unfair."

"Well, that's life," Hetia said. She scooted her chair out in a flash and hopped down. "We leave first thing," she added, before disappearing up the nearby stairwell.

"Excuse me," Troy told them, and went after Hetia in a rush.

When Sadie followed some time later, neither Hetia nor Troy were in their hotel room. Patricia had gone to make the phone call to Amadi while Sadie returned to her own room. Sitting at the vanity mirror, she began to take down her hair. She regretted finding herself alone. It gave her time to worry over the future. And to think of Jimmy, so far away when such trouble was coming.

Luckily, the door clicked open only a few minutes later. "There's no message, yet," Patricia said, coming to stand next to her. Sadie nodded in acknowledgement, keeping her eyes on her reflection in determination. The comb tangled in her hair and one prong snapped as she forced the issue. "Here," Patricia said, taking the comb and stepping in behind her.

"I don't know where they went, but I hope Hetia's okay," Sadie said. "Do you think she's more upset at not getting to solve the mystery of her father, or of the news about him disappearing the week of the fire?"

"I don't know, Sadie. You know her better than I do."

"And I don't know her at all," Sadie said, the stress making her exaggerate. Looking for an excuse to think about anything other than the terrifying news they'd just received, Sadie decided to prompt the topic now. "What about Troy? How do you think he's coping?" Patricia didn't respond right away, but Sadie could see the subtle shift in her demeanor. "I mean, you know him pretty well by know," she added, speaking gently since she knew her friend had been avoiding the topic.

Patricia sighed. "I know you can... see certain things. I've just been afraid... to talk about it." They watched each other in the mirror, and neither of them spoke until the tangles were gone.

Sadie pivoted and cupped the hand holding the comb. "Do you want me to do yours?" she asked.

Patricia took a slow breath. "Yeah. I'd like that."

They switched spots and Sadie helped Patricia remove her many carefully placed pins.

"Do you want to talk about it now?" Sadie prompted.

Patricia locked eyes with her as Sadie worked. "Last summer, when you and I met, there was that guy, VJ?"

"The one that was all into you, but bailed when he realized you were never going to sleep with him?"

"That's the one. I thought he really liked me, *and* I thought we were friends. Then I lost him, practically overnight." She chewed her lip. "It's... different with Troy. We seem to like each other a lot. Or, I like him." Patricia cast her a nervous look.

"It's mutual," Sadie said. "But you didn't hear that from me."

Patricia relaxed, then sighed contentedly as the comb scratched along her head.

"It's just – I feel *comfortable* with Troy. I enjoy being near him and... I like the way he smells." Her cheeks flushed with color at this.

It was Sadie's turn to chew her lip. "He does smell pretty nice," she admitted.

Patricia turned to look at her directly. "Are you okay with this?"

She frowned. "Why wouldn't I be?"

"Because you and Troy clearly have something going on. Earlier today you lied about what happened with that Lance guy, presumably just to make him jealous."

Sadie dropped her gaze, she'd forgotten Patricia would know that. "Yeah... I did, but – only because he annoys me. I'm not actually interested in Troy. I was just trying to bother him. I don't actually care what—"

Patricia was looking at her with such incredulity that she stopped mid-sentence. "I don't know who you think you're fooling, but I'm fairly certain the only part of that story that was true was the part about him annoying you."

"Okay. Fine," Sadie said, resuming the combing so that Patricia would look forward again. She huffed out a breath before continuing, "I don't know what I want to happen there, and maybe, yes, I have some residual attraction to him from that one night together."

"Getting closer," Patricia interjected.

"*But—*" Sadie sighed, "that's completely separate from you two. I'm happy you have someone you feel that way about. It doesn't make me jealous or anything." Their eyes locked in the mirror and Sadie found herself secretly hoping Patricia was about to tell her if that last line was true. She didn't, and Sadie didn't have the courage to ask.

"Well," Patricia stood up, "let's just keep talking about this, okay?"

"Promise," Sadie said.

"Because life is short and getting a lot scarier these days," Patricia added. Sadie nodded, and suddenly the weight of what tomorrow might bring returned in force. Patricia too, looked scared. Sadie hugged her carefully and they both held on surprisingly tight.

Then Sadie noticed something that had been becoming true in the gradual way such things did. "I love you, girl," she said.

"I love you, too," Patricia croaked a few breaths later, and the exchange of sentiments made their bond pulse stronger. Then instead of breaking apart they began to sniffle into each other's ears.

Troy cleared his throat and they both jumped, pulling back from the embrace. "Hey, it's gonna be okay. We'll figure this out," he said, assuming the crying hugfest had something to do with the end of the world. Sadie was a little embarrassed that it didn't, but she couldn't let herself think about the truly bad stuff yet.

"Yes, of course." Patricia waved at the air before disappearing to get them both tissues. When she returned, she gave Troy a long, considering look. Sadie frowned. A clear image of them cuddling in bed together appeared in the woman's mind. Sadie thought she could only see sexual desires or histories, of which Patricia had none, but this was unmistakable.

"Hey Troy, do you want to sleep in here tonight?" Sadie asked.

"What?" He looked between them uncertainly.

"I think Patricia would like it and I can stay somewhere else," she added, swinging back on her jacket.

Troy nodded. "Yeah, I'd like to," he said to the pretty, dark-haired woman with tears still in her eyes before turning back to Sadie, "but I don't think Hetia's going to go for that."

Sadie just laughed, turning for the door so she wouldn't have to look at Troy or Patricia studying her. "I'm a succubus. You don't think I can find a bed to stay in?"

She waited until she was out in the hall before dropping her smile. That had been the right thing to do, certainly. It had felt good as she was doing it. But as she leaned against the wall staring at the closed doors of their two rooms, she felt that sinking feeling of dread again. She still didn't want to be alone. She also really didn't want to go meet some stranger. If she'd been remotely hungry, her instincts would have driven her in search of someone, but as it were she just wrapped her arms around herself, wishing someone she loved was holding her.

Sadie stepped up to Hetia's door and pressed her ear to it. She thought she could hear the bathroom sink running. Taking a deep, steadying breath, Sadie raised her fist to knock. She hovered there so long someone would have laughed at the sight if anyone had been watching.

She dropped the arm, sighed, and walked away down the hall. A door clicked open behind her. Hetia was standing in the doorway when she turned. She didn't speak, but in a clear invitation to follow her, she held open the door as she retreated.

Surprised, Sadie followed her inside, her heart pounding with nerves at interacting alone with the woman. Hetia sat down on the desk in a casual sprawl and Sadie perched herself on the edge of the bed. The blond woman was fisting a bottle of gin. She took a sip and held it out.

"No thanks," Sadie said. "I don't like gin. Remember?"

"Yeah." Hetia gave her a wistful look. "I remember." She took another sip and then set the bottle down behind her. She watched Sadie in silence a while and then her gaze unfocused, softening as she stared at the wall. "The conversation between my father and Siphon, however, I don't remember at all," she said, speaking as if her mind was elsewhere. "I was playing with a puzzle in the corner. Thinking about childish things. I wasn't memorizing details."

Sadie kicked off her shoes and tucked her feet under her, waiting for more. But Hetia just looked her over with her light gray eyes, which never failed to appear as if they were penetrating right to the heart of her.

"How does it work?" Hetia asked in a voice just above a whisper.

"What?"

"Amadi explained a little. You follow people's desires to drop into their memories."

Sadie swallowed. "Yeah. That's about it."

"Is there a way... for the person to know which memory you saw?" Hetia asked.

"No. They don't even know it happened. It's quick. It happens in a flash, usually in the middle of the... climax." Her skin heated as she spoke and she bit her lip anxiously as Hetia considered this.

"Did you do it to me? When we—"

Sadie blinked. "No – I... didn't even know I could do it back then." She grabbed at a strand of her hair to twist around her finger, glad to be given this opportunity to explain, even if she was nervous.

"So you can see any part of a person's past and they don't have any idea what you did or didn't find? What about memories in which they didn't have any desire for anything?"

Sadie couldn't think of any safe way to address the first question, but to the second she said, "Everyone always wants something."

Though it hadn't been her intention, the comment significantly changed the mood in the room. If it had been anyone else, Sadie would have stood up and walked over to her, but since all of her previous attempts to get close to Hetia had been shut down, she remained awkwardly rooted in place. But the image of herself pressed against the wall with Hetia's mouth hot on hers bloomed sharply in the other woman's mind. It morphed into the memory of them kissing in the middle of the battle a few days ago. Hetia had felt alive the way she only did when in a fight, and her whole body had pulsed with desire at the surprise encounter with Sadie.

Hetia finally released her from her gaze and moved to staring at her hands. "This was my one shot to learn what happened, and now we're out of time." She lifted herself off the edge of the desk, and moved to join her on the bed. Suddenly Sadie could hear her own heartbeat pulsing in her ears.

"You can always come back, when the war is over," Sadie told her, continuing to fiddle with her hair. She wrapped a curl in one tight loop around her finger and released it. She wasn't sure why she was so nervous. It seemed clear where this was heading, and... hadn't she wanted this?

"When the war is over? The war will never be over. And the chances that I live to ever come back here aren't good." She put a hand on Sadie's knee. "No. This is my chance."

Sadie stopped her fidgeting, took a deep breath, and then placed her hand over Hetia's. "Are you sure? I don't want you to do something that—"

"I have no other choice," Hetia cut in.

"That's not – I'm not okay with that," Sadie said, finally realizing her anxiety. The fact that they shared an attraction had never been the problem. Their interest had been mutual from the beginning. The problem was the fact that apart from that first night they'd met, Hetia had never let her back in emotionally. And she didn't want to now. Sadie squirmed at the thought of her doing so only because she had to.

"This is our last night here, Sadie. Read me. You *need* to read me." Hetia's expression softened slightly. "It's okay."

Sadie chewed her lip. "I wish there was another way."

"There isn't," Hetia said, scooting closer. In a rush, Sadie was hit with a strong wave of lust, pulsing strong and thick from the other woman, and it muddled her thoughts. "We – wouldn't have to take off clothes or anything," Sadie said as if in a trance. "We could just hold hands. I can even do it fast. And – and not look at you or anything." Was she trying to make Hetia more comfortable with this suggestion, or only pleading with herself not to take advantage of the situation?

She watched anxiously as Hetia considered this. As always, it was impossible to clearly interpret her expression, but the image that appeared in the front of her mind was sharp as day. It was the two of them entwined on this bed together. People were complicated, she knew, but regardless of Hetia's reservations about Sadie traipsing through her past, she was *very* interested in the required action to get there.

Pulses of lust continued to flow out of her, and the sight of the strong red light connecting them added to Sadie's arousal. She had been jealous of the green friendship lines that connected Hetia and Troy. The only thing that connected her and Hetia was desire. Lately, those lines had been much staler than the lust lines between her and Troy, though in the moment Hetia had sat down next to her, they'd began to flow red-hot.

"Okay. I would rather keep clothes on," Hetia said as if none of the present emotion in the air was real.

"Right. Okay," Sadie panted, trying to shake off the sudden ache building in her body.

"And I don't want to lie down," Hetia added as she moved to kneel in the center of the bed with her butt on her calves. She put her hands on the comforter in front of her and stared back at Sadie, who hadn't budged. With ongoing trepidation and conflicting emotions, Sadie moved to sit across from her. She peeled off one glove only, and her hands shook as she gently put it aside.

Then she reached out and slid her fingers into Hetia's palm. She ran her thumb over the back of her hand, the softness contrasting with the rough calluses on the underside. As she had been the last time she'd made contact with the woman, Sadie was surprised at how fast Hetia's heart was actually beating. Her always outwardly calm demeanor showed off none of what was happening under the surface. Hetia. The perfect soldier. Always in control – her body taut like a cat ready to pounce.

Sadie said she would try to go quickly, but she hadn't been prepared for what it would mean to actually cross this line. This was more than just a hurried physical task to be accomplished. She was suddenly inside the hard exterior the woman showed to the world, and it was a tumultuous place. A powerful place. And a beautiful one. Hetia's lust was like a hurricane thrashing around inside her; the tiny muscles of her abs tightening and releasing in sharp bursts.

As Sadie let the smallest pleasurable sensation spread through her like liquid heat, images of all the ferocious things she really wanted to do ran rampant in her thoughts. Since Hetia still didn't know she could see such things, Sadie had to play along with the exterior narrative that they were just doing this for the information.

Hetia licked her lips and Sadie couldn't help but stare at them. Most of her features were small: her lips, her nose, her fine hair. Unlike Sadie, who was all curves and big curls, Hetia looked almost breakable. Only she was the best combat fighter in Amadi's army, as Patricia had informed her. And she was an obscenely powerful earthquake nymph who had the control to precisely level several blocks in the middle of a city. And yet despite all that, Sadie had seen there was a kind of fragility to her, one that made her want to wrap her arms around Hetia and promise to always take care of her.

Sadie found herself panting as she went in deeper. Hetia's lips parted on a muted gasp as Sadie began to escalate the sensation quickly. Her gaze drew downward to the spastic clenching of her abs as she rocked slightly in place. She felt wetness pool between her own legs as she watched Hetia's reserved demeanor slowly break open.

The woman dropped her gaze to their hands as the tension built. Sadie couldn't help but eat up the site of the flush building up her chest and neck. Hetia was getting close now, and this would all be for nothing if Sadie failed to focus her thoughts on the task. She wouldn't let Hetia down like that.

Trying to relax her mind, she fought for self-control, but Hetia's desire pulled at her as if it had a mind of its own. Sadie closed her eyes, trying to escape it, but a quiet, desperate sound of pleasure hit her ears, pulling her back to the present. She took another steadying breath. She could do this. Ignoring the sweet sounds of Hetia's suppressed panting, she forced her mind to calm.

A moment later, Sadie gasped and her eyes shot open as Hetia pushed her to her back. She'd launched herself forward and landed with her weight between Sadie's legs, pinning her hands with her forearms. Since Hetia wore long sleeves, this put them out of skin contact.

Their heartbeats pounded against each other through their equally heaving chests. Hetia brought her mouth just above Sadie's and the image of them kissing as Sadie finished her popped into Hetia's thoughts. Sadie desperately wanted to feel Hetia's lips on hers, and she arched her back into the feel of her between her legs.

"I just can't. I'm sorry. I can't have you in my head," Hetia told her.

It was Sadie's turn to make a desperate cry of wanton desire. She clenched her thighs against Hetia's hips, not quite believing it was over. The woman pressed into her and Sadie writhed against the friction as the pressure on her wrists increased until it was painful. But she didn't complain. In fact, she wanted more. Sadie fought against the hold in a challenge and, as expected, found her struggles to be in vain. If Hetia wanted her pinned, she wasn't going anywhere.

She looked at the woman's clenched jaw and parted lips, red from the flush, and felt she would burst if she didn't kiss her. "Hetia. Please don't withdraw from me. Not now." Sadie again arched under her and Hetia groaned, looking desperate to continue. "I won't let you down, if you just—"

Hetia sat up suddenly, leaving Sadie alone and panting on her back. She snapped out of it quickly and pulled herself upright.

"I'm sorry." Hetia got to her feet. "I've got to go."

"But – this is your room." Sadie blinked, jumping up to follow her.

Hetia looked back at her, but kept her gaze on the floor. "Stay. I'll find somewhere else."

Sadie's feelings were all chaos, but Hetia said this with perfect calm, betrayed only by the stiff way she held herself. This, more than anything else, caused anger to join Sadie's other emotions. How could she act like this was nothing? Like what they had wasn't even worth getting worked up over?

Sadie gritted her teeth and moved to step between her and the door. And then because it seemed she had nothing to lose, she said what was most on her mind. "Why are you always running scared? If all you ever do is protect yourself, you'll never have any chance to see what could have been."

Hetia's cool gaze dropped to the ground, and Sadie saw her betray a clear emotion: shame. Then Hetia stepped around her and out the door.

Chapter 5

Bold Choices

Sadie slept poorly. The potential destruction of her world as she knew it didn't make for particularly restful thoughts. It also didn't help that the bed she was in smelled of both Hetia *and* Troy. She must have dozed off eventually though, because she woke to the sound of the door.

She bolted upright, still on top of the covers and found herself face-to-face with a sleepy-eyed Troy.

"Wha— You slept here?"

"Nothing happened," Sadie said, inexplicably defensive. Shaking off sleep, she felt around the comforter for her other glove. "We – we tried to do a memory reading. It ended badly."

"She let you do that?" Troy asked. "Did you get anything?"

"No." Sadie tossed the covers and shifted the chair as she searched. "And look, I wouldn't mention this to her, okay. It didn't go well. Let's just leave it at that."

He nodded, then bent down before emerging with her glove. Sadie halted her search.

She felt him pulse with desire as she approached, and she avoided his gaze as she carefully extracted the glove from his fingers without touching them.

"Troy, Hetia doesn't know all the things I can see, either."

"I know. Amadi talked to me," he whispered. She looked up to find him staring at her lips. Opting for a less confusing morning, Sadie quickly stepped around him and made for the door.

"Hey, umm," Troy began, pulling her attention. She faced him, pointedly not looking down at his semi-erection. "Thanks. For giving us the room."

Sadie swallowed. "Yeah. I'm glad you two are... well, you seem happy together."

"We are. And with everything that's coming. I wouldn't want to miss out on a good thing," he said. Troy observed her with a somewhat pointed expression.

Sadie looked away. "Good. Well, I'm going to go find something to eat. Maybe food can replace sleeping."

He laughed. "Good luck with that."

By the time she pulled open the door, she was desperate to get away from that room. Taking off in search of some fresh air, she tried to steady her thoughts. Too much had happened in the last few days, and she wished with a sharp pain that Jimmy had been here to ride it out with her.

With him in mind, Sadie wandered in the direction of the building they'd stayed in last summer. There had been a lobby full of card tables on the ground floor. She wanted to see that place again just to feel closer to him. When she stepped into the morning market, though, she got a distracting surprise.

Where was everyone? There were about half the typical number of people and it made the place feel empty. Also, the usual cries of "Fresh bread!" and "Morning press!" had all been turned down in volume. A woman barreled into Sadie from the left and she stumbled back. The woman didn't apologize, though she was openly crying and dragging a suitcase.

When Sadie walked into what had once been a bustling card room, she found only a few people playing. When they'd stayed here before, there had always been several tables going, even this early in the morning.

She sat down on the edge of the small fountain that marked the center of the room. This was bad. Everyone was afraid. In her memory, this place was so bright and beautiful and full of Jimmy's face. A chill crept up her spine as she thought of Siphon's army tearing through here, imposing a new way of life. She needed to call her parents. The last she'd told them, she was on the East Coast. She should at least let them know she was nearby. And how much danger was Jimmy in, exactly? Would he fight with Amadi's army? She needed to—

"Sadie?" a man said behind her, making her jump.

She blinked up at the smiling face as he came around and sat down next to her. It took her several long moments to recognize him as the man she'd fed off of her first day in the city. He was the first stranger she had propositioned after becoming a succubus. She looked back at her embarrassingly clumsy attempt and inwardly laughed at the memory.

"Samuel?" she said, worried she had it wrong. She'd met a lot of strangers that year. Also, half his face was melted, which was something she hadn't really noticed last time she'd seen him. Back then she'd been too overwhelmed with people's sexual histories to pay much attention to their physical forms.

"That's right." He smiled. "What are you doing here? Have you moved back to the city?"

"No. Just visiting a while." She looked him over; there was something different. A woman. There was a woman all over him who hadn't been there last time. That was why it had been hard to recognize him. "How have you been?" she asked.

"Getting married." He smiled. "And I'm glad I got to see you again. I wanted to thank you. Last summer I was in a real low point in my life. You helped snap me out of it."

She smiled back, but couldn't fight away the feeling of sorrow at the thought of anyone trying to get married in the midst of what was coming. "That's great," she said, trying to sound enthusiastic.

"Are you staying long?" he asked.

"Probably leaving today actually. I should get home before— Well, I think it would be a good time to be close to family. But I wanted to show my friends this beautiful place."

"Did you go to the inner city?"

"Yes. I took them to see the museum at the big tree. The one that—"

His smile faltered. Sadie suddenly wondered how his face had come to look like melted wax.

"Yes. I used to live there. I left after the fire." He gestured to his face. "Lost everything that day."

"I'm sorry. I didn't know."

"Yeah, well. Let's just say it was the start of a lot of bad years. Those men took my mother and grandmother from me." He scoffed. "Things got so bad I even went to try and kill them."

"What?" Sadie tucked her feet up to turn and face him fully.

"That's right. I went the next day, sneaking in past the angry mob outside their cells. But they'd already escaped."

"You went to the jail?" she prodded, before getting an idea. "Could you direct me to where that was? With all the dangerous stuff that's been happening, I wanted to find out more about the men who were never caught."

He clucked his tongue. "Whew. I don't know. I mean I will of course if you ask me to. But I wouldn't get too caught up in digging up the past. It only leads to unhappiness. And we can't do much to change things, anyway." He stood up and twisted his engagement ring around. "That's why I'm going to enjoy the good parts of life while they're here."

Sadie stood, too. "That sounds like a plan, Samuel. I wish you and your fiancé the best. I think I'll go check out the sight of the escape anyway, if you wouldn't mind..."

"Of course." He patted his pockets. He had a pen, but neither of them had paper, so he told her exactly where to go. She said it on repeat to herself the entire way there.

A couple hours later, in a sharp turn to her morning, she found herself walking into a jailhouse that looked centuries old. "Excuse me," she said to a squat man behind a desk. "I'm writing a story on local history. I'm wondering if I could ask you a few questions about the men who started the fire and their escape the following day."

He stood up and came to lean against the side of his desk. "You want to know about the infamous three, eh? Well, you're in luck, girl. Mitch is on duty today. And he *loves* to tell the story. He was working that night and he won't let you forget it."

He pulled open a grate and pressed in a code to open the door behind him. "Mitch! Reporter coming your way!" he shouted to the man at the end of the hall. Sadie hadn't realized they'd think she was a reporter. She did her best to recall the name of the local newspaper as she stepped into the dimly lit cavern comprised of prison cells on either end of a long, straight pathway.

"Don't worry, it's perfectly safe," the man told her, misreading her hesitation. She stepped past him and he shut the door behind her, latching her in. There were cells on either side of her as she walked and she looked back and forth at them in fascination.

The prisoners were mostly reading, sleeping, and in one case, playing stones. No one took much notice of her as she passed, though a man in a cell filled with wildflowers did wink when he caught her staring. She smiled before turning her attention to the elderly man slumped in the chair at the end of the hall.

"Mitch? I'm... Mia... Baker." She wasn't sure why she gave a fake name, and she flinched inwardly at her silliness. "I hear you were on duty the night the prisoners disappeared."

"What's that?" he asked, holding a hand up to his ear.

She said a bit louder, "I hear you were on duty the night the prisoners disappeared."

"From under my very nose," the old man said, tossing aside his well-worn paperback and leaning back. "Over here." He pointed at the cell behind him. "It's the most secure room, totally flame retardant to contain prisoners of the fire nymph variety. And while I was sitting here, keeping a good lookout mind you, I feel the slightest little tremor. I look around. Everything looks fine. And then what do you know? The back wall of their cell has collapsed. Just the single wall. Was like someone hit it with a large, silent hammer. I rush out through it and the back alley is completely empty. The men are gone. Dead. Gone. Never to be heard of again." He gestured dramatically with both hands. "I'm writing a book if you want to see some excerpts."

"Perhaps tomorrow. I'm wondering, did you get to see any of the celebrations as everyone helped rebuild? I heard some big names came to town. Siphon, Ma—"

"Siphon? Oh, he was a wonderful man. He told me personally that he thought I had something special. Even put a word in for me with the boss, got me promoted to this position."

"You met him?"

"Oh yes. He came around to tour the city. This was back five years before the fire, when he was still a young lad. He was a part of some committee from Washington responsible for making sure prisoners were being treated well. His recommendation got me this job."

Sadie stopped listening as the man recounted everything he knew about prison safety. Siphon had got the prisoners out. Possibly with the help of a very skilled earthquake nymph. Which meant Eirik Pierce, Hetia's father, was probably involved. Maybe this had been the *keys to the city* Siphon had been referring to when he'd asked for his help. Or rather, paid for his help. Perhaps it hadn't been the literal keys he got from being a contractor, but his skill as a nymph that Siphon had been after. Though if he'd planned to help the prisoners escape, why?

And then Sadie remembered. She nodded and made a sound like she was still listening, but her eyes flared as she recalled exactly where she had seen that man before. The one who'd helped start the fire.

It was as she was racing through Mia Siphon's memory, trying to find the day in which her father might have shared their family secrets with her. The fire nymph had been a friend of Siphon's daughter growing up. They'd played together. Their families had dined together. He had popped into view all throughout Mia's memories of her teens. And if that was true, there wasn't any doubt that he was with The Coalition.

And it looks like Siphon hadn't just been taking advantage of the opportunity to act as savior after the fire. He was also likely responsible for planning it. Which he had certainly done to build resentment against humans and win over more nymphs to his cause. Which had worked splendidly.

Sadie felt rage, raw and hot, roiling around inside her. She hated that man. He was destroying everything and doing it all with a well-planned, cold calculation that was decades – no, generations old. Him, the Maddoxes, the Griffiths, and the whole Coalition. They were vile. And she couldn't stand the thought of them getting away with this.

Sadie burst into Troy and Hetia's hotel room after pounding twice on her own door. The nymphs were sitting on the bed in heated conversation, while Patricia appeared behind Sadie a few seconds later. She had been fuming so hard the whole way there that she hadn't really worked out what she was going to say.

"I remember. The man. Siphon knew him. The bastard planned that attack and then bailed out the attackers. All to build nymph hatred toward humans. I'm sure of it. And it's just too much of a coincidence that the bomb was finished the same week all this went down. I bet he had something else planned. Maybe it fell through. Maybe he's waiting and it's still coming. Either way." She stopped her pacing to look at each of them. "We can't let him pull us out of this just to go fight a losing battle against his now-ginormous army. It feels like he's setting all the rules and we're left to dance to them. And I don't want to play along. I want to learn more about what happened here. Get some kind of evidence. I want to track down what happened to that bomb."

"You think we should stay?" Troy asked.

"I think we should definitely stay. Siphon has kept his dirty little secrets long enough. The fighting isn't going to be over any time soon. It could be years before The Coalition has suppressed all the resistance. Because I assume they're going to win, given they've been setting up this moment for decades. But if we can find that bomb or uncover evidence of what he did here, then we might have a real weapon we can use to fight back."

Hetia nodded once, slowly, and then directed at Patricia, "Still nothing on the message machine?"

"No update. He'll send word soon, I'm sure. They're dealing with a lot right now," Patricia said as she pulled on a jacket. "But I'll go leave him a message immediately."

"Tell Dee we're staying here a week, unless we hear from him,"

Hetia told her. "Don't put any other details in the message in case the number is compromised."

Patricia nodded and disappeared in search of a pay phone, while Sadie relaxed slightly. She'd been ready to argue her point, but Hetia just looked at her with a rare smile. "Let's raise hell," she said, her eyes darting up and down Sadie's body. And the image of herself all fired up bloomed at the forefront of the woman's desires. Sadie glanced at Troy and saw the same image of herself reflected in him.

She was glad she'd convinced them, but life as a succubus, it seemed, only grew more complicated.

Chapter 6

Side Effects

The group went back to the original room assignments and stayed that way. Sadie barely saw Hetia as the woman began to get up early and return late.

"She's been interviewing everyone she can find who lived near the sight of the fire," Troy told them one afternoon while they were sprawled out on the floor eating lunch in his room. "She's determined to find something."

"I offered to go with her," Patricia said. "Help check if the stories are true, but she said she hasn't found anything worth my time yet."

"I'm following some leads at the jail. I might snag you tomorrow," Sadie told her.

"This is silly. If we could just get a peek at that conversation." Patricia pushed away her bowl.

"Hetia doesn't want me in her head," Sadie said.

"Yes, but—"

"She said no. It's not an option," Her voice came out a little too brusquely given that she agreed completely and it was frustrating that what they really needed was right in front of them, but out of reach.

"That's why she's trying so hard. She's determined to find another way," Troy said. "She feels guilty. Though really, she does have the right to not have someone dig through her memories."

The door shot open and they fell silent. Hetia had come back early. "I found something. I need you," she said, looking at Patricia.

"Really?" The hag jumped up and secured her heels.

"I think this guy's lying to me. I'm sure he knows something," Hetia said as she led the way into the hall. The door closed on the rest of the explanation, leaving them in silence.

Sadie darted a quick glance at Troy. The residual lust in his body from their encounter hadn't decreased over the past several days, and she too, found herself thinking about him far too often. She could feel him watching her as she lifted her bowl to sip the broth.

Troy shifted to lean back against the bed and she made the mistake of looking at him right as his thoughts turned back to the day they'd slept together. He thought about it as much as she did. More, actually, as he was usually the one that pulled her mind back to it. Despite everything that was happening, Troy woke up every morning hard and thinking about her bound and helpless and hungry. Sometimes he would have such intense wet dreams that the lust pouring from him would wake her in the night.

She was sure that the only reason he didn't grow an erection every time he saw her was because he took care of business right beforehand. But that morning they had shown up early enough that he hadn't had the chance. Which meant he'd spent most of the meeting sneaking glances at her and hiding the fact he was aroused behind bent knees. She knew though. And what was worse, he knew that she knew.

"Can I ask you something?" he said in a very different tone than he'd used when Patricia had been in the room. It was heavy with the burden of desire. Sadie nodded, not daring to speak.

"These... side effects from... what we did? Did they happen to Jimmy?"

She chewed her lip. "Yes."

"So they're – normal? They happen to everybody?" Sadie looked away. "The stranger you were with yesterday. He'll be experiencing a similar thing for the rest of the week?" She took another sip of broth, slurping loudly. "Sadie?"

She gave out a guttural sigh of frustration. "No."

"No?" He raised an eyebrow.

"No, it only happens when the experience is particularly intense. With Jimmy it happened because we are in love and it was our first time together, *and* I was hungry. With you—" She scrubbed at a spot of food on her pants. "I was also really hungry. That's probably why."

"So it'll go away?"

Sadie thought about it, uncertain of exactly how any of this worked, but not wanting to reveal her ignorance in front of him. "Eventually."

"Well how did Jimmy deal with it? Because hot and cold showers aren't helping." He ran a hand along his jaw, his eyes glinting as he added, "Not that I mind the showers themselves, or the dreams, but it can be a little inconvenient when we have so much work to do."

Sadie swallowed, and her face flushed, not with embarrassment but with heat at the implications of what she was about to share. "We... just satisfied those urges whenever they came up. Together. And eventually he stopped thinking about it all the time." She stacked the dishes as she spoke so as not to have to look at him. He kept staring silently at her, though, and eventually she had to acknowledge it. Glancing over, she kept her gaze on his as he adjusted himself. "I should go. Let you take care of that," she said, getting to her feet.

"What about you?" Troy asked. "Are you having a similar – reaction?" Her skin felt too warm now, and Troy looked satisfied at whatever he saw in her expression. "So... it's not just me then?"

She had no response for that so she simply dusted off her clothes. She was suddenly very hungry and considered going to find someone right then. It had been a challenge in a city so full of fear, especially first thing in the morning, or she would have done so before coming over. It was easy to find drunk people, but she had no wish to be with someone who wasn't coherent enough to properly consent.

She turned, but stopped as he said, "I have one more question."

She crossed her arms. "Yes, Troy?"

He stood up and moved to right in front of her. "When you're next door, and I'm in the shower? Can you feel it? From that far?"

She intensely regretted ever having told him anything about succubi.

"No," she said, but by the reappearance of an all-too-mischievous grin, it was clear he could tell she was lying.

Sadie turned her back on him, deciding that if he spoke again she would just ignore it. But he was silent as she escaped to the hallway and into her own room. It was only a few seconds later that she felt him. He was unbuttoning his pants. Only, instead of the feeling of warm water, he seemed to be lying on his back on the bed. The image of it popped clearly into her mind as if he'd sent it intentionally.

Her suspicions were confirmed when something new happened. Typically, Troy's fantasies involved that one memory, replaying it again and again. But this time, a scene began to play out like a movie running through her thoughts. She could have suppressed it, or gone downstairs, but instead she lay down on her own bed and let it come. After all, he wouldn't know she had stayed; that he was reaching her.

Troy imagined coming into her room and pushing her down, exactly in the position she was now lying. She felt him grow harder in his hand, as in his thoughts he pictured her struggling against the force of his weight even as she writhed hungrily against him.

Sadie unbuttoned her jeans and slid them open as Troy sent the image of himself pressing her knees open and resting on top of her. He imagined kissing her, softly, sweetly. Sadie could feel the moisture pooled between her legs as she reached for it with a finger. He imagined sliding his hand up her shirt and massaging. She mimicked the scene with her own hand.

He grabbed her wrists and pressed them above her head, and they were suddenly bound in the same tiny ropes she'd been tied with while a prisoner. The fantasy had no explanation for where the ropes were secured.

Troy kissed his way down her body. In his thoughts she wore the exact outfit she currently was. Except as he pictured removing her jeans, he imagined black panties instead of the cotton white ones she was actually in.

He spread her knees with his shoulders as he kissed along her inner thigh. Sadie arched into her own hand right as Troy pictured her arching against his tongue. She moved in the rhythm he set in his fantasy. Every now and again she caught a glimpse of the real Troy lying on his back, stroking himself to the same rhythm.

She could feel him fighting to prolong his climax, but he was too impatient. Lost in his own lascivious thoughts, he seemed to have no self-control. If he'd actually been licking her, she would have taken over his orgasm. She would have made him feel so good. As it were, he came only a minute or so in, his groan piercing the thin wall.

The scene he was firing at her died a few seconds later and Sadie was left chasing her own release alone. The room suddenly felt too quiet and she could hear the sink turn on in Troy's bathroom. She sped up her own motions and finished herself in a rush, feeling lonely and unsatisfied.

Pushing herself up, she glared around at the furniture. She was still panting heavily. "Asshole," she said out loud. He thought he could use her mental ties to people's lustful thoughts to send her suggestive scenes. And he knew she couldn't do it back. This was an entirely one-sided game and she definitely had the losing side. He was probably feeling pretty smug right about now. She should go over there. She should storm into the bathroom and give him something real to think about. Not just some quick flash as he released a little pent-up tension.

Sadie resecured her own pants and washed her hands. Then she stormed out into the hall and into his room.

"Sadie? You're back." He had on the most innocent expression she'd ever seen on anyone. It was comical. And decidedly intentional. She crossed her arms.

"Yes," she said, changing her mind about her next action. "I just wanted to let you know that I'm going in search of someone to feed from and won't be back for several hours."

"Oh? Alright then," he said, securing the buttons at his wrists. "Well, you don't need to tell me. I was just heading out to get to work."

He stepped around her, swung on his jacket, and pulled open the door. Holding it for her, he looked back expectantly, a twinkle in his eye. Sadie pushed past in the narrow space of the threshold, but paused facing him. The mood shifted. Troy's innocent little smile disappeared, his gaze growing hot on hers.

Sadie was tired of these confusing games. She wished they could just put it all aside and act without consequences. If only they didn't bring out the competitive side in each other. As she stood there, his hand landed on her hip and she was surprised to see she'd moved closer. Sadie could practically feel the tension radiating from every muscle in his body and his expression was suddenly deadly serious. She pressed against him before she could stop herself, but hesitated with her lips a few inches from his.

Troy closed the gap, his mouth crashing into hers with a hunger that nearly knocked her flat. She heard herself moan loudly as his desire pulled at her, his hand traveling to grip her lower back. He ground his hips against her in a spastic motion that looked unintentional, and it was all she could do to keep herself from tearing open his pants and reaching for the suddenly very hard cock between them.

"Sadie," he whispered against her mouth, rocking against her to the motion of his tongue.

A door closed at the end of the hall and it snapped her from her blissful state. Her rational mind caught up to her instincts and she broke off the kiss. Troy groaned, pulling her tight against him, but kept his mouth an inch from hers. He was looking at her desperately, a question in his eyes.

Suddenly she was scared. She wanted to give in, follow her instincts, but the force of her desire overpowering all other intentions frightened her into withdrawing. She had come over there to taunt him, to one-up the game he had played with her. And now all she wanted to do was drop to her knees and suck him into her mouth.

She staggered back, trying to suppress her panting so he wouldn't see her struggle. Troy, however, stood there like an open book, precum coating the mound in his pants and his whole body still unconsciously undulating.

"Thanks for the appetizer," she said, trying to sound cool, but giving herself away with the husky sound in her voice. Adjusting her clothing, she forced herself to step backward down the hall. She wanted to turn her back to him, but couldn't quite seem to take her eyes off the sight of him staring at her with an open plea on his face.

Good. That was what she had wanted from him, she told herself. He definitely wasn't looking smug now. And she wasn't going to give in to everything he was begging for. She forced another retreating step. She was going to leave him like this. One more step.

Sadie turned in a rush, immediately grateful to be free from his gaze. Troy didn't call after her, but she could feel the pull of his desire all the way to the elevator. When she turned back to face him as the doors closed, she caught one last glimpse of him holding himself through his pants. He looked beautiful, leaning back against the door-frame, his hair still damp from the shower and every cell in his body full of wanting her.

Sadie practically collapsed against the back wall when she was finally alone. The force of resisting having left her depleted of energy even as her body cried out for more action. Despite what she'd told Troy though, she didn't particularly feel like feeding off a stranger just then. One person never replaced another, and in that moment she wanted exactly one and only one thing.

Scrubbing at her face as if she could wash him away, she stared at a spot on the floor as she forcibly slowed her breathing. Sadie was sure that the second she calmed down she would be glad of having pulled off what she just had. She tried to conjure up his tiny, smug smile, but unfortunately all she got was his pained expression as she'd pulled away.

The elevator doors opened and several strangers were suddenly staring at her. Grateful for the pull back to the present, she smiled and stepped out past them as if everything was perfectly normal with her. Not sure what else she should do with her time now, she went to hang out with Mitch at the prison for the rest of the day.

It turned out that the guard was a wealth of knowledge, though he spent more time with his head in books than actually paying atten-tion to the prisoners. She filed away anything that might be useful in the little notebook she'd been carrying around and returned to her room just after dinner with a feeling that she'd at least done something that day, even if nothing spectacular had come up.

Hetia and Patricia stepped out of the stairwell just as Sadie was exiting the elevator. Hetia looked windswept and tired, and yet the look just highlighted her sharp beauty. Her long blond hair was down, a rare thing, and Sadie had to resist the urge to run her fingers through it. She'd wanted to touch her in any way, to connect, ever since their failed encounter, but Hetia seemed to be holding her even further away.

"Any luck?" Sadie asked them in greeting.

"Ha." Patricia laughed. "The guy was just having an affair the day of the fire. Thought his wife had hired us to question him. Nearly pissed himself when Hetia—" The door opened and Troy appeared. Sadie froze as they stared each other down. The tension in their non-verbal exchange must have been palpable because Patricia's speech faltered. "Anyway, no we didn't get anything."

They stood there in silence a minute before Troy directed at Hetia, "Do you want to get in some training tomorrow? I'm getting soft just sitting here."

"Yeah." Hetia sounded relieved for the suggestion. She nodded goodnight to Patricia and to Sadie's feet, since she hadn't actually looked her in the eye for days, and the two of them disappeared.

The door clicked shut with a firmness that annoyed Sadie. Patricia patted her on the back. "Come. Tell me what happened," she said. And they disappeared behind their own locked door.

Chapter 7

Thin Walls

They were eating lunch at the bar downstairs when Hetia and Troy swept in, full of excited energy. The pair were equally sweaty and it looked good on both of them.

Where'd you go?" Sadie asked.

Troy went to sit next to Sadie, but Hetia tripped him. He exaggerated his reaction, turning it into a chance to give her a surprise kick, but she stepped back just out of reach as if she'd seen it coming. Troy laughed. "Nice try though," Hetia said, sitting down next to Patricia.

"We found a park," Troy replied, leaning across the table to steal a fry from Patricia's plate.

"The ground was perfect. Muddy and inconvenient. And Troy kept the sun in my eyes," Hetia explained with a surprising amount of excitement in her tone. And if Sadie didn't know better, she might say the woman was even a little... giddy. "And then a band of local boys asked if they could join in."

"And Hetia fought all of us at once," Troy said. "Only cheating a few times." He grinned at her.

"Harnessing the power of the earth is never cheating," Hetia said, grinning back now. Yep. Definitely giddy. Sadie loved Hetia when she was like this. She hadn't realized just how down she'd been recently.

Her only regret was that it was never *her* that seemed to make her this happy. Sadie glared at the green friendship line between Hetia and Troy with a sharp pain of envy.

Things were looking up though, because Hetia looked right at her as she asked, "How was your morning?"

Sadie was so taken aback that she stuttered out a few false attempts before getting it under control. "Uh... you know. Nothing new." Despite her ineloquent response, Sadie risked smiling at her and Hetia smiled back.

"Well, I'm going to eat a horse and then catch a shower," Hetia said, stealing one of Sadie's fries before heading for the bartender. Sadie chewed her lip as she watched her walk away. Troy and Patricia looked knowingly at her, but Sadie managed to ignore them. She missed the woman's presence already and kept her eyes on her as her companions talked past her.

Hetia must have ordered for Troy, because a few minutes later three full entries were brought to the table. As Sadie watched them be devoured by the two of them, in between talking animatedly, their good mood became infectious. For one meal, Sadie forgot to be worried and afraid. She hadn't seen Patricia laugh in days either, but she soaked up the blow-by-blow fight as Troy told it with elaborate flare.

Eventually, Hetia rose.

"Where are you headed?" Sadie asked, feeling like the barrier between them had finally loosened enough for casual conversation.

"Time to wash away the mud," Hetia said, acknowledging each of them, including patting Troy on the back, before leaving.

"Sadie?" a man said to her right, pulling her gaze away from Hetia's retreating form.

"Oh, hi! Umm..." Sadie looked over the hulking figure.

"Cliff," he said.

"Cliff, yes." She swept a curl behind her ear, embarrassed she'd forgotten his name already.

"I was hoping to run into you again," he said, darting an uncertain glance at Troy and then at Patricia. "Have you already fed today?"

Cliff was direct. It had been the thing she'd liked about him. He was also tall, broad, and attractive in a rough sort of way. None of those things had meant much to her when she'd fed off him a few days ago, but at the glare Troy was shooting him now, Sadie was suddenly quite satisfied at Cliff's appearance.

"No, actually." She smiled and turned to Patricia. "Do you mind if we use the room?"

"No. Of course," Patricia said, casting a worried look at Troy.

"Great," Sadie said. "It's this way." She took Cliff's hand in hers, nodded back at her companions and led him away.

Though making Troy jealous had become her second favorite way to annoy him, if a bit disgraceful, at least she *was* actually hungry. And all the pent-up tension between her and Hetia and Troy had left her in the mood for more than just the casual-feeding quickie she usually had with strangers. She wanted something rough. Her whole body was buzzing with it, and Cliff would be the perfect medicine.

"You wanna be inside me this time?" she asked outside the door as he pinned her against it to steal the first kiss.

"More than anything," he said, hiking her legs up around him and holding her ankles with one hand. Cliff took the key and opened the lock for her. Within seconds they'd crashed onto the bed and begun tearing at each other's clothes.

Sadie didn't want to leave a mess on the comforter that she shared with Patricia though, and Cliff had just gotten her naked when she panted, "Bathroom" and pushed herself off the bed. He didn't immediately make to follow her so she grabbed his hand and walked backward toward the other room, clarifying her intention.

Cliff still wore his pants and Sadie began by kneeling on the bathroom floor to unzip them. She smiled up at him as he came free, but she didn't take him in her mouth. She'd already decided what she wanted, and it wasn't that.

As she rose to her feet, however, Sadie noticed something. A wave of lust was hitting her from a source that wasn't the man pulling her back into an embrace. She broke off the kiss immediately, not interested in it, as the pull from next door was accompanied by the pleasurable sensation of hot water.

Hetia was getting in the bath and Sadie was heavy in her thoughts.

Her heart sped up, as she realized what was about to happen. Though Troy had been hitting her hard with erotic imagery for days, Hetia had clearly been trying to tamp down any thoughts of her, since Sadie hadn't felt anything like this.

"Behind me," Sadie told Cliff, pushing him out of the way so she could step against the sink. She suddenly didn't want the distraction of interacting too much with the man. "You're going to fuck me like this. Hard." She arched her back as she looked at him in the mirror.

She didn't have to ask twice, but she did have to help him get inside her. Once several hands had him lined up, he thrust in one long stroke and Sadie braced against it, her body stretching satisfactorily.

As she let the man drive, she felt the wave of lust from next store change in quality, the feeling of wet heat engulfing Hetia's body. Sadie was shocked at the strength of the sensation coming from the woman.

Sadie felt some guilt for her ability to feel it when Hetia didn't know, but it hadn't been her intention to eavesdrop. After all, it was the other woman's thoughts on her that were tugging at her attention in the first place, Sadie justified. She never picked up on such things from her other neighbors. She couldn't feel someone else's lust from this distance unless it was directed at *her*. And right now, Hetia was clearly thinking about only one thing.

Cliff groaned behind her as he slowly thrust in and out until he was slick with their juices.

Sadie barely noticed as the feeling of Hetia's fingers sliding up her thigh in the warm bath hit her hard. When one hand continued upward to pinch her nipples, Sadie copied the movement on her own body.

Cliff held her hips as he pumped into her, and Sadie closed her eyes. She wanted him to use her body and feed her hunger, while she got to fall into the scene next door. And she was getting exactly what she wanted.

Hetia slid a finger between her legs and encircled her clit, but the image that overlapped the real scene of her in the tub was that of Hetia playing with Sadie. Everything she did to herself, she imagined it was Sadie she was actually touching. As Hetia rocked into her fingers, Sadie moved her hand down to mimic the other woman's motion.

"I'm close," Cliff said. Sadie ignored him. She didn't feel like explaining that he would stay hard as long as she wanted him to. Hetia was firm and slow and Sadie matched the pace precisely, even though it didn't go with Cliff's rhythm at all. She arched her back into her hand at a totally different pace than the man thrusting into her and the effect was chaotic and rough. Which was just perfect.

Cliff's grunts were getting louder and Sadie shushed him, not wanting him to disturb Hetia. "You feel so goddamn good succubus, do you know that?" he leaned down to whisper in her ear instead.

"Yeah? Show me. If you go fast enough, I might even let you come," she said, opening her eyes to look at him. At her words, he growled in excitement through gritted teeth as he sped up until his thighs were slapping loudly against her ass.

Cliff worked her hard and she loved the way it mingled with the feeling of her finger moving over her clit. Sadie lightened the touch, realizing she was about to climax. She wanted to wait for Hetia and the woman was taking her time.

"God. Fuck yes," Cliff said in her ear.

"Shhh," Sadie told him again.

"This is what you want?" he panted, staring at her breasts as they jiggled under the rough movement.

"Yeah. Just like that." She closed her eyes again as Hetia began to get close. "Don't speak to me. Just do it. And the harder you go, the better I'll make it feel."

He obeyed, sticking to rough grunts, and she kept her promise. She didn't want this man to come chasing her down all week, though, and she planned to tell him this was the last time, so she kept the pleasure within a reasonable limit. She was going to show him a good time, but not too good.

All the same, the lust and pleasure pouring off him was as intoxicating as what was happening next door, and she ate it up. Hetia wanted it now, and she'd sped up. The sound of the water lapping from the quick movement became the backdrop of the other woman's rising pleasure.

Sadie softened her own touch as her climax threatened to hit any second, but it was in vain. Her body was ready to explode. The long build-up made the orgasm sneak up with a powerful, gradual build. First, her legs went nearly numb until she was practically relying on Cliff's grip to support her. Then, a searing heat spread outward from between her legs.

It was Hetia beginning to spasm that sent her over the edge. She convulsed, clenching around Cliff. Her own climax was entirely out of her control and it shook her in several long bursts. Toward the end she released Cliff and let the feeling of his last few pumps, now slick and slow, accompany her own final spasm.

Sadie relaxed against the sink to catch her breath, taking her time to recover from what had just happened. After a minute, she said. "Thank you, Cliff. *That* was exactly what I needed to get through this week."

He laughed. But when she opened her eyes to look at him, he had that puppy dog look strangers got when she went a little too far with them. Sadie sighed inwardly. She might as well talk to him now, because she really wanted to shower alone.

Chapter 8

Misconceptions and Breakthroughs

Hetia's good mood didn't last long, which was entirely understandable. They were approaching the end of the one week they'd given themselves and still they had nothing. Nor had they heard from Amadi.

When Sadie and Patricia walked in with breakfast on day six, everyone was somber. Hetia mumbled a "Here goes nothing" before taking her croissant to go, and the rest of them sat down in silence to eat together.

"Last night here," Sadie grumbled. "What a waste of time." She threw her napkin down.

"Yeah, I think if we were going to find something by talking to people, we would have done it by now," Patricia said. It was true, and Hetia seemed to be the only one of them who hadn't given up on that notion.

"Should we even stay through the night? I'm worried about what's happening out there. Jimmy..."

"It's not over," Troy said. "We have one more place we can look." They stared at him with betrayal. Had he been holding out? "I mean Hetia. If we're going to do something useful with our last night, how about we focus on trying to get her to open up? I know that nothing scares that woman more than having someone snoop around inside her head. Especially," he looked at Sadie, "you. But maybe if we could get her talking about her past, she'd loosen up. Perhaps we should have spent this week focused on the mystery that is Hetia, not this city."

Patricia was nodding, but Sadie was skeptical. She'd been on the outskirts of that maze several times. She was pretty sure there wasn't a way through. "Any ideas on how to do that?"

"I could talk to her," Patricia said. "I know we're not close, but I *am* a hag. I'm also a little hungry right now and when I'm particularly ready to feed, people find themselves wanting to tell me their stories. I could take her out tonight. We can go get some drinks, just the two of us."

"That's not a bad idea." Troy leaned back. "I wish we'd thought of it sooner, actually."

"Do you think getting her to share is enough to work?" Sadie asked.

"It's something we haven't tried yet." Patricia shrugged, renewed hope in her tone. "And honestly, I can't think of anything better to do today. I was considering going to find some old person in the bar to tell me their life story and then taking a nap."

Sadie nodded. "You're right. We haven't got anything good all week. It's worth a shot."

Patricia looked suddenly anxious. "What is it?" Troy prodded.

"Oh. It's nothing. It's just... I'm hungry *now*. I don't think I can wait all day."

"I got you," Troy said, jumping up. "I told Annie I would come back and see the rest. Here's my last chance."

"Who's Annie?" Sadie asked.

"The woman from the museum. I told her I'd be back, remember?"

"Oh. I thought you were just being polite. I mean, people say things like that all the time. I'm sure she's not actually expecting you to return." Sadie frowned.

"Yes, people do say things like that. And isn't it obnoxious when they don't really mean it? Besides, why wouldn't I want to go back? That place was fascinating."

Sadie looked at him a long time. She really had thought he'd just been smooth-talking that woman to get what they'd wanted. But now a new thought occurred to her. Maybe Troy was good with people because he actually did like them in general.

His easy way with strangers was both something she admired about him, and something she'd always assumed he put on like a performance. Was she too hard on him? She tried to remember exactly what he'd said to Annie that day and why she'd interpreted it as if—

"Sadie?" Troy snapped his fingers in front of her face as if she'd zoned out. "Do you want to come?"

"Uhh. No. I think I'll stay here." She gathered up her trash, but added, "Thanks though," and smiled at him.

He returned the sentiment with a slight delay, possibly due to his surprise at her friendliness, "See you tonight then?" he asked, a bit wistfully.

"Sure." Sadie bobbed her head in goodbye and returned to her room, where she spent the day alone, full of heavy thoughts about what kind of person she was, and wondering if her own mistrust of other's intentions colored the way she often viewed Troy's behavior.

Eventually, she fell asleep on her stomach, still wrapped in the towel she'd secured after getting out of the shower. She must have been pretty out of it, because she didn't hear the door open and yet someone was saying her name as if far away. Sadie groaned, but forced her eyes open.

Troy was standing there looking down at her uncertainly. "Sorry," he said, as she sat up, adjusting the towel as she did so. "You can keep sleeping if you want. It's just, Patricia's off with Hetia and... it's our last night in the city. Our last night before joining the fight. And I was wondering if you wanted to go get a drink with me. Or something."

She stared at him for a long time. Was he asking her out? Sadie cleared her throat and swished her hair back behind her ear. "Uhh, sure. I'll just... get dressed."

Troy went back to his room and she began to move in a rush. The idea of going out with Troy on their last night there had her nervous in a way she couldn't entirely account for. Their interactions had gone through so many ups and downs that week, and she wasn't quite sure how to prepare for this next encounter.

Sadie combed her hair and scooped it up into a loose gather, held by a single clip that could be easily removed. It was her preferred style when she was around Jimmy as it kept her curls out of her face during the day, but meant they didn't have to waste time taking down her hair anytime they wanted to suddenly and frantically get her on her back.

A sharp pain of longing hit her at this thought. They'd had such little time to explore that part of them before being separated. Though in her opinion, years wouldn't have been enough. All the while, each day apart felt like an eternity. And now here she was, putting her hair up like this before going out with Troy, and the fire nymph was part of the reason Jimmy had told her he needed some time.

Sadie pulled the clip back out and tossed it aside. She'd come back to the hair. Instead, she opened the closet to glare at the five outfits. There were two dresses from her time spying that Patricia had inadvertently stolen when she and Troy had left in a rush to join Amadi's army – abandoning the mission early after Troy had become convinced Sadie couldn't be trusted. So much had changed so quickly.

Sadie chewed her lip, wondering what Troy was planning on wearing. She didn't want to get all dressed up and then have him show up in the same jeans he'd been wearing earlier. She could just see him looking her up and down and then shooting her a knowing grin. Then again, if he came over in that suit he had and she was in jeans then she'd have to be at his side all night while he looked amazing and she looked casual.

Ugh, this was stupid. They were just going to get some drinks while Patricia did all the hard work tonight. But Troy had been right, this could be their last night to relax at all, so Sadie pulled on the knee-length green dress with the low back. It was meant to be worn without a bra, and it especially flattered her hips and breasts.

She hadn't actually had a chance to wear this one before, but as she looked herself over in the mirror, she decided it was definitely her favorite. She wished Jimmy was there to see it.

A knock came at the door.

"Just a minute!" she called from the bathroom before reaching to put on some light make-up. It came again as she was putting on the mascara and she decided just to leave her hair down. She checked herself out one last time in the mirror and realized this was way too much.

It wasn't that it looked overdone, it was that she looked somewhat stunning in a natural way. She wiped off the light lipstick, but then chewed anxiously at her lips, which made them swell red anyway. Third knock. There was no going back now.

Sadie went to the door, took a deep breath, and then tried to look nonchalant about her appearance. Her first thought when she spotted Troy was that she was certainly not over-dressed. He was in the suit, the one that looked especially good on him, and he'd done something with his hair that made it appear windswept in a flattering way. They looked each other over and she was immensely grateful she'd had this dress, or else he definitely would have been prettier than her.

"Whoa," he said. "Where were you keeping that?" He pulsed with desire and she was glad that he'd spent half of his time getting ready on making himself orgasm, or else he definitely would have sprouted an erection just then. Which was both the exact reaction she wanted from him and also the one which would have made her even more nervous.

The fact she was nervous at all was a little unusual. She'd casually picked up three different strangers that week and she'd pretty much adjusted to life as a succubus. But as Troy looked at her with his lips parted, she found herself growing hot in the most pleasurable way.

He stepped forward as her cheeks tinged pink and he lifted a hand as if to touch one, only he kept it back an inch from her face. Then he smiled. "Is this a date, Sadie?"

"No." She pulled back. "Why would you think that?"

"Because you look amazing, *and* because you were just checking me out."

"You look fine, too," she hurled in what she realized belatedly was a poor defense. "And I didn't wear this for you. I was just looking forward to finding someone to feed off later tonight and wanted to look nice for our last night here." She stepped forward to point a finger at his chest. "And I wasn't the one who came to your room to ask you to go out. You were clearly the one who wanted this to be a date."

"I never said I didn't," he told her, stepping back and waiting for her to join him in the hall.

To that, she had no reply. Sadie blinked, feeling flustered in the way Troy alone seemed to elicit. She did her best to recover as she stepped up next to him, repeating the words *be nice, be nice, be nice,* mentally to herself.

That was her motto for the night. She had decided that day that she was going to start being kinder to Troy. She wasn't sure why he pushed her buttons so easily – maybe it was just their messy history – but he was a fairly decent guy and she wanted to do better. Actually, he was pretty great. Apart from the fact he'd hated her for the first few weeks they'd known each other, and the fact he'd been hard up for Mia, another succubus, before he'd started to develop an attraction for her.

This last thought left a fresh taste of bitterness in her mouth as she remembered it. As they stepped into the elevator, she glared at him. She'd intended to go on and list his good qualities to herself, but she'd got caught up with the bad ones and was now feeling sour again.

"What is it?" Troy asked, suddenly concerned.

"Whatever precisely happened with you and Mia Siphon? You never told me the full story."

"Mia? Do we have to talk about her tonight?" he asked, looking disappointed.

"I want to know," Sadie said, following him out the elevator.

He didn't speak again as he led her into the street, but she could tell he was thinking, so she waited. She hadn't realized they would be going outside and she wrapped her arms around herself.

"Where are we going?" she asked as he turned down a tiny alleyway.

"I found this place earlier. I thought you might like it. We're both overdressed, but who cares, right?" He led her into a pub. It was bustling with people, and a live band played fiddle and drums on a tiny stage. They were, in fact, *incredibly* overdressed, and Sadie felt a little embarrassed. Troy just smiled at her and took her hand. "Come on," he said, but she didn't budge.

"Troy, my arms. I can't walk through the crowd like this. I might graze someone."

"Oh, right." He took off his jacket and wrapped it around her, looking into her eyes as he pulled it snug at the base of her throat. The intimate gesture left her feeling a little shaken as she moved into the warmth of commotion, music, and food.

Troy spoke to a barmaid just inside the main room before reaching for Sadie's gloved hand and leading her to a private booth in the far corner. Her stomach churned at the smell of sautéing onions. She hadn't eaten since breakfast.

The booth was small, and even though she sat across from him their knees touched. She jostled around trying to find a better placement for her feet, but gave up and put one of them between his. He looked at her seriously as she slid off the coat and set it between them.

Troy took a deep breath. "You'll like this story, I guess, since it involves me playing the fool." For a brief moment Sadie had forgotten she'd asked about Mia, but her brain caught up as he continued. "Some of this you probably know. After I got a little local fame for doing what any decent human being would, I got swept up in the glamour of Siphon's world, and Mia was part of that. When I'd moved to D.C., I had just wanted to get involved in politics – to make some kind of difference."

She laughed.

"I know. I was a bit naive. But then Siphon latched onto me and I was high with the attention. I also found I did well in his world. People responded to me, and I thought I was really making something of myself."

"Can I get you something, loves?" a plump, rosy-cheeked woman asked them. This place was a welcome retreat from the generally somber mood of the city that week.

Sadie glanced quickly at the menu. She didn't want to have to wait for the woman to come back. "The pot pie. And some mead, please."

"I'll have the same," Troy said without glancing at the menu. He took another long breath as the woman walked away and then froze, staring intently at Sadie.

"I don't have a type," he said.

She blinked. "What?"

"Sorry. I had meant to lead into that somehow. This is the second time you've asked me about Mia, and I just figured out why. I was unfair to you when we met. And yes, I did have a bias against succubi because of what happened. You were right... about a lot of things actually. It scared me the way I continued to want Mia even after all the terrible things her family was doing. It messed me up a bit. I was afraid of how I felt about her."

Troy scooped his fingers under hers. "But Mia isn't terrifying because of her sexuality. She's terrifying because of her power in the world, how she holds herself above everyone – her lack of concern for the suffering of others. And she wasn't desirable because she was a succubus either, and it *wasn't* the reason I liked her." He ran a thumb over the back of her hand. "I liked how she was bold and forthright. She was powerful and self-assured."

Troy leaned forward. "You're also bold. And playful. And sometimes cruel." He grinned. "But I don't have a type. You," he dropped into a tone of such abrupt tenderness that it frightened her, "I like for too many reasons to name. You're big-hearted, and impulsive with your feelings. You're brave and resourceful. And you give your whole self to the people you love. I've seen the way you are with Jimmy. And I know we got off to a *really* bad start. And I know I piss you off. Sometimes, it's even intentional." He grinned again, which briefly broke the intensity, but continued seriously. "But I really do like you."

Shit. This was actually happening. He was dead serious and she didn't know how to reply to this new tone. She watched with her succubus vision as a small black line connected them. It was flowing only from him to her, but the love line punctuated his words like a bolt of truth.

The rosy-cheeked woman set down their food in front of them and reached for her tray to grab the drinks, but neither of them looked up at her. "Thanks," Troy said, throwing her a quick smile just before she left.

Sadie's gaze dropped to the food, but she didn't really see it. She obviously liked him too. Or at least she was attracted to him, and had been even when he hadn't liked her. But she just couldn't relax around him enough to feel more than that. And even if she did, what did that mean? She had Jimmy. And yes, she knew Mae had multiple lifelong lovers, Amadi being only one of them, but now that she was actually faced with that possibility, she wasn't sure if she could picture the logistics of it. If they made it through this war, she was going to have to ask Mae more about her life.

"Tell me about your Becoming," Troy said, drawing back her attention. He was letting her off the hook from responding just then and she heaved a grateful sigh. "I've always been curious about it." He picked up his fork. "I mean, most feeders develop slowly during childhood, and it's only succubi that turn rather suddenly during puberty. That must have been crazy."

Suddenly the smell of the food caught up to her and she reached for her own fork. "Yeah." She cleared her throat. "It was a shock. I didn't know I had any succubus blood. And then one day I started having all these feverish dreams. Then Gabriel's there telling me I'm about to turn." She took in the rich, savory bite and groaned.

"That's right. I forgot you'd mentioned that he was with you."

She nodded, swallowing. "Yeah, it was him who helped me through it. He made it a good experience for me. I was really grateful and... a bit sad to find out how tight he is with The Coalition."

"Yeah. No shit. That sucks. How old were you?"

There was a pause while she got down another bite. "It was last summer."

"Last summer?" he said, sounding confused. She nodded. "Then you've only been doing this for half a year."

She shrugged. "Why does that surprise you?"

He shook his head, blinking as if struck dumb. "You're just so confident all the time. The way you approach people. You seem more experienced than... half a year."

She liked this assessment of herself even though it wasn't entirely true. "Well things move fast after you change. I mean, I need to feed almost every day. It's kind of a necessity that drives instinct."

He nodded.

"What was it like for you?" she asked.

Troy sat back. "Let's see... Both my parents were fire nymphs, obviously."

"Why obviously?" she cut in.

"Because, it's actually rare that a nymph and a non-nymph produce someone other than human. Anyway, my mom was brilliant. She started teaching me control when I was five. She passed when I was thirteen, but her mom took over working with me. It was when Nana died that I decided to move to D.C. and carve out a life for myself."

He took a swill of the mead and Sadie said, "I'm sorry about your mom. What about your dad? Where's he?"

"He's a bit of a recluse now. All of his family stayed back in Korea, so it's just the two of us. I'm glad he's removed from society a bit. He should be safe for a while. He probably doesn't even know what's happening yet, which means I have some time before he starts worrying about me. I send him a letter every week though. Haven't missed one in three years." He paused with his fork to his mouth. "What?"

Sadie shook herself. "Nothing. It's just. That's good of you. I promised Mom I'd make a weekly phone call, but I've missed half of them. I should do better. They live not far from here, in a small farming community."

"Any idea how they're going to vote? Your town, I mean. Will they side with The Coalition?" Troy shoved a large bite into his mouth as he looked at her with concern.

Sadie shook her head. "I hope they just vote to comply honestly. I know it wouldn't exactly help the resistance, but it would keep my parents safer. For a while, anyway."

"That's understandable," he said.

Sadie shrugged. "Though, they might vote otherwise if enough other towns do, since... well, they're pretty anti-human feeder. It's kind of why I left. I hadn't wanted to, but they made it pretty clear I wasn't welcome there." She glanced up from picking at the remnants of her dinner to find Troy wearing a frown. "What?"

He shook his head. "I just didn't know. I'm sorry."

She sighed and reached for the mead. "Well, there are bigger problems to worry about." She looked around at all the people enjoying themselves. "Though no one here seems to know it. This is a breath of fresh air." She cupped her fingers around his hand, which had been resting nearby. "Thanks." She squeezed once before hurriedly retreating.

Suddenly self-conscious that they'd managed an entire civil conversation, Sadie held her breath as she waited for one or the other of them to ruin it. But she was feeling warmed by the atmosphere and relaxed by the mead, and after a minute of silently watching each other, Troy asked if she wanted to dance, and Sadie began to trust that they were capable of civility after all.

Her hasty reply caught in her throat as she stared down at her bare arms. "Maybe, but—" She shot a look at the dance floor. "I think it might be a little tight for me there."

Troy looked around as he got to his feet. "This way," he said, holding out a hand for her. She smiled as she accepted it, fighting back the urge to mockingly say something like *what a gentleman*. He led her to the empty hallway leading to the bathroom.

Troy put a hand across her lower back, a necessity given her open-backed dress, and pulled her in. They paused there briefly before joining in on the lively pace of the music. He led them around, swinging and stomping along until she was grinning in full. He released his hold only to spin her before pulling them tight again, and when the occasional person passed for the bathroom, he dodged them easily.

After what must have been an hour, the music dropped to a slow ballad, and they paused to catch their breath. Sadie leaned back against the wall and Troy stayed close, loosening his grip only slightly. They were both panting and he darted a glance at her lips.

She shouldn't kiss him here – he probably didn't want an erection in public. But even as she thought that he went hard anyway. He looked down and then pressed in closer to her, hiding it against her body.

Sadie couldn't help the smile that escaped in response. "How are the side effects going?" she asked, still breathing heavily.

"I think you know." His breathing was already back under control, but his smile had morphed into a heavy-lidded expression, hot with desire, and his shallow panting now seemed to have nothing to do with their recent physical exertion. "You said you wanted to find someone to feed from tonight," he said. "Should I release you so you can get busy on that goal?"

She wrapped her hands around the small of his back and pulled him closer. "I think you know my answer."

"No." He placed a hand tentatively around her hip. "I wouldn't ever presume to know how you're about to react, Sadie." He pulled back just enough to look at her. "But you know what I want. What about you?"

She shot a quick glance at the hallway entrance to see if anyone was coming, but decided she didn't care either way. She had wanted to kiss him again for days. Not in the way she had during her game in the hallway, but in the way they had the day he'd rescued her, when the pressure to run for their lives out of the Siphon estate had taken precedence over the tender exchange. Since then, she hadn't been able to get back to how she'd felt about Troy in that moment, all soft and vulnerable.

Though she certainly felt those things now. He'd been nothing but direct with her this evening, and it made her feel safe. She also, if she was being honest, felt an overwhelming desire to play with him without restraint; to give both of them exactly what they'd wanted all week. The idea made her hot all over.

Sadie didn't hesitate as she pressed her lips to his. The contact sent a wave of pleasure through him, and as he released a little moan, she found she didn't care about maintaining any kind of control, despite their public location. She moved on instinct as his body pinned her to the wall and his tongue prodded hers with equal urgency.

As Troy ran his hand from her hip to just under her breast, someone walked by behind him, but Sadie didn't even open her eyes to acknowledge it. The bathroom door closed at the end of the hall and Troy scooped up her heavy flesh, hanging loose under her dress.

He massaged the areola before swiping his thumb once over her hard nipple.

Sadie moaned into his mouth, shooting a strong pulse of pleasure through him. She knew Troy couldn't climax right here against their nice clothing, but what was the harm in playing a little? After all, they just looked like two people kissing, not overly inappropriate public behavior for this kind of establishment.

To that end, as he continued to play with her nipple, she responded in kind, matching the rhythm of his thumb until he was practically vibrating against her. After she'd gotten a little carried away and he'd bucked in an involuntary jerk against her, she broke away the kiss to catch her breath. Troy panted against her mouth, their lips parted in identical expressions.

"Is that something you're doing intentionally?" he breathed.

"Sort of." She swallowed. "I mean, I can have a lot of control when I try, and I can be totally out-of-control. Right now, I'm somewhere in between."

"It feels good," he said and reclaimed her mouth. Sadie soaked up the feeling of him wanting her, his body pressed tight, but it wasn't enough. Staying in this hallway wouldn't do. She broke off the kiss and looked up into his carnal expression.

"Let's get out of here," she said, having long since made up her mind about who she was going home with. There was no turning back for her now. Not when her body was crying out exactly as much as his.

Sadie was going to take every little thing she wanted from him and give him back everything he wanted in return. She was going to pull him apart and lap up all the pieces. She only wished that those strong lines of red lust which were pulsing out of him were not wrapped around a black line, a love line which had been growing stronger by the minute. That, she had absolutely no idea how to handle.

Chapter 9

Gloves Off

It took Troy three tries to open the door to his room. It probably would have been faster if Sadie hadn't been kissing the back of his neck the whole time, but now that they were alone again, she didn't want to wait any longer to touch him. He'd carried his jacket to hide his arousal on the walk home, which they had made rapidly and without talking.

He spun around to pull her into the room as he pushed the door open with his back. She fumbled for a light switch, but most of her attention was on the feel of his mouth on hers.

"Will you do it again? That thing you were doing to me before?" he breathed.

Sadie found the light and the room grew bright. She pushed him away with her hips and went to sit on the bed. He moved to follow but she held up a hand. "Wait. Stay there." He stopped a few feet from her. "When you came to rescue me that day... I was naked and I felt so exposed. I want to see you like that."

She flicked her eyes up and down his body suggestively. Troy didn't hesitate. He unbuttoned his shirt, starting with the clasp at each sleeve. His body was all lean muscle, solid and with just the right amount of bulk, and he didn't take his eyes off her as he undid his belt and threw it on top of the shirt.

The pants he unzipped carefully over the strained bulge before bending to remove the last of his layers. He stood up, pausing for her to take in every inch of him. Troy looked like perfection, standing impatiently, his muscles half-flexed in anticipation, his cock hard and wet.

She knew exactly what she wanted. It wasn't what he was picturing, but she doubted he'd complain. Sadie crawled backward on the bed, ripping off her gloves. He followed her, cupped her face between both hands, and pressed his tongue deep into her mouth. She fought to keep the embrace as she pushed him to his back and straddled his legs.

Sadie sat up, pushing Troy down with both hands so he wouldn't follow her. Though he was certainly much stronger, he let her direct him. She pulled her dress off in one swoop over her head, leaving her in a thin pair of cotton panties, and Troy ran his hands up her body as he looked her over.

But she was too impatient for that. Her eyes were locked on the part of him standing at attention between them as she slid her hips out of reach and dropped her chest to his thighs. Troy's abdomen tightened in a quick jerk as she wrapped her fingers around the base of his shaft. "Oh god," he said, his muscles going rigid as he realized her intention.

He lifted his head to look down at her, his jaw clenched with need, before collapsing back onto the bed. She watched him blink up at the ceiling as she lowered her mouth to his inner thigh and licked. Troy gave several little thrusts into her grip as she kissed along the line separating his hip and abs, but his earlier moans had dropped into utter silence.

He was frozen, barely breathing, but his whole body began to rock under her in anticipation as she took her time kissing and caressing all around the rigid cock in her hand. Finally, she dragged her lips up to the tip and gently took it into her wet mouth, tasting the salty precum as she spread it down the upper half of his shaft.

Troy sucked in air through gritted teeth before groaning loudly.

"Ahh, fuck. Fuck that's good," he said as she rolled her tongue in circles around the tip before pulling him in deep again, stroking her hand up to collide with her mouth.

Sadie knew her kiss was particularly potent, which was why this had fast become one of her favorite activities with Jimmy, but doing it to Troy had a new kind of excitement. She sat up in a rush and moved to pull the blanket over Troy's legs. He let out a tiny cry as she broke contact. "I want you as focused on this one point of contact as I am," she said as she resettled onto his legs. She wrapped her hand back around him and he bucked hungrily into her touch.

"And I want one more thing." Her lips grazed his shaft as she spoke, and she felt the coming spurt of precum pass under her grip. "Since last time I fed off you I couldn't move, not even an inch, I want the same from you." She stroked him once and he growled deep in his chest. "Put your hands behind your head and keep them there. Just let me work you."

Troy's chest heaved at these words, but a moment later, he obeyed. "God. Yes. Anything you want, Sadie," he said as he settled into the position. He writhed under her, his hips pressing into her hand as his abs convulsed. She hadn't even really begun, his reaction was all from anticipation, and she liked it enough to take her time scooting her hips back down.

Sadie took one last look at the taut muscles of his arms stretched on either side of his heated, pained expression, and then leaned down and took him back into her mouth. Her panties grew wetter at the strength of his reaction. This was just what she'd wanted. Her mouth met her hand and she worked them in tandem while Troy groaned in loud approval. She had been dreaming about this, but the sounds he was making now were far better than the ones in her imagination.

Last time she'd touched him, she'd been lost in her own hunger. This time, she let herself savor his. She reveled in the feeling of him sliding under her tongue, in the tiny bucks of his hips, holding nothing back as Troy's pleasure-crazed thoughts carried her away. And every time she felt him mentally beg for more, she took him higher.

"Ah god. I'm so hard. That feels so good. What are you doing to me?" he rambled in between moans. Sadie began to lose control in her excitement and Troy jerked as the first orgasmic wave hit him. Out of her peripheral vision she saw his hand appear next to her head as he clutched the comforter. Forcing herself to keep her word, she sat up. Since he was mid-climax, she kept a hand wrapped around the base of his shaft to keep him from finishing.

"Wha—" he gasped, convulsing as he looked at her in confusion.

"You moved. Did you want me to stop?" she asked.

He thrust in her hand and she pulled him back from the climax. She was getting better at that particular trick. "No. I—" He bit his lip and then replaced his hand behind his head. "I don't want you to stop." When she didn't immediately resume, he added, "Please," his thighs clenching underneath her. The barest hint of desperation in his voice nearly broke her, but she bent back down as slowly as she could and wrapped her mouth back around him.

He was back to being right on the edge and Sadie took her time, sucking, licking and stroking. "Yes. I won't move. I won't move. Just don't stop," he breathed.

And he kept to that. He let Sadie play until they were both gleaming with sweat, until it seemed he would explode from the stored tension. And when she couldn't hold back a moment longer, she let the climax hit in slow, steady waves.

"I'm coming," he said unnecessarily. "Sadie," he cried before his sounds of pleasure became incoherent. Every muscle in his body strained and she stared at the line separating his thigh and abdomen as it twitched. She ran one finger along the crease, tracing his lower abs, and the muscles trembled under her touch.

She could tell he was attempting to hold his hips still, but all the same they jerked in tiny spastic motions as she prolonged the peak of his pleasure. And when she couldn't hold out any longer, she took him deep into her mouth in one slow motion and drew out the final climactic wave along with a rush of fluid. Troy cried out one last time before collapsing, his muscles going limp.

Sadie swallowed down the sweet, musky fluid and sat up. He was panting harder than she'd ever heard him as she crawled up his body to look down into his flushed face. They were both trembling now, and it showed in her voice as she asked in hungry self-satisfaction, "Was that everything you wanted?"

He half laughed on an exhale. "Shit, Sadie. I didn't know it could be like that." He pulled her mouth to his and inhaled her breath as he kissed her like a lifeline. "I've been thinking about you almost constantly, as I guess you know, but I'd never imagined it like this. Your mouth on me—" He ran his thumb over her wet lips. "The things you can do…"

Troy moved, rolling them until he was on top of her. He pushed her legs wide so he could fit between them, and tucked his knees under her thighs as he sat up. "Tell me what you like," he said, running his hands down her waist to her hips. His eyes dropped to between her legs. The image of the wet patch on her cotton panties bloomed in his mind and she felt his excitement.

She'd liked playing with him, liked being in control, but she wasn't sure she wanted to really let him in. Her body was tense, both with arousal and with that nasty competitive streak that made her want to close her legs and say something stupid like, *I don't need anything from you, Troy Hyun.*

He slid her panties off her ass and reached for both her ankles. Straightening her legs in front of him, he removed that last layer. Her thighs fell back around him and she caught sight of him smelling the white fabric before tossing it aside. "Tell me, Sadie," he said again.

When all she did was chew her lip, he gripped her upper thighs and pulled her toward him in one rough movement until the sides of her ass collided with his inner thighs. His wet cock landed on top of her exposed clit and she sucked in air at the pleasurable sensation.

His eyes lit up. Troy's gaze raked over her as he ran his hands down her stomach and inner thighs before scooping his palms under her lower back, causing her to arch against him as he pulled. She gave a breathy moan, secretly loving the way he was handling her.

"I want—" Her mind raced through possible answers to his question. Would admitting how much she wanted him feel like losing the upper hand? Her gaze traced the muscles of his shoulders as he continued to rock her hips with his hands.

She was embarrassed at herself. She'd never struggled to tell someone what she'd wanted before, and Troy was asking directly, looking at her as if he was ready to devour her answer. But there was still a part of her that felt like she was in some kind of competition with the man. And yet, her traitorous body arched in the grip he had on her hips.

"You have nothing to say to me? That's a first," he said, and to her annoyance, she blushed.

"I want you to fuck me," she said, her voice coming out raw. "I want something hard to squeeze when you make me come," she added, regaining confidence. He groaned deep in his throat, his grip tightening on her hips. "And I want to watch as you work me with your hands."

His whole body had gone rigid as she spoke and a pool of precum landed on her belly. Then in one rough motion, he lifted her hips to align with the slick head, and she used her hand to help guide him just inside. He pulled her down onto him as he scooted forward on his knees. Only her upper back and head were on the bed as he held her lower back in place with his right arm, and his abs tensed as he began to thrust slow and deep.

"I can't believe after what just happened that I'm ready for more, but I feel like I could do this all night." Sadie moaned at the thought and his lids grew heavy as she sent a pre-emptive pulse of pleasure right to his cock. Troy's gaze went momentarily soft and then sharpened on hers like a promise.

He traced the lines of her breasts with his free hand before tentatively cupping them. Desire pulsed out of him in sharp waves, punctuating his actions. He seemed in no rush and Sadie tried to relax into his care as he explored the feel and sight of her body. When he finally dropped his thumb to stroke her clit, every inch of her responded in an involuntary convulsion. Her sensitive nipples puckered and her skin grew hot.

Sadie closed her eyes, momentarily getting lost in the feel of him moving in her as he slowly encircled her with his thumb. He was watching her face when she reopened her eyes, and she stared back as if in a challenge as her body spasmed with the first orgasmic wave. As ready as she'd been, he hadn't had to work hard for it, but she didn't care. She would make him work plenty hard throughout the rest of the night.

"God," she cried, her voice high and unrestrained. Her gaze dropped to his strong body working her as she spasmed around his slick shaft. Her lack of control caused him to climax with her, but he didn't falter in his utter focus on her pleasure.

His muscles were tight with the effort of holding her up and she looked him over unabashedly as she continued to cry out, her gaze landing on the triangle that defined the area right above where their bodies were connected. She watched his slow thrusts as she rode out her own climax.

Troy collapsed forward the second they'd finished, supporting himself with his forearms as he panted above her. His gaze was on fire and the energy pouring from him was as fierce as it was intoxicating.

"What happens if I don't pull out?" he whispered, shifting to settle his hips firmly over hers.

"Then in a few minutes it'll start over. You'll keep climaxing, though without ejaculating. And... we will probably need some water."

He groaned and scooped her knees up around him as he ran his lips along her neck. "And what about you. Will you come again?"

"Eventually. Not as quickly or as many times. But your lust fuels me. It keeps me turned on even when my body gets tired."

Troy looked into her eyes, desire and disbelief coating his features. Sadie couldn't help herself, she lifted her head and claimed his mouth, moaning with contentment. He was frozen for just a second, before meeting her with equal force. The embrace became a battle to see who could take more and Sadie wrapped her legs around him as he held the back of her neck.

After a minute, Troy groaned and pressed his hips into her as he began to move again. He broke off the kiss to ask, "Do you want to stop?"

"No," she said without hesitation. Sadie wasn't sure if it was the way he'd just kissed her, or their conversation that night, or the extremely good way her body felt just then, but she decided to tell him the absolute truth. "No, Troy. I want to do this with you all night. I want you to take me in every way we can think of. I want you to make me feel so good that I can't walk for days. And I want to watch your face as I make you cry out again and again."

He growled at these last words and gripped her hips in a bruising hold. Then he hooked her knees over his arms so he had absolute control of the movement and began to pump her with force. "I'll cry out for you, Sadie," he said in that deep, husky voice he fell into when he was aroused. "All night long. Whatever you want. I'm yours."

And with that, the protective exterior she'd had with Troy since the day they'd met melted a little. It seemed they were about to cross a line she'd never crossed with anyone, save Jimmy, and yet not a single piece of her could fathom turning back.

Chapter 10

Memories So Sweet

A tiny breeze smelling of pine needles stirred the skin on Sadie's arms just enough to spring goosebumps, despite the soft warmth of the morning sun. Though she didn't notice as she turned her back on the breathtaking view of the valleys below.

At first, Sadie was aware that this might be a dream, but as the memory mingled with her partially unconscious mind, the intensity of the vivid portrait distracted her from any objective analysis.

The cliff on which they'd made camp allowed them to see for miles in almost every direction, but right now Sadie saw only one thing. A man with sun-dyed skin and dark hair stood taut, an arm-span away. He had the start of a three-day old beard and her favorite pair of brown eyes. It was the most familiar face in the world. He was the person she'd spent more time with than any other, from the moment they'd been old enough to run.

Though right now he stared at her with such intensity she barely recognized the boy she'd known. His determination to give her what she needed had never wavered throughout the turmoil of her transition into the succubus life. He'd taken such good care of her that summer. He had been a friend when she'd needed one, her self-control when she'd had none of her own, and a loving partner even though she couldn't give him everything he'd wanted from her.

But now she needed something different. She stepped into him slowly and placed her hand against his chest. His pounding heart was the only physical sign of his frantically churning emotions. Their rigid bodies and patient movements were the calm before the storm as Sadie hesitantly pressed her lips to his.

Several minutes later, when Jimmy slid inside her for the first time, she looked up at him in utter shock. She had wanted this so badly, and the reality of him, her Jimmy, deep in her body, was even better than she could have dreamed. It was full of all the tiny things that distinguished reality from fantasy. The bead of sweat about to drip from the end of his hair. The way his throat moved as he swallowed. The feel of the muscles of his arms encasing her as he held himself above her.

For once it was him that lost control. The tightly bound knot of his suppressed lust broke free in a rush. Instead of Sadie controlling the wave of heat and pleasure as it traveled through his body, she observed in surprise as he tugged it into himself. He pulled until she filled all his senses. He inhaled the smell and taste of her as he kissed her neck. He took her face between his hands and reveled in the feeling of her tongue against his, the sound of her soft moan echoing through the hollow chambers of his long-repressed desires.

Sadie got lost in the sensations as she experienced them from his perspective.

"I didn't know it could be like this," he said in a tone she'd never heard on him, and something about the words felt familiar. Had he said them before?

Jimmy watched her with an expression of raw hunger as he took her hips in a demanding grip. She could feel him pulsating in her and she fed hungrily off the ecstasy of his pleasure. They could stay like this forever, she thought. Let it never end. Because nothing could compare to this. This was her Jimmy that she held between her thighs. It was him whispering her name.

"I love you, James," she managed to say.

He didn't respond in words. Just looked at her with lips parted as he neared his first climax inside her. Her face a few inches from his, she watched pleasure consume him. *Forever*, she thought. *Let us stay like this forever.*

Chapter 11

Trouble in Paradise

She opened her eyes to find Patricia staring down at her. "Sadie. Wake-up. It's ten o'clock." She bolted upright, clutching the sheet over her breasts as her mind reeled from her dream. It had felt so real. Was that why her head was pounding – she'd spent the night tossing and turning over lascivious memories of Jimmy?

No. Wait. She'd been awake most of the night. Her eyes shot to the empty space beside her, remembering for the first time where she was.

"He's in the shower," Patricia told her.

"It's morning," Sadie mumbled.

"Yeah?" Her friend looked at her with some concern.

Sadie scanned the floor for her dress. The room was a mess. What had they done? Patricia, who Sadie realized belatedly was holding the dress, handed it to her. She shot the woman a guilty look. "Where was Hetia? She never came home, and I forgot – I lost track of time." The truth was, she'd completely forgotten that her and Troy were not housed in the same room. If anyone had walked in on them last night, she would have been surprised at the interruption. Where had her brain gone?

"She stayed with me. Troy... well he might have asked me ahead of time to take Hetia to your room if it was empty when we got back."

"Did he?" Sadie said, pursing her lips as she pulled the dress overhead.

"I think he was just trying to be prepared."

Sadie stood up and straightened out the fabric, but she caught Patricia's eye and chewed her lip. "Were we loud?" she asked.

"Only if you have ears and are in the room next door," she said and Sadie cringed.

"I got carried away. I'm sorry."

Patricia sat down on the bed and her eyes fell on Sadie's arm. She had a dark, hand-shaped bruise there. She wrapped her arms around it to cover herself up.

"Don't be," Patricia said. "It's good this happened. Troy's been wanting it so badly he could barely focus." Sadie sat down next to her. "I've been up for hours, waiting for the rest of you, and I've had some time to process. I think this thing you two have... it might even be good for Troy and me." Sadie raised an eyebrow.

Patricia looked at the ground, seeming to search a minute for more words. "I mean, I'm not interested in sex, you know that, but this week it was all he could seem to think about. I saw him sprout an erection at least five times. I even once caught him staring at my chest, which hasn't happened since the day we met. I'm glad he has an outlet."

Sadie found herself nodding. "Also," Patricia continued, dropping her voice in an uncharacteristically conspiratorial way, "I kind of liked listening to him with you." Her friend hugged her own waist as a light blush highlighted her beautifully painted face. Sadie's eyes went wide and then out of nowhere she giggled, some of the tension leaving her. A moment later, Patricia followed suit.

"So... you're okay with this?" Sadie asked.

Patricia nodded. "I think so. I think, well, it's nice... hearing him feel good."

Patricia flushed deeper, and this time Sadie copied her. She very much agreed that it was *nice* hearing Troy feel good, though her whole body felt warm at the thought. And there was something exciting about Patricia feeling the same way. It was something they could enjoy together.

The shower went off and they both jumped.

"I should get one of those too," Sadie said, heading for the door before the man could appear.

"Hetia's still sleeping."

"What? The woman of 5 a.m. wake-up calls?" Sadie said, coming to a halt.

"It's a surprise, I agree." Patricia nodded.

Sadie remembered then what the actual point of last night had been. "How did it go?" she asked, feeling guilty it had taken her that long to do so.

Patricia shook her head. "Hetia is a closed book. I have never failed to get a good story from someone when I'm hungry. All she wanted to talk about was military tactics and the coming war. Any prompt about the past returned one-word answers. It was almost comical how badly I failed." She sighed. "And you should know, I'm pretty sure she was onto us. She looked pretty damn suspicious at times and kept turning the questions back at me."

"Shit," Sadie said.

"If you really like that girl, Sadie, I'm sorry. I don't envy you."

Sadie groaned. "Hetia's no girl. And, yeah, I do like her. There's just something about her that—"

The bathroom door opened before she could follow that train of thought. The sight of Troy was a powerful distraction. Memories of the night before flashed through both their minds. She was the first to look away, shyly tucking a strand of hair behind her ear and heading to the closet. She grabbed a towel and turned back to him. "I think I need to borrow your shower," she said in place of the million other things that came to her mind.

He stepped aside so she could pass, but when she was next to him, he whispered "Good morning" and leaned in to kiss her. She froze at the soft feeling of his lips. It was a tender hello, fitting for the night they'd had together, and yet it frightened her. Despite how good he felt, she pulled back quickly, glancing at Patricia.

Her gaze dropped to Troy's erection, then the love lines that flowed from him to both of them. She was so shaken that it took her a moment to notice that the black love line that ran between her and Troy was flowing both ways, though his was still much stronger than her own. Sadie batted at it, as if that would dislodge it from the air.

Troy and Patricia looked at her with raised eyebrows.

"Sorry. Bug," she said, ducking her head as she turned toward the bathroom. Closing the door on the confusing situation in the bedroom, she pulled the dress back off. She'd never been more in need of a hot shower to clear her thoughts. Pausing to examine herself in the mirror, she made note of the bruises and scratch marks so she could tend to them later.

Sadie didn't regret a moment of last night, and yet the reality of where it left them was another matter. Had she made a mistake, taking things so far? She could have just fucked him, once and done, so they both felt better. Her stupid hormones had been riding shotgun all night. Actually, they'd been firmly behind the wheel. And now she was left to face the aftermath. And the aftermath, it turned out, was a whole batch of emotion she had no idea how to handle.

Sadie emerged from the bathroom fifteen minutes later, still going commando in the green dress, and with no resolution to her tumultuous thoughts. Patricia and Troy were sitting in their usual spots on the floor, except this time there seemed to be little space between them. Their shoulders touched as they prepared breakfast, a simple bread and cheese thing. When they sat back, Troy put his arm around Patricia's shoulder.

"Uhh... I think I'll sneak in and grab some clothes," Sadie said before escaping into the empty hallway. She was a little embarrassed that she was the uncomfortable one. After all, shouldn't a succubus think this was natural? She'd never thought twice about sleeping with strangers every day all while being in love with Jimmy, but this felt like something entirely different. Someone who wasn't Jimmy was looking at her like she was the sun and moon. And on top of that, he had been steadily falling in love with her friend. She had no road map for such a thing.

Sadie carefully opened the door to her own room, and the

daylight peeking past the curtains fell on the sleeping form in the bed. And then on top of everything with Troy... there was Hetia.

The woman looked so tiny like this. Her long hair spread out around her and her body curled up in a ball, as if hiding in a protective cocoon. Sadie loved the brief moments in which Hetia let her in, even a little. It was the reason she hadn't completely given up. Hetia was worth it, if only she would take the risk.

Her face looked pretty and almost soft without the intensity of her piercing gray eyes. Sadie looked from it to the wall that separated her and the man she'd spent all night with. Perhaps, Troy felt the same way about her that she felt about Hetia. How much had she been letting fear keep her from what she really wanted?

But it was too early for such thoughts. She was tired and hungry and in need of clean underwear. Sadie crept over to the closet and fished a pair out of the drawer. She slid them on without turning around and became acutely aware of the exact moment Hetia woke up and noticed her. A wave of desire hit her from behind accompanied by a clear image of her ass peeking out as she hiked up the panties. Sadie suppressed a smile and waited a second before turning around.

When she did, she found Hetia's eyes closed. She walked over to the bed and intentionally stubbed her toe on nothing but the ground. "Ouch," she said, leaning on the bed to grab at her foot. Hetia blinked open her eyes. "Sorry. Did I wake you?" Sadie asked, feeling completely foolish. Why was she being so silly?

"S'okay," Hetia mumbled, clearly still sleepy.

"It's almost eleven. Did you have a good night last night?" Sadie asked.

Hetia pushed herself up, looking increasingly alert as she settled back against the headboard. "You mean the part where Troy told me he wanted a night alone with you and so asked if I would take Patricia out, or the part where Patricia spent the night trying to get my life story?" She dropped her voice an octave. "Or maybe you mean the part where I got to spend all night listening to you two go at it in my room."

Busted. Sadie sat down on the edge of the bed. "Sorry. That was selfish. I wasn't thinking right." She looked up at her sheepishly, not quite sure how to make up for so many mistakes, but Hetia wasn't giving her that stern look she wore. The woman was staring at her breasts. She blinked and looked away when Sadie caught her.

"I like your dress," she said, and Sadie caught the memory of her own moans echoing through the walls still ringing in Hetia's mind.

A compliment. That... was unexpected. "Look, Hetia, about Patricia. It wasn't just her idea. We all thought that maybe—"

Hetia leaned forward and kissed her. Sadie had a brief moment of panic before she recovered enough to kiss her back. But before she could properly settle into it, Hetia had pulled away.

Wow, this really did seem to be her lucky dress. Sadie opened her mouth, searching for what to say, but the woman was already scooting off the other end of the bed.

"Is there breakfast over there?" Hetia asked, desire pulsing from her.

Sadie cleared her throat, "Yeah."

"Then I'll be there in a minute."

She watched Hetia disappear into the bathroom before standing up, still feeling a bit dazed, and grabbing a sweater before returning to the other room. Talk about out of the frying pan and into the fire. Had this been what Jimmy was picturing when he'd said they each needed time to figure out who they were? Because if so, Sadie was more confused than ever.

Troy latched onto the sight of her the second she entered, as if he'd missed her the five minutes they'd been apart. "You didn't change?" Patricia said.

"I'll... change later. Hetia's awake. She'll be here in a minute." Sadie pulled on the sweater to at least put the dangerous dress out of sight.

"Is she upset about last night?" Troy asked.

"It's... hard to say," Sadie said.

They both raised their eyebrows in a question. Sadie held up her hands in a shrug as if to say *I got no idea* but dropped into a neutral posture as Hetia appeared suddenly.

"Morning. Did I wake you when I left?" Patricia asked, looking as nervous as Sadie felt.

"No. *You* didn't wake me," Hetia said, staring pointedly at Troy as she took a seat. He actually blushed and cast a contrite look at the ground. Sadie felt the instinct to jump in and defend him, but couldn't quite think of how to phrase an apology around *I'm sorry for causing Troy to make all those sounds. It's my fault, really.*

Luckily, Patricia rescued them all from the awkward moment as she sat up, looking suddenly serious. "Good, we're all here. I've been waiting to give you the news until we were together. I got through to Amadi this morning." Hetia and Troy looked suddenly alert. "I called to see if there was a message, some kind of direction on the machine, the way I have every morning, but he was there. I'm not sure where *there* is exactly, but he actually answered the phone."

Patricia took a deep breath. "There's a nymph, uhh, Tucker Stone, I believe." Sadie and Troy exchanged a look. "He's leading an all-nymph army that exists as a separate branch of The Coalition. This last week, The United has tried to fight off both the nymph army and the feeder one against two different towns who had already come out against the feeder coup. Both times The United had to retreat, but they did learn one thing. Tucker's army doesn't want to kill civilians. They swept into the town and took away their weapons and stole some food. All in all, it wasn't that bad. While the Coalition army wiped out half the town where they attacked. Of course, the rumor mill has made it sound like the Coalition army is somehow the victim."

Patricia sighed and looked at Sadie. "And now they're splitting up. Tucker's army is taking the East Coast, while The Coalition... is moving this way."

"Jimmy?" Sadie said, praying Amadi had mentioned him.

"Amadi said to tell you *Mr. Baker is fine,*" Patricia told her before turning to Hetia. "He also said to stay put. Arlington is a hotspot of nymph power. Everyone is looking to them to see which side they'll take. If they vote against the feeder government, then this is the next place the army will strike."

Troy let out a whistle. "So basically... everyone's coming this way."

An alarm went off as if punctuating these last words, and everyone but Hetia jumped. "Is that the fire alarm?" Sadie shouted to Troy.

He tilted his head, pausing there. "I don't think so."

Hetia went to peer out the window. "There's something happening in the streets," she yelled, before pulling her small utility belt out of a drawer and sliding two small knives and several metal objects into it.

Adrenaline shot through Sadie's system. "You're preparing for a fight? Now?"

"Just being prepared," Hetia told her.

"One sec," Sadie said. "Don't leave." She practically ran next door. It was hard to know what to prepare for. The future was like a black hole looming on the horizon. It was too unreal to actually picture. Pulling on pants under her dress and grabbing a hair tie, she looked around, wondering if she should hurriedly pack their bags. Deciding there was no time, she just snatched up some gloves from the floor and went out to face the unknown threat.

Sadie was still securing her hair when she entered the hall to find everyone waiting. They glanced around at each other, and Hetia nodded once, as if signing off that all was in order before leading them down the hall.

Sadie had expected to find the ground floor crowded with people coming to see what was happening, but it seemed for that most, fear was beating curiosity. The commotion outside though, was a sight to see. The street was full of identical tables laid out in one long row down the center. Behind each table were two people dressed in some kind of uniform. The letters SC were printed in a fancy script across their breast pocket.

"Species control," Patricia whispered just as the alarms stopped.

A few seconds later, the ringing was replaced by a woman's voice. "The deadline for this city to register has been shortened. Given the history of violence here, the government is intent on ensuring the safety of nymph property and life. You have three days to register your species and declare allegiance. Ample locations have been set up in every major street to assist with this essential task. Failure to comply will result in arrest and relocation. Thank you for your cooperation."

Sadie felt a hand on her arm. "Come on," Patricia said in her ear. She turned to find the others had retreated and were waiting for her.

Cold fear pricked over her skin as she stumbled after them. The bar was closed and only a few other people were around on the ground floor, every one of them exchanging a look of panic.

Hetia led them back into the elevator and Sadie felt safer the instant the door had closed them in. "Hey. It's okay." Patricia put a hand on her back. "We're going to tackle this one step at a time."

"We'll need fake IDs," Troy said, sounding calm and matter-of-fact. "We don't want to be easily findable if Siphon comes looking."

"I'm sure there's already a booming market for them. I'll ask around," Patricia said, still rubbing Sadie's back.

"I'll go with you," Troy told her as the doors opened. Sadie stepped out, then looked back when no one had followed her.

"I'll scout out more of the situation on the ground," Hetia said. "Why don't you stay here," she directed at Sadie.

Sadie blinked at them. They were leaving her alone? They were all staring at her expectantly and so she nodded, absently. The thought she should offer to help reached her brain slowly and she opened her mouth, but Hetia cut her off. "Just go back to the room. We'll be back soon," she said with the tenderness of someone speaking to a dying person.

Sadie wondered why she was using that voice, but nodded again before floating away down the hall. The army was coming this way. Jimmy, Amadi, and everyone she loved was going to go up against them. Her parents. Her home.

Sadie couldn't find the room. Why couldn't she remember the number? Eventually she faced a door on instinct and found that her key worked. She went straight to the bathroom and threw up. It took her a while to recover from the surprise of her reaction, but eventually she stood up and stared at her pale face in the mirror, shocked at how she looked.

Okay, perhaps she was a little shaken, but she wasn't going to be the only useless one. She'd have to pull herself together before they got back. She didn't like them thinking she was falling apart and in need of special care just when things were getting bad.

A hot shower would be a good start.

Sadie washed away the remnants of the night with Troy, immediately regretting the loss of his scent on her. Then she rinsed her mouth and brushed her teeth, the minty smell helping to clear her senses. No one had returned by the time she'd repacked her own bag, so she moved onto Patricia's. When that was done, she began the very important task of anxious pacing. Ugh, why had she been so out of it? They wouldn't have left her here if she hadn't reacted so badly.

Well, she clearly had to do *something*.

Sadie stepped back into the elevator in an entirely different mood than she'd left it an hour ago and jammed at the button for the lower floor. If she couldn't find Hetia, then she would at least talk to some people, get the lay of the land.

The doors to the ground floor opened and her eyes went wide. It was packed. She had gotten used to seeing a crowd of people around the bar, coming and going to the various elevators, but this was an entirely different scene. Everyone was on their feet, huddled in pockets of whispered conversation.

The bar was closed but lit up, with a crowd of people behind the counter, which happened to be the only space that wasn't completely filled. Sadie spotted one of the waiters she'd gotten to know that week.

"Jalen?" The man turned as she whispered his name. "What's going on?"

He adjusted his tie as he shook his head. "The city council is counting the votes. Everyone who lives here just cast their ballot last night. Which is why The Coalition is here early. If the vote goes in support of the feeder government, then a lot of us in the outer city are going to resist." He narrowed his eyes. They'd been friendly up until now, but she realized that Jalen was aware that she and her friends were all feeders, two of whom feed off humans.

"If I lived here, I would have voted against," she hurried to tell him. "Though it wouldn't be the safety of my own home I'd be risking." She chewed her lip. "What will you do?"

He assessed her a moment longer and then seemed to decide she could be trusted. Dropping back into a conspiratorial whisper he said. "If the vote is a yes, we're to tear down the registration tables. If it's a no, we're going to give the city a chance to coordinate its own response." He put a hand on her shoulder. "If you don't want to get swept up in that, you might want to get back upstairs. It'll be starting soon."

Sadie put her hand over his. "Thanks, but I think I'll stay." He nodded and they released each other. "Actually, I'm looking for my friend. The blond one?"

He opened his mouth to say something, but was drowned out by a loud whistle and pop. When she spotted smoke and lights raining down just outside the door, she realized it was a firework.

"The signal! It's a yes! Arlington voted to comply!" someone shouted, and Jalen ran off before saying another word. Sadie scrambled up on the countertop as the crowd rushed the street. If Hetia were here, would she be headed to the elevator or helping the resistance? Sadie scanned the heads, eyes falling on any lighter hair, but none of them were her.

The sounds of fighting exploded as the room in front of her cleared. Eventually, Sadie couldn't help but be drawn to the commotion outside. She had to see what was happening. At least if she witnessed it, she'd have something to tell the group about when they came back – that was if Hetia wasn't already in the thick of it.

Sadie peered out from under the ledge, keeping most of her body behind one of the supporting pillars. It was clear that the registration officials had not been overly prepared for this level of response. Every table was overturned as far as she could see. No one was fighting to injure, and so far no guns had been drawn. Which meant that at least The Coalition wasn't armed enough to distribute weapons to every official doing their bidding. A small mercy.

Feeling secure in this knowledge, Sadie stepped out from under the covering and took a better look up and down the old marketplace. She was rewarded with the sight of Hetia standing in an alleyway several blocks down, observing the outbreak.

The officials were surrendering. With their arms in the air, they were backing up in one long line as the resistors destroyed the tables. Sadie waved an arm, trying to catch Hetia's attention, but the woman was looking past her down the road. Sadie jumped as a gun went off, dropping to a crouch. When she stood back up, Hetia was gone and the crowd was scattering.

Sadie backed up as a swarm of local police charged into the fray. Most of them were armed with batons which helped to beat back the largely unarmed crowd. Heartened by the support, the registration officials began to fight back as most people retreated. The ones who stayed were nymphs making use of their affinity. There were a fire and air nymph working in tandem to destroy the tables, while the police danced around them, trying to find a way in without getting singed.

Sadie hugged the pillar with her back as she frantically scanned for Hetia. She would have to retreat before the fight fell on her, and it was rapidly moving her way. The earthquake nymph could certainly take care of herself. Sadie would just have to trust her not to get into too much trouble. Sadie stepped back under the building, tossing one last hopeful look up the road.

The sight of Troy and Patricia stopped her dead. What were they doing? Troy was pulling off his shirt while Patricia gesticulated, as if arguing with him. He ran toward something Sadie couldn't see and she stepped into the street to keep sight of him. One of the archways had caught fire from a burning table. The nymph who had set it was being arrested, she was looking at the flames desperately as her hands were forced behind her back.

Troy held out his arms and began to consume the flame. At least that was what Sadie assumed he was up to. Unfortunately, the nearby officers made a different assumption. One of them struck him hard on the back and Troy landed on his stomach briefly before bouncing up to his hands and knees. Patricia rushed forward at the same time as Sadie, only she was much closer.

Two men easily stopped the woman, binding her arms behind her in one swift motion. Troy rushed them, releasing the flames from his torso as he did. He pushed one of the men and attempted to pull Patricia free. Sadie screamed as he took a blow to the face. A moment later three officers had subdued him. He stopped resisting immediately. As they pulled him upright, he shook his head to clear the blood dripping down his face. Then, with his hands tightly bound, he let himself be dragged away.

Chapter 12

Secrets and Seduction

Sadie stopped running. She was on the edge of the fight now and it seemed there was nothing she could do. Her friends disappeared behind the swarm of officials coming her way, and she was forced to retreat back to her pillar.

Sadie hugged her waist as she thought about Troy being dragged off, dripping blood. Just a few hours ago he'd been inside her. She could still feel him. And now he was completely out of reach and in pain. Chills ran down her spine, her body hit with a sudden emptiness.

And poor Patricia. Sadie couldn't picture her sitting in a jail cell. She was grateful that at least no one had struck her, but she hated the sight of her being forced to the ground. Then an even worse thought occurred to her. What if Hetia had been arrested too? She'd be left all alone to figure out what to do next.

But before she could stew on that notion, a hand closed on her wrist. "Time to go, succubus," Hetia said in her ear. Sadie faced her as Hetia pulled her back from the edge. She threw her arms around the woman before she could overthink it. Hetia stood there stiffly until Sadie released her.

"Sorry," she said.

"Later." Hetia took her hand without looking at her, and led her back into the lobby. They stepped into the elevator alone, and Hetia immediately released the grip. "We'll find the others," the woman said. "Then we should discuss moving to a room on the edge of the city. The yes vote is good for us in the short run. It means we won't have an army descending on this place, but we might need to flee if— What?"

"The others?" Sadie said. "Didn't you see? They were just arrested."

Hetia merely froze, blinked once, and then nodded. After a minute of thoughtful silence, she asked. "Was Troy injured? Fire nymphs aren't easily handled."

They stepped into the hallway as Sadie replied. "He seemed hesitant to use fire in the fight. I don't think he wanted to hurt anybody." She cast a nervous look sideways.

Hetia shook her head. "People get hurt all the time. That's life. We're not going to get far in this war if our best fighters are pulling their punches."

They stopped outside their rooms and Sadie turned to her. "They were just local police, Hetia. Troy wasn't going to set them on fire."

The woman sighed and inserted the key. "You're right. He did the right thing." She kicked the door to open and took a swill of a bottle on the counter. She offered it to Sadie, but she shook her head. "It's just water," Hetia told her, pushing the bottle into her hand.

"Thanks." Sadie took it and gulped at the cool liquid. It suppressed her desire to throw up again, but did nothing to calm the knot in her stomach. Hetia sat on the edge of the bed and searched the ground with her eyes as if reading a large script written there.

Sadie had seen Hetia under stressful circumstances many times now, but she had never seen her express so much outward concern over it.

"What do we do?" Sadie asked, kneeling at her feet. Hetia just chugged the rest of the water and tossed aside the bottle. "We have to get them out of there. Somehow. I mean, if we need to leave the city, we're not going to get far with half of us locked up." Hetia just glared at her so she kept pushing. "And with the fight coming to this coast, it's not like we could have stayed here long anyway. We've failed in our goal. The city just voted to support The Coalition, and their army is coming."

"You're going to read me," Hetia said.

Sadie blinked up at her. The words had been quiet enough she wasn't sure she'd heard them right. "If there's nothing to find... at least we'll know," Hetia added.

Sadie propped herself up. "Are you sure?"

There was a short pause and then she nodded once.

Sadie was hesitant about trying again, but as she searched through everything that had happened that day and everything that might be about to happen, it seemed like this was even more important than ever. "That's good. And if there is nothing useful, we'll have no reason to stay here. We'll have a chance at breaking the others out and leaving the city before we get in trouble." Sadie chewed her lip. "Assuming we can find them."

"We'll find them," Hetia told her.

Sadie looked up to find Hetia's piercing grey eyes on her and a different kind of nervousness hit her. Would she go through with it this time? Or would they get all worked up again only to end badly? "How—" Sadie swallowed. "How do you want to do this?" She swept a curl behind her ear, not quite able to look the other woman in the eye.

Hetia stood up. "I'll be back."

Sadie too hopped up. "Where are you—"

"I want to make sure Troy and Patricia are being sent to a local jail. I wouldn't put it past The Coalition to be rounding them up somewhere."

"Oh... okay. Should I—" Hetia was out the door before she'd finished. She didn't return promptly. An hour passed. And then two. Sadie paced the empty room until she thought she would go crazy.

Everything was such a mess, and if Hetia had just agreed to this earlier, maybe they wouldn't even be here. Sadie went from nervous excitement over her return to frustrated anger. When she finally walked in, Sadie rounded on her with all the pent-up emotion of someone left with nothing to do at such a critical time.

"Where the hell have you been?" she said the second Hetia

returned. The woman stopped short, probably because Sadie had never spoken to her like that before.

"I said where I was going," Hetia told her.

"Yes. But you left me for hours. And Troy and Patricia are in jail and Jimmy's far away and the war is coming toward us." Sadie scowled at her. "And if you had just let me keep reading you last time, maybe we would already be gone from here."

Hetia lifted her chin. "No one should be forced to share their memories."

"I know that." Sadie crossed her arms. "But this is important. And you wanted to do this earlier and only stopped because you ran scared. You're like, the bravest person I know and also a complete coward, you know that?"

Sadie immediately regretted the words, but Hetia just pulled off her jacket, looking unphased. "You don't know me, Sadie," she said almost sadly, tossing the warm layer on the desk.

"Because you haven't given me a chance," Sadie lamented.

"They're in a local jail. We'll break them out before dawn when the guards are the least alert." Hetia's tone was calm. Too calm. It made Sadie want to scream, which must have shown on her face because the woman sighed. "Look, all we have here is a shared goal. There's no reason we need to make it more than that." She kicked off her shoes while Sadie's mouth fell open. She couldn't believe Hetia had just said that.

Looking at her more closely, Sadie could see the long night Hetia had spent listening to her and Troy. The sounds of her own cries of pleasure echoed around in the other woman's thoughts, accompanied by the strong desire to relieve the throbbing tension between her legs. Hetia's body was so ready she was practically in heat.

"That's not remotely true," Sadie said, kicking off her own shoes, which she'd kept on this whole time in case she needed to run out suddenly at the sound of yet another disaster.

Hetia shook her head, coming over to her. "Here. You want to know me. Just do it." She held out her bare hands for Sadie to take, looking almost bored. Only, Sadie felt the desperate pulse of sexual anticipation and knew her act for what it was: a lie.

No. She wasn't going to let Hetia get away with this. She couldn't just pretend like it was nothing.

"I'm not hungry," Sadie said, crossing her arms.

Hetia frowned. "Is that even possible?"

"Yes," she said stubbornly. It was true. She wasn't remotely hungry after having spent all night with Troy. But that didn't matter. She would want Hetia under any circumstance. Though if the woman was going to be this stubborn, Sadie decided two could play that game.

"How long until that changes?" Hetia asked, looking slightly anxious now.

Sadie shrugged. "Hard to say. I can probably get in the mood, but it will take some work."

Hetia's eyes narrowed the tiniest fraction. "What kind of work?" she asked, and Sadie thought she detected the barest hint of excitement in the tone. Though it was the wave of arousal that poured from her that made it clear Hetia was quite interested in this turn in the conversation.

"Well," Sadie said. "Maybe if we talked for a while... gave me time to warm up to you. And maybe you could stick especially close to me."

Hetia's posture softened at the suggestion, but Sadie knew well enough by now that any response could come out of her. "Okay," she said quietly, and Sadie blinked in surprise. Watching her like she might bolt at any minute, Sadie moved to sit back down on the bed. Hetia followed her, taking Sadie off guard when she scooted in so that one knee touched Sadie's lower back, and swung the other leg across her lap.

"How's this?" she asked, undoing her miniature utility belt and tossing it on the floor. Sadie almost asked her to keep it on. She imagined Hetia naked wearing only that belt and found herself biting her lip. Hetia's gaze dropped to her mouth, and Sadie released the lip with a little pop.

"That's a good start," she said in a breathier voice than she'd intended, as she was hit with such a powerful wave of lust that she had to dig her fingers into the comforter to stop herself from responding to the call. Hetia rolled her hips forward as she sat up and Sadie caught her desire to do that again just for the friction between her legs. Only, she held perfectly still. How did the woman have so much control?

"So... what did you want to talk about, Ms. Hall?" Hetia said, in a mockingly formal voice that contrasted with the intimate way she looked over Sadie's face. Her mind went momentarily blank as she fought down the urge to push Hetia to her back and rub herself against her like a cat in heat.

Attempting to focus on the question, Sadie searched her brain for where to go from here. She knew she couldn't ask anything about Hetia's past. She'd have to find topics in the present, and there was only one topic currently dominating both their thoughts.

"I guess... since the goal is to get me back in the mood, we could talk about our fantasies."

Hetia's eyes flared and a million different images passed through her mind. Knowing how private of a person she was, Sadie felt some guilt at being able to see them. She made a desperate attempt to block them out, but their strength and focus around her made it an entirely impossible task.

"Okay," Hetia whispered. "You first."

Sadie squirmed a little under her gaze. Dropping her eyes to the hollow of Hetia's throat, she watched her quick shallow breaths until her thoughts calmed enough to focus. With her gloved fingers, Sadie caressed the soft skin at the base of the other woman's neck. It was one of her favorite places on Hetia's body, the bones of her clavicles giving depth and texture, smooth skin over hard ridges.

Sharing fantasies was actually a tricky business. She couldn't be too honest, since saying something like, *I fantasize that you beg me to touch you,* was sure to make Hetia withdraw. Cheating a little, Sadie looked for overlap between her own secret desires and Hetia's.

"Sometimes... I imagine that were alone together in some public place; maybe some bar or park with a lot of people, and I'm staring out at the crowd." Sadie ran her finger down Hetia's body and caressed the upper outline of her breasts. "We're talking about something unimportant and you stop suddenly and step in behind me."

Sadie remembered the times in which Hetia seemed to lose

control of herself. In the fight in the woods last week, she'd kissed her without preamble or restraint, and this morning, she'd done the same, almost on impulse. For someone who always appeared in control, these surprise moments stood out in contrast. Just the thought of them was exciting, but Sadie decided it was probably best not to reference them directly.

"I briefly feel your breasts against my back and then you push me forward until I'm bent, gripping the railing in front of us."

"There's railing?" Hetia asked, arching a brow.

"Of course. That's how fantasies work, after all. When I need something to grip, exactly that thing appears." Sadie grinned up at her in time to see Hetia's mouth quirk. "And of course, I'm wearing a short, flowy dress, so when you slide your hands under it to my hips you don't have to travel far to find my panties."

Hetia's lips parted a fraction as she rocked forward, moving her hand to rest on the inside of Sadie's thigh. All of her fantasies fixated on getting into Sadie's pants and touching her while holding her down in some way. Sometimes Hetia was rough and punishing, sometimes gentle, but she was always in control.

"It doesn't take much to remove them, just a little push off my hips and they pool around my feet," Sadie continued, satisfied at the growing heat in Hetia's eyes. "You make me step out of them and then kick my legs wide. Air hits the wetness between my legs and I feel open, exposed."

Hetia's hand had moved up to caress the crease between her inner thigh and pelvis. She continued to rock against the hard seam of her pants almost subconsciously and Sadie had to fight the instinct to reach out and give Hetia what she was seeking. It was hard to tell how much of the woman's reaction was intentional since Sadie could feel the overwhelming arousal pulsing off her. Her lids had grown heavy and lips flushed as she continued to look at Sadie like a moth mesmerized by a flame.

"Though I feel even more vulnerable when you press down on my lower back, forcing my hips to arch into the air." Hetia gave out a little whimper and Sadie was sure this time that she hadn't meant to. The sound made her own body grow hot and the wet heat between her legs throbbed. Suddenly, she couldn't resist a moment longer. As much as she wanted to wait until Hetia couldn't help but initiate, her own self-control just wasn't as strong.

"It would be something like this," Sadie said, rising to her feet and pulling Hetia to the edge of the bed with her. Sadie reached for the buttons of the other woman's pants as she stood and Hetia watched her pull them open with rapt attention. Sadie knelt as she stripped her lower half. Nervous to look directly into Hetia's eyes, she stared at the wet spot glistening in front of her as the sweet scent hit her senses.

Sadie pulled off her gloves with her teeth as she enjoyed the sight of Hetia's abs tensing and releasing in anticipation. When she ran her bare thumbs up the insides of her thighs, Hetia let out a high-pitched gasp, her hands landing on the top of Sadie's head. As much as the woman actively fantasized about being in control, Sadie could see another layer, one that longed for the opposite.

Standing in a hurry, Sadie turned her by the hips, pushing her hands down to rest on the bed in one fluid motion. Hetia arched her back as her body trembled. It seemed she'd said something, but she'd bitten down the words with her lip between her teeth. Though when Sadie pushed her feet apart, she couldn't help but give an audible cry of longing.

As Sadie stood up to run her bare palms over Hetia's undulating hips, she could feel the other woman throbbing, heavy between her legs. Hetia's ass was tiny, like the rest of her, and Sadie ran her finger down the crack as she appreciated it. The contact continued to send pulses of pleasure through the woman's body, but she could feel her silently begging to be touched directly.

Sadie had never seen Hetia this tense, this wanton, and she couldn't resist the pull. Kneeling so she could watch, she spread Hetia's wet folds wide until she could see the pink nub of sensitive nerves.

"Yes," Hetia breathed, as Sadie's thumbs ran on either side of the swollen peak. She arched her back even harder, pressing hungrily into the touch. Sliding her thumb inside to wet it, Sadie slowly pulled out to stroke the sensitive underside of the woman's clit directly.

Hetia cried out with such a satisfying reaction that it rivalled the many moments Sadie had recently shared with Troy. And though she appeared to be fighting down the words that threatened to surface, Hetia couldn't seem to help any of her other responses as Sadie played with her in little circles, the wet friction adding to the pleasure from the skin contact.

Sadie forgot why they were doing this, where it had all started. Her mind was wholly focused on the building tension that filled every cell of Hetia's body. At the way the woman seemed unable to fight back her reaction as she slowly came undone.

But the pleasurable heat was reaching a peak too quickly. As Hetia's lust spurred her onward, Sadie began to struggle for control. When her whole body jerked with the first orgasmic spasm, Sadie quickly stopped touching her directly, wanting to extend the moment and show off the skill she'd acquired since last they'd slept together.

Keeping one hand on Hetia's ass to keep the orgasm going, she tickled the other up and down the insides of her thighs. "Oh god. Wha—" Hetia panted as her body jerked involuntarily through the rising pleasure of the climax. Sadie felt half-crazed by the other woman's ecstasy as she stared at the swollen clit pulsing in front of her. Before she could doubt or question her behavior, Sadie reached out and flicked it right as the second spasm struck.

Hetia cried out at the sting. "Yes. Fuck," she said loud and clear, and Sadie could feel the way every muscle in her body had tensed with the pleasure of the moment.

"You like that," Sadie said in a tone that was only half-question.

Hetia didn't answer right away, as she was busy jerking with the next climactic wave, but she eventually drew in air as if emerging from water and panted out a breathy, "Yes." Her hips bucked as Sadie flicked her again. Through the awareness from the contact, Sadie could feel the way the pain mixed with the pleasure, and Hetia's reaction to it was utterly intoxicating.

"How about this?" Sadie asked, slapping her ass as her thumb slid back over the sweetest part of her.

"Oh god," Hetia cried, and this time Sadie lost sight of anything else. She slapped her again, harder as she reached up to pull down on Hetia's lower back. Her hips arched further and Sadie found her sweet center with her mouth. Holding her in place with one arm, Sadie licked her directly as Hetia bucked spastically in her grip.

Though the woman had gone beyond using words, Sadie could feel her sheer enjoyment at being treated this way. And Sadie's behavior must have surprised her, because Hetia's high-pitched cries had an undertone of shock, while her typical control fantasies were rapidly dwarfed by a desire to be overpowered. When Sadie slapped her the third time, it was hard, intended to hurt, and Hetia's hips responded with a violent jerk, finally letting go of her remaining reserve.

Sadie felt the woman's body melt as she took her through the final waves, experimenting several more times with the painful punishment as she drew out the final moment with all she had. Hetia was the third person she'd taken to such heights, though the other two had never surrendered as completely as this woman currently was. Despite the intensity of the mixed sensations, Hetia was utter putty in her hands as Sadie played her through the final note.

Sadie sat back as the last wave passed, landing on her knees to stare at the woman before her. Some of Hetia's juices pooled enough to drip down her thigh and Sadie leaned forward to lap them up. The woman whimpered, and for a minute her stance wavered, as if her knees might give out. Sadie nuzzled her ass before following the curve to the handprint she'd just left. She kissed its outline as Hetia moaned with complete satisfaction, all constraint out the window. It seemed they were finally communicating.

It took several long minutes of her kissing the developing bruise and Hetia responding with abandon, before Sadie recalled what had started this. Breaking the contact at last, she rose to her feet. Hetia turned, blinking in confusion as she faced her. Sadie immediately stepped forward to pull off Hetia's shirt. When she was entirely naked, she pushed her to her back, without removing any of her own clothing.

Hetia looked soft, her body still trembling as Sadie climbed on top of her, resting along one side. It seemed they'd successfully talked some things out. At least, Hetia was no longer denying her desire as she cupped the side of Sadie's face with an expression of unrestrained longing, hot and raw.

Reminding the other woman about what was about to happen, Sadie broke away from her gaze to stroke the bare skin of her arm.

"I'm not going to dig through your memories. Not all of them anyway. I'm headed for just a single one," Sadie said. "I'll see things along the way, but I'll try not to linger too long."

Hetia tensed a fraction and Sadie felt her heart speed up. "Sure," she said with a shrug that would have appeared nonchalant if she hadn't looked so visibly anxious.

"You don't believe me?" Sadie said, feeling another rising wave of frustration.

"I have no way of knowing what you'll see." Hetia swallowed.

"I'll tell you," Sadie said, looking back into her eyes.

Hetia pursed her lips. "Okay."

"You don't trust me," Sadie said.

"I never know who to trust," Hetia whispered, reaching to entwine her fingers through Sadie's in a gesture whose intimacy contrasted sharply with the words that accompanied it.

"I'll try to go fast," Sadie said, leaning down to gently caress Hetia's lips with her own.

"Just do it," Hetia said against her mouth.

Sadie complied before she could overthink it. Hetia grew hot with excitement for another orgasm as Sadie kissed her through the build-up. She drove the tension to a peak with ease, propping herself up at the end and clutching the side of Hetia's face as it contorted with pleasure. Neither woman blinked and Hetia looked up at her with complete vulnerability as Sadie's gaze softened to look inside.

It was a good thing she was so overfed as it made it easier to memory dive, and she needed the strength to look past the beautiful sight of Hetia wrapped in ecstasy and dig under the surface. Not wanting to waste a second of this important opportunity or draw out this task which made Hetia so uncomfortable, Sadie relaxed her mind, forcing herself to focus. With the woman's tiny gasps reverberating intimately in the space between them, Sadie launched the last orgasmic spasm. She rode Hetia's longing for it down into the recesses of previous such moments, letting the lust carry her forward until she could get her bearings.

Hetia's past was filled with strong desires. They jostled Sadie around like a hurricane while she tried not to look too hard at any particular thing. She'd already seen the day she sought in Mia's head. It shouldn't be too hard to relocate that particular moment. Only, one person's memory of an event was always quite different from another's.

Sadie focused on locating that general time in Hetia's life, searching out moments she might have shared with her father. She had looked about ten or eleven in Mia's mind. What did it feel like to be a ten-year old Hetia? She could only imagine. Though as soon as she'd formulated the thought a scene sharpened. A moment later, Sadie found herself looking up into the face of Amadi, the man that had helped raise Hetia and her father's closest friend.

Hetia wanted him to stay. Why was he grinning at her like everything was just dandy? "Dad's right. Mae distracts you," she said, crossing her arms. "She takes you away from your odligations."

Dee chuckled. "My *obli*-gations are to more than just the work. And I'll be back in a few weeks." He put a large hand on her head in a comforting gesture that only annoyed her.

"But how do you know she can be trusted?" Hetia crossed her arms. "What if she's just like Mom?"

Dee crinkled his forward and kneeled in front of her. He paused there a while, observing her. "Sweetie. Did your dad tell you some things about your mother?"

She was glad he looked so concerned. Maybe now he would stay and take care of her. "Yes. Mom was a spy, sent by the enemy."

Sadie bucked, remembering she wasn't supposed to get distracted, but she couldn't seem to look away from Amadi's sad expression. His eyes glistened as he searched her face.

"Hetia, your father is hurting, but I want you to remember something, okay?" She nodded. "Most people out there are good people, and they don't want to harm us. Mae," he rubbed his hands up and down her arms, "doesn't take me away from anything. I love her and she's a part of my life. An important part. But she won't take me from anything or *anyone*," he said pointedly, "who is also important to me."

Hetia pouted.

"Okay?" Amadi pressed.

She nodded. Sadie pulled backward, casting around for nearby memories, attempting to free herself from this one. A second later and she was staring into Amadi's face again, only this time they were closer to the same height.

"Did he kill her?" Hetia said, her whole body pulsating with emotion.

Dee blinked in surprise. "No, of course not. Why would you even think that?" He had on that excessively worried expression he seemed to wear permanently with her these days.

"Because, you just told me Dad was actively trying to infiltrate The Coalition when she died. If Mom was a spy, *and* if she had been able to pass information back to the enemy, then he wouldn't believe his identity to be safe. Therefore, she must *not* have had the chance. It's just logical. He killed her, didn't he?"

Dee was shaking his head seriously. "He didn't kill her." But then he sighed and Hetia tensed for the truth. "I'm going to tell you something, okay?" he continued. "It's something no one but me and Mae knows. You know Luciana's husband, Sherman?" She nodded. "He can tell when someone tells an untrue story. It was how we found out that your mother was lying about her past. Your father should have told you the whole truth, but you were so young and he was in so much pain."

He sighed again. "When we confronted her, your mother confessed. Sherman validated her new story was absolutely accurate. She had been sent to get close with your father and learn what kind of danger he was to the Coalition cause, that is true. But something very different happened instead. She fell in love with him. She began to lie and cover for him without ever telling anyone how she had come to be in our lives in the first place. She never revealed anything about his identity. She even burned the few photos she'd taken with him. That day the truth came out, she asked to run away with him. She wanted your family to leave the country. But he couldn't forgive her. He said he couldn't ever really trust her. He told her to leave." Dee tried to take Hetia's hands, but she brushed him away and stepped back.

"Then how did she die?" Hetia asked. "Tell me!"

Dee swallowed, looking weary. "She took her own life, later that night," he said in a small voice.

Sadie pulled away. This was wrong. She needed to go back the other direction. She'd been closer before. She'd never had this much trouble navigating someone's head. Where was a memory containing the father? Father. Father. Father.

Everything blurred around her as she pushed toward the earlier thoughts. She caught snippets of her young life. Quick snapshots, but there seemed to be a hole right where she wanted to look most.

She felt a desire for Hetia's father to be alive. A strong impulse that seemed to consume an entire period. The months immediately before that time were a fog. Sadie clawed her way into them blindly, unable to latch onto anything specific. She could feel the present day calling her back. Her time was running out. She searched frantically through half-formed images, but before she could make out a single clear moment, she had returned to facing Hetia.

The beautiful woman in front of her gasped on a long inhale and then shuddered in her arms. Sadie held her by the back of the neck as she came down from the high. Eventually, Hetia ran her nose along her cheek, still catching her breath, and asked, "Did you get it?"

Sadie shook her head. "I couldn't get in. I think there's some memory trauma. That day in Siphon's office is... buried. It's in the middle of a thick cloud."

Hetia scooted away, breaking the contact. Her body was visibly shaking as she sat up and reached for the water bottle. She watched Sadie as she drank down several large gulps. "Did you see anything else?"

Sadie knew she would be asked this and had decided it would be best not to get caught in a lie. That would probably hurt Hetia's trust more. "Yes. I saw some stuff about your mom. Why she died."

Hetia didn't react to this. She just laid back down. "Go again," she said.

"Wha— Right away?" Sadie asked, caught up with worry, and

desperately trying to process the terrible information about Hetia's past.

"No use waiting," Hetia said, moving in beside her.

"I'm not sure I'll do any better the second time," Sadie said, the renewed contact revealing just how hard Hetia's heart was pounding.

"Try," Hetia said, sounding angry now.

Sadie ran her palm up and down the other woman's arm. Hetia's body was still recovering from the recent orgasm, however, and the touch didn't immediately send the early flutter of excitement. They were in that brief moment in which they could touch in a not directly sexual way.

Sadie ran her thumb over the smooth skin of Hetia's cheek, her gaze flickering from eye-to-eye as she enjoyed the simple sensation of touching her. "It'll take a minute," Sadie whispered. Hetia gave a single, slow nod.

And then she blinked and a sheen glistened over her piercing eyes. Between one moment and the next, Hetia's hard expression disappeared, and Sadie's heart skipped a beat as she realized Hetia was about to cry. She opened her mouth to say something comforting, but didn't get the chance.

Hetia's lips closed on hers. Sadie was too surprised to respond immediately, but as the other woman parted her mouth and sought her tongue, she was struck with an entirely new emotion. The lust and frustration that had fueled her evening melted into the softness of the sweet kiss. She inhaled the feeling of the tender embrace as Hetia tentatively claimed her mouth, uncertain and vulnerable. The movement was far too hesitant for the woman's usual behavior. She looked fragile as Sadie pulled back enough to kiss the wet tears leaking from the creases of her eyes.

Sadie put an arm around her and pulled her close, moving tenderly as she scooped a strand of blond hair behind Hetia's ear. She desperately wanted to comfort her, to take away all her pain and fear. She'd never felt that impulse about a person who wasn't Jimmy, but right now, while Hetia seemed like a breakable thing in her arms, all she wanted to do was scoop her up and protect her.

Hetia let herself be held until the tension in her body eased. The pleasurable flutter of early sexual excitement from the contact began, but they both ignored it. Sadie kissed her temple, her cheek, her tears as they slowly dried up.

"I want to be different," Hetia whispered after a while. "I want to let you in."

Sadie's body melted with sorrow, and she wished she knew the right thing to say. But then Hetia lifted her head to look at her and her expression was clear and calm and wide open. "Try again," she said, and this time it wasn't filled with angry emotion.

Sadie leaned forward to kiss her, and it seemed there were no more barriers between them. Hetia began to undress her, caressing each new patch of skin as it was revealed, and by the time they were both naked, their bodies had ramped back up into overdrive. They made love, soft and sweet, and it was some time before Sadie responded to Hetia's suggestion.

As the fifth orgasm threatened to consume her, Hetia was again on her back, and Sadie was ready to make a second attempt. She pulled the hair tie from behind the woman's head and thin blond hair cascaded across the sheet as Sadie sat back up to stroke the insides of the other woman's thighs.

Hetia was beautiful like this. She was all lean muscle under soft skin, her tiny nipples puckered from arousal. And most importantly, she looked completely at ease, her legs as open and inviting as all the rest of her. Sadie gripped her hip with one hand as she stroked her and Hetia arched into the touch, her lips parting in a silent cry, as Sadie disappeared into her past.

She could tell immediately that something was different. It took her only a moment to rediscover the dark cloud that covered the time around Eirik Pierce's death. And when she did, she found it much easier to penetrate. Though, when she began to look around, it was all the same dust-covered gray. The memory had no color or emotion, as if any desires Hetia had had during that time had been suppressed out of existence.

Sadie marched in a steady pace toward the last time Hetia had seen her father, and eventually she found herself in the office from which she'd stolen the bomb plans. Little Mia was playing in one corner, while Eirik and Siphon discussed business on the couch nearby. All Hetia wanted was to get the hell out of there, but the desire was small. Mostly she just played with the puzzle her father had given her. She turned the thing around in her hands, looking for a way to align the pieces.

"Mia, hush. No, this is a private affair. I need to get in without notice, before the repairs happen. Me and several of my men. You would be compensated enormously for your discretion and help in this matter," Siphon was saying. Hetia didn't like the sound of his voice, but she wasn't really listening. She tried to put the man out of mind so she could enjoy the puzzle.

"You're about to have a teenager on your hands. You could retire early, a rich man. I'm offering you the chance to give your little girl that kind of life," the man continued. All Hetia noticed were the last words. *Little girl my ass*, she thought. Who does this guy think he is? She was nearly eleven for Christ's sake. Adult men were the *worst*.

Siphon's kid sobbed louder and Hetia looked up as he scooped her into his arms.

"I accept," her father said.

"You're a smart man," the asshole said. "Now if you'll excuse me a minute. I need to take care of my daughter, and then we can talk details." His girl sobbed louder and Hetia looked up as he tossed her into the hands of a maid. The woman must have been right outside the door, just waiting to serve him or something. It was gross. Hetia rolled her eyes and went back to the puzzle.

"That's better." Siphon sat back down. "Now, I will be leaving for Arlington today. I will have someone escort your daughter home. You will stay at my side throughout the excursion. After that terrible fire this morning, the gates have been locked at every entrance to the catastrophe. There is one that will be unguarded tonight. You will provide us passage that way. You have a master key, no?"

Hetia twisted the puzzle several times in the silence.

"Good," the man continued. "And the special code they gave out this morning?"

There was another pause.

"Good. I have some philanthropy to do in the afternoon and you will be free to leave. I will pay you half now and half tomorrow."

Hetia looked up at the silence this time. Were they done yet? She paused at the expression on her father's face.

"Thank you for this job, sir. You can trust me to be discreet. But may I ask which entrance I will be opening?"

"It's in the southeast, on north pine."

"That's the largest one. That street is a tunnel. Are you sure you don't want to sneak in through the north? I know a little place I could show you."

"As I said, I will be bringing in something rather large. And the tunnel leads right to our destination."

"Where will that be?" Hetia watched her father. He looked casual and comfortable, but she could tell he wasn't. He'd asked that last question in the same calm voice he used when he'd asked her if she'd told anyone where they were going that morning. He was very interested in the answer.

The other man took forever to answer. "I have a... device that I wish to bury at the base of the largest tree."

"The one where the fire began?" her father asked.

Siphon turned to look around at Hetia, and she dropped her gaze to the puzzle.

"Yes. It's a protection against this kind of thing happening again. We will bury it before the repairs happen. It'll be safest for everyone if I'm the only one who knows it is there. Hence the secrecy."

There was silence a minute longer, before the men began to shuffle around. Siphon was handing an envelope to her father as Hetia got to her feet. A few minutes later, a tall woman was coming to collect her.

"Hetia. This lady will take you home, okay?" her father said.

"What?" Hetia crossed her arms. "You're not coming with me?"

"No. It turns out I have some work to do here. I'll be home tomorrow evening. There's dinner in the freezer and—"

"No," she said coolly. "You can't leave me alone. I won't just wait around for you or—"

"Hetia! You'll do as I tell you." Her father turned to the other man. "May I have a private word with my daughter before we go?"

The man shook his head. "I'm sorry, but I can't permit that," he said, before turning to her. "I'm sorry I'm stealing your old dad. It's all my fault. Will you forgive me if I have Bet make you her best chocolate cake?"

Hetia just scowled at him.

Her father ruffled her hair. "Go with the lady. I'll see you soon." She continued to glare at them both, but they'd already turned away from her. She considered screaming, but she didn't want them to treat her like a child. In the end, she let the woman put a hand on her back and lead her away. The only protest she made was to refuse to give even a backward glance at her father.

Chapter 13

An Explosive Revelation

Sadie emerged with a jerk as if expelled and collapsed next to Hetia. She scooted away just enough that their skin wouldn't touch as Hetia rolled onto her side to face her. "You got in," she said. It wasn't a question. The shaken way Sadie felt inside must have shown in her expression.

She nodded, searching the ceiling with her gaze. Sadie processed the information rapidly, coming to the only conclusion she could.

"Tell me what happened after they led you away. Your father went off and a maid, Bet, took you home."

Hetia shifted, rolling to her back as Sadie faced her. "She made me a cake in the kitchens downstairs. I refused to eat it. Then she made me hot chocolate. I told her I wouldn't eat and drink anything until my father came home." Hetia swallowed. "I was so angry. Eventually she took me to the little house Dad and I had rented in town that year. She left me tucked in bed."

Hetia reached for the sheet and covered them, the sexual moment clearly passed. Sadie scooted closer, and with the sheet as protection from skin contact, she wrapped an arm and leg over the other woman, resting a palm above her beating heart. Hetia paused a while, searching the air with her gaze as if struggling to dredge up the rest. Eventually, she continued, but in a much slower, uncertain voice.

"Later that night I heard someone come in. Briefly, I thought it was my dad, but they didn't turn on any lights. I got up and hid under my bed. They entered my room. I remember their muddy brown boots in front of my face as they reached and touched the place I'd just been lying. I figured it must still be warm and that they would probably look under the bed as their first guess of where I'd hid."

Hetia heaved an impatient sigh. "I was terrified, young, and inexperienced. I called a quake that brought down most of the house and did significant damage to the houses next door. I was lucky none of the neighbors died, but the man who'd come into the room was killed by a blow to the head from the chimney. It collapsed directly over my bedroom, trapping me under my bed and taking out my guest."

Her fingers closed over Sadie's from the other side of the sheet. "Before any sirens came, Dee appeared. He climbed through the wreckage and pulled me out. He told me to be quiet as we snuck away. But before we could leave, he started a little fire in my broken bedroom, using an oil lamp. Which I realize now was probably to cover up the quake." Hetia's face screwed up in thought. "I remember that moment so well. I remember thinking, he's going to destroy all my books. Why would he do that? I became fixated on saving my copy of the *The Little Nymph that Could*." She laughed. "After we had put some distance between us and the scene, he told me that some bad men had come to try and hurt me, and it was best if they didn't know I had survived."

Sadie sucked in air and Hetia looked at her. "Siphon. He tried to have you killed."

"Probably."

"Then he killed your father," Sadie added, her eyes tearing up.

Hetia looked down at her. "We've never known that for sure. Sadie, tell me what you saw."

She didn't hesitate, wanting to give Hetia all the information she could. "Siphon hired your father to help plant something large in the center of the city, under the great tree. I think it was the bomb. And I think when the task was done, that he must have... permanently silenced your father."

Hetia sat up. "The bomb is here?" Sadie had expected her to react to the news about her father's murder, but that seemed far from the woman's thoughts as she swung out of bed. "We should move."

Sadie sat up. "Dawn's hours away," she mumbled, feeling suddenly exhausted.

Hetia refastened her bra. "We'll catch the first train out of town."

"Today?"

"As soon as we collect the others," Hetia added in a tone that allowed no argument.

Sadie slumped, but didn't lie back down. She knew she should be more afraid, but if the bomb had been here for over a decade, it hardly seemed like an emergency.

"What's the rush? Can't we wait till the sun comes up at least?" Sadie reached out a hand in Hetia's direction as if she could draw her back to bed by grasping longingly at the air between them.

"We'll get the news to Dee. But first, the war has started. There's a chance The Coalition was waiting for just this moment to use the bomb. It would be foolish to linger." Hetia sounded matter-of-fact rather than afraid, though she was making fast work of dressing herself.

Sadie just pouted at her, struggling to feel the urgency in her predawn, post-sex haze.

Hetia caught sight of her face and paused, a slight flush and flare of her eyes betraying a hint of a reaction before the image of Sadie mussed up in bed appeared in Hetia's mind. She cleared her throat. "There are five jails in the outer city. It'll take time to locate them, but we'll—"

"I think I might know," Sadie cut in. Hetia looked surprised and Sadie was quite satisfied she had something so useful to contribute. "I've been turning it over. My prison guard, he gave me a very thorough picture of the city's judicial system. I've been struggling to remember, but I think there are three places they might be. And I'm guessing they're at the largest one."

She stopped to tug her shirt over her head, pleasantly aware of

Hetia's gaze on her body as she pulled the fabric over them. "Only problem is, if I'm right, it's also the most heavily guarded," Sadie added, speaking with the same confidence as Hetia had when she'd casually mentioned their impending jail break last night. Bolstered by their now *shared* conspiring to rescue their friends, she felt a little thrill at being a part of the dangerous world Hetia seemed to inhabit with ease.

"Alright, Sadie. I'll follow you," Hetia said, reaching out to sweep her hair behind her ear, not bothering to avoid the skin contact. For a brief moment, they paused to remember what had just happened, moving simultaneously to exchange a slow kiss.

Sadie's eyes teared up as she noticed the tiny black love line pulsing out from her to Hetia. Though the woman wasn't returning the color, the gentle feel of her lips and the soft caress of her hand in Sadie's hair added an intimacy that gave weight to the moment all the same.

As Sadie relaxed into the embrace, she recalled her recent confusing emotions regarding her feelings for Troy, and her struggle to handle them in light of what she already felt for Jimmy. But then she imagined trying to love Hetia with as much ferocity, and in this moment the idea made complete sense to her.

Patricia had told her before they'd come here, that in such dangerous times, all a person could do was suck up all the good things while they were still in front of them. Seeing Troy and Patricia dragged away from her, and having Jimmy so far away, Sadie was suddenly desperate to cling to this thing she felt for Hetia. She couldn't know what tomorrow might bring, but falling in love with this woman now seemed not only possible, but inevitable.

As Sadie pulled back and paused to take one last look at her, she wondered if Hetia could ever feel the same. In light of what she'd just learned about her past, Sadie understood now why she was so guarded, and she resolved to do her best not to add to the hurt of her past. But she wasn't going to let Hetia push her away again. Sadie would be patient, as she showed Hetia that she was safe in her arms.

They broke contact, and the second the spell of the moment was lifted, they both moved swiftly to prepare to leave. Ten minutes later, they were in the elevator, loaded down with two backpacks each. "I can't believe the bomb's been under our feet this whole time," Sadie said into the silence.

Hetia gave her a long look before turning back to the doors. "You did good. Stealing that folder from Siphon's office." Sadie felt a small rush of pride at these words as she shifted to get more comfortable in the heavy packs. Hetia moved to help, running her fingers under the straps and lifting them higher on Sadie's shoulder. "We wouldn't be here today if you hadn't been so bold. And this could turn things. Give us an edge."

Their eyes met and Sadie was hit with a wave of emotion as the slow rumble of the elevator stopped on a ping, and she pushed aside the million things she wanted to say. *I'm sorry about your mom. And your dad. What just happened was amazing. What do you think the chances are the city blows up while we're in it?*

Sadie sat on her multitude of thoughts as Hetia led them down an alleyway so dark she had to hold her hand to direct her. They stashed their bags behind a dumpster, Sadie watching in surprise as Hetia shoved them in. "How will we find them again?" she asked as Hetia lifted the second bag off her shoulders and disappeared with it.

"I scouted this place out ahead of time, in case this happened."

"You prepared for if some of us got arrested and we had to break them out in the middle of the night?" Sadie asked.

"I prepared for a lot of things," Hetia replied quietly, her words sounding like a threat to the world, which left Sadie with a sense of awe as she recalled precisely who this woman was and of what she was capable. She followed her with increasing nerves over what they were about to do, all the while trying to guess exactly what a jailbreak might entail. Luckily, Hetia appeared far from nervous as she followed Sadie with confident determination.

Freed by the weight of the packs, they moved swiftly through the city. It was less than an hour later when Sadie grabbed Hetia's arm and pulled them to a stop. "There. Whew. I told you I'd find it eventually." She smiled over at the woman, but Hetia wasn't listening. Her eyes were darting over the brick walls and guards, taking in every detail. It looked nothing like the other jail Sadie had seen. This was a prison, and they had clearly called in reinforcements after yesterday's events.

"I'll be right back," Hetia said.

"Wait, wha—" Sadie tried to protest, but the woman was already gone. She watched her light hair disappear under a dark hood as she moved forward through the shadows. Sadie lost track of her until she emerged near the corner of the prison. Lights illuminated the guards and Hetia's black attire the instant she stepped into view.

It happened fast. Sadie almost screamed as seven guns turned in the direction of the tiny figure, but before anyone could lock on they began to shake. It was hard to tell the cause from so far away, but Sadie knew the nymph was producing a controlled earthquake under their feet. Several of them fell to their knees, while Hetia moved swiftly to trip the ones still standing.

Sadie jumped as one of them fired. The sound pierced the night, but Hetia closed in before the man could reload. He swung his nightstick full force, and the momentum carried him easily over her back and to the ground. She had their weapons tossed in a heap before more guards emerged through the doors. In less than a minute since she'd stepped into the light, Hetia had disappeared through the front entrance.

Sadie moved closer. She wished they'd talked more ahead of time. She wanted to help. What if something went wrong? She had no idea what to do. Those guards and their guns were terrifying. Or they would be if they were coming at her. How could Hetia just leave her here?

Just as she was beginning to get worried in full, a loud rumble came from the left-most wall. It grew, until separate bricks began to move against each other. When it finally came apart, it seemed to crumble all at once, forming a heap of rubble over which a stream of people immediately began to climb.

Sadie moved to the edge of the action, staying just inside the shadows. She chewed her lip as she frantically looked around. She was waiting for more guns to appear, but nothing happened. On the backs of the large dose of adrenaline now pumping through her, she darted forward, past the stream of people, and peered inside the open hole in the building. She recognized none of the faces running past her, but behind several fractured bars, she caught sight of the tiny-hooded figure that was Hetia.

"Sadie?" a man said, screeching to a halt. It took her a moment to realize it was the bartender.

"Jalen?"

"What are you doing here?" he asked.

"Uhhh, helping, I think." She looked over his dust-covered clothes. "Was anyone hurt?"

"Yes, a guard got trapped under some bricks. One of your friends, the guy, is digging him out.

"Sadie!" Patricia's welcome voice hit her. Sadie turned to smile at the woman running her way, but grabbed the bartender's arm before he could disappear.

"Jalen, look, you should know, there's trouble coming for this city. More than just the yes vote. You might want to get people out of here."

His gaze darted back and forth between her eyes. "What do you know?"

"Just that staying here much longer might be a death sentence. It won't be something you can fight either. It'd be best to get people out and far away."

Jalen lifted his chin. He wore a look of a man about to play the hero, but in the end he said, "Okay. I'll see what I can do."

Her shoulders relaxed. "Good luck to you," she said.

"And you." He squeezed her arm once before turning away.

Patricia pulled her into a hug before Sadie could face her. "You're here. I mean we knew you would be, just not so soon." She released the embrace. "How did you find us?"

"Sadie's a wealth of knowledge on local jails, apparently," Hetia said, pulling up between them. Patricia looked at her with raised brows.

Sadie looked back at the rubble. "And Hetia's good at destroying buildings *now*, asking questions *later*. Apparently."

Hetia looked up at her from under the deep hood. She looked intense and beautiful like that, especially since she was covered in the images of their recent encounter. "Well, I am my father's daughter. I was just testing the building was up to quake code. It wasn't."

There was a brief pause and then Sadie and Patricia both laughed. Of course, if Hetia was going to make a joke it would be about something destructive. Sadie just shook her head as the tiniest smile appeared on Hetia's lips.

The last stragglers disappeared into the darkness as Troy crested the heap of rubble. Sadie's heart skipped at the sight of him. She'd forgotten how present he still was in her body. No wonder her skin had seemed to buzz all morning, with everything that had happened in the past few days.

He pulled up next to the group, looking windswept, and Hetia said "Let's go" before they could even greet him. But Troy smiled at Sadie before following the hooded figure into the shadows.

She and Patricia had to half jog to keep up with their pace, and the instant they'd dropped into the safety of a dark alleyway, Patricia called them to a halt. "There're rocks here, and I can't see," she said, sounding distressed.

"She's barefoot. We lost her shoes," Troy explained.

Sadie could just barely make out Hetia dropping her sack and digging around. She jumped when someone reached for her hand in the dark, but relaxed as she caught the familiar scent of Troy. He appeared in front of her and she put a hand on his chest and relaxed against him.

"Here. Try these," Hetia said from somewhere to her left.

Troy was practically vibrating against her and she could feel his erection despite the fact they hadn't touched skin. With urgency, he scooped a hand behind her neck and kissed her. Sadie was a little embarrassed at the proximity of the others, but she stopped thinking straight a second later as she matched his intensity. He drew her as close as he could while wearing clothing and consumed her furiously.

"Those'll do," Patricia said.

Now that they were touching, Sadie could feel the extent of his pent-up desire from their night apart and again regretted how far she'd taken things with him. They needed to run for their lives, not fool around in a dark alley.

She heard movement as the others took off and her heart pounded at the overwhelming situation. Just as she was about to push Troy back, however, he broke off the embrace and ran after them, leaving Sadie confused and aroused to pull up the rear. Luckily, an hour of jogging on no sleep shook off any distracting feelings that lingered in her body.

The sun came up as they were retrieving their bags, and Hetia popped out of sight, emerging in a soft yellow dress, heavy enough for winter, her hair loose. "Wow. Uhh... you're certainly unrecognizable," Troy said. Sadie disagreed. Hetia always looked like herself; beautiful and powerful. If she was the one searching for her, this dress wouldn't fool her for a minute. But she kept silent about those thoughts as Troy added, "In fact, I might even be able to trip you in that thing."

Hetia gave him a cool stare. "No. You wouldn't," she said, before leading them out of the alley. Troy winked at Sadie and Patricia behind her back before following. When they pulled up next to her, Hetia directed at Troy, "That's what holds you back. You interact as if the world is in your way. You need to learn to move with it. These skirts," she lifted the heavy things around her legs, "are just another medium." Her casual tone made Sadie relax. If she was chatting conversationally, and moving at a slower pace, they must be out of immediate danger.

Sadie dropped back as Hetia and Troy launched into a serious conversation about fighting technique, the green light of friendship pulsing strong between them. Patricia's gaze was on the feet ahead of her, looking as tired as Sadie felt, and the moment gave her a chance to look around at the four of them. Their relationships had evolved rapidly, and the tangle of lights between them was a web of color.

The sight of all the love, lust, and friendship lines made her miss Jimmy with a sharp pain. What was going to happen when they were all back together? Troy was behaving as if they were engaged now, and she and Hetia had definitely taken a strong left turn last night. Sadie couldn't help but be overwhelmed by juggling so many strong emotions at once. How did Mae do it? She felt a little ashamed that she was a succubus, and yet none of this seemed to be coming easily to her.

Though when they joined back up with Amadi's army, it would all be a moot point, anyway. Troy and Hetia would go to fight, and maybe something horrible would happen to them. She, Jimmy, and Patricia would do... something. They'd probably fight too, before the end. And her parents. Her home. This was really no time to be falling in love. Perhaps she'd do better by guarding her heart against what was coming, despite Patricia's sage words about seizing what you can from life.

"We need breakfast. Let's stop here." Patricia nodded to a bakery just as a man flipped the sign on the door to open. The place was empty, but all the same, they took the most secluded table in the corner. They ordered a loaf of banana bread to share, and Hetia selected several baguettes and cheeses, packing them all away in her pack.

Sadie spotted a brightly colored bracelet around Patricia's wrist as she reached for her slice across the table. Patricia followed her gaze, looked self-consciously at the store owner, and quickly tucked away the clear indication of their recent incarceration.

"We have to get rid of these." Troy rubbed his hand around his own wrist.

"At least they didn't take your clothes. I thought in big cities they put you in orange or something," Sadie said.

"I don't think they had enough to go around," Patricia said. "They didn't even search us, just piled us in together. The bracelets are metal though, and Troy thinks he might be able to melt them off."

Troy's gaze flickered to Sadie's as she recalled intimately the last time he had broken through metal with heat. "We'll just have to keep them out of sight for now," Troy said, pushing his further up his sleeve.

"What's the plan?" Patricia asked, dusting away the last crumbs of her breakfast.

"We get out of town, find Dee." Hetia chimed in.

"What's the rush?" Troy frowned. "He said to hang tight, right? That they were coming this way. You could keep a low profile, and we could take a room on the edge of town." Sadie felt a pulse of desire waft off him at his mention of getting a room.

Hetia and Sadie exchanged a look. "Umm." Sadie cleared her throat. "We know where the bomb is," she said in barely more than a whisper. The other two turned to her with rapt attention. "It's here. In the heart of the city."

Troy flinched, and Patricia pushed her chair back as if readying to run. "What? Why the hell are we sitting here?"

"Because a couple hours isn't going to make a difference," Hetia said, "but we *are* leaving today."

Patricia cleaned up their table and stood up, giving them all an impatient look, and without pausing to discuss further, they headed for the train station. An hour later, they were on the first train out of town. It happened to be heading east, but one direction was as good as another until they heard from Amadi.

They found a car to themselves and piled in with their packs. Sadie and Patricia shared a bench and Hetia and Troy sat across from them. It wasn't until the train started, that any of them began to relax.

Troy sunk down in his seat, putting his feet between Sadie and Patricia. "Prison sucks. I didn't sleep a wink last night. It was so bright and loud." And as if these words were a catalyst, Patricia yawned. She too, put her feet up, and the two of them were asleep within minutes, her friend's form slumping against Sadie's shoulder.

Hetia glanced over at Sadie and they exchanged a long, intimate look. All the memories of a few hours ago returned and Sadie's body warmed when Hetia's expression softened. It was a look she only wore in the bedroom, and the sight of it again made it hard to think straight.

"We should get some sleep, too," Hetia whispered. It was true. They too had been up most of the night. Hetia scooted down into a sleeping position, stretching her boot to touch against the edge of Sadie's. She licked her lips, and cast her one last confidential look, before shutting her eyes.

Sadie could feel her own exhaustion, but she was sure her mind was buzzing too much to sleep. It wouldn't hurt to just close her eyes though. Just for a minute.

That was the last thing she could remember thinking before jerking awake. The train was slowing down, Hetia and Patricia were gone, and Troy was still passed out across from her. His hand was loosely resting on the prominent erection and Sadie swallowed down the wave of lust as she pushed herself upright.

Where were the others? Sadie held on as she stood up and peeked out the door. The train conductor was leaning against the far wall.

"Morning miss," he said. "Almost there now. I hope your journey was comfortable."

He smiled and bobbed his head.

Sadie cleared her throat. "Yes. Uhhh, thank you."

She withdrew back inside. Troy was sending out a distracting, frantic set of images, and she hated to wake him in the middle of them, mostly because she was nervous to face an awake Troy, but there was nothing for it. She shook his shoulder. He grumbled and tried to turn away. Sadie noticed then that his bag was missing, he'd been half-leaning on it before. She glanced around and her heart stopped. All of their bags were gone.

She shook him harder. "Troy. Get up." He woke on a gasp. "Something weird is happening. Get up."

"Sadie?" He looked up at her and then around. "Where— Oh, right. The train." He ran a hand through his hair and sat up. He looked at the erection and blew out some air. "I should find a bathroom." He said, putting a hand on the seat next to him and then looking confused. "Where's my jacket? Wait, where's our stuff?"

"Not here. The others were gone when I woke up, and the train's about to stop."

"Shit." He put his head between his hands. "Just give me a minute."

She could feel him pushing down his desire as if by sheer force, and he rose exactly as the train stopped moving. Troy avoided looking at her as she assessed him before turning to the door.

The conductor was still right outside. He smiled again at her. "This way, miss. Sir." He nodded at Troy over her shoulder. He didn't even seem to notice they had no bags as he led the way. She'd never seen a conductor behave like this, and it only added to her confusion of what to do.

"Actually, we need to find—" Sadie began, but stopped as several things happened at once. The conductor had turned back as she spoke and Hetia had come up behind him and pulled him to his back, just as a hand closed over Sadie's wrist and Patricia hissed, "This way."

Her friend tugged hard and Sadie obeyed the summons, glancing back only to see Hetia's hand covering the conductor's mouth. Patricia pulled them into the corridor between coaches, where their bags were piled in a corner. "Take a pack," Patricia said as Troy came in behind them. Two women tried to enter through the opposite door. "Other way," Patricia told them. "This section's blocked off."

The second they were gone, Patricia shoved open the door facing away from the station. The bright world darted past outside as the train moved toward stopping, and Sadie nearly screamed as Patricia just hopped off. Troy put a hand on her back. "Let's go," he whispered in her ear.

Sadie looked back at the door to the hall. Where was Hetia? What if they couldn't get back to her and she needed help? But then Troy too jumped out, and Sadie was left alone with her worries. It seemed there was nothing for it. She just had to trust the others in this since she had no idea what was happening.

She leapt down, crumpling to her knees under the weight of the fall and her bag. Troy ran over and pulled her up. Patricia was gesturing them to follow in the distance, and without preamble, they ran after her as she hopped over the other tracks. Sadie couldn't look back as she had to watch her footsteps. They were lucky another train wasn't coming, because they had to stick to the tracks for several minutes before reaching an opening in the fence to wriggle through.

As they cleared the back end of the train they'd just fled, someone from the station caught sight of them. "Hey! What are you doing? Get outta there!"

The words chased them as Sadie squeezed through the opening and out onto the grassy field beyond. The horn of an incoming train sounded somewhere in the distance and Sadie stopped. "We need to keep moving." Patricia gestured.

"Hetia," Sadie whined.

"She'll catch us. We're the slow ones."

Her friend took her wrist as Troy said, "What the hell is going on?"

"Later. We need to move," Patricia said, panting with the effort of exertion and talking. Sadie let herself be dragged onward and when Patricia broke into a jog, Sadie did the same. She, too, was panting after only a few minutes, the bags feeling heavier than ever.

Despite this, Patricia seemed determined to keep moving as if their lives depended on it. Head down, she plowed on in a fast trot. Sadie kept her eyes on the hem of the dress in front of her as a million questions darted through her head.

Clearly, they had been tracked from the prison break. Hetia's attack on the conductor made it seem like he was assisting in some way in an attempt to arrest them, which would explain his strange behavior. But none of it made a lot of sense. Hetia wasn't around when he had been fixated on leading Sadie and Troy off the train.

"Let me take your bag for a while," Troy told Patricia.

"I've got it," Patricia snapped, but the woman wasn't accustomed to physical exertion. Even for Sadie, who had a good deal of muscle under her curves, this was a lot, while Troy appeared to have barely broken a sweat.

"Patricia, Troy is strong. Let him help," Sadie pleaded through her panting, and she found that she felt no reservation at siding with him on this, or competition over the fact he could lift more. If he'd offered to carry her bag instead, she would have accepted.

They paused as Patricia handed off the bag, and Sadie bent to catch her breath. "Almost there," Hetia said from behind her, making Sadie jump as relief flooded her. "I made it look like we went south, left some things behind," Hetia told Patricia. "We just need to get to that farmhouse and out of sight." The women nodded in agreement to each other and took off running.

Sadie and Troy exchanged a frown before following. With renewed energy, Sadie peered at the little red barn in the distance, glad they had an end destination in mind. Though it wasn't until they got close and began to slow, that she was able to get out the words, "What happened back there?"

It was Hetia who answered, breathing as easily as if they'd just been lounging around. "Patricia and I removed the bags. Slowly. The conductor didn't seem to notice, despite his hovering. I left him passed out to buy us time."

None of that seemed to answer her real questions. "And why was he hovering around us and not you?" Sadie pushed.

Neither woman spoke. Patricia was heaving now and she dropped to a walk, causing the rest of them to do the same. Hetia didn't answer, but after a while, Patricia managed to choke out, "Because they're not after Hetia."

Sadie and Troy's heads snapped to her, but she didn't elaborate, and they turned back to keep their eyes on the prize as they approached the barn. Hetia led them around the back, keeping out of sight, and Sadie clutched at her side, grateful to be done running. Especially since she didn't know what they were running from.

There were voices in the distance, but none of the human inhabitants were visible. Some cows cast them a decidedly suspicious look, however, as they invaded their space. Sadie leaned back against the inside wall of the barn and shut her eyes. She was thoroughly annoyed with the lack of information coming from the other women, but she would have to wait to catch her breath before she could lay into them. She stood upright and Hetia shoved a newspaper into her hands.

Troy rushed to read over her shoulder as Sadie's mouth fell open. Their faces were on the front page. Troy and Sadie, dressed as they'd been the night of Phoenix Maddox's birthday party, were front page news. Siphon had put a five-hundred-thousand-dollar award on their capture. Wanted alive only.

"It seems he knows you've left the United army," Patricia said. "And he really wants you back."

Chapter 14

Running Hot and Heavy

"Why?" Sadie gasped, feeling tears and panic threaten to overtake her.

"The bomb. He must know you stole the file on it." Patricia shook her head in dismay as she spoke. "He needs to know what happened. They can't control the information if they don't know who knows what." She took a swill of water and tried to hand it to Sadie, but the effort was in vain. She passed the bottle to Troy instead.

He drank and then blew out a whistle. "For that much money, we're going to have a hard time finding friends. We'll have to stay out of sight." He shrugged. "Or we could turn each other in and retire rich. You know, after they torture and kill us." Catching the look on Sadie's face he dropped his bitter grin. "Sorry, I didn't mean—" He put an arm around her. "We'll stay out of his hands, don't worry."

Troy must have become suddenly aware of their proximity, because he stepped several feet away before clearing his throat and adding, "We need to get to a phone booth."

"We'll head north the rest of the day," Patricia said. "It's wide open that way. Eventually we'll hit some small town, contact Amadi, and take it from there."

"We'll rest here briefly to take care of the necessities," Hetia said, pulling toilet paper and food from her bag.

The matter-of-fact response of the others helped calm Sadie considerably, and she felt some of the tension release from her muscles. They had a plan, they were currently somewhere safe, and they would soon be joining back up with Amadi's army.

Troy took another swill of water, watching Sadie as he did so. Catching his expression, and the thoughts behind it, made it clear that he was no longer worrying over bombs and war as he disappeared without a word.

For a second, she considered following him, but her mind was on too many things to get swept up in the call of his lust, which had grown more potent than ever. Though she felt the exact moment he released his tenuous control and let the full force of arousal rush in. It was less than a minute before it peaked and dropped sharply. Sadie inhaled, accepting the piece of bread and cheese from Patricia. Her thoughts cleared in tandem with Troy's, making space for the fear-based adrenaline to rush back in.

Sadie's hands shook as she ate. "Does your mom know? I mean about what's happening?" She asked Patricia as Hetia sat next to her.

"Yes. She's known this was coming for years. It's why she got out of the movement. After Dad died and Grandpa was killed, she said she just couldn't forgive my grandmother for getting me involved. She'll stay away, protect her heart." Patricia gave a small smile. "Unless we win. That would change everything."

Sadie squeezed her hand. No one offered empty platitudes about everything working out. Instead, they looked around at each other as they ate, and it seemed the world was made more real by the immediacy of their presence. Here they were together, eating moist bread on a crisp, late autumn day, facing an unknown level of destruction. The future felt unreal.

"I don't want to lose you," Sadie blurted out, looking from one woman to the other, her eyes tearing up. "Whatever happens."

Patricia squeezed her arm. "I'm here with you. Today. And tomorrow."

Sadie put her own gloved hand over her friend's.

"We should get moving," Hetia said, standing up, but not before Sadie caught the emotion in her expression. A tiny thread of green light was flowing from Hetia to the two of them, and Sadie's gaze softened on the way the one connecting them was laced with black. It was thin, almost undetectable, but it was flowing both ways. This really had been a world-changing couple of days.

Troy returned and they readied themselves in silence, a state that persisted as they trudged over rolling fields, each person lost in their own thoughts. Occasionally, one of them would look up to glare at the heavy rain clouds ahead, but they made no plans to try and avoid it. What would come would come, Sadie figured, and she'd certainly seen her share of rain growing up.

Luckily, they hit a small farming village before the weather struck in full. "I'll be back," Patricia said, as the rest of them stepped under a tree to escape the few droplets splattering around them. They covered their packs with rain jackets and waited for the verdict.

Patricia returned a few minutes later, running and ducking away from the moisture. She smoothed out her bound hair and stood up straight. Then she sighed. "There's no one answering the phone, and no new message. They're coming east and we should stay put in Arlington. That's it."

Sadie's shoulders slumped. Jimmy felt impossibly far away. Not knowing exactly where he was or what was happening left her with a constant buzz of worry. When they'd parted, she thought they'd spend a couple weeks apart, which had seemed like an infinite amount of time, and then she'd return to the camp. Now, she had no idea when or where they'd meet again.

"Also, this place doesn't have an inn. Someone suggested the next town over if we want a place to stay. Though," she shifted, "we'll have to sneak Sadie and Troy in since their pictures are up everywhere."

"Already?" Troy asked.

"The Coalition must have sent out a bunch of posters all at once." Patricia sniffed, looking irritated.

"All over the country?" Sadie asked. "Or do you think he knows we're here somewhere?"

"How could he?" Patricia said. "He has no way of knowing we've connected the bomb to a memory from his daughter's perspective a decade and a half ago."

"Unless someone spotted us," Hetia said. "They have spies everywhere."

"I bet he was having the inner city watched, given its significance to his plan," Patricia said. "If the bomb is there and we happened to visit its exact location unknowingly, someone would've sent word to him that day."

"How far was the next town?" Troy asked.

"Too far to make it tonight." Patricia tapped her toe, glancing around. Sadie looked from her to the now-pouring rain.

"This way," Hetia said. She led them back the way they came. Back to a small house on the edge of town. The residents appeared to be away, and the property contained a workshop that was blissfully clean, apart from a little sawdust.

The temperature was dropping rapidly with nightfall, however, and Patricia, insisting they not freeze, made Hetia go in search of bedding. She returned with two sleeping bags and a thick wool blanket. "We'll have to share," she said, casting a look over at Sadie.

"Good," Patricia said. "It's warmer that way." She'd been by far the most stressed about roughing it, but her whole demeanor relaxed as she laid out the fluffy sack. When she finally looked up, she paused at their expressions. "What?"

"Ummm... who sleeps with who?" Troy asked.

Sadie caught both his and Hetia's eye before she could stop herself. "I think I share with Patricia, like the rooms."

Hetia nodded and turned to spread the other sack. "Makes sense," Troy agreed, but Sadie noticed he pulled the other bag closer to theirs as they unloaded. When they climbed in a few hours later, Hetia took the spot closest to Sadie, however, and she found herself snug and warm with Patricia at her back and Hetia nearby in front of her. It was a tight squeeze, and she watched the other bag wriggle as the two found a way to fit, Troy facing away, and Hetia facing her.

Though Sadie wasn't remotely in need of feeding, she was slightly grumpy about the logistics of this situation. The conditioner smell of Hetia's hair reminded her of all that had happened last night, and with the hectic day done, Sadie had time to think of it. And she wasn't the only one. The other sleeping bag was a succubus feast's worth of carnal thoughts. It didn't seem likely the three of them would be getting much sleep that night.

She was wrong. Everyone but her drifted off quickly. Hetia and Troy carried their thoughts happily into the dream world, undisturbed, and it was Sadie alone who couldn't seem to get away from the tug of desire.

It reminded her of many nights spent close to Jimmy, not touching, but wanting. Wanting so much that her whole body was a constant aching mess of pent-up energy. Despite her complete lack of hunger, she couldn't wriggle her mind free of the feeling of Hetia's hips under her hands, or Troy's mouth on hers.

Her scattered thoughts, thick with rich sensations, drifted to the night Troy had taken her out. She was enveloped with memories of the warm room as they'd danced and the heavy aroma of her shepherd's pie as she'd broken the surface with a spoon. It was a blanket over all her confusing emotions. She wanted to wrap herself in it with everything she loved and stay there, safe and warm.

It must have been with that feeling that she slept, because she dreamed of only pleasant things, and awoke with a general sense of contentment, even if she couldn't remember where her mind had taken her.

Hetia's eyes were open, watching her. Sadie took one look at her face, still wrapped in drowsy sleep, and thought clearly, *I love that woman*. She could see it was increasingly true, in that she was falling in love with her now. The black threads which had appeared between them were growing stronger, and Sadie felt the weight of it. The feeling was frightening in a different way than it was with Troy. Hetia was a force of nature, one that might go off and play the hero soon. One that might disappear at any minute.

Hetia's hand was visible above the blanket. Tentatively, Sadie reached out and clasped it. She thought she could see her own emotions reflected in the other woman's gaze: fear, longing, and hope. Though Hetia was hard to read, and it might all be her own wishful projections.

But then, Hetia pulled the hand up to her lips and kissed her fingers through the gloves, and when she looked back up at her there was no doubt. She kept her gaze locked on Sadie as she kissed again along every knuckle and the gesture seemed to say, *Yes, I feel it too. I love these hands.* Hetia pulled back Sadie's fingers and pressed her lips to her wrist. *I love this wrist.* Then she reached out and cupped a hand around the back of Sadie's neck. *And I love this person.*

Hetia's expression was suddenly punctuated by another surprising thing. Her eyes welled up and a tear leaked across her face. It was the second time Sadie had seen her cry in two days, and yet it was no less shocking. Was it because of the night they'd had together? Or perhaps from what Sadie had seen in her memory – in having someone else know the truth of her past?

Either way, Sadie was so caught off-guard that her heart nearly stopped. Yesterday, when she'd tried to tell both the women how she felt, Hetia hadn't responded. She'd suggested they leave and hadn't even looked back at her. But now, in this quiet early morning space, in their little bubble of privacy, Hetia cried silently as she held Sadie in her hands.

And Sadie, honored to be witness to such vulnerability, felt her heart melt in full.

~

THEY AGAIN SPENT the day on the move. Everyone agreed it was better than staying put near the place they'd been last seen. They traveled north and west, and it donned on Sadie that it was almost as if they were headed toward her hometown. She longed to see her parents, and she did her best to trick her mind into believing that she was merely on a pleasant trip with friends, on her way to introduce them to her family.

They stayed the second night at an inn with still no word from Amadi about their whereabouts. Patricia snuck the other three in after dark and they piled into the single room. The inn of the tiny town had no central heating, but each room came with a small fireplace. At least it was cheap. The money Amadi had provided would last longer now that they were out of the city, for which Sadie was grateful as she hated wasting the precious resource. The United was not a rich organization.

Troy set to warming the place while Patricia claimed first shower with a gusto with which no one dared argue. As Hetia prepared a meal of reconstituted soup using the kettle over the fire, Sadie began to get hungry for more than just food. Uncertain what to do with their present circumstances, she stayed far from the other two, staring out the window as they bustled at her back. Troy always got a rush from fire that was sensual in nature – she knew because it flavored his desire in a way unique to him.

Hetia was even more distracting, however. Unlike Troy, she could hide the arousal that had been building in her since their encounter, and so she'd been making no efforts to release it herself. Sadie had felt it like a heavy pulse all day, and it was both fueling her hunger and adding to her impatience.

She was downright irritable by the time Patricia reappeared, and she wasn't alone in the feeling since the meal passed in moody silence all around. When they'd finished repacking the bowls, Troy directed at Hetia, "You can have next shower if you want."

She nodded without looking at anyone and disappeared.

Patricia put on her shoes. "I'm going to the bar. I haven't fed since the jail," she said with the same exasperated tone she'd had during this whole unruly affair. A shower and a story would probably go a long way to calming her. At least Sadie hoped so. Though Patricia's sudden departure left her and Troy rather abruptly alone, and now she'd have to decide what to do with their limited time.

Sadie swallowed before facing him. His back was still turned as he stoked the fire, but she could feel that he too was aware it was now just the two of them. They hadn't really talked since the night of their date, and she wanted to slow things down, take a few steps back. But her desire to have that conversation now was overwhelmed by the knowledge that they had only a few minutes. And she was hungry.

She went to stand next to him and held her hands out to the fire. He didn't look over at her as he stood up, but his arousal was evident, and she turned to watch as he went erect. Troy held himself through his pants, but still avoided her gaze. She was surprised. Sadie would have thought he'd jump her at the smallest opportunity.

"I can see why this was hard for Jimmy," he said. "If I could crawl in bed with you for a month right now, I think I would die happy, but wanting you this much all the time..." His gaze flicked briefly to hers before landing back on the fire.

He looked uncharacteristically shy. "I really like you, Sadie." He shifted. "And I don't want you to feel any pressure. This," he rubbed his hand over himself, "isn't your responsibility, and I'm taking care of it. I just want... I want you to want me as much as I want you." He looked at her. "And I can't tell if you do."

The shower turned on and she knew they wouldn't have long now. Sadie decided to respond with action. His sweet words warmed her, and she didn't want to try and articulate a worthy response. She pulled herself against him and pressed her mouth to his. She could see clearly how they each felt and she did, in fact, have an answer to his question. Yes, she did want him as much as he did her, but his other feelings were certainly stronger. He was falling hard and fast. Love and sex seemed to be intimately entangled in the world of Troy, and his all-consuming desire for her had grown hand-in-hand with the deeper emotion.

Sadie pushed away her worries over the mismatch in their romantic feelings. She wanted to drown out thoughts of it in the feeling of his mouth on hers. He was so hungry for this contact that his body had cried out at her touch. Troy scooped her face up in both hands and consumed her furiously as she let pleasure course through the rest of him.

She pulled at his belt, and quickly freed him from the restraint of his pants. Then she gathered him up, warm and slick, and he groaned. "God yes, Sadie," he breathed against her mouth. "I've wanted to be back in your hands for days. I could barely sleep that night in jail." She stroked him gently. "I couldn't stop thinking about you. I can't stop. And I don't want to." He punctuated this last line with a deep thrust against her.

Sadie reveled in the sweetness of his open-hearted lust even as she withdrew from his words. A light fear of the intensity of his emotions added uncertainty to the moment.

"What is it?" Troy asked, concern showing through on his features.

She was surprised he'd noticed something was amiss when his thoughts were so occupied elsewhere, but she didn't want to try and explain. If she did, she was sure he would make them stop to talk about it. And she didn't want to talk. She wanted to do, to feel. "Nothing," she said, and pulled him back against her. How long had Hetia been in the shower? Sadie doubted the woman would take long, especially since for some inexplicable reason she was not taking advantage of the privacy to relieve her body of the pent-up arousal.

Sadie resumed stroking Troy with complete focus this time, soaking up the longing in his tense muscles, the call for release. When he began to pulse in her hands, she knelt in front of him. The shower clicked off and he seemed to put in every effort to muffle his cries, but as she wrapped her mouth around him, he sucked in air through gritted teeth before groaning loudly.

Sadie looked up in time to see his head fall back, jaw clenched, as she slowly drew out his warm fluids, musky and made sweeter by the sound of his masculine moan. She held his hips with both hands as he jerked in little spastic motions. Troy was lovingly stroking her hair when she pulled back and their eyes met.

He appeared utterly content and Sadie quickly shied away from his gaze. She rose quickly to her feet, and they worked together to put back his clothing. Before she could pull away entirely, however, he put a hand on the back of her neck and pressed his forehead to hers. His panting filled the space between them, and she couldn't help but enjoy the sound of it.

"Troy?"

"Yes? Sadie." He said her name as if it were something rare and precious.

I really like you, too. That was what she wanted to say. The words were just under the surface, trying to come out, but for some reason she didn't understand, they lodged in her throat. "I wish we had more time," she said instead.

He laughed once. "I wish we had all night. At least there's always tomorrow. We'll find a way."

Tomorrow. Always tomorrow. If only that were true. Hetia came out of the bathroom and they separated. Troy pulled back casually, but Sadie jumped a little in her retreat, feeling oddly guilty. Hetia's eyes flicked over the two of them. "I tried to be quick, but there's not a lot of hot water." After a brief pause, she added. "You might want to share."

Troy looked at her hopefully. For some reason, Sadie blushed. "Okay."

They moved toward the bathroom, stopping when Hetia said Troy's name. He looked back at her. "Don't waste the water or you'll be bathing in the cold."

Sadie couldn't help but read a double meaning in the warning, and it only added to her anxiety. When the door closed and Troy moved to kiss her, she shook her head. She knew Hetia would be able to hear them if they did anything now, and since the pull of her immediate hunger had subsided, she had room for her own self-consciousness.

She wondered at what in the world was happening to her. She'd been in several orgies, and slept with countless people since she'd turned, and yet the idea of two people she really liked being so close together left her shaken and confused. Jimmy's words, "I just need some time, I think we both do, to deal with the Troy situation," they came back to her now. And it was clear to her that what was happening was nothing like what had come before. And sooner or later, she was going to have to deal with it.

Troy didn't seem at all disappointed at her rebuff. He watched her undress with pleasure, and let her climb under the water first. They didn't speak as they took turns quickly washing away the sweat of the day. She slid against him as they switched, and Sadie leaned back against the wall to watch him lather himself down. He smiled at her, relaxed and content at what was happening. She tried to return the expression, but her stomach was in a knot and her face felt frozen.

It was the first time she'd seen him naked and not erect. He looked carefree, and the black love lines flowing from him pulsed with increasing ferocity. It seemed every time he shared his body with her, they grew stronger. While every time she touched him, smelled him, looked at him, she wanted more. Only her wanting was mostly physical, and even as she looked at the tiny threads of black emanating outward from her, they seemed to cower and shrink under her observation. She couldn't meet him where he was at, and she feared where it was all going.

Eventually the weight of the wide and unknown future became too much for her to continue to ponder and she relaxed. Sadie smiled back at him then, and this time, she too felt almost content. He turned away to rinse his face and she ran a hand down his back. *What a unique person you are, Troy, falling with such ease.* Unique, and beautiful, and hers, whether she was ready for it or not.

~

THEY STOPPED EARLY the next day at another inn, afraid to get caught out in the cold again. This one had no shower and no fireplace, though they were assured that the three rooms upstairs stayed marginally warm in winter from the heat coming from the common room below.

It was a challenge to sneak them all in, as the only way to get past the watchful gaze of the woman who owned the place was to climb a tree and clamber up through the window. Hetia went first and then held Sadie's hips as she lowered herself through the high opening. Sadie slid against Hetia's body as her feet touched ground, and she was sure she wasn't imagining the way the woman stayed pressed unnecessarily close.

Hetia still hadn't done anything to release the growing tension that had been building in her since their night together. Sadie wasn't sure why she hadn't taken matters into her own hands, but she regretted increasingly that they hadn't had a single moment alone together all day. Whatever self-control nonsense the woman was employing, Sadie would happily do away with if she could only have the chance.

If Troy had behaved like this, he'd be walking around with a permanent erection and everyone staring at him, but in Hetia's case, she seemed outwardly unchanged. In fact, the others appeared to not have even noticed.

But Sadie noticed. She couldn't help but feel the constant ache like a throbbing between her own legs, an unrelenting heaviness. She'd barely slept last night, even as Hetia rested deeply in pleasant dreams. This was becoming unacceptable. Sadie was sure her own nipples had been hard for hours, and even the light friction of her underwear against her as they'd walked had been a teasing distraction.

Uncertain as to what Hetia was playing at, or when or how they were going to be able to talk about it, Sadie had become an increasing mess of desire and anxiety. And now they were about to stay in a tiny room fitted with a single slim cot, and it hit her with a wave of claustrophobia.

It was a strange kind of claustrophobia, born of her desire to be alone with a few of the people in the room more than her feeling that there were too many of them in general. Patricia, still moody from tramping through the rain all day, claimed the cot. Which left Sadie, Hetia, and Troy to share the rug. At least everyone agreed that they should get the comforter.

No one spoke much as they bustled around, readying for bed. Hetia seemed to be watching her, casting sidelong glances when she thought she wasn't looking, while Troy smiled at her every time she accidentally caught his eye. Sadie wanted to scream in frustration. Why couldn't they have found two rooms, and then she could have demanded a few hours alone with Hetia and then a few with Troy.

Or perhaps that was too weird. Though... was it? All it would take was openly acknowledging exactly what she wanted and then intentionally arranging for it to happen. She'd certainly done such a thing many times before. And Hetia and Troy didn't seem particularly tense over the situation, so she didn't have their feelings to worry about.

In fact, as they climbed under the comforter, Sadie in the middle, she was surprised at the spike in desire that hit her from both sides. It was the flavor people gave off immediately before something was about to happen. Which meant that some part of each of them believed they were about to do more than just sleep next to her.

Troy shifted around behind her, adjusting his jacket that was serving as a pillow, while Hetia slid in front of her, biting her lip as she looked into Sadie's eyes. Patricia blew out the candle on the bedside table and cast them into darkness. Hetia's glowing face disappeared, but not the heavy feel of her presence.

There was absolutely no way Sadie was going to get any sleep like this, and she was already immensely tired. She slid a hand down to rest between her legs, just to remove the pressure. Despite the feeling of excitement coming off the two people beside her, neither of them made any move to touch her. Sadie found herself increasingly annoyed at this fact, even though she wasn't sure what she would do if one of them did actually make a move in this crowded environment.

Her frustration culminated in a blinding peak when an hour later everyone around her had fallen asleep. Sadie heard the familiar light smack of Patricia's lips that she only made when she was deep in slumber. The lust from Hetia and Troy took on the flavor of dreams, scattered and free. And Sadie wanted to claw her way out of her own body.

She rolled her hips against the side of her hand, arching her back. A small wave of pleasure traveled through her. She knew from experience sleeping next to Jimmy before they had begun touching, that doing this now would only make her hungrier, but she didn't think she could help it.

Making as little movement as she could, Sadie gradually began to rock faster. The comforter moved with her in an obvious way and she strained her ears to listen for a change in breathing of the people beside her. When none came, she sped up, feeling the heat rising between her legs. She was getting close, she just needed to move a little more.

She pressed her forehead into the ground and rolled over her hand, as the tiniest sound escaped her. It had been so small and yet was unmistakable as a sound of pleasure. Troy and Hetia woke up at the same time, as if her little cry had called them from the depths of the dream world.

Sadie froze, but it was too late. She could tell by the feeling coming off them that they knew exactly what she'd just been doing.

Troy put a hand between her shoulder blades, her heart was still pounding and her body throbbed from the denied release. He slid his palm up to her arm and followed it down to her hand, still in a fist between her legs. Troy adjusted himself to move against her back, the length of him settling at the top of her ass.

Shit, this was trouble. Trouble, trouble, trouble. She arched into him and against her hand, but he pulled at her wrist, removing it from its desired location. He pushed her right knee forward with his own as he reached around to slide a hand inside her many layers. His fingers found her wet and swollen.

She sucked in a quivering breath as he pressed a finger just inside her and slid it ever so slowly up over the tight cluster of nerves begging for attention. Hetia's face came closer and she felt the woman's lips on her forehead. Tentatively, Sadie reached out and slid a hand around her waist, pushing up her shirt to access skin. She no longer wore her gloves to bed as they got wet during the day, and her palm slid smoothly over the soft surface of Hetia's side.

Troy pressed in closer as Hetia claimed her mouth. They both must've been aware of the movement of the other one, Sadie was sure Troy could feel Hetia's presence and hear her breathing, and yet neither of them seemed overly concerned. In fact, as intent as they were on touching her, they seemed entirely devoid of reservations. When Troy disappeared under the covers and began working off Sadie's pants, Hetia scooted her hips back to make room.

Sadie lifted her own hips so Troy could work off her panties. A second later, he had scooped her thigh over his shoulders and nuzzled his head between her legs. Hetia grabbed at the back of her neck, pulling her in tighter. Her lust felt like a feral thing. The pleasure building inside her at their skin contact seemed to grow without Sadie's input as if Hetia was pulling it out of her.

Sadie slid a hand up to cup Hetia's warm breast and the woman trembled under her touch. Troy kissed around her folds and Sadie dug a heel into his back, silently begging for more. It seemed to take an eternity for him to flick his tongue under the hood of her clit, but when he did, she had to bite down a silent cry. Her own unrestrained arousal passed on to Hetia, and she too, released their kiss to chew on her lip. Sadie squeezed Hetia's nipple between her fingers as Troy continued to tease her in quick, long strokes, his head moving in little circles which passed over her swollen center even as he licked the most sensitive nerves.

Sadie felt her climax coming on slowly. Troy took his time, savoring her, until the heat built to a boil and began to overflow. Hetia bucked under her hand as Sadie's hips convulsed involuntarily. As the waves built and crashed, Hetia experienced them simultaneously, though Sadie wasn't intentionally controlling the other woman's pleasure. It all happened naturally. They climaxed together, clutching each other in the dark, their muffled panting reverberating in the inch of space between their lips.

When Sadie finally stopped shaking, Troy turned to kissing the insides of her thighs. She became aware of how hard he was fighting back his own climax, which would be quite messy on the inn's rug if it came. She regretted the sudden loss of contact when he extracted himself from under the covers. Sadie briefly wondered where he was going, until Hetia grabbed her face. The woman wasn't done, not even remotely.

It seemed her body had just woken up after days of hunger, and she wanted more. Sadie responded by pulling her closer and sliding her thigh over Hetia's. The woman relaxed on her back, but took Sadie's hand with urgency and guided it down her body. Impatiently, she silently asked to be touched. Hetia opened her legs as Sadie slid her finger inside. And when she slicked the wet finger over her directly, she arched her back dramatically.

Troy reappeared behind Sadie. At a tap from him she lifted her hip and he slid something underneath her. It felt like a towel, but she wasn't sure where he would have gotten one. A minute later he was pressed against her back again, his presence coming with a wave of desire so strong it nearly rivaled Hetia's.

With Sadie's leg still over the other woman's thighs, Troy grabbed her hips and arched them up toward his. She felt the head of his shaft encircle her entrance, spreading out their wetness before pushing inside. He groaned as he slid all the way in and she froze. Patricia appeared to still be sleeping. The sound was tiny after all, and yet Troy's pleasure always sounded loud to Sadie.

He stuck to heavy breathing after that, not letting another sound escape him as he began to move inside her. Sadie became suddenly aware of what was happening. Troy was making love to her from behind, kissing her shoulder as he held her hips, and she was playing with Hetia, stroking her gently as she writhed under her touch.

She'd been in threesomes before, but they were nothing like this. These were two people she liked, desperately, and in their own way. She'd never imagined them mixing. Troy and Hetia had no direct attraction to each other – they were fellow soldiers, friends, and allies, but not this.

And yet it worked. They each seemed wholly focused on her, uncaring to the presence of the other, though not unaware of it. When Troy wanted to speed up, he pressed his right knee against the floor for traction, and Sadie felt Hetia slide her legs a little wider to make room for him. And as he thrust into her, deeper and faster, her own hips rocked against Hetia's to the rhythm Troy set.

Hetia clutched at her, finding her lips again in the dark. In all that had happened between them a few nights ago, she'd never seemed so desperate. The frantic, avid pleas in her movements were so out of character it almost scared Sadie. She had wanted more than anything for Hetia to let her in, and now that she was, she found herself with the most powerful human weapon she'd ever seen coming apart in her arms. Sadie's mind went blank with her own ravenous desire. Lost in the strength of her power, she caressed Hetia in slow, teasing strokes, responding to her silent calls for more by taking her higher with every heartbeat.

Troy pulsed inside her and Sadie's mind went to him. He gripped her hip, pumping into her desperately as he came. Like Hetia, she could feel him fighting to stay silent as his mouth closed on her shoulder. His unrestrained excitement fueled her own, despite his silence, and Sadie fought off his final release.

Hetia began to convulse under her as Troy clutched at her thigh and waist in desperation. His hips moved spastically against her as he continued to pulse in climax. His weight on her pressed her breasts against Hetia's as the woman arched her back, caught in the throes of her own ecstasy. Sadie's right nipple, hard as a rock, rubbed against Hetia's, and the sensation was almost painful in their heightened sensitive state.

She released Troy first and he gasped in her ear as warm fluid filled her. Sadie followed the euphoria of his release into Hetia's, drawing it out in one final wave that brought her shoulders off the ground as her back bowed. Then her body went limp, falling still except for the heavy breathing, a thick sound that was now emanating from all three of them. Sadie relaxed her weight into Hetia's side and ran a finger up between her breasts. She rested her palm there and soaked up the sensation of her pounding heart.

Troy kissed between her shoulder blades as he lay his head down behind her, but she could still feel the slight sting of where he'd bitten her shoulder. Through her hazy thoughts, came flashes of worry and contentment. She could stay here forever and die happy. What had they just done? God, they both felt so good. *Troy hasn't pulled out, he wants to go again, should I allow it? What if it makes tomorrow even harder? Hetia's nipples are so hard, I wish I could move and suck on one.*

A few minutes passed like that. Then, as if they'd planned it, Troy scooped up her breast in his palm as Hetia simultaneously found her lips. And before she could worry another second about the consequences of their actions, Sadie was lost in their insatiable hunger. And in that moment, it felt like even eternity wouldn't be enough time to quell the aching inside them.

Chapter 15

Under Pressure

Sadie woke up in a fit of anxiety, though it took her a minute to remember all the reasons why. The light streaming through the window felt like a spotlight as she opened her eyes to face the world. Hetia and Troy were already up and had left the room. She sat up, clutching the blankets over her breasts as she spotted Patricia lacing up her shoes at the foot of the bed. Her skin was tingling, and she felt a little drunk. She'd been feeding way too much recently and last night had been out of hand.

"You slept well?" Patricia asked and Sadie fought to detect an accusation in her words, but there was none.

"Yes. Sort of. You?"

"Finally, yes." She groaned dramatically. "I slept very well. Sorry about my crankiness these past couple days." Patricia stood up and straightened out her clothes.

Sadie thought her behavior was to be expected given their circumstances. "You don't need to apologize, really. I understand."

Patricia shrugged. "All the same. We have bigger things to worry about than dry clothes." She pulled on her bag. "I'll meet you down there."

It seemed Patricia was being a little hard on herself. After all, there were worse things one could be focused on right now, Sadie thought guiltily.

She felt light as a feather as she stood up. Her body seemed unusually alive. As she strung her legs out the window and prepared to grab at the nearby tree, she felt strong and confident. Maybe excessive feeding had its perks. She could certainly use the boost in energy to get through what was coming.

An old woman squealed as she jumped from the tree and landed next to her. "Sorry," Sadie mumbled, turning her face away. She made a quick stop at the outhouse before heading to the edge of town and finding the others under the large oak at which they'd agreed to meet. Her heart pounded at seeing Hetia and Troy standing together in the light of day. They were talking casually and looking as animated as she felt.

Sadie met their eyes briefly. Hetia too looked nervous, but Troy smiled at her warmly. "Good morning," he whispered as if they were alone, sharing an intimate moment. He bent as if to kiss her, but stopped himself, looking down. "Maybe that's not a good idea in public."

"Speak for yourself," Hetia said, pulling Sadie's lips to hers. The exchange was brief, but she couldn't help but smile at such a romantic greeting from the woman. Sadie ducked her head as they separated, tucking back her curls and biting her lip as she looked from one to the other of them.

Patricia arrived at her side, looking more put together than when she'd left the room, and smiling contentedly. Troy greeted her in the same tone he'd used with Sadie. Touching her shoulder, he asked, "How did you sleep?"

"So much better. I feel like last night changed everything," Patricia said. She smiled at the rest of them, unaware of just how true those words were. Sadie blushed in confusion.

"Where to?" her friend asked, wrinkling her forehead at Sadie's behavior.

"We'll head back south and to the east," Hetia said, securing the straps of her pack. "The change in course will throw anyone who might be tracking our behavior."

"Tracking our behavior? Is that something we should be worried about?" Sadie asked.

Later, Sadie would think what happened next was all her fault, her skepticism clearly tempted fate. No sooner had she asked the question then four men on horseback tore out of the nearby bush and surrounded them.

"Sadie Hall and Troy Hyun, you are under arrest. Keep your hands where we can see them," a man boomed as he dismounted. Troy immediately moved between Sadie and the officer, displaying his hands in a pacifying gesture.

"And who are you to threaten us?" Patricia asked, straightening her back to her full height. "Are you really going to do the bidding of an imposter government?"

"This town is in adherence with the true government, and you are under arrest for crimes unknown." The man moved toward Troy with a thick baton, but to their left another man cocked a gun at Sadie's head. She couldn't see Hetia behind her. A fear that the woman would make a rash move and be shot drove Sadie to hold out her hands and step nearer the man with the gun.

"And we're cooperating, as you can see," she said. A third man came in to cuff her and Sadie waited in fear for the ground to begin shaking, but no such thing happened. As the man drew nearer, she realized that his uniform and badge looked rather suspect. She glanced around and saw the nature of makeshift uniforms. This explained how one tiny town had come to have four sheriffs. They hadn't. These were just ordinary town folk. Why the costumes? Did they think it would make it easier if they treated it all like an arrest? Or perhaps that they would be less likely to resist if they were real officers?

She watched Troy peer over his shoulder as he let himself be cuffed. He seemed to be waiting for a signal. Sadie was too, but Hetia remained still and small, out of the minds of the men. "Where will we be able to visit our friends?" Patricia asked, glancing from Hetia to Sadie as the man led her back toward his horse.

"You won't," responded the one who had cuffed Troy.

"You don't have visiting hours at the local jail?" Patricia asked.

"They won't be there," a different man said.

"Surely you'll need to get permits of some kind, to transfer them across the country," Patricia pushed, and Sadie finally understood what was happening. This was just an interrogation. Patricia would be able to tell which parts of their story were true, and Hetia wasn't going to make a move until the woman gave her a signal that she was finished.

"There'll be no need for that. Government troops will be arriving later today." The man holding Sadie by the cuffs grinned. "On top of showing our strong support for their bravery, we'll be able to deliver the single most wanted fugitives."

Troy moved first, and no sooner had he knocked down the nearest guy with a hard swing of his elbow than the ground began to shake. The gun went off behind Sadie's head and she flinched and fell as she turned. Hetia had already moved on to the other men as Patricia crouched over the one who had until recently been armed, but was now unconscious.

Her friend approached her a second later with keys and quickly removed her handcuffs before tossing the keys at Sadie and running after one of the horses. Hetia stepped into Troy's fight with the last man standing. He'd been holding his own pretty well given his bound hands, but he stepped back to let her take over. Sadie pulled his attention to her by grabbing the cuffs.

"Hold still," she said. He did as she asked while Sadie fumbled the key into the lock with shaky hands. When they fell to the ground he reached down and picked them back up. Then he stepped closer and gently took the key from her. He pocketed it all with a wink and Sadie chewed her lip. Could he really be thinking that now? She could see he was.

"Let's go!" Patricia called. She was sitting on top of one of the horses and holding the reins of a second. Sadie and Troy turned to look at the large animals. They exchanged strongly skeptical looks.

"Here," Hetia said, running past them and directing her gaze at Troy. She ran a hand soothingly over Patricia's horse before helping Troy get his foot into the stirrup. He hoisted himself awkwardly behind Patricia, grabbing her hard as the beast shifted.

"He can sense your fear. Just relax," Patricia said. She looked entirely comfortable herself. Sadie hadn't realized she knew how to ride.

Hetia looked to her next and Sadie let herself be hoisted awkwardly onto the second horse. She might have made a slightly silly squawking sound as she settled into position, but no one was in the mood to laugh. Patricia looked around worriedly, as if the coming army were about to descend on them any minute.

Without delay, Hetia swung up in front of her and reached over to take the reins of their horse from Patricia. Sadie held on gratefully as the two women directed the horses into motion. She wasn't surprised to learn Hetia felt comfortable on a horse, but she was awed by Patricia's fluid control over the animals. She was definitely the better rider of the two of them, and she took the lead in setting a fast trot heading southeast.

The sun came out briefly in the afternoon and Sadie's adrenaline over what had happened that morning grew stale. Hetia's body gyrated against her front and Sadie expected the situation to become a lot more sexually distracting as she relaxed, but the pain of sitting so long in the saddle was the biggest thing on her mind.

She held tight to Hetia's waist though, and took some small comfort in her close presence. She could feel the worry of the others simply through their lack of sexual thoughts and emotions. For the first time since they'd fled Arlington, their minds were fully engaged elsewhere.

They traveled over rolling fields most of the day, and though her ass and legs felt like they might fall off, Sadie did her best not to complain. She suspected she'd be even worse off if her body wasn't still riding the high from the excessive feeding she'd engaged in the night before. Despite that, she nearly cried when Patricia finally pulled them to a stop.

They'd run into a little creek. It was approaching late afternoon, and the horses had had no water. The other women led the animals down to get a drink while Troy and Sadie hobbled around, trying to regain use of their lower halves. He recovered before she did, and came up behind her as she sat down on a large rock.

"Why horses? Why?" she complained as he began massaging her shoulders. "Hmmm." She melted into the feel of his hands on her sore muscles.

"They really are the worst," he agreed, and then she felt the spike of his change in mood before he added, "I bet they would be a lot more enjoyable if we were on the same horse."

She laughed. "Neither of us knows how to ride. There's no scenario that involves us sharing a horse."

"I know. I just like the idea of getting to cling to you while it jostles us around." She looked back at him. "What?" he asked, his grin faltering at whatever he saw in her expression. He stopped rubbing her and came and sat down while she bit her lip in thought.

"I'm just surprised you can be thinking about such things with everything that's happening," she said, though in truth the comment was more directed at herself than him.

As if he'd read her mind he asked, "Am I the only one?"

She glanced at him then looked away guiltily. The buzzing under her skin that she'd woken up with seemed to hum louder as she let herself focus on her body. "No. It's not just you." She sighed. "I'm surprised... at all of it. Everything's changing so fast, and – well, it scares me."

He took her hand. "Sadie, I know we can't make any promises about the future. What happens next," he shook his head, "is going to be dangerous any way we spin it. But this," he squeezed her hand, "I'm sure of." He leaned in and kissed her then. It was brief, the barest touch of lips, before he pulled back. "The more I get to know you, the more I want to know more. And I hope you feel the same way."

She dropped his gaze. The motion was too quick, almost a flinch, and she flushed at the accidental confession. He went still, the stroking of his thumb on the back of her hand halted. Shit. She looked at the ground, frantically searching for a way to respond to the intensity of his words when she wasn't quite in the same place as he so clearly was.

"Troy—" she began.

"It's okay," he said with a shrug that was just a little too forced.

"It's not that I don't like you," she said in a rush. "It's just... I can tell your feelings for me changed rapidly after we slept together that night you rescued me. And – I worry I made a mistake." She swallowed at the hurt look on his face and pushed on, trying to get a hold of what she was saying. "I know we had something between us, but it just became so intense after that night and I think it was because I took things too far. I shouldn't have done that. I was selfish, just wanting to play with you because, well, I wanted it and I liked you. But now... every time you look at me—"

Troy stood up. Kicking at the ground, he ran a hand over his jaw. Sadie, too, got to her feet, feeling like she was really putting her foot in it now.

"I do really like you," she added, her voice sounding far too weak.

"Hmm," he said, in a grunt of partial acknowledgement.

She stepped toward him, but he folded his arms over his chest in a protective stance. "And I love – well, I love sleeping with you." His gaze shot away from hers. "I just want to slow things down a bit. I'm not ready to be so – that is... I'm just not where you're at."

Sadie immediately regretted this whole conversation. Why did she have to go and say it all like that? She reached to wrap her arms around him, but he stepped back. "Okay," he said. "That's... okay. We don't have to be in the same place. I'm glad you told me." He was still not looking at her. "Excuse me," he added and walked off toward the river.

Sadie watched him go with sorrow. *Nice work*, she chided herself. She couldn't have just let things develop as they were? No. It seemed she had to pre-emptively turn a good thing bad by telling him the exact details of how she felt.

The feeling of his loving hands on her shoulders still lingered, and she was filled with self-loathing as she searched her bag for that bit of stale bread. Coming up shy, she decided it was for the best. She didn't feel much like eating anyway.

The other women reappeared a minute later. "Where's Troy?" Patricia asked. Sadie nodded toward the river. "Well, when he gets back, we'll head for that farm. It's time to find a place to hunker down for the night." Sadie followed her gaze to the horizon, barely making out a little farm, complete with a red barn. She just nodded.

Then without bothering to explain where she was going, Sadie moped off to be alone, if only for a few minutes. She heard the gentle trickle of the creek before it came into view. She shot north of where Troy had gone, not wanting to run into him just yet, and found herself in a quiet little alcove. The creek turned out to be a decent-sized stream, almost a river, but it was traveling slowly in this particular place, spread out wide as it was. A pool gathered behind a hillside of rocks and the hazy autumn sun glinted off its surface.

Sadie kicked off her shoes and waded in up to her ankles. The water was ice-cold, but she didn't care. The shock was refreshing and seemed to calm her worries. In fact, as she stood there, glancing around at the glistening rocks, she began to feel a sense of calm contemplation. It was a clear and strong feeling. She had a desire to stand there all day, gazing at the changing surface of water and thinking about life.

A year ago, she might not have noticed this sudden change, or she may have attributed it to some internal stirrings, but she'd seen a lot since then. This was clearly a nymph home, and their presence had imbued this place with emotion, with a sense of being even more of what it was, a quiet little river.

Sadie looked around. There was no one in sight, but she thought she heard voices. She waded in further to peer behind a nearby boulder and her breath hitched on the sight. There were two half-naked women, deeply in love, bathing in the cold water. One of them had a cloth and was dripping water over the back of the other. Sadie swallowed.

Feeling like an intruder on an intimate scene, she decided not to say hello. She went to step out of the water to let her feet dry before sheathing them, but instead she tripped on a little rock and found herself falling backward. A bolt of ice traveled up through her butt and hands as they landed in the glacier water.

Sadie squealed and two heads turned to look at her. Before she'd even managed to get back on her feet and scramble to shore, Hetia had appeared at her side. She looked around furiously for a threat, realized the only danger Sadie was in was from her own clumsiness, and relaxed.

The nymphs came around the bolder, still naked from the waist up. Hetia's head whipped in their direction and Sadie watched an appreciative expression pass over her face. Her eyes quickly darted away, though, and she and Sadie exchanged an intimate look.

Sadie shook herself and cleared her throat. "Sorry to intrude. We're just passing through."

"That's alright," the shorter one said, pulling up her sleeves to cover herself. Troy tore around the corner, apparently also having heard her cry. He glanced briefly at the nymphs before looking her over in concern.

"I just fell," Sadie assured him. Like Hetia, he relaxed.

Troy turned to the women. "Sorry for the commotion." Unlike her and Hetia, his reaction to the half-naked nymphs was entirely absent. He barely seemed to notice that one of them was only just then covering her breasts as he repeated Sadie's words, "We're just passing through."

"A strange time to be traveling around," another voice said. Three heads snapped to their left as a third woman appeared. She was heavily covered in a thickly layered dress and carrying a bucket. She shared green lines of friendship with the two nymphs and so clearly wasn't new to the area.

"Yeah, uhh, we're just heading to my aunt's place for the night," Sadie explained.

"No." The woman stepped closer. For a long minute, they were all silent as she gave Sadie a long, scrutinizing stare. "You're not just heading to your aunt's place. You're Sadie Hall." She looked from Sadie to Troy and smiled. "It's okay. No one here is going to help the feeder government." She held out a hand. "It's Tamira," she said, not offering a family name.

Sadie shook her hand through her wet gloves, then apologized when the woman winced at their soggy coldness. "Let's get you out of those," Tamira said, hiking up the bucket full of water and backing up toward the shore. "My family owns the farm just south of here. They're backing the feeder government, like most of my town, but our barn is warm and I can help you sneak into it for the night."

Sadie relaxed a little. Could they trust this woman? She looked up at the riverbank for Patricia. But before they could make any decisions, the day took a drastic turn.

Hetia dropped to a crouch next to Sadie. She put her hand to the ground and closed her eyes. "What is it?" Troy asked.

"The earth is trembling," Hetia whispered. The water nymphs exchanged a look of fear. A few seconds later, a faint sound became audible over the trickle of water. It was a rumbling mix of a distant roar.

"Patricia," Troy said, and ran back up the hill to the flats above.

"We got word from a friend downstream this morning," the taller nymph said. "A town was subdued just south of here. They had refused to comply. Word of what happened is traveling only slightly faster than the army seems to be moving, but trouble is on its way."

"On its way now," Hetia said, standing up. Even as she spoke those few words, the noise grew and Sadie could feel the slight tremble of the ground. Troy and Patricia appeared with the two horses on the bank above.

"Should we ride? Get out of here?" Sadie asked, unable to keep the panic out of her voice.

"No," Tamira said at the same time as the shorter water nymph. "I can take your horses back to the barn. They'll spook otherwise. You should stay here – out of sight." The woman dropped her bucket and headed up the bank. Sadie watched the retreating form of the stranger full of uncertainty. This was a dangerous time to be trusting anyone.

"We can hide you," the taller nymph said. Instead of answering, Hetia turned to Patricia and gestured for her to come down. The urgency must have been clear since the woman hurried down the banks, Troy at her side.

Hetia turned away and spoke quietly into Patricia's ear. This was followed by her friend directing several rapid questions at the nymphs. In short order, she had concluded they could be trusted. On a quick nod back at Hetia, it was decided. Hetia said simply, "Where?"

One of the women grabbed the bucket and they turned their backs to them as Troy appeared at Sadie's side. "What's going on?" he asked. "That stranger just took our horses."

"We're staying here. Patricia trusts them to keep us safe for the night," Sadie whispered, starting to shiver from the cold.

The boulders surrounding the overhanging bank went far deeper than Sadie realized. As they approached, the nymphs disappeared entirely, though she couldn't quite make out the place they'd passed through. It wasn't until they were right up against it that the overlap of two tall stones revealed a tiny gap. As she stepped inside, she found herself in a little cave, dark except for a candle at the back.

Troy bumped into her as she came to a sudden halt, blinking as her eyes adjusted. The cave was deep and water trickled over the stone ground for several paces before the floor rose. A little table and cot filled one corner, but apart from that small sign of human life, it seemed like an ordinary creek running under a hillside.

Sadie moved toward the back, and the smell of earth and cool water invaded her senses. She shivered in her wet clothes and wrapped her arms around herself as the others found their way in, the nymphs coming in last.

"People rarely find us by accident. You should be safe here," the shorter one said. "I'm Shaya, by the way. And that's Asha." The other bobbed her head.

"We've never had so many guests," Asha said. "I'm sorry we don't have more seating."

"Here." Shaya dug through a bin and offered some coarse wool blankets. "I know people typically find the stone cold."

Patricia accepted the offering and she and Hetia worked together to spread them out. Troy lifted his hand next to her and Sadie realized he had grabbed her shoes. She'd entirely forgotten about them.

"Thanks," she whispered, bending to slip on her dry socks over damp and frozen feet, but she perched on the edge of the blanket, not wanting to infect it with her wet rear.

The river nymphs sat cross-legged directly on the stone. "Tamira knew your name, but you clearly didn't know her. What's your story then?" Asha asked.

They were relieved of the burden of answering, however, as they all fell silent at a horrifying sound. Above them, as if they had appeared all at once, began a thundering ruckus of hundreds, possibly thousands of feet. They caught the roar of engines and the whinnying of horses. Through the gap in the stones at the entrance wafted in the chatter of dozens of conversations, laughter, and shouting.

Siphon's army had arrived.

Chapter 16

Heating Up

Sadie felt like a rabbit caught in a trap. She looked around at the dark corners of the cave as the roar above their heads grew. "We should have run, got back on the horses and fled," she said to no one in particular.

"There's so many of them," Patricia whispered.

Asha reached out and clutched Shaya's hand. "No, you were right to hide. They're moving fast."

Sadie jumped as a pebble near the ceiling broke loose and landed with a tiny plop in the trickle of water nearby.

"Can this place hold up under all that weight?" Sadie directed at their resident earthquake nymph.

Hetia put her palm flat on the stone. "The tension is steady, there's no slippage in the near future."

"Our home has lived through several earthquakes, it will withstand the boots of men," Shaya said. "You're safe here. The army will pass."

The army will pass. Sadie shivered from more than cold this time. Up until just that moment, the threat of the approaching war had seemed an abstract thing. But now that it was quite literally bearing down on her, she could no longer ignore the bleak horizon of her life.

She didn't want the army to pass, she wanted it to turn back. To go away from her home, not closer to it. She pictured her parents' faces.

Last week, she had dialed their number from a little pay phone, ready for her weekly call home, but some strange panic had gripped her and she'd hung up. It was only after a guilty night of picturing her mother's concerned face that she'd tried again.

Her mother was worried that she'd called a day late, even though her track record for calling in the past had been spotty. Sadie tried not to cry as she'd apologized, and then asked with trembling reservations how their town was voting. Her mom had told her that they would likely go in support of the feeder government, not because there wasn't fierce debate about resistance, but because nearly every tiny town was making the choice to comply. They had no means to do otherwise.

Sadie had lied when her mom had asked her where she was. She said she'd stayed on the East Coast and was safe with friends. She could hear her dad breathing as her mom told her that was the perfect place to be. That she should stay where she was until this whole thing blew over. "Governments change all the time," her mother had said, assuredly.

It was only now, as the reality of the Coalition power was so vivid, that Sadie realized her mother might have been lying to her as well. What if her town did decide to resist? They were largely opposed to feeder power, after all. She'd left home because of that very sentiment. What would happen if they refused? Would Amadi's army burn down Main Street? Would people be killed? Would the deaths be indiscriminate, or would they spare people that were unarmed?

She thought of Jimmy's little sisters. They'd be so frightened if a force like this passed by, even if no harm came to them or the farm. *Jimmy.* Where was he now? Was he safe, behind the lines of Amadi's forces? Maybe he had decided to return home to be with his family. Would he expect she'd do the same and they'd find each other there? What if he was waiting for her there now, disappointed she hadn't come?

"I shouldn't be here," Sadie whispered, shaking her head, though no one seemed to hear her over the roar above.

After what must have been an hour of huddling in terror, the nature of the sound began to change. The clamor of feet and hooves morphed into a simple humming sound of many voices.

"They're camping here," Troy said. His voice was steady, as if just stating a useful piece of information. The lack of active fear in his tone heightened her own and Sadie's throat tightened as she fought back tears.

Patricia moved closer, taking her hand. Sadie could barely make out her features in the dim light, but she too appeared nervous. "Your family is going to make it through this. The army is here to make a show of power. Think of all their strategies so far. Assaulting a tiny farming town isn't their goal. They'll pass it by like a boot over an ant."

Sadie was only partially comforted by this assurance. Though Patricia was probably right. Siphon's army wasn't here to take out every small village that dared resist. It was here to show what it might do. If it truly fought, it would be against Amadi's army, the very place they'd been trying to get back to.

Sadie remained tense for a while longer, but like all things, her fear was not sustainable. When the little ray of light that had been seeping in through the stones disappeared and the smells of roasting meat wafted through in its place, she moved on to anger and impatience.

"They're probably completely destroying that poor farmer's fields. The cows will have nothing to eat," she said. It was the first anyone had spoken in a while and they all looked at her. She knew it was a small thing to complain about under the circumstances, but somehow their casual disregard for the destruction of someone's livelihood left a particular kind of bitterness on her tongue.

"Well, it seems they aren't going anywhere tonight," Asha said. "I suppose we should look to our own dinner."

Her words broke the spell of silence. Hetia stood up and dug her black jacket with the hood out of her backpack. "I'm going to take a look," she said. Troy opened his mouth as if to protest, but she was already gone, blending with the dark entrance of the room.

"I'm sorry, we weren't expecting so many guests," Shaya said. "Please make yourselves comfortable and we'll see what we can do about a meal." She sounded like Jimmy's mother the time she and her parents had come over after a pipe in their kitchen had broken suddenly. The tone seemed comical under the circumstances, but the two women began to bustle about as if an army wasn't camped on their heads.

"Troy?" Patricia said, giving him a look that he managed to interpret much better than Sadie, because he said, "Oh right. Sorry." He rolled up his sleeves and opened his hands. Two flames seemed to crawl out of his skin and bundle in a messy ball between his palms.

"Ahh, a fire nymph," Asha exclaimed. "Well, that'll make things easier. Tamira's always complaining about the cold in here. Are you all of that persuasion?"

"No, just Troy," Patricia said. They seemed to realize all at once that they hadn't finished their introductions. The nymphs turned their attention back as Patricia named them each in full, demonstrating that she must truly trust them.

Sadie bobbed her head at her own name, but she found it difficult to move. Her body had become surprisingly stiff. She'd been so distracted by what was happening around them that she hadn't noticed the icy cold seeping in. Her clothes were still covered in glacier water and were nearly freezing in the cool cave air.

She raised her hand to sweep her hair behind her ear and found her fingers were like a dead fish. "I'm cold," she croaked. It wasn't the most articulate sentence, but it got to the heart of the matter.

"Sadie?" Troy scooted over and perched on the edge of the blanket. "I forgot you're all wet." She nodded through chattering teeth. "Here." He held up the flames in front of her. She flinched backward.

"Too much," she said.

"We have a bit of wood," Asha said, "if you want to build a little fire."

"If I burn something it will produce smoke, which will be visible when it trickles out the front entrance," Troy said. "I'll have to be the heater."

The flames went out and Sadie blinked in the sudden darkness. When they returned Troy had removed his shirt. Tendrils of flame moved across his torso as he reached out and began exploring her wet clothing. Patricia appeared next to her.

"Sadie, we need to get you out of these. I'm freezing as it is, and I'm in thick, dry clothing."

Careful not to touch her skin, they helped her strip down to underwear. Patricia began digging around in her bag as Sadie stood up to remove the last of her layers, but her hands were still not cooperating. Troy watched them with concern as he crouched next to her.

"May I?" he whispered. She let him take her hands and his mouth parted in surprise. "I'm sorry. I always forget how cold people can get." He massaged her fingers, seemingly ignoring the spark of pleasure that passed between them at the contact. His hands were so warm they nearly burned her.

After a minute Troy moved from her hands to her feet, massaging life back in, while the flames around his torso quickly took the chill off the air. Sadie couldn't feel the difference in her skin, only in the way it felt to take air into her lungs. The cave was warming up, but her frozen flesh seemed mostly immune to it.

Hetia returned and Patricia jumped as she appeared suddenly out of the shadows. "You scared me," she admonished. Then added impatiently, "Well? How's it look out there?"

"Couple thousand. Armed. Well-provisioned. Also, they're all in uniform. It gives them an official look, which is going to contrast sharply with our own army. It might hurt recruiting and increase fear."

"Can you see our fire light from outside?" Patricia asked at the same time Troy followed up with "Weapons?"

"All armed. Lots of automatics," Hetia said. "And no, the light's not visible." Her eyes dropped to Sadie in her underwear. "You're going to get hypothermia like that." Hetia squatted in front of her, looking her over in concern. She ran a thumb over Sadie's lips and the ripple of sensation drew Sadie's mind to her, but like Troy, Hetia ignored it as she said. "You're turning blue."

"Here." Patricia spread the second wool blanket over the first and indicated Sadie should get under it. "Troy?" her friend directed at him.

"I won't be able to do both," he said.

"Heat Sadie. The room is fine for now, and we'll be able to see by the candlelight once our eyes re-adjust." Patricia stroked Sadie's hair as she spoke.

Troy let the flames die completely and followed Sadie inside. He removed the last of her wet layers and tossed them out before snuggling close, pulling her forcibly into his arms as the others tucked them in. She rested her head in the crook of his shoulder and relaxed while he ran his free hand continuously over her skin. His touch was firm, and yet non-sexual despite the faint arousal coursing through him.

It calmed her to be held like that. Her body seemed to melt and for a moment she felt safe. After a few minutes, she began to shiver. Though as her shaking resumed so did a sharp pain – her skin burned as it reheated. She tried to be grateful for the defrosting, distracting herself from the discomfort by focusing on the pleasant sensation of being in Troy's arms.

Perhaps it was her lack of sexual appetite in that moment, or maybe it was just her weakened state, but the contact with Troy didn't escalate as they lay against each other. A steady feeling of pleasure kept him hard, and she could feel the heightened beat of his heart, but it didn't become more than that as he slowly rubbed heat back into her flesh.

Her earlier words to him lingered in her thoughts. It seemed like a silly thing to have told him. Why did it matter if she didn't feel for him exactly what he felt for her? The world around them seemed to be ending, the future was literally bearing down on their heads, and these connections they had were precious things.

Sadie squeezed his far bicep and pulled herself closer until her chest was resting entirely on his. Then she brought his hand to her mouth and kissed the knuckles, before sighing in audible contentment.

Troy tensed, each one of his muscles going rigid as he stopped rubbing her. A few seconds later, he shifted and she realized he wanted her to move. She rolled back off her pleasant resting place and looked up at him.

His face was barely visible in the dim light, but he blinked down at her uncertainly. She considered the idea that maybe this wasn't the best time for them to be so intimately pressed together. Sadie cleared her throat. "I'm feeling better now," she whispered. "If you want to go."

He was silent for a long time, and the sensation from their contact began to grow, while the others bustled around on the far end of the cave, exchanging news and stories. Patricia would be well-fed by morning.

Troy resumed rubbing her arm and back. The sounds of the army overhead were loud, but he leaned in to reply quietly to her question. "I want to stay until you're warm. Just..."

He seemed to struggle with his request, so Sadie jumped in. "I'll try to hold it back from escalating too quickly.

There was a long pause before Troy whispered, "It's not that. I just can't... cuddle – right now."

Sadie couldn't help but be hurt by this, but she understood. After her confession earlier, she should give him whatever space he needed. Trying to fight the escalating sensation of pleasure, she curled in on herself as she lay stiffly next to his body heat and tried to pretend he was nothing but a furnace to her. A task she was certain to fail at.

She gave it her best effort as she listened to the chatter from the other side of the room in an attempt to lose herself in it, but after a few minutes of only partial success, the situation with Troy took a sharp turn. She knew he'd been fighting down the arousal in his body as much as she was, but he seemed to give up all at once as he grabbed her hand and drew it downward, shoving it forcefully into his pants. He closed her fingers around him on a muted groan, and Sadie was uncertain what to do with the very hard and wet shaft when they were lying on someone else's blanket with their friends a short distance away.

Though for the moment, neither of them seemed to care about consequences. Troy rotated into her, rolling his hips in demand, and Sadie, wanting to repair their conversation earlier, stroked deeply and frantically. With their respective reserve cracked, Troy's pleasure escalated like an avalanche.

Sadie bent to find his mouth in the dark, needing to feel his tongue against hers. Troy pivoted his face away. For a second, she thought it was a coincidence that he'd moved. She slid further on top of him, again seeking his lips, but this time his reaction was unmistakable.

He pushed her back off him, grabbing her wrist simultaneously to ensure she kept stroking him. Sadie blinked in a mess of confused emotion, as his rebuttal contrasted with the needy feel of his hips thrusting into her hand.

He didn't want her to kiss him. Though he clearly *did* want her to keep touching him. And he was chasing down his climax with sudden abandon. The background sounds from above them should be enough to cover the heavy breathing coming from their side of the cave, but Sadie knew she couldn't take things very far or Troy would no longer be able to keep quiet.

Shit. What was she supposed to do? What did he want her to do?

Tentatively, she leaned forward enough to whisper against his ear, even as their movement jostled her face awkwardly against his cheek. "Do you want me to release you? I can keep it small, and quick; you'll be able to stay quiet, and... I can swallow it."

She felt his jaw tighten against her lips as he sped up the pace of his thrusting, but he didn't reply. She could feel him getting close now. If he didn't instruct her soon, things were going to get messy. Just as she was considering taking charge and moving down his body, he grabbed her face and took her mouth in a bruising kiss. It was brief and hard and as needy as the rest of his exertions. And then it was over.

He withdrew from the kiss at the same time he pulled her hand off him. He scooted to the other end of the blanket, breaking the contact entirely. She could still hear his heavy breathing and feel the overwhelming call of his desire to climax, but he just lay there on his back, knees bent to make a tent of the harsh wool blanket.

He had been so close to the edge, and she could feel him fighting back the threat that he might spill anyway. Amazingly, he managed to stay perfectly still for several minutes as the immediacy of his need slowly lessened.

Sadie had been pushed to her back by the kiss and she stayed there, blinking up at the cave ceiling, wondering if there was something in particular she should do. Troy was clearly feeling vulnerable. And he was struggling to contain his need for her all the same. The net effect was a mess, and she felt increasingly terrible about the situation as she listened to him slowly gain control of his breathing.

"You're warm now?" he asked in a raspy voice after what felt like a lifetime later.

"Yes." Sadie couldn't keep the sadness out of her voice.

Without another word, Troy slid from the blanket. Flames licked to life along his torso as he walked away, and her gaze stayed mesmerized on him as he joined the small group huddled in the faint light on the other side of the cave. Sadie curled in on herself, feeling suddenly very alone. The sounds of the army overhead returned to her attention, and she immediately regretted the loss of the sexual distraction.

If there hadn't been anyone else around, she might have attempted to go talk to Troy. Mostly because she was now desperate to pull him on top of her – inside her. She didn't know how he'd managed to break their contact, but she certainly didn't have such restraint herself. Which meant it was probably a blessing that they weren't alone. Troy needed space. She knew he needed space. And yet, she would have been much happier to fuck now, and talk about their differences later.

Sadie sighed into the dark. Which was exactly their problem. Troy didn't feel the same way about intimacy, and she had learned this about him after she'd already taken things too far. All her teasing – all their games – shone in a new light as she remembered the way he'd looked at her during his various attempts to ignite something since arriving in Arlington.

What if her own feelings never became more? Would he still be interested in sleeping with her? The thought of losing him made something ache in her gut. Though she might lose him soon anyway if they succeeded in finding Amadi's army.

The sounds of heavy boots and laughter, along with the scent of meat, continued to invade her senses as her thoughts turned to Jimmy. She wanted to be held by someone she loved. She wasn't sure how she was going to make it through this night otherwise. Sadie stared at the backs of Hetia and Troy's heads – at the outline of Patricia's silhouette – and began to cry.

Through her tears, Sadie watched them pass around smoked fish as they took turns telling stories late into the night. Eventually, the sound of their voices distracted her from her fear just enough to let sleep find her. With a mess of conflicting emotions, and held only in the embrace of the coarse wool blanket, she drifted off before anyone else had come to bed.

SADIE HAD BEEN afraid she would have nightmares all night with Siphon's army so near, but as her mind began to focus back on reality, she found herself fighting to stay in the pleasant feeling of her dream. It hadn't been fantasy she'd just been lost in, but a very specific memory.

It was of a time shortly after she and Jimmy had left home. They'd been sharing a room in Arlington. She'd been foolishly trying to keep herself from feeding off him; keeping him at arm's length. He'd been trying to suppress his desire for her in the wake of her telling him she didn't want him; of her outright lie that was.

But Jimmy never seemed to be able to get away from his own sleeping thoughts. He always woke up heavily aroused, and she'd been discretely trying not to notice the number of mornings there'd been a large wet spot on the sheet between them. And that particular morning, Jimmy had woken up with such an aching desire that she had scrambled out of bed and turned on the shower just to keep herself from jumping him.

He hadn't waited more than a second after the door closed before he started stroking himself. She didn't get in the shower, just turned on the water before leaning against the bathroom door to get lost in the feeling of lust pouring off him just a room away.

Sadie had wanted him so badly in that moment, it had been nearly unbearable.

And then a few months later, she had gotten exactly what she'd wanted. She'd had him in every way she'd craved. But it had all been too brief, and now where was he? Somewhere in the middle of the resistance, possibly in danger. She knew he wouldn't do anything stupid, but in the midst of all that was happening, it wouldn't take much for harm to find him.

As she lay there, panting over the intense memory, she felt more strongly than ever that she had to get back to him. She couldn't stand to be apart a moment longer. And then, once they were back together, she wanted to go home.

She only hoped he wanted the same. What if he was glad to be free of their intense relationship? After all, he had been the one to suggest she go to Arlington without him and give them some space to grow on their own.

Though she had to admit, he *had* been onto something. After all, she'd been glad for this time to explore her feelings for Hetia and Troy without the complication of Jimmy around. Perhaps he had been wise in suggesting they needed this. Then again, being apart was like having a constant hole in her soul. And in her body. Her entire life had been filled with his smell, his voice, his presence. Then more recently with his desire. And now that was gone. All gone. And she had let it go so easily.

Sadie could hear the steady breathing of the others around her. They'd left a good amount of space between her and them, likely because she was still naked. She slid out the top of the covers, taking care not to jostle anyone, and found that the stone underfoot was still warm from Troy's efforts the night before.

She could barely see in the dim light shining through the crack at the entrance, but she managed to find her bag and get dressed. Everything was so quiet. Sadie strained her ears for sounds of movement above them, but couldn't make out anything but the light breathing of her friends and steady trickle of water.

Wanting to relieve the pressure in her bladder she popped just outside the cave and found a little corner. Still, she couldn't hear anything from above. Were they all still asleep? Her curiosity would be the death of her, she thought, as she climbed the rocks to peer over the top of the bank.

The field was empty.

The green grass had been trampled into a muddy mess, but there were no soldiers in sight. Sadie jumped out of her skin at the blur of movement in her peripheral vision. She turned toward it ready to scream, but it was only Hetia.

Sadie put a hand over her heart. "You scared the shit out of me," she hissed.

"Sorry." Hetia hopped up to stand next to her.

"They're gone." Sadie looked back out over the sad field.

"For now."

Sadie looked a question at her. Hetia was tall and beautiful in the morning light, but the thing that caught her attention most was the way her eyes were blazing. "Hetia? What is it?"

The woman looked to the horizon and then back at Sadie. "The fight's coming," she said with reverence – the hint of a grin dancing on her lips – and every inch of her radiated power.

Chapter 17

Where Armies Clash

For a second, Sadie was afraid of the woman, but her fear was quickly overpowered by the strong burst of desire that hit her like a force of nature only a second before Hetia's mouth found hers.

Distant thunder broke the silence of the morning as Hetia desperately took what she wanted. Sadie let herself be consumed, lost in the feeling of the woman's overwhelming pull. Sadie didn't hold back in meeting her hunger with waves of pleasure, and it wasn't long before Hetia was panting in quick shallow gasps against her mouth.

The thunder grew louder and mingled with Hetia's cries of pleasure as she came, and when she retreated a minute later, Sadie felt as if she'd just been struck by a storm. Her body was warm and she could feel sticky heat between her legs. But before she could gather herself, and ask Hetia what was going on, Troy appeared next to the river below them, and she was momentarily distracted by his somber expression as he locked eyes with her.

Thunder struck again, much louder this time, and Sadie could see storm clouds coming in from the distance. "They're here," Hetia whispered in her ear. Sadie couldn't read the tone of her voice, and she was confused about the words.

She tilted her head and mumbled "Wha—?" through her haze of confusion and arousal.

"That's no ordinary storm coming in so fast. That's the work of an unusually powerful storm nymph; one who can call and control storms at will," Hetia said, and this time Sadie was sure she detected pride.

"Amadi?" Sadie said, turning to look over at the farmhouse in the distance. Thick black clouds were gathering overhead. They were moving fast; coming their way.

Hetia stepped back as Sadie readjusted her clothing. The blaze in Hetia's eyes had only grown stronger. "Time for you to get back in that cave."

"What?" Sadie's heart began to pound. "Why?"

Hetia looked left and Sadie followed her gaze. Sunlight glinted down on a horde of figures in the distance. The Coalition army was returning.

"This is a good place for a fight. They're coming back to meet them here," Hetia said.

Sadie put a hand to her heart as her stomach dropped. She looked left at the clouds and right at the approaching force. Then her eyes fell on the tiny farmhouse. Hetia put a hand on her chin and drew Sadie's gaze back to hers. "I'll go warn them; make sure they evacuate. Get in the cave, succubus. And stay there."

Hetia's mouth met hers in a bruising kiss before she bolted for the tiny red barn. Sadie wanted to scream watching her go. Hetia was right to tell her to hide – there wasn't much she could do to help – and yet the sight of her tiny figure running off in the large field made Sadie's mind go blank with fear.

She jumped at the feeling of a hand on her arm. Before she'd even finished turning, Troy's mouth closed on hers. He kissed her with an urgency that momentarily distracted her from all other thoughts. Then he too stepped back in a rush.

"Tell Patricia I love her and… I'll see her after," he said, and then turned and followed Hetia.

Sadie put a hand to her lips. She'd seen Hetia go up against armed men just fine before and still, the thought frightened her, but Troy seemed in even more danger. After all, last time she'd checked, bullets could pass easily through fire. She could only hope he'd keep himself safe, but she hadn't seen him shrink from a fight. In fact, he would probably do everything he could to help.

Sadie regretted not having kissed him back.

A flash of lightning lit up the distant sky and this time, when the thunder reached her only a few seconds later, it reverberated through her whole body. The sounds of distant chatter hit her ears and she looked back toward Siphon's army, surprised to see how much closer they'd come.

Sadie ducked down next to the rock. If she could see them, they would soon spot her. But she didn't want to go inside; leave behind the two figures running in the distance. Troy caught up to Hetia right as they reached the front doors of the tiny home, and they disappeared inside, making Sadie's heart beat anxiously until they re-emerged.

She watched as five figures came out, three of them hopping in a truck and driving off. Behind the house, she could just barely make out movement in the falling rain. Amadi's army was approaching fast, but by the sounds coming from her right, Siphon's would reach her first.

It was time to obey Hetia and get back in the cave. Ducking, she crept around the stone and made her way down the bank. Amazingly, despite all that had happened with her in that past fifteen minutes, the others were still fast asleep.

"Ouch." Sadie stumbled in the dark and caught herself as she fell at Patricia's feet.

"Sadie?" Patricia asked sleepily. "Where are you going?"

"It's time to get up," Sadie said, rubbing her stubbed toe.

"S'dark still," Patricia mumbled.

"We're in a cave. It's morning and time to get up."

"Hmmm." Patricia made the sound in half acknowledgement and rolled over.

Sadie found the place the candle had been the night before and managed to light it. The soft glow illuminated the sleeping forms of the nymphs in the little cot in the corner and danced across Patricia's sleek brown hair; a pleasant mess across the blanket. Sadie sat down next to her and stroked her fingers through it.

A tear trickled down her face and she beat it away. There was no time for that now. "Patricia," she croaked. "I'm sorry, but you need to get up now."

Patricia rolled to look up at her. "Sadie?" she said, sounding a little concerned this time. Then she caught sight of her face. Patricia pushed herself rapidly into a seated position and looked left to right at the empty blanket. "What's wrong?"

"They're gone," Sadie said. It wasn't where she should start, but those were the words that came to her first.

"Where's Troy?" Patricia said, impatiently.

"They've gone to join the fight."

"What?" Patricia was on her feet before Sadie. Sadie almost grabbed her wrist before remembering she'd taken off her gloves.

"Wait," Sadie said, moving to block Patricia's panicked scramble toward the door. "Siphon's army left this morning, but they're coming back. They're about to reach us, and Amadi's is on its way. They're going to clash right over our heads. There's nothing we can do... but wait."

"Oh god, Tamira," Asha said. They were both sitting up in bed, staring at Sadie now.

"The farm has been evacuated," Sadie said, holding out her hands in a pacifying gesture. "I saw them drive away myself."

They fell silent, and in the distance the sound of many feet rumbled nearer in the way it had the night before. Only this time, the roar was matched by thunder. Patricia sat back down, looking dejectedly into the dark. Sadie redonned her gloves and joined her. They reached for each other's hands at the same time.

"We always knew we were heading here. I just thought we'd have more time," Patricia said. "A chance to say... that is, to talk before we separated."

"Troy says he loves you. He told me to tell you that."

Patricia nodded. "How large was the army? Could you tell which side—"

"No. It looked big, but I could only see a piece of it. And Amadi was still far away."

A gunshot went off and they both jumped. Sadie stared at the ceiling for a long time as the sounds of boots passed overhead. They were moving quickly, as if in a charge.

"It's gotten harder," Patricia whispered after a while and Sadie looked at her. "For me. It's gotten harder to do this work, to be ready for this fight, ever since I met Troy." She shifted on the stone. "All I had, for years, was recruiting and preparing. And *now*... God, I just want to curl up in a little corner of the world and spend our lives together. I want children. I want to see my mother again."

Sadie's mouth parted in surprise. Patricia wiped away a tear. "I'm sorry. And here I thought I'd be the one comforting you."

"You do comfort me. I've never been more terrified in my life. Almost everyone I love is in danger today, and I don't even really know how much." Sadie batted away her own tear. "Is Jimmy in that army? Will he fight? And my parents, will they be threatened next? I just want to go home. Whatever happens next, I need to be back *there* for it. I need to be with my parents, and," Sadie squeezed Patricia's hand, "and with my family."

She hoped Patricia understood she meant her. By the look in her eyes it was clear she did, and a second later they were hugging. "Whatever happens," Patricia said, "we're together."

"I don't want to lose that," Sadie added. "Promise me. We'll *stay* together."

"Always. I swear it." They were clutching one another with some desperation now, and Sadie felt Patricia's chest shake against hers. She thought for a second that she was actively sobbing, but it turned out to be laughter. Strangely, the emotion was catching. Sadie laughed too and they broke away to look at each other.

Eventually, their laughter stopped and they cleaned away the last of their tears. "How strange life is," Patricia said.

And that was the last anyone spoke for several hours. The roar of fighting continued overhead, and they could do nothing but stare at the ceiling. Eventually, the sound of heavy rain came, and it echoed noisily off the nearby stream. The comforting sound of water plopping into water was a stark contrast to the angry shouting and blasts of gunfire.

But in time those other sounds died, and all that was left was a light trickle of rain.

Asha moved first; coming to stand in the center of the cave. She took in a long, slow breath. "There's blood in the river," she said, her eyes closed.

The rain died as the four of them emerged. Sadie blinked at the sudden brightness, surprised to see sunlight glinting off the water. It sparkled like a little piece of paradise, with trees and mountains in the distance. But Asha had been right. As they climbed around and up the bank, Sadie caught glimpses of blood streaming past.

The field was a muddy mess. As far as she could see, there was nothing but brown spotted with the bodies of the dead. She'd never seen anything so horrible. The battle she'd been caught in earlier that year hadn't ended like this. There'd been a retreat, and those that had died had been few and out of sight from the little Sadie had seen of it.

But there was no missing this. They picked their way across the field toward the little farmhouse. The place was still standing, though the barn and fields had been completely destroyed. Sadie wondered idly what had happened to their horses.

Most of the dead wore the new uniforms of Siphon's army, but she frantically scanned the faces of the ones who didn't. Asha and Shaya wandered in the direction of the farmhouse while Patricia and Sadie spread out in their search across the field.

Figures moved in the distance. As Sadie drew nearer to the far field, she could see that members of Amadi's army, noticeable by their random garb, were gathering people onto stretchers and carrying them toward a white tent that was only now being erected.

Every time she spotted someone with dark brown hair and no uniform, her heart skipped. If someone she cared about was dead, would there still be lines of light connecting them? The cries of pain of the injured increased the further she went. Two men passed her carrying a woman she recognized on a stretcher. She'd been burned and her leg was bleeding heavily.

Sadie felt an odd sense of calm numbness. Her fears about the future had so far been an anxiety about some unknown horror. But now that that future had arrived, she was almost relieved. This was exactly what war looked like. It was horrible, but at least it was known.

There was a trail of burnt grass, and her attention locked on it. Only a fire nymph could have made such a thing in the midst of that storm. She began to run along it, looking left and right at the injured and dead. The trail ended abruptly. No Troy.

But then she caught sight of something in the corner of her vision. It was streaks of red light flowing between her and someone, both bright and deep. They pulsed around strong cords of black and green. She turned toward him with her mind blank, not believing it was real. Pushing away her succubus vision, she took in the sight of Jimmy across the field.

He hadn't yet spotted her, focused as he was on lifting a man onto a stretcher. She moved closer as if under a spell. It was really him. He was safe. He was here.

Jimmy had his sleeves rolled up and a smear of blood across his chest in the shape of a handprint. He also had a full beard. She'd never seen him like that. It made him look so much older, and... well, she liked it.

"Jack," Jimmy called to someone nearby. "Take this, will you?" He handed off his side of the stretcher to a young man that looked about sixteen. Then he turned and squatted next to a woman with an arrow coming out of her side. She was in a uniform.

"Get away from me, scum," she spat out through her pained panting.

"You're losing too much blood. We need to wrap that wound," Jimmy said in an entirely calm voice that sounded out of place as a response.

"No. I'll die here. Like my sister," she sucked in air through gritted teeth. "She also died because of your kind. I hope you sleep well tonight, thinking of that."

"I doubt I will sleep well for a while," Jimmy said as he broke off the arrowhead.

She cried out in pain at the movement. "Leave me alone, you bastard. I don't want your help."

He pulled something out of his pocket and fiddled with it while the woman glared daggers at him. Sadie was standing only a few yards away now. Jimmy moved in a flash, jamming a needle into the woman's side. Almost immediately, the excruciating look on her face disappeared.

"We don't have a lot of this to spare, but that should take the edge off." He put a hand on her shoulder. "I'm going to pull the arrow out."

"Why? Why should I let you feel good about yourself? I told you what I want."

He paused and seemed to consider this for a moment. "Was it true? Do you actually want to die today?" The question sounded genuine and dead serious. Which was perhaps why she seemed to think over her answer. Her eyes darted to Sadie's, then up at the sky.

Finally, she relaxed. Her body went limp and she breathed, "No. I don't want to die."

Jimmy nodded and launched into swift action. Sadie watched as he successfully stopped the bleeding in just a few minutes. Some of his skills she recognized – they'd needed to clean and dress wounds growing up, especially since Jimmy had often refused to put animals down when they got a little injured. But he'd clearly learned some new ones in their time apart.

By the time two people had returned with the stretcher, the woman had passed out. They carried her away and Jimmy stood up, wiping his blood-soaked hands on his pants. The injured had mostly been removed from the field, and he did one last scan of it, turning slowly as he surveyed the surrounding bodies.

His head snapped to her as he realized someone was standing behind him. His hand flew to his waist and she saw he was armed. Jimmy's hand had closed on the hilt of the long knife before he'd frozen, his lips parting in surprise. Sadie realized then that she was dressed in dark green, the same color as the uniformed soldiers. Perhaps it would've been better not to sneak up on him.

She took a hesitant step forward.

"Wha— Sadie? You're here? How?"

"We had to leave the city. And then," she moved a little closer, "there was this bounty on my head and we had to hide. We've been waiting for you to get here. I've been waiting." Her eyes filled with tears and she blinked them away, not wanting to blur her vision. She just wanted to keep looking at the man in front of her. He had a rugged look to him, and despite being covered in blood, he'd never looked so attractive.

He went to put a hand on the side of her face, but stopped. Jimmy wiped his palm again on his pants before putting both hands in his pockets. "God, I was so worried," he said. "I heard about the bounty yesterday morning. I wanted to send you a message today, but we were too busy trying to catch this army before they got to Marysville. They voted against The Coalition and they'd been planning to make an example out of them. Amadi wanted to catch up while there weren't many people around. This field was the perfect place."

Jimmy stepped closer, but kept his hands in his pockets. "Sadie." He whispered her name. "I'm sorry. We should never have separated. I didn't think about the danger we were in; what it would be like if something went wrong."

She choked on all she wanted to say, but managed to get out the words, "I missed you."

He pulled back, and his gaze fell from hers. "I should go clean up. They're setting up tents back there. If you head that way, you should be able to find people you know."

He stepped around her and she pivoted to face him. "Jimmy?" Sadie wanted to go with him. She didn't want to be separated again so soon. But his behavior was strange, and a small fear that he didn't want her to follow stilled her tongue.

His love and lust lines were as strong as ever, perhaps stronger. It didn't seem like he didn't want her, and yet, there were so many emotions succubi couldn't see. What if he had some other reason for his reserved behavior?

"I'll meet you over there," he said, still not looking her in the eye, and left in the direction of the river. Sadie watched him until he was out of sight before turning to look past the destroyed barn.

Tents were going up at a rapid pace. As she wandered through the commotion, it seemed like everyone had a clear task to engage them, making her feel conspicuous from her lack of clear intention.

Maybe she should return to the field, keep looking for Troy. But the muddy mess behind her was filled only with the bodies of the dead now, and she just couldn't have so little hope as to start looking for him there.

"Sadie?" a woman said behind her.

It was... "Cobie." Sadie's favorite general was coming toward her, flushed from battle and wearing a broad smile.

"I hadn't heard you were back with us. I thought you were off hiding somewhere."

"We were accidentally swallowed by the fight."

Cobie smiled. "You seem to have a habit of that. I guess some people just can't stay out of trouble."

"Yeah." Sadie tucked her hair behind her ear, remembering that the last time she'd seen Cobie had been after she'd intentionally tried to cross from the Coalition camp to the United, getting caught in the early morning battle. At least this time, it was the fight that had over-taken them – she'd just been trying to stay low.

"Speaking of such people, have you seen Hetia? Or Troy?" she asked, hoping to change the subject.

Cobie pointed. "Hetia's in there." Sadie felt a small release of relief wash over her even though she hadn't been too worried about her. "And thank goodness for that," Cobie added.

Sadie raised her eyebrows in question. "The armies were pretty evenly matched," the general said. "In fact, we just learned that Siphon split his army into thirds, to head in different directions. The one he sent back here was meant to handle us easily. Only, he hadn't factored in Hetia. She held back during the previous fights, trying to keep a low profile as to what she can actually do." Cobie grinned. "But today, Amadi let her go all out. She had half the army on their knees by the time we charged them. She changed the whole game." Her face grew serious.

"The bad news is.... that this was only a piece of Siphon's forces. But at least his underestimation gave us a chance to take a bite out of him." Cobie shook her head. "And I was so critical of Amadi's choice to under-utilize his daughter back east, but he had a good strategy. He usually does." Sadie was smiling now too, hearing of Hetia's victory. A wicked part of her wished she could have seen it.

"Listen to me rambling on. I'll catch you later, Sadie. Glad to have you back." Cobie put a hand on her shoulder before hurrying away.

Sadie, rather grateful for the rambling update, ran toward the tent Cobie had indicated. She found Hetia surrounded by a smiling crowd. A man was recapping the battle, but people kept jumping in to add their piece.

Sadie caught a thorough description of Hetia's contribution as they all launched into an animated retelling of precisely how it had gone down. When they were done, Hetia laughed, took a swill of a large bottle of whiskey, and passed it to the guy next to her. Sitting in a wide-legged sprawl on a table in the center, her tiny body seemed to take up as much space as any of the men's.

Deciding this wasn't the best time to ask if she'd seen Troy recently, Sadie snuck back outside to continue looking for him on her own. She ran smack dab into Patricia. "Shit, there you are," her friend said. "Have you seen the others?"

"Hetia's here, and... I found Jimmy," Sadie said.

"Jimmy's alright! Oh, that's great news Sadie. I'm so happy for you." She was looking around her. "Where is he?"

Sadie kicked at the ground. "We decided to split up. He needed to clean up and... uh, I needed to find the rest of you."

Patricia narrowed her eyes slightly, and Sadie wondered if her story hadn't rung entirely true.

"Did you find Troy?" Sadie asked, hoping to distract her.

It worked too well as worry returned to Patricia's face. "Not yet, but I looked all over the field. I was just heading to the medic tent when someone told me they'd seen you come in here."

Without another word, they took each other's hands and took off toward the large white tent. The smell of fresh blood assaulted Sadie's nose as they entered, and wasting no time, they exchanged a look before silently agreeing to split up. She'd run up and down several rows of cots before she caught sight of Patricia stopping in her tracks on the opposite end of the tent.

As she moved in her direction, it became immediately clear by the lines connecting Patricia with the person on the cot that she'd found him. Sadie slowed, a bit nervous now. She wasn't sure if she was relieved or not at the thought of Troy injured. It meant he was alive, that was what was important, but how bad was it?

There weren't any medics nearby. Did that mean he was fine or too far gone to help? Patricia was facing away from her so she couldn't even read her expression. What if he was really hurt? What if they were about to watch him bleed out in front of them? For the first time, she imagined Troy disappearing from her life; never seeing him again. Her chest constricted and it became hard to breathe as her gaze stayed fixated on the top of his head, his hand clasped in Patricia's.

No. She couldn't lose him. Not now. Not when... Sadie watched the black love line, which had been a weak strand flowing out from her ever since it had appeared, strengthen and pulse. She sped up and closed the distance at a run.

He looked up in surprise at her sudden appearance. His eyes were alert and he was smiling.

"Troy," Sadie said breathlessly before dropping to her knees next to Patricia. She looked him up and down, searching for harm.

"It's just a scratch," he said, indicating a large bandage across his side.

"Lie," Patricia said as a fact.

"Okay, it's a deep gash that didn't penetrate any major arteries and will likely heal quickly," he corrected.

"Entirely true." Patricia smiled, nodding in satisfaction.

Sadie's chest shook in a half-sobbing, half-laughing motion. She took his shoulder in her hand and squeezed while he looked at her in surprise.

"Are you okay?" he asked.

"Yeah. It's just been an emotional day. And I was worried about... all of you," Sadie said, lifting her chin and standing back up.

Patricia narrowed her eyes again, and Sadie looked away, though Troy was still looking at her and didn't notice. "Hetia? Did you find her?" he asked, sounding only mildly concerned.

"Yes, she's in a post-battle congratulations orgy, drinking and talking with the soldiers," Sadie said, feeling suddenly jealous.

Troy looked annoyed, too. "Dammit, and here I am lying around because of a cut. I bet there's going to be a big celebration tonight." He turned to Patricia. "Promise you'll help sneak me out of here."

She pursed her lips and glared at his bandage. "We'll see."

A little while later, they learned Troy had been right. After hours of helping dress wounds and carrying water up from the river, Sadie caught the distant sounds of merrymaking. She looked longingly in its direction.

"Just go," Troy said. He too, had asked her where Jimmy was when she'd informed him that she'd run into him. She'd been awkwardly dodging the topic as she continued to help out in the medic tent, but it was time to go find out what was going on with the man she'd been so desperate to see ever since she'd left his arms several weeks ago.

Sadie stared down at Troy's face, glowing from the surrounding firelight now illuminating the dark tent, and wished she could also curl up in his arms a while. "Here, I brought this for you." She handed Patricia a bottle of water and a package of dried meat. Sadie had been checking in on them now and again as she worked, but Patricia hadn't left Troy's side.

"Thanks," the woman said, taking the package absently.

"Are you coming?" Sadie asked.

"No, I think I'll stay here," Patricia replied, looking back at Troy.

"In that case, I brought you this, too." She handed over the ratty deck of cards she'd just bought off one of the soldiers.

"Ooh," Troy said, pushing himself upright, before cringing.

"Here." Patricia bent to help him.

Sadie watched them with her heart aching, wishing she could be everywhere at once. She was afraid to leave Troy's side now with the next leg of her journey so uncertain, but she had a powerful pull elsewhere, and her increasingly desperate desire to see Jimmy helped her take the first few steps backward.

"I'll see you later," Sadie told them. Patricia made a sound of acknowledgement, while Troy looked over at her retreating form. She saw her own fear reflected back in his expression and wished there was something she could say to reassure him that everything was going to work out for them.

"I'll be right here," he told her.

When she could think of no reply, Sadie simply ducked her head and walked away with the powerful feeling of Troy's eyes on her back.

Chapter 18

A Reunion Old and New

Sadie had passed Jimmy several times as they'd worked that day, but he would just squeeze her hand without looking at her and hurry on. She didn't know what it meant, but she didn't like it. He'd said he was happy to see her, and she could see it was at least in part true, but he certainly wasn't acting like it.

She wrung her hands as she moved toward the commotion. The festivities were taking place on the ashes of the old barn, and bonfires lit up the night around them as the smell of roasting meat filled the air. Sadie walked into the crowd and everyone fell silent. For a confused second, she thought it had something to do with her, but then she looked around to see Amadi standing on a stump nearby.

He'd spotted her earlier in the day but had been too preoccupied for her to feel comfortable approaching. Now, he looked out around the crowd. "Before we all get too far into celebrating such a welcome triumph of a terrible nature, I have a full accounting of those who didn't make it. Eighteen of our people lost their lives today. You can pay your respects to those close to them in the grieving tent. But here, I'll read out their names."

They took a long moment of silence, Sadie copied those around her and bowed her head.

When it was over, the mood was somber for a while. She passed through the crowd, nodding at faces she recognized, and looking for Jimmy. Eventually someone laughed in the corner and conversation resumed. A few minutes later, the celebration broke out in full.

When her eyes finally landed on Jimmy, he was sitting in a corner, staring intently at her. How long had he been watching her search for him?

Unnerved by his behavior, she made her way over and sat down on the log with a foot of space between them. She looked at him over her shoulder, but he kept his gaze fixed on her knee.

"I missed you," she said, just barely loud enough to be heard.

He took her hand in his. "I've missed you, too." His eyes flickered up to hers and memories of their weeks apart bloomed at the forefront of the sexual images surrounding him. He'd been aroused almost constantly. She caught scene after scene of his right fist moving rapidly while he looked around. She assumed there hadn't been much privacy to be had, and it seems he'd perfected the ability to make himself come in just a few breaths.

She might have been in a similar state if she hadn't been busy having intense encounters with Troy and Hetia. Even so, she'd missed him beyond what she could stand, and for far more than just sexual reasons. Why was he hesitating with her? Was he about to share more bad news? If he had something to say, she wished he would hurry up and spit it out. She reached for his face, wanting to feel its new rough texture.

He flinched.

"Jimmy? Talk to me."

Her mind raced through possibilities. He was upset at how much he'd craved her. He didn't want to share her with anyone else. He'd decided it was best if they stayed permanently away and he was regretting her sudden appearance.

Finally, he put her out of her misery and said, "What I want to say to you, can't be said in words." It took a moment to comprehend and then her whole body relaxed, only to immediately reheat with the implications of that sentence. She'd learned to recognize with Troy when someone was trying to fight down arousal. It seemed it was something men did a lot more often than she'd realized.

She hadn't noticed it before with how distracted she'd been at seeing him, but the lust coming from him was fiercely contained and ready to explode. This was why he wouldn't look at her? If so, why hadn't he just taken her down by the river when she'd first shown up?

As if reading her thoughts, he said, "There's so much I want. So little privacy."

She jumped to her feet, impatient now. When she tried to pull him up too, he looked down significantly, and she could see on him that behind his raised knees he was very, very hard. Sadie looked around. No one was specifically staring at them, and they were on the edge of the festivities.

She bent down and whispered, "Just stay close."

He let her pull him up and the prominent erection pressed against her. With their faces only a few inches apart, it became hard for him to avoid looking at her. Before she could pull them around the log and get them out of there, he'd grabbed her face in both hands. She got her wish to feel his rough beard when his mouth closed suddenly over hers.

Jimmy's hips rolled against her as he drew her in tight. His tongue fought hers with a demand that left her completely distracted. She forgot that they were surrounded by people, that they were clothed, that she'd been meaning to take them into the shadows.

As he pressed her to him with a piercing need, clutching her face in his hands, she responded to his call. He groaned against her as pleasure shot like rapid fire through him. Seconds later, he climaxed in several agonized bursts.

He released her immediately, looking down in shock at the wet spot now on both of their clothes. They blinked at each other as a mortified expression took over his face, but the people nearby weren't looking at them.

"Sorry," she said, panting like they'd just run a mile. "Let's... get out of here."

He let her lead him into the shadows. Sadie didn't look over at him as she directed them toward the nearby house. It was dark except for a small porch light, and would shelter them from view if they went around to the back.

Only, he didn't let her get that far. As they stepped up to the side of the house, he pushed her roughly against the wall from behind, her breasts pressing into the hard surface as he began fumbling with her long winter skirt.

"Tell me to stop," he said in her ear, his voice a husky growl she barely recognized.

Sadie just helped hold up her layers and arched her ass into him, her chest heaving in surprise and arousal at his behavior. He pulled down her underwear and she heard it tear before falling, pooling around one ankle. Before she could catch her breath, he was lining himself up with her entrance, and he cried out the second the head of his cock touched the slick flesh between her legs.

In one rough thrust, he entered her and immediately began pumping hard and fast. There was no pause to get comfortable, no slow build, no move to caress her. His hands closed over hers against the wall as he did nothing but take what he wanted with a violent ferocity. The alarming demand with which he fucked her was both terrifying and thrilling in a way she'd never experienced.

Jimmy had always been so attentive, loving. Even the first time they'd slept together, he had been more preoccupied with a desire to kiss her than anything else. Not now. Now he moved with complete abandon, thinking only of his own desire.

And she'd never found anything more intoxicating.

She could barely breath against the onslaught of his body beating into her. She wanted him to use her, to fill her up, to leave her in broken pieces. She tried to brace herself against the rough wood of the house, but his uncompromising movement left her with nothing to do but surrender.

Jimmy didn't stop when he climaxed. He continued to move with the same brutal abandon, and Sadie felt his recovery period pass within a few short breaths. He resumed his deep groans right into the next orgasmic cycle.

It was only after he'd cried out again a minute later that he let up. He dropped into several slow thrusts as he ejaculated into her, coming to a stop on a final groan. Sadie was panting out of control, and he matched her, breathing hard into her ear.

His heartbeat pounded against her back as the evidence of his release dripped down her leg. "Fuck." He released the grip on the backs of her hands and ran his palms over her hips as he stood upright. Though he didn't pull out as he asked, "Are you okay?"

The first sound to escape her was a whimper, but she cleared her throat and added, "God yes."

He kissed the back of her neck. Above the skirt, he pulled on her shirt until he could slide his hand under it. Jimmy squeezed her breast in his palm, emitting a light groan as he pulsed inside her.

"I didn't dream it," he said. "How good this feels." He began to move slowly in and out of her. "I've touched myself a hundred times since we've been apart, thinking of how much I wanted to fuck you, just like this." He punctuated his words with a deep thrust.

With the side of her face plastered against the house, she stared at the bonfires in the distance, her heart beginning to pound again. He had never spoken to her like this before.

"Could you see it on me? Could you see me stroking myself and thinking of you?"

"Yes," she breathed. Jimmy pulled on her collar and freed her shoulder. His lips kissed, sucked and then bit at the skin there before he said. "I want more. I want you to do that thing you do, where you bring me to climax and then hold me there."

"Yes," she said again, in a tone of encouragement.

He picked up the pace of his hips as she moved to comply with his request. He kissed her shoulder again as he squeezed her to him with the hold on her breast.

"My own hand was nothing. My hasty climaxes, they fought off the constant ache like a band-aid. None of it was enough," he said in that shaky, husky voice. "As I dream, as I walk, I'm consumed with thoughts of you." He thrust deep inside her, letting out a heavy groan of pleasure as he did so. "I want you with everything I have, Sadie. Forever."

She let out a gasp as liquid heat pooled between her legs at these words. Needing to release her own tension, she slid a hand under the pile of skirts and applied the tiniest bit of pressure. Her legs began to tremble with the build-up of her own need.

As her pleasure grew, she found herself wanting to match his debauched tone. "Faster." She said, her climax right around the corner. "I want to feel you moving in me when I come." He groaned and sped up. "I want your hard cock to clench when I spasm."

He growled at her words. And despite her desire for release, she lightened the pressure of her fingers, finding she suddenly had so much more to say. "I want you to use me, to take me, while I touch myself."

Jimmy took the forearm of his free hand and pressed it down on the small of her back. Continuing to hold her with a hand on her breast, this new motion caused her back to arch forcibly and gave him better access to her hips. He burrowed himself deep inside her, barely pulling back between thrusts, as he held her in this restricted position.

"And once my body is soft, and spent and pliant, I'm going to make you feel better than you ever have before. I'm going to over-whelm you with the agony of pure pleasure; assault all your senses with it, until you can't think, can't cry out, can't stop."

Her mind was so caught up in her own words, and the sounds of excitement Jimmy was admitting, that the first spasm of her climax took her by surprise. She immediately backed off on her touch, stroking as lightly as she could. The effect was to make her pleasure rise, but with such a measured pace that it only grew, far beyond anything she'd ever experienced. When it finally broke, she lost track of all other intentions as she let it consume her.

Somewhere, on the other side of the pounding of her heartbeat in her ears, Jimmy was saying her name – crying out in sympathy with the excite-ment of her release. As her thoughts refocused, she noticed he was right on the edge, and she immediately pushed him over. He pulsed in her, emit-ting a feral sound, and she had to grab hold of the reins in order to keep her promise. Now that she was less distracted, she called on all that she had learned that year to bring the full force of her skills to this moment.

And she did to Jimmy exactly what she'd told him she would.

As he convulsed in her, Sadie stared at the noisy gathering in the distance, glad of the sound of their cover. Her body went numb and her mind dropped into a rapture she didn't know was possible as Jimmy rode out the ecstasy of his elongated bliss.

When she finally let it pass, her legs felt on the edge of collapse as he slowed to a stop inside her. Her insides were sticky and sore, and she reveled in the feeling of it as Jimmy stood upright on a final thrust of release. With her hips in both his hands, he moved to caress the top of her ass with loving gentleness as they came down from the high. He bent to nibble at the back of her neck and she sighed in between the panting. The smell of sex permeated the air, and she soaked up the way it mingled with Jimmy's contented breathing. They didn't speak as he tickled her back and stroked her hair, all the while remaining buried happily inside her.

Some infinite time later, they made their way down to the river to clean up. They kept smiling over at each other as they walked, and every time she looked at him for more than a second, he would scoop her up and resume kissing her.

"This feels different," she panted against his mouth.

"For me, too," he said.

"But I like it. There's so much I want to explore with you. So much of life I want to live."

He just moaned contentedly and resumed kissing her. "We'll stick together," he said after a minute. "Whatever happens next."

It must have taken an hour for them to reach the water with the way they kept stopping. The moon was high overhead by the time she squatted in the stream and scooped up handfuls to clean between her legs, squealing at the cold.

As they washed, she filled him in on what they'd learned in Arlington.

"Why would they put a bomb in the city and not detonate it?" He paused in his scrubbing to shake his head as he spoke.

"We don't know. Maybe they're waiting for the right time... like this war to start. Which, clearly it has."

"Or maybe they tried and it didn't work," Jimmy suggested. "There wasn't any hint about it in Hetia's memory?"

Sadie dropped her gaze. "Uhh, no. Nothing." She scooped her hair behind her ear and bent back to the water.

There was a long silence in which she tried to think of something to say next.

"I'm okay with it," Jimmy said.

"What?" she asked.

"You and Hetia." He sat on the rock at her feet and clasped his hands around his knees. "You and Troy."

She just looked at him, searching his face in the moonlight.

"I don't like the idea of having to *share* you, especially when I want so much of your time." He smiled. "But maybe it's for the best if I don't get what I want. After all, if I had that option, we might never get out of bed."

She laughed. That was most definitely true. It was hard to imagine what would have happened if they hadn't started touching right in the midst of this war. Her face fell. Though it was hard to imagine anything about the future. How exactly would they build any kind of life for themselves in the middle of all this? And Troy and Hetia were fighters. They were going to stay with the army, and she...

"Jimmy? I – I want to go home."

He'd bent over to scrub at his pants, but his gaze shot up.

She chewed her lip. He'd clearly made a place for himself here, helping with the wounded and even fighting. What if he wanted them to stay?

"Sadie, I—" He seemed to search for words. "I want that more than anything."

Her stomach unclenched. "I know I still have a major bounty on my head and I know the army needs all the help they can get, but—"

He took her hands. "I'm just a drop in the bucket here. And in such a dangerous time, there's no wrong place to be. I want to be with my family. The only reason I haven't gone home is, well, I was waiting for you."

She nodded. "I'm ready."

Jimmy stood up. "You'll have to stay hidden. No one can find out you're back."

"No one can find out either of us are, since they won't believe I've returned without you." Sadie's teeth began to chatter as she spoke.

"We should get changed," Jimmy said.

"I'll head back to the cave, my backpack's still there. Meet me back at the barn?"

Jimmy grabbed her, also shivering, and pulled her back against him. "No. I don't want to separate."

They stayed at each other's side until they were both warm and dry – well, dry at least – and by the time they'd returned to the festivities, the music and drink were flowing freely. They paused to watch the people dancing, making an even muddier mess out of the ruins.

"I guess we know how we're going to warm back up," Jimmy said, grinning at her before pulling her into the fray. It was an hour later, when Sadie had extracted herself from her most recent dance partner and was heading for the sidelines, when she spotted Hetia. She was locked in conversation with Jimmy, looking relaxed in a way Sadie had barely seen her. Though the fervor in her eyes from the battle still lingered.

"I've been hearing stories of your triumph today," Sadie said, grinning down at her.

Hetia's expression shifted in some subtle way as she looked up. "Maybe we can get you a front row seat next time," she said, still beaming. Sadie smiled before exchanging a somber look with Jimmy, secretly knowing there wouldn't be a next time.

Sadie looked at the dance floor and then back at Hetia. "Do you want to dance?"

Hetia's smile dropped and she stiffened. Taking her boot off the nearby log, she sat up straight. "No, I – I don't dance."

"Luckily, there's plenty of folk here who do." Cobie came to a stop next to her, and held out a hand. Sadie beamed and let the woman pull her away and back to the dance floor. The second Cobie released her, a man stepped forward to take her place. It was... she couldn't remember his name, but he'd traveled to the East Coast with her as part of Cobie's troupe. She had slept with him a couple times, which she mostly remembered now because of the memories she could see on him.

She did her best to enjoy the dance while not giving him any encouragement that something more was going to happen with her. Looking around, she realized how many sexual history lines she actually had with the people in the room. As distracted as she'd been by Jimmy's return to her life, she hadn't realized the furtive looks being thrown her way.

She glanced over at Jimmy, missing the sight of him, but he was engaged in conversation with Cobie. Hetia, however, was glaring at Cobie and looking entirely somber now. Sadie couldn't see where that look could be coming from. It seemed the women were so alike. She would have thought they'd be happily sharing war stories or something.

"You and Jimmy come from the same town?" the man she was dancing with asked, pulling back her attention. He was semi-hard against her, and under a different circumstance his interest might have attracted her.

"Yeah, and, uhh, we're pretty much together." How did she explain their situation in a way that captured the truth? Sadie decided it was best to just include the most relevant part. "I'm not really looking for someone else to feed from tonight."

"Oh." He pulled back. "Sorry, I was being a little forward. I wasn't trying to – I mean, I *was*, but—"

"It's okay," she cut him off. "No harm done." But he withdrew from her all the same. When she turned back to Jimmy, she found Hetia glaring at *her* now. The woman took a swill out of her bottle and came toward her. She looked so serious that Sadie froze in fear. What was about to happen? They'd never really talked much about their situation, was she about to initiate that? Had Jimmy told her they were leaving and she was upset?

As Hetia approached, a man nearby held out his hand for Sadie. "Can I cut in?" he asked.

"No," Hetia told him, and he backed up at the sight of her cold stare. She turned back to Sadie and cleared her throat. "I'll be taking this one," Hetia said, quietly, still looking utterly determined. Then before Sadie could be surprised, she pulled her close and began to dance with her.

Hetia's tiny frame fit nicely against her, and Sadie's heart pounded at her sudden nearness. Hetia wasn't actually a bad dancer, and it left Sadie wondering why she'd always refused to do it.

Whatever the reason, Hetia seemed to have no reservations now. Waves of lust pulsed from her as she moved, keeping Sadie close. Her hair had come down, and Hetia tucked a loose strand behind her ear, her fingers brushing the bare skin of Sadie's cheek.

"You'll be staying with Jimmy from now on?" she asked, as the spark of pleasure at the touch subsided. Sadie dropped her gaze. When she looked back up, Hetia's face had become expressionless. "It's okay. I never expected this to be more than it was."

Sadie frowned. More than it was? What was it?

"Hetia, I need to tell you something," Sadie said in a tone that made the woman stop moving and cast her an intent stare. "I've decided to go home to be with my family." Hetia lifted her chin as a shadow passed over her eyes. Then she nodded once, pulled her back in and continued dancing. "But I don't want to be apart from you," Sadie whispered in her ear. Taking a chance, she ran her lips along her cheekbone.

Hetia's hands tightened on her as the wave of pleasure rippled through her. She was still so wound up from the battle, her body was practically humming. With their skin in contact, Sadie could feel every sensation that passed through the other woman. The sensitive tickle of her own lips on her face, the way she felt warm under her hands, the way the fabric of her panties rubbed against her aroused body.

Sadie caught an image of Hetia dragging her into the dark and pushing her against the same building Jimmy had earlier. She found herself emitting the same shallow panting as the woman in her arms. She waited, thinking of nothing else except the desire for Hetia to take what she wanted.

But she only pulled back, breaking the contact. "It's been a pleasure, Sadie," she whispered. "Dancing with you." Then without looking at her, she turned and left the festivities. Sadie watched her retreat, trying to memorize everything about her. She was struck with a sharp fear over saying goodbye to the woman, and suddenly she dreaded the uncertainty of tomorrow.

Would they ever see each other again if she left for home now? Yes. Sadie would make sure they did, because she knew Hetia would always be worth fighting for. If only she could convince the woman that regardless of where they each went next, she was never letting her go.

$\sim$

THE NEXT MORNING came far too soon. Sadie woke to the sight of Jimmy watching her sleep, and she blinked contentedly at him as the realization that they were really back together struck her for the hundredth time. And since the five people he shared the tent with had long since left, they were blessedly allowed some privacy. Deciding it would be cleanest if she swallowed the mess, she immediately pushed him to his back and slid down his body.

When they emerged an hour later, the camp was in full swing, helping to reconstruct the barn. Sadie waved to Tamira and the river nymphs as they stood around, watching it go up. They didn't stop to chat, however, since Sadie was too fixated on her destination. With her hand in his, she led Jimmy to Troy's sickbed.

Her chest grew heavy as they crossed the tent and she spotted not only Troy and Patricia, but Hetia too. They all three looked up at them at the same time.

"Troy, it's good to see you're alright," Jimmy said.

"You too. We were getting worried when there was no news." Troy pushed himself more upright.

Sadie looked between them, trying to read if there was any tension there. Before she could arrive at a conclusion, however, she saw the three of them focus on something behind her, and she shifted to see Amadi coming their way.

His progress was slow, as he was stopping to check on every wounded person he passed. He hadn't stayed for the celebration the previous night and he looked tired and somber as they exchanged greetings. He patted Troy's shoulder, examined his bandage, and looked around at them. "This information about the bomb could be invaluable. Thank you for pursuing this." He faced Sadie. "Now I hear you're ready to return home."

Her eyes shot to Patricia and Troy, before returning to Amadi's. Jimmy must have talked with the man last night. Sadie swallowed. It all felt so fast. She hadn't had time to figure out what this meant for the group of them.

She nodded, numbly.

"This bounty makes that a bit tricky, you know? We can't have you getting caught when you have such valuable information."

Sadie swallowed. She hadn't thought of the larger repercussions of her choice. "But," he continued, glancing down at the bed, "we can't exactly leave Troy here to recover like we've been doing with the other wounded along the way. Siphon has split his army into thirds: one we decimated yesterday, one is heading north, and the third south. A new, mostly nymph army has sprung up in southern California and is making its way north to join forces with this faction. Support for The Coalition is growing much faster than for our side. Soon, even Hetia might not be enough to keep the fight in our favor." He pushed up his glasses, looking more weary than ever.

"I think it might be for the best if we hide you and Troy out of sight. If either of you are captured, Siphon will stop at nothing to learn what you have uncovered, and who you have told."

Sadie's shoulders fell. Siphon would certainly look for her in her own home. *Of course* she couldn't go back there now.

"Siphon has had a lookout outside your house for days," Amadi said, reading her thoughts. "But I sent lookalikes of the two of you heading south, spreading rumors about a succubus and a fire nymph. And I got word this morning that the lookout was recalled. The coast is clear, and I think that hiding you in the most obvious place might actually be the safest. Siphon isn't one to take chances – he likes absolute control. If he's recalled his man, it can only be because he already thought it highly unlikely you would return there."

Sadie half-sobbed, half-laughed in relief. "Thank you," she said, batting a tear away as it slid down her face.

"And I'd like you to take this." Amadi handed her a wooden box with two handprints on its lid. It was the succubus box that had gotten them into all of this in the first place. The memory of the ocean nymph that had died in Jimmy's arms flashed through her mind. The nymph that had died trying to get this box into the hands of Amadi and had been forced to entrust it to Sadie and Jimmy instead. And now the box was coming back to her. "You can hide it someplace safe," he said. "Away from all this."

Sadie nodded, accepting the box somberly.

"And," Amadi looked at Hetia, "it could be dangerous getting you there safely. I think Hetia should accompany you. The next battle will take place up north. She can get you settled in and then meet back up with us. You will have four days before she'll need to return, but I have a truck to help you make the journey in two. Just make sure to abandon it when you get close and walk the rest of the way."

Sadie looked to the blond woman, relieved they didn't have to say goodbye yet, but Hetia kept her gaze on Amadi's as she gave a curt nod.

"Well then, that's settled," he said, clapping his hands together like his old self. "I'll leave you to get ready." He turned to Sadie. "But first, may I have a word?" She looked around, surprised he wanted to talk to her in private. What could he possibly have to say that couldn't be shared with current company?

She followed him out of the tent and he waited until they were alone before he spoke. "I know I said in there that we may lose this war. And I have to be prepared for the worst. But I still don't quite believe it. I hope for a future in which I can see the next generation grow old in a better world. The tide sweeping across this country is a frenzy, a reaction pumped up by a well-planned campaign. I think it will take the smallest of things for it to break, for people to realize what is happening. And in case our luck turns, I want to say something... about Hetia."

Sadie blinked. She hadn't seen that coming.

"She was a hard kid to raise. That is – I'm not complaining. She saved my life at the time. I was too focused on the fight. Working was all I had; her dad and I both. Then once she was my responsibility, things changed for me. For her too, obviously. Before Eirik died, she always hated how hard he worked. But once he was gone, little Hetia just wanted to do more of the things they had done together. He had taught her how to fight and how to harness her skills as a nymph. She'd been resentful of these lessons with him. He pushed her hard. Too hard. And he was one of the best. But once he left us, Hetia wanted me to continue to train her. Since she only opened up to me when I engaged with her in that way, I relented."

Sadie wrinkled her forehead. As interested as she was in hearing this, she couldn't imagine where it was going.

"I was gentle, much more than Eirik was." Amadi laughed. "She used to get so mad at me. She would train for hours, wanting me to push her harder. It was never enough. All through her teens there would be big tantrums. *I was ruining her life. This wasn't what her father would have wanted.* I knew she didn't mean it though. And sometimes, when she was just exhausted enough, she would come curl up in my arms and let me hold her while she slept." He handed Sadie a piece of bread and she accepted it gratefully. "If you want to know how to date my Hetia," he paused to smile knowingly at her, "just don't let her fool you. When she acts like she doesn't care if you're around, hang around anyway. When she says she isn't hungry, put food within her reach all the same. And when she lets you in... take care of whatever you find there. Just promise me that."

Sadie couldn't believe it. Andre Amadi was actually having a your-intentions-with-my-daughter talk right here on the muddy battlefield. And he was the leader of the resistance. She smiled, realizing exactly what this meant. He must actually think they might win.

"I promise, sir," Sadie said.

Chapter 19

The Sweetest Scent

Sadie left that strange conversation feeling almost giddy. An image of getting to spend the rest of her life with Hetia had bloomed in the back of her thoughts, and she floated around on a bed of hope as they packed up to leave.

Jimmy drove the beat-up truck as he was the least recognizable out of the bunch, while Hetia crouched in the bed with her hood pulled up over her head, scanning the surrounding woods. Sadie tried to talk her into coming inside when it began to rain, but she wouldn't hear of it. Sadie and Patricia, who had refused to leave Troy's side, were crammed in the back with Troy laying across their laps.

He fell asleep almost immediately, and Sadie watched Patricia stroke his hair as the truck jostled them over the rocky road. Sadie was heading home and taking everyone she loved with her. Despite the temporary nature of the moment, she couldn't help but feel a sense of peace.

"How's he healing?" she asked in a whisper.

"The wound is almost completely sealed. The stitches came out this morning. Drawing on fire from the fight definitely sped up his recovery time, but it seems that healing so quickly has taken it out of him." Patricia stroked his cheek. "We almost lost him."

Sadie hugged Troy's thighs to her with her left arm and reached to take Patricia's hand with her right. "Well, we're together now," she said, and she thought she saw her sense of peace mirrored in Patricia's eyes.

When night came, they pulled off the road and slept in the truck. Jimmy woke early and dragged her into the woods with unabashed intentions. Not wanting to return to the others smelling like sex, she turned him around and held him from behind. After he'd spilled twice over the forest floor, she withdrew her touch.

Jimmy zipped up his pants and faced her in the predawn light. He had a small frown and she looked a question at him. He shrugged. "Sometimes I worry you'll get bored of this. That it's too much."

She almost laughed. "Jimmy, I'm a succubus, remember? And it's you. I will never get bored of you." She shook her head, bemused.

He looked in the direction of the truck. "If you've been sleeping with them, do—" He cleared his throat. "Do they feel the way I feel?"

She thought for a moment. "It's less intense, but only a little. Troy is wiped out right now, but that will pass. Hetia is dreaming of me, but Jimmy, she still doesn't know I can see these things."

He nodded and made a zipped-lips motion. "I guess we'll have to find space for you to be with them too."

She took his hand. "We'll work it out. For now, let's just get home."

They accomplished that first task by the end of the day. Abandoning the car in a patch of woods, Hetia created a quake just large enough to sink the truck into the soft dirt. They covered it with leaves and continued on foot.

Gradually, Sadie began to recognize the surrounding forest as her own. She exchanged a grin with Jimmy. They were close now. As they neared, she realized she was nervous to see her parents. What would she tell them about her year? She'd definitely be leaving out the dangerous spying part, and the sexual escapades. Which pretty much left talking about the food.

"And the people," Jimmy said, when she voiced her concerns out loud. "We'll tell them about the nymph-woods in Arlington and the casino-owning siren family."

"But not the part where they tried to shoot us," she said.

"Yes, we'll skip over that."

"What about the bounty on my head?" she asked.

"If we're lucky, they won't have heard about it yet. And if they have, we say as little as possible," Patricia jumped in. "You just got a little mixed up with Siphon's succubus daughter, and now he mistakenly thinks you're some kind of threat."

"Right. Just what my mother wants to hear. She'll be so proud," Sadie said, wondering suddenly if this was such a good idea.

But then she caught sight of a little house through the trees, and her body melted in a pool of longing. The forest came to an end on the edge of a wide field. Their cows were out to pasture, and the corn had already been harvested. She wondered exactly how they had managed it all on their own. Though as they passed by the gardens, she noticed that most of the earth hadn't been tilled at all. She felt guilty for leaving her parents here without help. When she'd gone, she'd thought they'd at least have Jimmy, but then she'd stolen him too. Well, she was bringing them both home now, and she vowed never to abandon her parents again.

The fading light of dusk struck the side of the house as Sadie walked up the steps. She secured her gloves and adjusted her clothing to make sure she was entirely covered, took a deep breath, and knocked.

It seemed to take forever before she could hear the faint patter of footsteps. The door didn't have a peephole, but it opened a crack and then stopped. The left side of her mother's face appeared in the tiny fissure. "Hello?" she asked, sounding weary and a bit confused.

Then recognition bloomed and Sadie found a mane of auburn curls coming at her a second before two mom arms enveloped her. "Oh, sweetie," she cried. "This is such a – oh, it's just the best surprise."

Her mom seemed to realize they weren't alone as she released her in a rush and, wiping away her tears, said, "And you brought guests. Pardon my manners. Please, come out of the cold." She backed up. "Here, I'll take that," she added to Patricia who was already unbuttoning her floor-length jacket.

The house was warm and smelled of Sadie's favorite casserole. The cheese and onion scent filled her with a fresh wave of homesickness even though she was now, in fact, at home. Her father appeared around the corner, leaning on his cane and grinning at her with tears in his eyes. She rushed forward to hug him too. "My daughter. You've come back," he said softly, patting her firmly on the back with one arm.

Jimmy extracted himself from her mother's grip and swept in behind Sadie to hug her dad. "Ahh, James. You're safe. And looking well," her father said, hugging him like his own son.

Sadie beamed at the two of them, and then turned to make introductions. When she got to Troy, he reached out to shake her mother's hand and flinched slightly at the sudden movement. He was also the only one of them not loaded down with a backpack, and her mother missed nothing.

"You're hurt. Where are my manners? Let's get you all seated." She led them into the dining room, and Sadie and Jimmy went to gather the extra chairs from the back of the house. They were stacked there, just as they'd always been. But one thing had certainly changed. Sadie's mouth fell open at the sight of what was in the backyard.

The foundations that Jimmy and her father had begun last summer now supported a finished home. Sadie crossed the field as if in a trance and pulled open the smooth wooden door. It had a living room, bedroom, and a bathroom with a simple toilet and sink, though no shower. She heard Jimmy flip on the tap as she peered into the bedroom.

"The water's hooked up," Jimmy called from the kitchen. "But it only runs cold."

"And there's a bed," Sadie said.

The king-sized mattress took up most of the bedroom, and was the only piece of furniture in the place, but it was made up. She ran her hand over the thick comforter. It was ready for her. Ready for if she came home unexpectedly. Tears pricked her eyes and she blinked them away as Jimmy pressed to her back and wrapped his arms around her. "Welcome home," he said in her ear.

When they returned to the kitchen a few minutes later, they

found her mother had already extended the table and brought in the chairs. They were all taking their seats as they answered her many questions.

"What do you think?" her father asked her with a grin as she took the seat next to him.

"I love it," she whispered back. "Thank you."

She smiled at Jimmy across from her as her mother took the seat at the other end of the table between Hetia and Patricia.

"Dig in," her mom said, gesturing to the bread in the center of the table. "I've just popped in the extra lasagnas. We'll eat late, but there'll be enough for all." Then she smiled around at them and asked the dreaded question, "So how do you each know each other?"

Sadie cleared her throat, feeling it was her responsibility to take this one. "Well, Hetia and I met in Seattle shortly after we arrived. I was just starting to make new friends there and we hit it off right away." *Then we had a great night of sex before she disappeared from my bed, and later turned out to be the one-in-a-million daughter of the rebellion, capable of leveling cities and raised by the leader of The United, training her whole life for this current war.*

Sadie tucked her hair behind her ear and gestured palm up to her mother's right as she continued, "Patricia and I met later that summer, after Jimmy and I had moved to another neighborhood that was more friendly to human-feeder relationships." After they'd heard her speak as the voice of The United in Seattle, where she single-handedly recruited and vetted hundreds of new people for the resistance. Patricia was basically her best friend now, and the only new friend she wasn't actively sleeping with.

Sadie recrossed her legs and turned to the man sitting between Patricia and Jimmy. "And Troy and I met a month later through a mutual friend." Sadie smiled, satisfied at her ability to say enough without giving any actual information.

"Oh," her mother said. "Well, with the bounty on your heads and Troy's injury, I just assumed you'd gotten involved in the resistance. Also, aren't you the earthquake nymph that brought down Seattle?"

Sadie choked on her water and Hetia's eyes went wide. They

hadn't heard anything about her being tied to that incident, otherwise she would have been keeping a lower profile.

"Where did you hear that?" Patricia asked.

"I mean I can't be sure," her mother continued, "but I saw a sketch of the woman in the papers."

"The papers? There was no national news with a sketch of Hetia in it," Patricia said, absolutely certain.

Her mother shifted. "No, but there was a small local paper and I signed up to have it delivered to me monthly. You see, my daughter was living in that city at the time and I followed all the news I could of it. And you really do bear a resemblance to the sketch, poor as it was."

Sadie struggled to process the implications of what she'd just heard. The only way her mother could have signed up for a local newspaper was if she'd traveled to the city, just to get news of it. She could picture her mother debating with herself whether to come find Sadie, and then deciding not to let her know she'd even been there.

Sadie took a deep breath. The table went so silent she thought she could hear actual crickets. "Let's start again," Sadie said, then began the tale from the beginning, this time leaving very little out.

Her mom put a hand on her heart when she got to the part where Alec, the manipulative siren from Seattle, had tried to kill them. She downplayed the danger she'd been in during the forest fire in the middle of a battle incident. And decided to skip entirely the events of her capture by Siphon, making it sound as if Troy had burst into the room to rescue her a second after she'd been caught as a spy.

Sadie didn't tell her about the bomb, either, leaving it at the simple fact that she and Troy had stolen something valuable from Siphon. "Which is why we have to stay out of sight," she finished. "If anyone in town sees us, I doubt they would hesitate to turn us over."

"How's the sentiment around here regarding the war?" Patricia asked.

"Split," her mother said. "And a little... tense. After the recent, well... trouble, everyone has agreed we will publicly go along with the wishes of the new government, but there's some who want to resist in other ways. There's a town meeting in three days from now to talk it all out. I'm baking five hundred muffins."

"Well," Sadie said to her mother's rosy-cheeked pronouncement. "At least you won't be doing that alone." She was glad she hadn't had to lie to her mother, and equally glad to be back home helping out.

When the casserole and lasagna came out, Sadie launched herself, rudely she was sure, to steal a big piece of the limited casserole. She held up the plate to her face and inhaled the smell of her mother's cooking for several long breaths before savoring her first bite of home. Troy and Patricia did a fine job of entertaining the table as Sadie scarfed down three whole helpings before it ran out.

The conversation continued long after dinner, and happy as she was to have everyone she loved in one place, Sadie could find no energy to worry about the future. A state that changed only slightly when her mother asked, "So where should we put you all tonight? We have a guest room, of course. And your room is just how you left it, dear. The little house out back will do as well. Though you'll need to get a fire going, or else it'll be freezing."

All heads turned toward her, and she realized the burden of deciding was entirely in her hands. Sadie cleared her throat, looking nervously around. "Well, I guess Jimmy and I should try out this new fireplace. And Troy and Patricia could take my room – with Hetia in the guest room." She didn't like that Hetia was the only one sleeping alone, but she wasn't sure what other arrangement made sense. Plus, she really did want to spend the first night there with Jimmy in their new home. It felt right.

Jimmy stayed to help her parents clean up while Sadie showed the others upstairs. She turned to face Hetia, Troy, and Patricia in the tiny hallway, a bit shocked to find them in her childhood home. "We have two bathrooms," she said breathlessly. "The one I used to use is there." Sadie pointed down the hall. "Extra towels are in here." She stepped past the closet and pushed open the next door. "And this is the guest room."

Hetia passed her in the narrow doorway, so close that Sadie could feel the heat of her body. Naturally, the woman had been in a high state of arousal all day, and Sadie thought they were lucky she was able to so easily hide such things, but it seemed to spike sharply as she briefly caught Sadie's eye on her way into the room.

Sadie swallowed, not wanting to leave her, and not being able to start something with Troy and Patricia watching. "Well, goodnight," she said in the end.

"Goodnight," Hetia replied, looking uncharacteristically small as she sat on the edge of the bed.

Not looking at the others, Sadie continued down the hall. Flipping on the light to her old room, she found it looked exactly the same, only smaller. She was surprised to find herself back in it, and some part of her just wanted to curl into her covers alone and remember her old self. But then she found the faces of her new friends and could feel nothing but warmth that they would be sleeping in her bed together.

Okay, maybe there was the smallest pain of jealousy that Patricia would get to snuggle into Troy's arms when she couldn't. Though, even if she was the one staying in this room with him, there would be no platonic snuggling anyway, which only increased her envy. But *mostly*, she was warmed by the thought.

Sadie hugged Patricia goodnight, pseudo-kissing on the cheek, and turned to Troy. He went hard the second she looked at him, and he coughed before grabbing the bulge in his pants. "Sorry, I'm... I'll go take a shower soon," he said. The image of her on her knees in the shower with him bloomed in his mind, but then disappeared so quickly she could tell he hadn't intended it as a suggestion. His cheeks tinged just slightly.

"Glad to see you're feeling better," Sadie said, hesitating in between wanting to pull away and wanting to hug him. She settled for running a finger over the bandage peeking out from under his shirt.

His breathing quickened and he said, "Yeah, I think I'll be my old self by tomorrow."

"Well, if we're going to be fugitives here together, I'll have to find some time to take advantage of that," Sadie said with a grin, enjoying the pulse of lust that burst out of him. Then she blushed, too, and looked sheepishly at Patricia watching them from only a foot away. Strangely, Patricia was biting her lip, looking a little hot around the edges as well. Though the traditional sexual desire most people wore was entirely absent in her case, her gaze did hold the barest hint of curiosity and was that... heat?

Sadie was a mess of confusing emotions by the time she'd joined Jimmy in their new house. Luckily, he simplified her feelings rapidly when he forced them into sharp focus with a kiss. She ran her hand over his beard as he pushed her against the wall.

"Do you like it?" he asked.

"The beard? Or being here with you?"

"Yes," was all he said.

"Yes," she replied with a smile.

He went to hike up her shirt, but the house was so well-insulated that it was even colder inside then out.

"Whew, let's leave that in place," she said, laughing. "At least until we heat this place up."

"What if I heat you up?" he asked, turning her around and sliding a hand down her waistband.

"That might work." She arched back into him and slid her palms up the wall as his hands slid into her panties.

They froze as a tiny knock came at the door. Since Jimmy wasn't fit for company, she moved to answer it, her face flushed despite the cold.

Troy was standing there, looking incredibly nervous. "I'm sorry. It's just your mother said the new flue was untested, and on a cold night like this... Well, it might be hard to get the first fire going. She sent me to help."

His hair was still wet from the shower, and the image of him stroking himself and thinking of her was fresh in his thoughts, but as he wasn't picturing anything happening now, she concluded he was genuinely there to just get the fire going. And by the embarrassed look on his face, he had clearly overheard them and was feeling sheepish about interrupting.

"I can go if—"

"No. Thank you, Troy. It's freezing in here."

She stepped aside, and let him in. Jimmy had withdrawn to the bedroom, and Sadie hovered in the doorway, where she could both see him waiting for her and stay in conversation with the man building the fire. Troy tossed a few large logs into the fireplace, not bothering to mess with kindling. Then he rolled up his sleeve and gave a burst of flame so hot she could feel it from across the room.

No one actually spoke as he held it for several long minutes. It must truly be a cold night if it was taking this long. Eventually though, the chimney began to draw and the tiny hint of smoke that was escaping into the room disappeared into the upward pull. Troy withdrew his hand from the burning logs and Sadie raised her eyebrows as Jimmy appeared at her side. He put an arm around her and whispered into her ear. "I have you all night, if you want some time..."

She swallowed, bit her lip, and looked from Jimmy's face to Troy's back. Jimmy was nice to suggest it, but she knew it wasn't at all what he really wanted. It only made her love him more, though, that he would even offer. No. She wanted to be with him in their new bed. More than she wanted anything else right then. But knowing he was capable of sharing was the icing on the cake of that perfect evening.

Troy turned around, his gaze flicking briefly to Jimmy's pants, which were still quite noticeably strained. "Done," he said, running a hand through his hair, his gaze solidly on hers.

"Thank you. Goodnight, Troy," she said, decisively.

He nodded and left in a hurry. When they were alone, Sadie and Jimmy put in their own work to heat up the little house, and though it took hours, they fell asleep having thoroughly christened their new bed.

She woke up in the middle of the night with some of her euphoria having worn off. As happy as she'd been to fall asleep in Jimmy's arms, the thought of Hetia alone in the guest room continued to nag at her. In a few days from now, she would be here with Jimmy and Troy, but Hetia would be gone, off to fight in another dangerous battle.

Sadie didn't want to miss the chance to spend more time with her, and she could feel the pull of her even in sleep a house away. She kissed the top of Jimmy's head and slid her feet to the stone floor, still warm from the fire. She cleaned herself as best she could in the bathroom sink, despite the coldness of the water, and her heart pounded at the idea of sneaking into her own house to awake a beautifully aroused and yet emotionally guarded woman. But she remembered her promise to Amadi. *If she says she's not hungry, put food in her reach anyway.*

Sadie skipped the first and fifth stair so as to avoid the creaking sounds they always emitted. She carefully opened the door and found Hetia out of bed, standing at the window. The woman turned her head, a small smile visible in the moonlight. Sadie crossed the room in a few strides and stood next to her. The familiar field outside was a welcome sight and she took it in fondly. "You're awake," Sadie said unnecessarily.

Hetia took a minute to reply. "Too much on my mind," she said eventually, and Sadie felt her tiny fingers twitch next to her own.

"Anything you want to share?" Sadie asked.

Hetia just turned to face her, pulling her close with two hands around her lower back. She sighed as she gently touched Sadie's lips with her own. As thoroughly as the gesture had succeeded in distracting away from the question, Sadie had been hoping that Hetia would talk to her. Not that she didn't have every intention of satisfying their base needs, but right then she wanted Hetia to open up in words the way she had in other ways.

"You didn't eat much at dinner," Sadie said, trying for a safe topic.

"I didn't want to put your mother out."

Sadie chewed her lip, feeling suddenly guilty about her own three helpings. She knew Hetia could eat, after all, and she hadn't realized she'd been intentionally holding back.

"Come on," Sadie said, taking her hand.

They crept to the kitchen, making it just inside before Hetia pushed her against the wall and kissed her. Their bodies pulsed with a rush of excitement, and Hetia gasped at the strong wave of pleasure that Sadie was unable to hold back.

She wouldn't be distracted though. Sadie pushed her away, a small giggle coming out with the action. "I thought you were hungry."

Hetia grinned. "I think I'm making it pretty clear that I am."

Sadie lifted her chin, giving her a wicked smile that was full of promises before disappearing into the pantry. Flipping on the light, she frowned. The shelves were surprisingly bare. What was going on? Had they rearranged stuff?

Pulling out the little step stool, Sadie looked on the top shelf. She was in luck. There was a little box of chocolate chip cookies still shoved behind the flour. Her mom had bought ten for the house last winter, and after seeing the speed at which her father consumed them, Sadie had decided to ration a box for later. She removed the secret stash, feeling it was a lifetime ago that she'd placed it there.

She held out the opened package to Hetia who looked briefly torn between her and the cookies, but the woman went for the box in the end, making Sadie smile that she'd successfully tempted her with the sweet treat.

Moving on to a riskier topic than food, Sadie said, "The first time we slept together, there was a little earthquake." Hetia's eyes snapped to hers. "Not enough to do any real damage, but enough to give everyone in the casino a scare."

It was clear the comment was meant as a question because Hetia averted her eyes back to the cookie. She didn't push away answering though. "I hadn't been expecting it to be so... intense," she ran a finger down Sadie's collarbone, "with you. It took me off-guard. I didn't have time to prepare myself."

Sadie bit her lip. "So that means that since then... you've been holding back."

Hetia stroked a hand over her hair. "Always," she whispered, leaning in to kiss her. Sadie pushed a cookie up between them and took a bite, cutting her off with a smile. Hetia groaned at Sadie's diversion and pulled her closer before reaching back into the box. She ran her palm up Sadie's waist and over her breast, watching her with rapt attention as she ate.

"Is there any way to get you *not* to hold back?" Sadie asked, meaning the question in so many ways.

Hetia answered it in just one, however. "Water." She frowned. "I can't feel the earth when I'm on the water. But I don't like it. That feeling. It's as if I suddenly have no control."

"Hmm." Sadie swallowed the last of her cookie and dusted off her hands. "Follow me." She pulled away from Hetia's grip, and didn't look back to see if she'd be followed. Hetia was too intent on her to let her walk out the back door alone. Sadie led them to the side of the house and pulled open the storage closet. She grabbed several heavy wool blankets, piling most of them into Hetia's arms when she appeared at her side.

They didn't speak as Sadie took off through the garden with intention. Hetia did make a sound of uncertainty when she continued right on into the trees, but she followed nonetheless. It wasn't far to the river. The moonlight was muted under the cover of the forest, but Sadie knew the path well, and her footsteps didn't falter. It was strange to be the one moving with confidence while Hetia fumbled behind her, but this was her terrain they were on now.

Sadie led her by the hand until the sound of water hit them. They emerged into the place that had always been her and Jimmy's, and for a second, Sadie was confused in her emotions. Then she looked back at Hetia and smiled at the woman with her hair glowing in the moonlight. "Come," Sadie said, leading her to the little boat moored on the shore. She would take Hetia downstream a bit, someplace that could be just theirs.

Hetia froze as she spotted Sadie's destination. She flipped over the little vessel and tossed in her blankets before returning to retrieve the ones in Hetia's arms. "Succubus," Hetia said, sounding exasperated as she shook her head. Sadie took the blankets from her and tossed them in as well before pulling the tense woman against her.

"You don't have to," Sadie said, brushing her bare lips along Hetia's neck and intentionally sending a strong pulse of pleasure through the slight connection. "That is, if you're afraid of being... unmoored." She smiled as she pulled back and hopped into the boat.

Hetia stared down at her, and Sadie could see her chest rising and falling in a pant. "You're the devil," Hetia told her, and though she didn't budge, Sadie had a feeling that the woman was going to cave on this one.

Sadie just leaned back, adjusting the blankets under and around her. Once she was comfortable, she smiled up at the narrowed eyes above her. Hetia took a tentative step forward and glared down at the little raft. "I won't be able to protect you," she said, "if I can't feel the earth."

"We'll just have to fight off the salmon with our bare hands," Sadie said, beginning to shiver and hoping Hetia was going to join her soon.

Clucking her tongue in response to Sadie's comment, Hetia jumped into the boat, putting out her arms as it wobbled. It was quite the sight to see from the woman who could stand in the middle of an earthquake and remain calmly on her feet. She sat down tentatively, and Sadie held open the blanket in invitation.

Hetia moved next to her, and she pulled the layers tight against the cold before reaching to unloop the rope holding them to shore. Hetia grabbed her knee as Sadie pushed them off with one oar. The river was always calm here, and she easily steered them around the one rock without even turning to look at it. Sadie parked them around the corner in the little alcove of an island and retied the rope to the horseshoe buried in the rock there.

Hetia still looked tense, but her attention shifted as Sadie ran a bare hand under the hem of her shirt. "Let me take you somewhere new, Hypatia Pierce," Sadie whispered in her ear. "Can you trust me?"

Hetia spread her legs as Sadie pushed herself between them. The woman gave out a sigh that turned into a moan as she dug her hands into Sadie's curls and claimed her mouth. Sadie pulled Hetia off the wooden seat and onto her back, adjusting the blankets to cover them.

"I want to," Hetia said. "I wish—"

She hesitated a long time. Sadie pinched her nipple with her bare fingers, running her lips along her neck. "Tell me," she commanded, willing her to go on.

Hetia arched into the touch, gripping Sadie's hip as she gasped, but eventually she finished her sentence. "I wish I knew how to love you," Hetia breathed, and her voice was low and throaty, as if fighting off emotion. Sadie swallowed, fighting down the lump in her own throat.

"It's hard," Sadie said. "To let people in. I know." Sadie thought of the way her hometown had treated her after her transformation. And before it. Then she remembered the dangerous way her so-called friends had turned on her in Seattle. It was best not to trust too many people. But the shining face of Jimmy popped into her mind, and her heart went soft. "But you don't need much to be happy. You just have to find your little family. You can blot out the rest. Though if you never let anyone in at all, well, what kind of life can you have?" Sadie grabbed her face between both hands and kissed her. "And our time is short, Hetia. So short." Sadie held her as if the strength of her embrace could somehow fight off the future.

Hetia pulled Sadie directly on top of her and swept a strand of hair behind Sadie's ear. The moonlight lit up their faces as she said, "Okay." Her chest heaved. "Okay, I'm yours. Tonight. Just... help me turn off my brain."

Sadie wasted no time in responding. And Hetia had been right. Though the water lapped at the rocking boat, no earthquakes accompanied her surrender. The decadence of the moment dragged them both under, and when the sun began to rise hours later, Sadie was lost, her thoughts entirely at peace as she kissed the silent cry from Hetia's lips.

They crawled back into bed while the house was still asleep, and Hetia curled up against her, a sheet between them to prevent skin contact. Sadie waited to hear the shallow breathing of the edge of slumber that would make it possible for the other woman to feign sleep if she wished to, before whispering, "I love you, Hypatia."

Hetia didn't speak, but in a clear admittance that she'd heard her, brushed her lips against the back of Sadie's hand, and it all but felt as if she'd said it back. A minute later, Hetia dropped into easy sleep and went soft in her arms.

Chapter 20

A Perfect Day

Sadie awoke to a quiet knock at the door. Hetia's eyes shot open and she tensed as if responding to a threat, before she noticed the surroundings and went slack. Daylight was streaming in through the curtains, falling softly across her cheek and making her hair shine. Sadie cupped her face in one palm and scooted closer. She brushed her lips against Hetia's before the knock came again, reminding her of why they had woken in the first place.

Good morning, Sadie mouthed. Hetia scooted closer in reply, and pulled her into a kiss. The knock came again and Sadie groaned before breaking away.

"I could bring the house down, leave just this room standing," Hetia whispered.

Sadie laughed, and Hetia cast her a contented smile.

"It's tempting," she said, "But there's a lot of people in this house I think I'd miss."

Hetia looked at the door and then back at her. "Thank you. For staying with me," she said. "This... craving; it's intense." She pulled Sadie's hand from her face, breaking the skin contact. "But that's not the only reason I'm happy you're here." Her eyes dropped to stare at the pillow between them and she reached to pick at a little hole in the sheet. "I need time to—" Hetia stopped, swallowed, and seemed unable to find or at least get out the words.

Sadie took her hand from the other side of the sheet. "I know," she said, squeezing her fingers.

"Though I do like this." Hetia kissed her. "Being with you," she breathed against her mouth. Then she laughed, and added, "How did Jimmy do it? Go without you for weeks? I think I'm going to go crazy when I leave."

"I guess you'll just have to come back," Sadie said, and a wave of sadness swept over her, thinking of how little time they had together.

Hetia swept one of her curls behind her ear. "I will, you know?" she said. "Come back. When this war is over, I'm coming back for you."

Sadie propped herself up and took her face in both hands. "Swear it," she said.

Hetia looked up at her, glowing and beautiful in the sunlight as she said, "I swear."

The knocker had clearly given up on them, since they were permitted another half hour before emerging of their own accord. They could hear voices coming from the kitchen and the upstairs appeared empty as they scrambled to the bathroom to take a shower.

Sadie wasn't sure if it was her own good mood coloring her interpretation or if Hetia was actually smiling more than she'd ever seen, but it appeared that for the moment at least, the woman was totally at ease. The hot water ran out almost instantly and yet they stayed under the cold, washing each other and exchanging kisses on shoulders, necks, and lips.

Her mother was passing by the bathroom door when they opened it, still wrapped in towels.

"Oh," her mom said, her hand coming to her chest.

"Excuse me." Hetia ducked her head and disappeared inside the guest room.

"Well," her mother said, watching the door close behind Hetia before turning back to Sadie. There was a little pause before she added, "Maybe we should have built you a bigger house." Sadie blushed, before ducking her head and heading for the end of the hall.

Her mom followed her to her bedroom and dumped a load of laundry on the bed. She began folding it into separate piles as Sadie disappeared into her old closet to put on the first fresh pair of her own clothes she'd worn in months.

"So how many of them are you dating, dear?" her mother asked with only slightly exaggerated casualness.

Sadie emerged in a good pair of blue jeans and fitted wool sweater, feeling like a whole new person. She sat on the bed to help with the laundry as she contemplated her answer. "It's... complicated."

Her mother laughed and it turned out to be contagious. Sadie hugged her knees to her chest as she giggled in precisely the same way her mother did.

"Whatever the nature of your relationships, I can see you care about all of them. I'm glad I got to meet the people who are important to you."

"Me too," Sadie said. "And I promise not to go so far from home again." She dropped her gaze. "Tell me, honestly. How have you been managing? I saw half the field hasn't been put to bed for winter."

Her mother heaved a big sigh. "Jimmy and your father have been out working on it since dawn this morning." She sat on the edge of the bed, looking tired. "I guess it's time to tell you about certain things. The truth is, it's been a struggle keeping a farm with just one child. I fear we put too much of a burden on you. Jimmy was always a blessing, but with both of you gone, well, the Wilsons asked to buy half the property to expand their farm. We're considering accepting."

"But--" Sadie blinked. "Without the space for the crops and the cows, how will we make enough to keep this place running?" Sadie said, in a panic.

"We won't, dear. But the sale will support us for years, until we're ready to sell and move into town."

Sadie slumped back against the headboard. She'd always imagined growing old here. She hadn't considered her departure would mean her parents would have to sell it. "That's not going to happen. Now that we're back, we'll get things back on track. I promise."

Her mom opened her mouth to respond, but had to pause to wipe away a tear. "I'm just glad you're back. Though I never wanted to keep you somewhere that would be unsafe for you. But it seems the whole world is unsafe now." Her mother put the empty basket on her hip. "Though if you helped too much dear, people would suspect you'd returned. The most important thing now is to keep you safe. The rest is out of our hands."

Sadie's shoulders slumped as she realized her mother was right.

"Though Patricia had a wonderful idea this morning. Clever one, that girl. She went to town to do the shopping and she's putting about the word that we've taken her in as some help. She's staying in the guest house, of course, which will explain the smoke coming from the chimney every night, but she's also helping us get the farm back in order."

"That's brilliant." Sadie sat up. "You see, so long as we're together, we'll work it out." Her mom gave her a somber smile before leading the way downstairs.

Troy was exiting the kitchen right as they appeared. He was swinging on a heavy jacket and her mother put a hand on her hip as she looked at him. "Where do you think you're going then?"

"I was going to help Jimmy plow."

"So you're entirely healed? All the stitches are out and the bruising's gone? Let me see." Her mother flicked her wrist at him.

Troy pulled up his shirt and she fingered the skin of the wound. He didn't even wince and all that was left was a thin scar. Sadie liked the sight of his exposed torso and she wished she could just drag him into the side house without ceremony. And she liked her mother worrying after him – it felt as if, without even blinking, he was now a part of the family.

"You're cleared," her mother said, her lips still pursed.

"Thanks, ma'am." Troy nodded. "And I promise to take it easy."

Patricia returned from town with all the ingredients they'd need to bake five hundred muffins, and the three of them spent the afternoon engaged in the monumental task. The chatter and laughter, combined with the smell of baking, created the kind of mood you could only get from being with loved ones in your own kitchen.

Hetia joined the men outside and Sadie and Patricia eventually brought them all lunch, forcing them to take a break to eat. Despite the crisp air, Troy and Jimmy both had their shirts off and were sweating in the late autumn sun as they worked the field. Sadie paused to enjoy the show before calling them over.

Hetia and her dad were rebuilding the fence around the chickens. Apparently, the local wolves had been having a little too much fun that season. Hetia, unfortunately, did not have her shirt off, but she did cast Sadie a wide smile as she accepted the sandwich.

Despite all the dangers in the world and uncertain future, it really was the most perfect day. The only thing which soured any of it was the feeling that she might lose something this precious. In fact, the happier she felt, the more her fear of the forces around them crept in to distract her. If only she could put a giant bubble around them and permanently keep out the rest of the world. Here, with these six people, she could die happy.

Troy went to start the fire in the side house right after dinner. "If he keeps this up, we'll forget how to do it ourselves," Sadie said with a laugh as she put away the last of the cleaned plates.

"It is a welcome save on the kindling," her mother replied, hanging up the little drying towel. "Ahh... the help today has been lovely." She smiled around at them. "Goodnight, dears."

Her parents departed as Jimmy whispered in her ear, "I'm going to squeeze into that shower while there's a bit of hot water." Sadie nodded, hugged Patricia, kissed Hetia, and went out the back door into the crisp air with a feeling of utter satisfaction.

The little house was as cold as ever when she joined Troy. He looked up at her from his crouch. "This won't take long, it's a much warmer night," he said, turning quickly back to the fire.

She knelt on the ground next to him, suddenly conscious of the fact they hadn't had the chance to really connect since before that horrible conversation in which she'd decided to tell him they weren't in the same place. She looked at the love lines between them now, and even in a few days hers had grown much closer to the clear pulsing black of his.

Sadie didn't think talking about it directly would help – she'd probably just muck the whole thing up again – but intimacy went a long way in communicating such things. She put a hand on his thigh, swallowing nervously. "Jimmy's in the shower."

Troy's breath hitched, but he kept his gaze fixed on his flaming hand. "I really don't think we should start something we can't finish," he said, but his voice was husky and he spoke as if forcing out the words. "And Jimmy won't be long. Your hot water tank is surprisingly small."

"No," Patricia said from the door, making Sadie jump. "We had a talk. Jimmy's staying in your room tonight." She bent to unbuckle her boots. "And we're staying here."

Sadie swallowed. "Wha— by *we*... do you mean—" she began, wondering if she was being kicked out or not.

"I mean the three of us," Patricia clarified.

Sadie didn't like this plan. Not getting to sleep with Jimmy and instead spending the night next to Troy without touching didn't seem like a good time at all to her. Troy stood up, the fire roaring at his side, and Sadie moved away from its powerful heat.

"Patricia, I don't think that's a good—" Troy began.

"I want to cuddle with you when you're not shifting uncomfortably all night. You've been pining for Sadie for days, and I'm not going to let you go another night wishing you could kick Jimmy out of her bed. So... I did it for you." She turned to Sadie. "If I'm out of line, and you want to leave, that's another story."

"No, I—" Sadie looked at Troy. "I want to stay, it's just, with the three of us..."

"I can stay in the other room awhile if you want privacy." Patricia took off her coat in the now-warm room. "Or," she dropped her gaze, seeming to lose some of her bold confidence, "I—" Patricia stopped, swallowed, and looked to Sadie as if for help.

Patricia had never been interested in sexual touch. It had been the first conversation they'd bonded over given that Sadie had been the same way before she'd turned. As she looked at her now, Sadie could still see none of that kind of desire on her. And yet, there was something else. Something new.

"She wants to watch," Sadie said as if in a trance. Patricia blushed, but didn't contradict her or look away from Sadie's gaze. Troy looked at the woman in the doorway, but she tilted her head as if taking extra care to avoid his eyes.

"If that's okay," Patricia whispered.

Sadie put a hand on Troy's arm to draw his attention back to her. They exchanged a long look. When it seemed they were in agreement, he glanced back at Patricia and nodded, his mouth still parted in surprise.

Patricia moved closer as Troy turned to Sadie. Her heart pounded at the heat in his eyes, and she caught a wave of excitement from him as he stepped into her. He hovered his mouth over hers, growing hard in the space between them as he drew out the moment. Sadie was less patient – closing the gap in a rush to claim his mouth. Her body pulsed as he groaned and pulled her in tighter.

All of their teasing and competition seemed a thing of the past. She wanted to make love with him, to make amends for her hasty words before and communicate something of how she really felt. She drew him onto his back by the fire, not breaking their embrace.

The rug under them was small and Patricia didn't try to join them on it. She sat several feet away as they undressed each other. Troy matched Sadie's mood as if it was what he'd always wanted. They moved slowly, pausing to kiss bare flesh as it appeared, and she held back the strong pull of his lust, forcing his pleasure to grow gradually.

When he flipped her to her back and made her climax with his mouth between her legs, Patricia stared at the fire. But when Sadie climbed on top of him a few minutes later and slid him inside her, the other woman moved closer. Patricia stretched out next to them, propped on one elbow and stared at Troy's face.

He tilted his head to look at her and Sadie stopped him with a hand on his cheek. She understood what Patricia wanted. "Just let her watch you," she said, rocking her body in a slow undulation over him. Troy caressed her hips as, very gradually, she let his pleasure build.

Sadie saw herself through his eyes, the feel of her around him as she rocked back and forth in the firelight. He cupped her breasts, and stroked her thighs, until the sensation in him grew to distraction.

Patricia rested her thumb on Troy's jaw as his expression began to contort. Sadie let the climax crash suddenly, enjoying the convulsion that accompanied his gasp. And as she almost always did these days, she drew out the moment. Patricia's mouth was parted in an O-shape as she watched him in fascination. Sadie ran her palms across his abdomen and let the sensation consume him completely.

"Fuck. God. Yes," Troy said between gasps.

For the other woman's enjoyment as much as her own, Sadie kept it going until he was bucking uncontrollably under her. She let the pleasure spread until every inch of him was sensitive to the smallest touch.

"He's in the middle of an orgasm and I'm holding back the ejaculation," Sadie explained. "See the flush here." She stroked her fingers over his neck as Troy closed his eyes. "That's how you can tell this is the most pleasurable part. His body's in peak arousal as he releases the built-up tension. Here, touch his nipples."

Patricia ran her nail over the hard nipple closest to her and Troy jerked.

"Everything's very sensitive," Sadie continued. She tickled her fingers across his abdomen. "See the tiny convulsions here?" She lifted his twitching fingers, displaying them for Patricia. "And here? That only happens during the climax."

Troy's eyes were still closed and he seemed to be holding his breath behind his clenched jaw. "Keep breathing, Troy," Sadie said. He broke into a shallow pant as his palms closed hard on her hips.

"Climaxes are normally just a few seconds," Sadie said. "But I've been learning how to draw them out." Patricia bit her lip as she stroked his nipple again. She smiled at the reaction before grinning up at her. "Jimmy and I have gone deep into this kind of play, but I've always held back a bit with Troy. But since I'm hoping he'll be in my life forever," Sadie added in a whisper, "I see no harm in giving him all I've got."

Troy opened his eyes and found hers. Though his face was still screwed up in an expression of agonized pleasure, his gaze was full of other raw emotions, love and desire. He seemed to understand her; she cared for him. She did. And she wanted him to know it.

Flames licked across his chest and they all three jumped in surprise. He stretched his left arm out and his hand landed in the fire a second before the flames doubled in size. And it was only then, when she began to worry they might burn the house down, that Sadie released him.

Patricia gasped as he finished, frozen in a look of agony as he clutched Sadie's hips. He shook with one final spasm, and relaxed under her, panting.

Sadie felt high off of all this feeding, and her body was alive like it had never been before. She could get used to this feeling. It felt absolutely right, as if coming home to herself.

"That was new," Sadie breathed, tracing the outline of where the flame had appeared on his chest, as Patricia snuggled her head onto his shoulder.

"I liked it," the other woman whispered.

Troy kissed the top of Patricia's head, still panting. "Me too," he said, his eyes locking with Sadie's.

She let his racing heart calm before she asked, "Want to see it again?"

Patricia looked up at her. "You can do that?"

"If you want," Sadie said.

Patricia pulled back and again propped herself up on one elbow, looking this time like a woman waiting to rewatch a movie she already knew she liked. Sadie looked at Troy and he shook with a husky half laugh. "If it makes Patricia happy, I guess we could do that again."

His attempted joking tone was undermined by the tremble that passed over him as he hungrily took Sadie's waist in his hands. He pulled her into a kiss and then tried for another quip as he said, "Just don't hold back this time."

She kissed him slow and long, savoring the love in his eyes and finding herself returning the expression. "Don't burn down the house then." She smiled, and sat back up to give Patricia another show.

When they climbed into bed, it was with Troy in the middle and Sadie fully clothed. Through her gloves, she held Patricia's hand, their fingers entwined as they rested on Troy's chest. It was the best night's sleep she'd had in months, and when she awoke, it was with the feeling that just about anything was possible.

Chapter 21

Things Found in the River

The next day, Sadie spent the morning in bed with Hetia, trying to get all she could out of their time together. They ate breakfast alone, talking more freely than they ever had before, and after she'd thoroughly worn the woman out, Sadie let her drift back to sleep, kissing her one last time on the forehead and sneaking out.

In the afternoon, Sadie and Jimmy insisted on going down to the river. No one ever came to their favorite spot anyway, she assured her mother, but all the same they took precaution to scout out the area before they approached.

They made love, keeping as much clothing on as possible, and then sat on their familiar bank, looking out at the smooth, slow flowing water.

Jimmy was the first to break the silence. "It feels unreal. The war, everything that's happened. It's all so far away. Now that we're home together, like this." He squeezed her hand. "It's everything I've ever wanted. And it's hard to feel anything but happiness. And guilt."

"I know what you mean." She rested her head in the groove of his shoulder.

"But I don't see how it can last," he said.

She sat upright. "What do you mean?"

"Well, we can't just hide forever. Never going to town, never seeing anyone."

Sadie thought that sounded like heaven actually, but she just said, "What choice do I have? Who knows if Siphon will ever stop looking for me."

Jimmy rubbed her arm. "I know." He cleared his throat and his muscles stiffened under her. "We'll just have to survive as best we can. Who knows how long this war will last."

They sat for several more minutes, silently contemplating that question, and then rose to do the task they'd come there for. They buried the succubus box containing the diary and mystery button next to the river and held the funeral for the ocean nymph that had died there. Sadie cried as she said, "We got it to Andre Amadi. You succeeded. And it helped. It helped so much, Ocean." They didn't even know her name, and so called her by the one Jimmy had made up. A tear fell from Jimmy's eye as he said, "Be in peace," and began to cover the box.

It was amazing to think it was only five months ago that Ocean had died in his arms, right here.

So much had changed.

They wandered home in silent contemplation, and found Hetia emerging from the house as they approached. She was dressed in her heaviest jacket. "Wha— Did you get through to him?" Sadie asked, knowing Hetia was to call Amadi for directions today. Her heart pounded as she noticed Hetia was sporting a packed bag.

"Yes," Patricia said, appearing next to her with Troy on her heels.

"I need to go," Hetia said.

"Yes, but not to Amadi, please Hetia—" Patricia said.

"I've made up my mind." Hetia's face was somber as she adjusted her pack.

"What's going on?" Sadie asked, looking frantically between the two women.

"Amadi's dug up the bomb and snuck it out of the city," Patricia said. "The army is vulnerable if Siphon discovers that both him and

Hetia are gone. He's asking Hetia to return to the troops immediately."

"He has a plan. One that might actually affect the progression of this war more than just a single battle or two," Hetia said.

Patricia made a sound of frustration and then turned to Sadie to explain. "Amadi has a spy deep inside who got word of a secret convention happening at the Siphon estate. Politicians and generals alike will gather to discuss the future of the new regime. They're going to sign a pact with the various army leaders that have sprung up around the country. Amadi's going to show up with the bomb."

"He plans to walk into the midst of his enemies to display it in an attempt to break up The Coalition. It will be both threat and evidence of how far Siphon was willing to go," Hetia said. "And it's a plan that just might work," she added proudly. "But it's also danger-ous," she directed at Patricia. "And I'm not going to let him do it alone."

Sadie flinched and stepped back. What was she saying?

"The two of us together are nearly unstoppable, the strongest storm and earthquake nymphs in the country," Hetia said. "And I'm going to make sure we make it out of there." She put her hands on Sadie's arms. "I promise."

"No." Sadie shook her head, her eyes welling up. "Don't do this, Hetia. It's dangerous traveling with a bomb. Who knows what could happen? And Amadi's right, the army needs you."

Hetia pried Sadie's hands from her shoulders and kissed them. "Don't worry. We'll drive the truck carefully. I'll be back within the week."

"Hetia," Troy stepped in, "she's right. Amadi wouldn't want this. If something happens to him, the movement will need you more than ever."

"My mind's made up, and he can't make me go to the army," Hetia said as if she were a child refusing to go to her room. "I'm going," she directed at Troy.

His shoulders slumped, and he held out a hand to shake hers before stepping back.

"This is wrong," Patricia said, shaking her head, but she too stepped back as if accepting what was happening.

"No." Sadie glared at the others before rounding on the woman adjusting her shoulder straps for a long journey. She grabbed Hetia's waist and pulled her close. "Don't do this. Please don't."

"Sadie," Hetia said in exasperation as she tried to untangle herself. They wrestled briefly with increasing struggle, until she suddenly found herself on her back. Hetia had tripped her with a hand cupping the back of her head to soften the impact. For the briefest instant Hetia's body was on top of her, warm and soft. She pressed her lips to Sadie's on a sigh, and then she was gone.

By the time Sadie could stumble back to her feet, the woman she loved was bounding away through the trees. "Hetia!" she called, before turning tear-soaked eyes of betrayal on the others.

"Sadie—" Troy said, reaching for her, but she stepped back. She didn't want to be comforted, she wanted him to chase after Hetia with all he had and hold her down. In the back of her mind, Sadie knew that wouldn't work, even if he could catch her, but she needed to direct her emotions somewhere. Troy and Patricia took the brunt of her feelings as they held her back until Hetia was out of sight.

It took her another ten minutes to come down from her initial panic, and then she climbed into bed and refused to speak for the rest of the day. Her mother brought her dinner and made her sit up to eat it, but she only got down a few bites. "I'm so sorry, sweetie." Her mother petted her hair, wearing the gloves she'd bought when Sadie had first turned. "But Hetia's a very competent woman. Maybe you just need to trust her. You'll see, this will all be over soon. She'll be back before you know it." Her mother still didn't know about the bomb, so Sadie just nodded numbly.

When Jimmy crawled in next to her an hour later, he didn't offer any false platitudes. He wrapped his arms tight around her and stayed there until morning. The immediacy of her fear and sadness softened with a night's sleep, and when Jimmy came to get her for lunch the next day, she decided she was ready to come downstairs.

She found only Patricia and Troy in the kitchen, and they looked over at her nervously.

"I'm sorry," Sadie said, wanting to apologize for her behavior yesterday, but Patricia waved the words away. Sadie sat down, staring at them with her shoulders slumped. Troy took her hand.

"We're here, if you want to talk about it," he said, while Jimmy rubbed her back. Sadie shook her head, not wanting her tears to return.

"Where's Mom and Dad?" she asked instead.

Patricia blinked at the sudden change in topic, and turned back to stir the potatoes as she said, "They're at the town meeting, deciding where they stand." Sadie looked at Patricia's hands as she cracked the knuckles anxiously, while Troy looked from Patricia to Sadie and added, "She's worried they'll decide to cause trouble and then we won't be able to hide here."

"Apparently your town is pretty against this new regime, maybe even to the point of being foolish in how they respond. Ow." Patricia pulled her burnt thumb away from the hot pan and stuck it into her mouth.

No one spoke after that, and they ate in utter silence, each one of them staring at their own plate as if in a trance. When her parents returned partway through, Patricia was the first to jump up. She rushed to help Sadie's father out of his coat as she prodded her mother, "What was the verdict?"

"Ridiculous," her mother said. "Every small town within a hundred miles has voted to comply."

"We didn't vote to—" Sadie jumped in, but her mother held up a hand.

"We did, but only to buy us time. We're sending out word to neighboring towns to see about a coordinated resistance."

"But that's so dangerous," Sadie said, the words coming out like a squeal. "All it would take is one of them reporting the attempt to The Coalition and we'd all be in trouble."

"I wouldn't worry about that – no one has love for the new government around here," her mother said, but her expression said she was far from convinced of her own words. Pushing on none-theless, she added, "I'm more afraid what will happen if they agree. What exactly are we going to do against these... these—" She seemed unable to locate the right words in her vocabulary. "Armed aggressors? This troublemaking will come to no good."

Sadie chewed her lip, in total agreement with her mother. Troy and Jimmy exchanged a look, and they averted their gazes when Sadie caught them. "What?" she asked, perhaps a bit aggressively.

Troy shrugged, "There are currently three Coalition armies: the Tucker Stone-led one in the East, the one growing in size coming up from the South and the one with Siphon nearby. But we only have two armies, and our support isn't growing as fast. If a whole region of human-heavy towns come out against The Coalition... it might give people courage, and every little bit helps."

Sadie huffed. "How is watching a boot crush an ant going to encourage other bugs to cross the sidewalk?" she asked, looking around at her father and Patricia for support. They made identical motions of holding up their hands in surrendered agreement. She turned to Jimmy.

He cleared his throat. "Nothing's going to happen overnight. Siphon's army will be long gone by the time we get our act together, but it might be good to be prepared for what we'll do when government officials sweep through here to register our species." Sadie relaxed just slightly at this line of reasoning. She looked to see what her mom thought.

"Let's finish lunch before it gets even colder," her mother said, forcing them all to take their seats. "Well now, the last farmer's market is coming up, we should start harvesting that cabbage," she pressed on, and no one dared bring up the war for the rest of the meal.

Two days passed without another mention of anything outside their little farm. They stored and stacked the last of the fall crops, and prepared the field for another year. In the evening, Patricia and her mother made them all play cards, and occasionally in the midst of one of the games there would even be the smallest outbreak of laughter.

But Sadie couldn't escape the ever-present dread that hung in the air. It felt like the calm before the storm as she waited for a future she hoped would never arrive. It wasn't until the third morning that some of the immediate tension began to soften under the normalcy of daily ritual. She woke up in her old room, snuggled safe in Jimmy's arms, and smiled up at him. She'd wanted to spend a night in a familiar place, and it hadn't disappointed. Jimmy in her childhood bedroom was a special kind of comfort. And to top it all off, the smell of bacon wafted in under the door and she could hear the voices of her loved ones in the distance.

Patricia and Troy were laughing at something her mother was saying. Apparently, Sadie wasn't the only one feeling better. She and Jimmy spent five minutes having hurried sex and hopped in the shower, discussing the need to get back to repairing the fence around the chicken coop.

They were emerging in towels when Troy appeared at the top of the stairs with a finger to his lips. Sadie fell silent at the look of concern on his face. There was a loud knock on the front door, and her father called, "Just a minute."

Sadie and Jimmy joined Troy on the upper landing and strained to listen. "Mr. Hall. Good day to you."

"Good morning, Aasaf," her father replied, sounding perfectly normal.

"I'm here on official business I'm afraid. You've seen the paper?"

"Uhhh, no. We've had a bit of a busy morning getting ready for market and all."

"Ahhh. Well, let's start there. I'm terribly sorry to deliver this to you."

Sadie's heart pounded and Jimmy squeezed her hand briefly before realizing she was ungloved. She and Troy exchanged a look. What could be in the paper? Hetia? The bomb? But then why would Aasaf be delivering it to them special? It must be something personal, something about her.

"There's a town meeting tonight to discuss this, and everyone will expect you and Ms. Hall to be in attendance, you understand?"

Her father audibly cleared his throat. "Yes. I – We'll be there."

"Seven o'clock."

The door closed. Sadie wanted to run downstairs demanding the news, but her mother appeared at the foot with a hand held up to halt her. She was looking toward the kitchen, frozen like that until Patricia said from somewhere in the distance, "He's gone."

They gathered around her father in the living room. She'd never seen him look so sad. He leaned on his cane with shoulders slumped. He'd tucked the paper into his back pocket, and it was a testimony to how somber he was that her mother didn't move to snatch it. They just waited, frozen, for him to speak.

"The Coalition army has... *intercepted*," he said the word strangely, "one of the letters we sent to our neighbors. They know of our attempt to coordinate a resistance." Her mother put a hand over her heart. "The army will be passing by to our east tomorrow. They said they will be making a detour to have... uh, a word with us before they move on. But," his eyes found his daughter's, "they sent a private message to our city council." He pulled out the tiny note stapled to the newspaper and read, "They will consider giving us a pass if we can draw in Sadie Hall and turn her over."

Sadie took a step back as her mom looked at her in horror. She was frozen while her mother grabbed the paper and began to read it for herself. "They can't really expect us to come lend our support for finding and giving up our own daughter? Who do the council think they are?"

"They're demanding our cooperation, actually," her father said. "I don't think they expect we have any choice. We've seen what the army does to towns like ours. This isn't an idle threat."

"Don! This is our daughter. How can you—"

"I'm not saying we cooperate, just that no one is going to suspect we'll resist. Look, they haven't even sent Sheriff Bray to watch us. They're certain we'll be there."

Sadie's body slowly unfroze. "I should get dressed," she said, so quietly only Jimmy and Troy heard her. The men followed her upstairs and she disappeared into her closet to pick out something. It looked like a cold day. She should probably wear a few layers, maybe even some wool underwear under her jeans. Yes. That would be smart. Wool underwear, jeans and then a couple of sweaters. The thin black one with the thicker green one on top. That made the most sense.

She put the pile of clothes on her bed and dropped her towel to pull on underwear. Jimmy was already dressed. He only had the clothes they'd traveled with, since he'd decided not to inform his parents they were there just yet. After all, his three younger sisters might not be able to keep the secret at school the next day.

She pictured the school surrounded by armed soldiers.

It wasn't fair that she got to wear new, warm winter clothing, and Jimmy was left with mostly threadbare summer clothes just because he couldn't go one house over and gather up some more appropriate clothing. She pictured a faceless soldier shooting her father as he swore he didn't know anything about her whereabouts. This underwear was so soft. It really was a blessing to have fresh undies again.

Jimmy sat on the bed, staring off into the distance with his lips parted, while Troy leaned against the window, watching her dress. She was still naked and yet there was no immediate lust coming off him. How strange? That had never happened before. They really should get him new underwear too. He deserved it. Why hadn't they taken care of something so fundamental when they'd been home for days? Sadie couldn't fathom what they'd been thinking.

She pulled on the sweaters and went to stand next to him at the window. She stared at the cherry blossom tree just outside. It always bloomed so bright in the spring, but it was preparing for winter now. Its gnarly twig branches looked shrunken, like little arms curled in on themselves.

A knock came at the door. They didn't wait for a reply though, and her mother, Patricia, and then her father shuffled in. Her bedroom had never been so crowded. Even when she was little. It wasn't like she'd ever had big slumber parties, after all. She'd never been particularly loved by her peers, at least not enough of them to do something like that. She remembered when she'd briefly been friends with the wood nymph posse, but even that had been because Ina had liked her. Once puberty hit, though, she'd felt nothing but awkwardness around other people.

No, this town had never much liked her. And now they were going to hand her over to her enemy. It was a fitting end.

"Sweetie?" Her mom ducked her head in front of Sadie's vision. "There's not much time."

"Wha—" she went to say, but found her lips had gone a little numb.

"You have to leave. The sooner the better," her mother was saying, but Sadie shook her head uncomprehendingly.

"Leave?" she managed.

"Before tomorrow, you need to get far from here," her mother said.

"We can head back east. Stay with my dad," Troy suggested, rubbing her arm.

"Leave?" Sadie repeated.

"I'll start packing," Jimmy said from somewhere in the distance.

"The town. They're going to destroy it," Sadie slurred.

"We don't know what they'll do, but there's nothing you can do about it now," her mother said. Sadie shook her head and Patricia put a hand on her shoulder.

"Sadie, I'm so sorry, but the truth is Siphon is going to make a lesson of this place regardless. We know him. He's just trying to get you thrown into the bargain. But whether you stay or not will make no difference. It's over. We have to run again."

The truth of what Patricia was saying sunk in slowly, but it froze on the edge of her brain. "Run," Sadie mumbled.

"Run," her mother said, and there were tears streaking down her face now. Her father held out her gloves, tears appearing in his eyes, too. Sadie pulled them on and reached to dry her mother's cheeks.

"I'm sorry," Sadie said, but the words sounded bland and devoid of emotion. She did want to say some things though. "I'm sorry I got swept up in this. I didn't mean to bring trouble home."

"Oh, sweetie. This trouble was already coming. All we can do now is keep you safe."

Sadie didn't respond, just stared numbly at her mother's face. A minute passed and then they all separated to make preparations. Patricia decided a trip to town was going to be essential if they were really going into hiding when they left. Her father went next door to discreetly invite over Jimmy's parents. In the living room downstairs, Sadie heard Jimmy saying a permanent goodbye to his mother.

Her mom helped Troy pack up their bags with everything they might need. All the while, Sadie stayed curled in the window, looking out at the cherry blossom.

She needed to see the river.

Escaping the tearful sounds of goodbyes wafting up the stairs, she hopped out the window and scaled down the tree in her usual way. The cold air was sharp when the wind gusted in her face. Her hair whipped around her as she walked directly into it, as if defiantly denying its order to turn around. She needed to get to the river. She needed to see its smooth surface.

Sadie traced the familiar path through the woods, her body carrying her on autopilot. An owl cooed above her and she stopped to lock eyes with it. She almost never saw owls during the day. That was all wrong. She scowled at its behavior before stomping past.

She'd run this path a million times. Images of her and Jimmy playing pirates and sirens or farmers and wolves appeared before her eyes everywhere she looked. She reached the river and, without hesitating, grabbed the rope and swung free of the land. She let go at its farthest peak and let herself fall backward into the freezing water.

They used to do this once a year. Come here and dive into their favorite spot in the coldest part of winter. Sometimes it was even snowing. Her hair swirled above her, obscuring some of the light from the surface, as she relaxed into the river's depths.

She held there for one long second as flashes of her life passed rapidly through her mind. Then the instinct to escape the cold gripped her, and she kicked for the surface. She gasped as she emerged, sucking in air that felt almost warm in comparison to the water. Sadie flopped up to the shore and turned to stare out at the once again smooth surface. It was as if nothing had even happened.

She was beyond shivering when his footsteps finally appeared behind her. Sadie watched as Jimmy, too, swung out and disappeared into the water. He pulled up only a second later, gasping and darted for shore. He'd brought towels, which he swung over their shoulders as he took the seat next to her.

Jimmy put his arm around her and tried to pull her head to his shoulder, but she didn't relax into him and he frowned at her. She was still as a rock.

"You once told me that I'm too sure that everyone doesn't like me. You said it was as if I decide before they do." Sadie pulled the towel tighter. "I remembered why Ina and I stopped being friends." Jimmy shifted away a bit to face her.

"I'd forgotten. We used to be so close. But one day, I was having a birthday party, my tenth I think. Ina had invited Ilda, Marisa and Sarah, but not Cassie. I asked her why she'd invited the entire wood posse and not Cassie and she said because I had told her I didn't like Cassie since she never spoke to me when we were in class." Sadie's eyes glazed, as the words came out in one long speech.

"I said I didn't want her left out though and asked Ina to invite her. Only, Cassie'd already realized she hadn't been invited. She was so upset, that she convinced the others not to go to my party. She called me a mean little brat. Ina still came, but no one else did. And shortly after that, even Ina drifted away." Sadie laughed. "That was it. That was all that happened. And that was the start of it."

She turned to Jimmy, feeling freer than she had in years. "I have a plan," she said, and despite the chilly air, her body seemed warm and alive.

Chapter 22

A Gamble

The town hall, which most often served as an indoor market in winter, was crowded with just about everyone who lived within a twenty-mile radius, certainly everyone Sadie had ever known. She'd come in late, wearing a thick scarf that covered half her face and a wool hat that hid her hair. Still, she found a corner far from anyone who might recognize her, avoiding old teachers, her doctor, their mailman, everyone she'd gone to school with and their parents.

No one glanced at her as she squeezed in to stand against the wall.

"Order. Order!" The elderly man who she'd always known as the head judge for the pie competition banged a hammer like a gavel from his soap box at the front of the room. "We have a grave problem to deal with," he said in his scratchy, but well-projected voice. "Our town has been threatened by a... a... bully, and we must stand together if we're going to do the thing in all our best interest. Now, anyone who has a suggestion can raise their hand, and we will call you to the front to speak *one at a time.*" He said the last four words as deliberately as possible.

A woman who'd had hurried sex with someone who appeared to be her husband just before they'd come here was the first to be called on. She climbed up on the little box and smoothed her skirts. "I think the choice is clear. Only question is, how do we pull it off? The Halls' daughter is clearly in hiding with criminals, and she knows the army is nearby. Why would she choose to come here?" She held out her hands to clarify she was asking rhetorically. "*Because...* her mother is dying and has requested to see her one last time." She smiled proudly. Sadie couldn't blame her. The woman was also sleeping with their mailman. She had a lot to lose.

Many heads nodded around the room at this first suggestion.

Her kindergarten teacher got up next. "I agree there's only one thing to do here, as horrible as it is. I say we tell Congressman Siphon that we're putting an ad in all local papers with Ms. Hall's dying wish. Even if Sadie doesn't respond, it will show we've done all we can."

Several men spoke next, simply to give full support to this plan, then Cassie's father rose. A strong man, with broad shoulders and an air of authority, he had always intimidated Sadie. But seeing him now, she could observe the powerful love lines pulsing from him to his family and friends. He had many caring relationships, and it gave him a somewhat different feel to her.

"I don't think Sadie Hall is gullible enough to come running home because of an ad in the paper. Clearly Siphon could have posted such a thing himself. She's a grown woman who has managed to avoid being caught by the most dangerous man in the country. We should give her intellect some credit. But I highly doubt that her mother has gone all year without being in contact with her only daughter. Lillia, please," he paused to give a long look to her mother, and Sadie was surprised to find they shared a solid green line of friendship. "Take the stand," he told her. "It is all our lives at stake here, and Sadie has clearly gotten mixed up in something dangerous. You can save us in this. Tell us, what do you know?"

Her parents had agreed not to speak, since if Sadie was going to take this risk, they needed time to see where everyone was at. Her mother shook her head and dropped her chin, while her father rubbed a hand over her back.

"He's right. They could find her if they wanted to," a woman shouted out of turn. "Tell us where she is!"

"Order," the elderly man said again. He called on the next hand and Sadie's stomach dropped as Ina Birch, her closest childhood friend apart from Jimmy, made her way to the little box. She looked so small up there and she kept her eyes on the ground as she spoke.

"Louder!" someone shouted.

It appeared Ina now had her first girlfriend, a woman from the graduating class before theirs whose name Sadie had forgotten. She could see her pretty face clearly in Ina's recent memory of the woman on top of her. Sadie smiled at this news.

Ina raised her voice a bit, but it still quivered as she said, "I don't think Sadie would believe her mother would put her in danger by publicly calling her home. I think we should come up with a fake plan just to make the – the congressman happy. But we shouldn't try to actually bring her home. Because Sadie... isn't coming back here. And no parents should be forced to turn over their own daughter." Her voice gained confidence on the last line. Sadie was warmed that Ina was arguing this. It gave her hope.

"Of course her school friends and her parents are going to try to protect her," the next man said. "But this congressman is dangerous. Very, very dangerous. And, I'm sorry, but we just can't take any risks. No one wants anyone to get hurt here, but please, I beg you," he held both hands out to her parents, "I beg you all." He spread them wide to the crowd. "We must turn Sadie Hall in."

It was time, Sadie thought. She'd heard enough, and she wouldn't know until it was over if she was making the right choice. Sadie raised her hand and the elderly man gestured her forward. The town was afraid, but conflicted. No one had said anything vile. They simply wanted to protect themselves. All she could do now was trust them and hope her trust wasn't misplaced.

Her legs felt like led as she walked slowly forward. No one recognized her until she heard Ina gasp. Even then, the faces stayed mostly passive as she stepped up on the box and removed her hat and scarf. Several people sucked in air and others looked around confused.

She cleared her throat. "I agree. Congressman Siphon is very dangerous. And the only way to keep our home safe is to turn me in."

•　•　•

THE UPROAR of chatter that followed this was too much to be contained by the old man and his hammer. Sadie caught snippets of "Thank goodness!" and "Lord have mercy, we're saved!" as well as, "Poor child." It must have taken five whole minutes before they fell silent again. Sadie didn't step down and she kept one hand up like a student in a classroom.

"Yes, dear? You had more you wanted to say?" the elderly man asked when it had finally gone quiet.

"Yes." Sadie cleared her throat again and stood up as straight as she could. "That person was right, I have gotten caught up in something dangerous." She nodded her head at the woman sitting at the end of the front row. "I stole something invaluable from Siphon when I was escaping from his estate after he'd held me prisoner." She pictured Amadi's face. He would certainly disapprove of the information she was about to reveal, but Sadie had made up her mind. This was the only way.

"It was the plans for a bomb, one that he had secretly planted in Arlington years ago." Foreheads furrowed in confusion. "When I left home last summer, I wound up being recruited as a spy for The United. Succubi make good spies." She was relieved to hear herself say the word succubi with pride.

"I got to see firsthand just how dangerous that man is. They've been carefully planning this war for almost a century, him and his friends. He won't hesitate to destroy our little town. He would do it to set an example. He would do it whether you turn me over or not. Siphon would destroy the whole country in his quest for power."

She swept a strand of hair behind her ear and took a steadying breath. "People follow him because they don't know the truth. They don't know what he's really capable of. So... I think we should show them."

An hour later, after she'd finished explaining the entirety of the plan, and everyone... *every – single – person* was in support of it, a kind of peace settled over her. She thought of Hetia and Amadi traveling east with that quite literal ticking time bomb, taking their own desperate gamble to end this war. Well, she was going to do all she could to help them.

Sadie inwardly smiled as she remembered the three factions of the Coalition plan. The Siphons were in charge of military matters, the Griffiths handled rumors and spreading discord, and the Maddox family dealt mostly with politics. Now in their own grand counterattack, it felt as if they'd be dividing and conquering. Hetia and Amadi showing up with the bomb while she launched her own war, a war of information. Only what she'd be broadcasting wasn't rumor: it was nothing but the truth. A truth that she, herself, desperately wanted to know. What exactly were Siphon's intentions with that bomb?

The meeting ended with the elderly man, who had finally put away his hammer, reading out their carefully worded letter. "Dear Congressman Siphon. We know the whereabouts of Sadie Hall and Troy Hyun. We request you come and collect them yourself without the army or we will be forced to keep them in hiding. Though you should know we are but farmers who pose no threat to you, we will allow you five guards for your personal protection as we wish you to feel secure in your visit."

They nodded and clapped in approval. "*And*, and..." the man pressed on, "we've enclosed the following cake from our finest baker." He looked exasperatedly at the woman who had insisted on putting this at the end.

"There's no use being inhospitable at a time like this. Cake fixes most things," the woman replied with a defensive lift of her chin.

Sadie's eyes teared up as she looked around at them. *Well now... this might just work*, she let herself think for the first time. They hadn't torn her apart or refused her idea. All they had to do now was work together and trust that not a single person there would break and confess the truth in exchange for clemency. That was the weakest part of the plan. After all, it would take only one of them to ruin it.

Chapter 23

The Siphon Estate

Gabriel slipped out the back of the gathering. Everyone had arrived and they'd begun the long self-congratulatory speeches over brandy. Apparently, such things were necessary before the rich and powerful decided precisely how they planned to rule the world. He wouldn't know.

The Siphon estate had become like a second home to him ever since he'd been welcomed into the family's good graces when he'd arrived to help with their daughter's Becoming. But he wasn't raised in this world, and it still seemed entirely foreign to him.

"Gabriel?" He stopped at the sound of his name on her lips. Speak of the devil. She must have slipped out after him. Of course she'd be watching him in particular.

"Mia." He took her elbow and kissed her forehead, but she turned and found his lips. He couldn't help but kiss her back, staring in fear at the tiny love lines that had been growing between them. In some ways this development was perfect – it would raise his status in Siphon's eyes. But in other ways...

"Where are you going?" Mia asked. "This is the most important meeting that will happen in our lifetime. You can't miss it."

"Mia." He said her name again sweetly, hating that this might be the last time he touched her. "I need some air... to calm my thoughts."

"I could calm your thoughts on my knees if you want to come take some air on my balcony." Her smile was sexual, but with an underlying air of warmth, of *caring*.

Gabriel sighed. If only he could pause time to take her up on such a thing. He'd been trying to keep her at arm's length for months, but recently his resolve had morphed into pushing her away in the hallway and then falling into her bed any time he'd had a particularly lonely day. A very ill-advised choice on his part, and he regretted ever having taken things so far. More than anything, he regretted the feelings that had developed both ways.

"Not today. I really need to be alone," he said, trying to resist the urge to check his watch. Then without warning, he grabbed and kissed her. For a brief second, Gabriel let that familiar thrill pass through him and his mind went soft, and then he broke the contact in a rush.

"Go back inside, Mia."

He turned before she could argue and strolled away as quickly as he could while still appearing casual. Gabriel peered back around the corner in time to see blond hair disappearing through the door, and knew she'd stopped following him.

He hurried to the east end of the house and snuck out a side entrance so as not to be too conspicuous. There was no one in the garden. Now that the meeting had started, everyone present was inside the giant mansion.

Gabriel jumped as he exited the gardens and almost ran into the backside of a guard. The man looked at him with a furrowed brow, but before he could ask what he was doing outside at a time like this, Gabriel grabbed his face and pressed his mouth to his.

The man went limp in a second and he had to carefully lower him to the ground to avoid cracking open his skull. Gabriel skulked to the front of the house and made a little noise behind the rose bush until the nearest guards came to investigate. Within minutes he had them both on their backs, pants still bulging with their brief erections.

Anyone who came by here would know this was the work of a

succubus. He really didn't have long. The estate shrank at his back as he bolted for the front gate, no longer trying for subtlety. The truck was waiting, large and imposing. He'd never seen such a big vehicle.

Gabriel approached the wrought-iron gate which surrounded the enormous Siphon estate, and shook Amadi's hand through the bars. "Welcome, sir. May I show you inside?"

Chapter 24

A Dual Interrogation

The town didn't exactly have a jail, but there was a single room which locked from the outside next to the sheriff's house. They'd had to release drunk Tommy a day early to stick Sadie and Troy in there. It didn't seem fair to force poor Tom to stay in case things turned south, especially not because of a little gambling debt.

To set the stage for an interrogation, they dragged in two chairs and secured both Troy and Sadie with their hands behind their backs. One by one, the others trickled away, first the sheriff, then Sadie's parents, until it was just her, Troy, Patricia and Jimmy.

Jimmy bent to kiss her, deeply, slowly, as if savoring every second of it. "I know you can do this. I'll see you on the other side," he said, but she saw the hint of tears bloom in his eyes before he could turn away. Patricia squeezed her shoulder before cupping the back of Troy's neck. She bent to inhale the scent of his hair and kiss his forehead. They didn't look back as they left, and Sadie couldn't help but get the feeling it was because they were both trying to hide the fear in their eyes.

The door shut with a definitive click and they found themselves alone in the little jail cell. Sadie smiled over at Troy. "You ready to end a war?"

He laughed. "I guess if we've nothing better to do. Though I'm a little disappointed that I finally have you tied up again and I can't even touch you."

She shook her head. "Don't start that. The last thing I need is you distracting me when we have to get this thing just right."

"I'm pretty sure if my hands were free, we could get a lot of things just right." He grinned.

It was her turn to laugh. She could see the nerves behind his joking, but she appreciated the banter. It seemed to do wonders to calm her.

"Troy?" she said, growing serious. When he looked at her, his grin too was gone, and her voice choked a bit as she tried to say the next words. "I'm really glad I met you." He swallowed, his jaw clenching. "And if we make it through this, I hope you'll stay in my life – forever," she added.

He tried to turn his body toward her, but their movement was rather limited. "Sadie, I—"

"Wait. I need to tell you this, in case something happens," she said, her voice breathy as her heart pounded. "I think... that I might be falling in love with you."

He made a half-laugh, half-sob. "Bout damn time," he said, but his face broke into the most childlike smile she'd ever seen on him. It made her unshed tears break free and stream down her cheeks. Troy started to blink, putting his head back to prevent himself from doing the same, but it was no use, a single tear slid down his cheek. He shook his head on a growl, flinging it away. "Well, you couldn't have picked a better time to tell me this," he said, back to smiling.

"Actually, this is perfect." Sadie snorted. "Siphon's going to find us both crying. Ha. Remember our training? This is just what we needed." She shook her head, full-on laughing now.

"We do look pretty miserable," Troy said.

"Good. Siphon needs to believe he's won if he's going to tell us anything." Her face grew serious.

"You should tell me you love me after he gets here, just to retrigger it."

"*Might,*" she corrected, "be falling in love with you. Don't push your luck."

"Might. Yeah, sorry," he said. Then he sighed. "Well, Sadie. As you know... I'm lost in you. Have been for a while." He smiled sadly at her and she returned the expression, desperately hoping this plan was going to work so she could spend the rest of her life with that smile.

The latch slid across the door, and they turned to see bright daylight streaming in, illuminating a figure. Derek Siphon strolled in with exactly five guards. They positioned themselves at the door, holding automatic weapons at the ready.

Siphon was dressed in a long traveling cloak and boots that made him appear even taller as he stepped up to them. He had newly tanned skin and a neatly trimmed beard, appearing in the prime of life. His gaze looked from Sadie's teary face to Troy's before he walked around them and began stroking the ropes and cuffs which held them in place.

"Leave us," he said without turning, and the men at his back disappeared. The room went bleak again as the door shut.

"You finally consummated your relationship, I see. I'm glad you at least got to have some fun." He leaned over Troy with a hand on each arm rest, and the rickety chair creaked at the added weight. "Because only one of you is making it out of here." He stood back up and positioned himself evenly in front of them. "After all, I only need one of you alive to give me what I need."

"Siphon," Sadie said, frantically shaking her head. "You don't have to do this. We gave the papers to Amadi. It's out of our hands now. We can't do anything anymore."

"What have you already done? I know you were in Arlington," he said, his tone and body language far too calm.

Sadie hung her head. He began to pull off his gloves. "It will only take me a second to suck the life out of the fire nymph. And it would give me great pleasure to snuff out that flame. I find—" and here he gritted his teeth, "that it is of no more use to me." The look he cast Troy was venomous, and Sadie thought she detected a hint of sadness.

"Wait," Sadie said. The thought that Siphon might actually do such a thing before they could get what they needed made it easy for her to put on the right show. Was he really so cruel? Were they taking too big of a risk? With genuine panic, tears again began to stream down her face.

"Wait. Siphon, I—" She hung her head as he looked at her. Then once she had his full attention she said, "We know the bomb is in Arlington. We know you planted it there years ago, after the fire that destroyed the inner city. The fire you were responsible for." She spoke clearly, praying he wasn't going to respond with a denial. Thinking subtle flattery could go a long way, she added, "Though it's a mystery to me why you would do something so challenging and with so much foresight and then never use the weapon."

Siphon smiled. "Thank you for your honesty. And yes, it was challenging. It took me years of my life setting up this particular plan. And I'll never even get to take credit for it. Though—" he brushed invisible dust from his lapel, "I'm sure Amadi will try to tie me to it. But there is no connection between me and that bomb, I made sure of that. Even the man who designed the weapon refused to make more. I buried him along with anyone else who knew of what I had done. There exists no evidence. Besides, the notion that I would have hidden it over a decade ago is too absurd to be believed."

"So that's the reason? You organized the fire so that you could plant the bomb and you did it so long ago so that you couldn't be connected to it?"

He smiled. "No. The fire had its own purpose. The city wasn't anti-human before then. It was a bustling place full of feeders and humans. We needed to create a nymph hotspot. Someplace that could be a symbol. So that when this war began with a group of human vigilantes blowing the place up, the whole country would react in a frenzy." He laughed. "Not that we've had much problem with that. But this resistance force has been a nuisance. We would have been able to squash out its existence immediately if that bitch Leah hadn't stolen the box."

Sadie's lips parted as comprehension sunk in. "Leah, the ocean nymph?" she mumbled in shock.

Siphon raised an eyebrow. "Yes. That's what I thought. A little birdie told me the other day that you showed up in Amadi's life sporting a succubus box. I believe you were in possession of my property. Something you seem to have a knack for."

"The box had a button," Sadie mumbled, her eyes glazing as she looked off into space.

"Sadie," Troy warned.

"Yes. A switch. One capable of sending a remote signal from my estate all the way to the other side of the country."

"You were going to detonate the bomb when the war started," she said, registering his comment about 'human vigilantes.'

"Last summer, before my forces made themselves known to the world," he said and Sadie's blood went cold. She and Jimmy had been in Arlington last summer. They could have been caught in the blast. Siphon continued, grinning devilishly at whatever he saw in her expression. "It would have been a much more compelling story, don't you think, if humans had attacked the beacon of nymph pride and then I swept in to put down unrest. This unfortunate resistance we've been experiencing is the result of a very good plan being thwarted by a single ocean nymph."

He shook his head. "It was remarkable. She didn't even turn back when I threatened to kill her husband. She just watched him crumple and kept on running."

She had nothing left to lose, Sadie thought numbly. That's why she'd let herself die. She'd already given up everything to bring that box to Amadi. The only question was, why had she been set to meet him *here,* in Sadie's little town?

"And to think... you gave away such a powerful bargaining tool," Siphon said, looking down his nose at her now. "Who knows what Amadi plans with it? After all, the best way to determine what a button does... is to push it."

Sadie couldn't help it – she exchanged a look of relief with Troy, immensely grateful that she and Jimmy had buried the box over the ocean nymph's riverside grave. It was at their secret spot. Safe. She pictured the tiny red switch, sitting on its side in a succubus box two feet under.

When she looked back into his eyes, she found Siphon watching her with particular scrutiny. And then something he'd said earlier finally occurred to her. She shouldn't speak. They'd gotten the confession from him they needed. It was sitting safely on the tape recorder nestled down the front of her shirt. But the words came out of her as if in a trance.

"If you're not afraid of being tied to the bomb, why have you put in so much work to find us? You know we already gave the papers and the box over to Amadi."

Siphon smiled. He bent until his face was an inch from hers. "Thank you, Ms. Hall. This conversation has been most enlightening." His long coat hit her in the face as he turned and left. The door clicked shut and Sadie began to panic.

"He knows it's here," she whispered.

"Doesn't matter. We got what we needed," Troy said.

Sadie nodded. "You're right. We just need to get the tape somewhere safe and then tactfully make the demand that he leave if he doesn't want it out in the world."

"It's important we play this just right, though. If he thinks we're capable of releasing it anyway, then who knows what he'll do," Troy whispered.

"We wouldn't dare." Sadie gave him a feigned look of innocence as she let her shoulders slump. "He has an armed force knocking on our door and we're just a bunch of farmers. We wouldn't give up our only protection against him," she said, practicing conviction. "At least not until Amadi is back to offer us protection."

"God, his confession was perfect," Troy said. "I can't wait for it to blare on every news station across the country. Let's see what people think of *that*."

She smiled at Troy. Whatever happened now, they'd done what they'd set out to. Soon, everyone would hear Siphon's confession in his own words. Sadie dropped her smile at the sounds of approaching footsteps.

"Did you hide it someplace good?" Troy whispered, clearly referring to the box.

"The best," she assured him.

The door reopened and two of the armed guards appeared. They untied them and dragged them to the village green, where they found a large cage that Siphon must have brought in for the occasion. It stank of gasoline, and Sadie felt ever so slightly light-headed as they shoved her inside it. Half the adults in town were gathered around them with the guards patrolling the perimeter, looking entirely out of place against the unarmed townsfolk.

Sadie was glad there were no children present, but clearly Siphon intended to threaten and intimidate by rounding them up like this. She pressed her hand over the tiny black box between her breasts. They had leverage. She had to stay calm. Keep a level head. Play this right.

Siphon stood in the wide gap between their cage and the surrounding crowd as he said in his booming voice, "Ms. Hall has taken something very precious from me. And today, she's going to give it back."

"I already told you we gave the papers to Amadi," she said, stepping back to lean against the bars. She wished there was someone else near their cage. This had always been the trickiest part of the plan. How to get the recording from its hiding place into someone else's hands. She wished now that the faction that had argued they put the recorder somewhere in the cell had won. Though it had been hard to know for sure that Siphon wouldn't take them out of the jail before questioning them. Hiding it between her breasts had seemed like the best option at the time.

Sadie caught the eye of her second-grade teacher and Ina, pacing slowly through the crowd. She could see the many calculating eyes of the people around her as they collectively tried to figure out a way closer without making Siphon suspicious. Worst came to worst, they would make the threat of blackmail first in order to protect themselves and then figure out how to get the recording to safety later.

"I'm not referring to the papers. As I told you, that's irrelevant. I want the box. And after our little chat, I have come to believe that it is in fact... here." Siphon held his palms to the sky.

Sadie tried to look impassive. Perhaps this was a good thing. If she could distract him with this conversation a while, maybe she'd have a chance to pass off the recording before things got too ugly.

"What makes you think that? Why wouldn't Amadi have it?" She shook her head as if in confusion.

Siphon frowned. "That, I'm not sure of. But I've had some recent experience of what you look like when you're lying." He stepped forward and his gaze bore into her. "And I am certain you have the box, Sadie. I'm also certain you're going to tell me where it is."

He nodded to a guard who pulled something from his pocket. It was a little match box. He struck once and then blew it out. Sadie understood. She couldn't help it. She cast a look of fear at Troy.

"It will be an interesting experiment," Siphon said. "Seeing how long my prodigy can suck fire into himself in an attempt to save you. But I don't think you're cruel enough to put him through that."

Sadie froze, everything in her tightening in icy dread. She took her time in responding, desperately trying to think of another way to stall for time. But when Siphon raised his hand in another signal, she blurted out, "Wait."

He stilled, and again she took a deep breath, stalling. She caught the eye of the sheriff, who seemed to be trying to silence her with his gaze. It was a risk to speak now. She'd have to be convincing. No fooling around now. This had to be the performance of her life.

She thought of Hetia traveling with a bomb, and Troy, who could die trying to save her. She thought of Jimmy, so far from them, hidden away so Siphon couldn't use him as leverage. What if she never saw him again? She felt tears coming back to her eyes and she leaned into that emotion as she spoke desperately.

"I do have the box," she said. He was already certain of it and it would only hurt her cause to lie now. "I buried it someplace safe. Somewhere only I can find it." Siphon's gaze flicked briefly, almost imperceptibly, to the guard with the matches. A second later, he cast her a suspicious look. Fearing she was digging herself in deeper with the half-truth, she quickly amended. "Only me and one other person knows where it is."

Again, Siphon looked to the man and this time his whole

demeanor relaxed a fraction. She understood. The guard was clearly a hag and had just confirmed her story. Sadie could have leapt with joy. If Siphon had a hag with him, he would know that her blackmail was real, though she would still have to be careful with her words.

"Please," she shook her head. "Forget about the box. You can't really think of using it. Siphon. Sir. Please just leave it in the ground and move on."

He looked at her with amusement. "And why would I do that?"

Sadie grasped for something to say. "Because, I've already made up my mind. I'm prepared to lose everything to protect it. I know what it does. And I can't let it into anyone else's hands." Though she was uncertain if her words were true, she managed to speak them with confidence as she watched Ina move closer over Siphon's shoulder. Sadie just had to stall a little bit more while they figured this out. Just stall.

"Is that so?" Siphon arched a brow. He nodded his head at the guard without taking his eyes off her. Sadie pivoted toward the man in alarm as he lit the match.

Shit. Cold fear filled her, and not just for their lives, but also for the tape. How much heat could it withstand? This was their only bargaining tool. They were out of time. "And because," she said rapidly, "we have a deal for you."

Again, she caught the warning glare of the sheriff in the background. But what could she do? It was clearly time for the backup plan. As the guard took a step closer with the match, Sadie threw her remaining reservation to the wind. Her heart was pounding out of her chest as she stood up as tall as she could, her shoulders back and chin lifted. "In the jail just now, we recorded our conversation and hid away the tape."

Did that sound like they'd somehow pulled off hiding it after the conversation? Someplace safer than down her dress? She hoped so. Her old science teacher had assured them that there existed stronger recorders than this dinky thing and that it would in theory have been possible for them to record from the jail window if they'd been in possession of better-quality equipment. Hopefully, Siphon would think they'd done something more professional like that.

"We'll make sure the recording never makes it onto the news," she added. "If you leave here today, leaving us unharmed, and never come back."

She watched as slow realization passed over his features. He looked to his guard and back as a hint of panic appeared under his commanding gaze. She'd never seen him wear an expression remotely like it, and she did her best to tamp down any look of satisfaction. He was a proud man, and this deal would be best struck if she didn't anger him beyond what was necessary.

He had her in a cage, with the threat of fire over her head and an army just outside of town. He wasn't the weaker party here, just a man about to cut his losses and walk away. *That's all you have to do, Siphon*, she thought with all her will. *Please*. Just realize this is a truce and walk away.

She slumped her shoulders, trying to look as desperate and pathetic as she could, as his expression went from fear, to anger, to rage. A vein popped out in his forehead and he stocked up to the bars. Siphon, who was usually an attractive middle-aged man, looked increasingly like a beast as he bit out the words, "You dare to threaten me? With blackmail? And how do you all plan on delivering this tape when you will be dead by then?"

He gave a signal to the guard and stepped back. Sadie turned just in time to see a line of fire twenty feet away traveling rapidly their way. "Troy?" Sadie said in a panic as he jumped between her and the flame. There was clearly a line of gasoline from the guard to them, and the ground she stood on was soaked in the stuff.

The flame flared wide as it reached the cage and Troy fell to his knees, arms outstretched in a desperate attempt to keep it from filling the entire cage. Sadie pressed herself as far back as she could as the heat grew nearly unbearable. *Shit. Shit. Shit.*

"Congressman Siphon!" she heard Jimmy shout somewhere to her right. Oh no. What was he doing here? "There's no use. The tape is already on its way out of town." She watched in horror as Jimmy stepped out of the crowd with his hands out in a pacifying gesture. "If you kill them now, the tape will be on every TV and radio station by this time tomorrow. Now I don't know what was said in the jail, but I know you're a smart man and this action is being done out of anger." Jimmy moved closer. "I understand. No one likes being blackmailed, but I know you will regret this in the morning." He sounded so calm, but she could see the dread on his face.

"Troy?" Sadie panted as the fire continued to swell ever closer to her.

He was entirely too focused to respond and she didn't intend him to, but her fear was getting the better of her. To distract herself, she turned to watch Siphon as he stared at Jimmy. He slowly regained some of his calm, the red retracting from his face. Slowly, he lifted his chin. And then after another long stare at Jimmy he turned to her just as Troy began to master the fire.

Siphon's eyes narrowed on her as the flames sputtered out. Troy was panting on his knees. His clothes were half burned off and his whole body was shaking as he looked around to find Sadie's tearful face.

Another guard appeared with a tank of gasoline and stood nearby. "That won't be necessary," Siphon said, sounding quiet calm again, almost pleased. It made her blood turn cold. He swirled to face the surrounding crowd. "I accept your terms. I will leave and not come back so long as you never release the tape. This town is of no consequence, anyway. It means nothing to me." He turned back to her. "But I'm leaving with the box. Where... is... it?"

Sadie shook her head, "No, the box is part of the deal."

"No. It isn't. The deal is this. I give your town a pass. That's it. But I want my detonator." He shouted this last word and Sadie jumped.

What happened next seemed to pass in slow motion. And despite this, she seemed unable to move. Siphon pulled a pistol from under his traveling cloak and pointed it at Jimmy. Then without even a hint of hesitation, he fired.

Several people screamed at once as Jimmy dropped to his knees. Sadie stared in horror at the sight of him clutching his hands over his stomach as blood spilled out around his fingers. She put her hands to the bars as Siphon aimed again, this time at Jimmy's head.

"Wait!" she shouted, but Siphon seemed determined to make a point. He was going to shoot first and ask questions later. He was going to prove he wasn't afraid to use this leverage over her. He would kill Jimmy. Then he would threaten Troy afresh. "Siphon!" she called, even as she knew it was in vain.

"James," she croaked as Siphon cocked the gun.

Jimmy's gaze found hers and it was filled with regret. *I'm sorry*, he mouthed. Sadie couldn't comprehend the reality of what was happening, even as time seemed to slow as if for her to process it. But she could do nothing but watch, her mind frozen.

Then, out of nowhere, Cassie Ash appeared on her knees directly between Siphon and Jimmy. His trigger finger stalled and Sadie stared numbly, her mouth half-open, at the wooden succubus box in Cassie's lap.

Siphon froze in equal surprise. His mouth, too, dropped open as he stared down at the little wood nymph who Sadie had never particularly liked. The feeling was mutual between them, but Sadie could see that the woman felt very differently toward Jimmy. A solid line of red desire flowed from her to him, bound by a thin love line.

"What is *this*, my dear?" Siphon asked, relaxing visibly, and repocketing the pistol.

"I collected it for you. Last night, after I learned of their plans," Cassie said in a meek voice that sounded ridiculous on her.

"Is this a trick? How would you know where Sadie hid it? You two are not friends." Siphon clearly wasn't in his right mind, as to most people there was no way he could know such a thing, and yet he offered up this fact casually.

"They have a secret spot. Sadie, and... this man." Cassie nodded her head to Jimmy bleeding out on his knees behind her. "They were burying this there a few days ago. I saw them and went back for it." Cassie got to her feet and carried the box forward with her gaze still on the ground. Siphon took her chin in his gloved hand and lifted her face up to meet his.

"I'm not in agreement with my town," she said, more confidently now. "I never wanted to blackmail you. I believe in what you're doing.

Please don't destroy my home, sir. There are people here who support your cause."

Siphon smiled. "That there are." He was peering at Cassie with satisfaction and approval. "Well, since you are so loyal, perhaps you can assist me in opening this beautiful gift you've brought me." He ran a thumb over her lips and her eyes went wide. Then she blushed and looked down, clearly understanding this meant something sexual.

But she nodded. Siphon drew the young woman to him and lightly touched her lips with his. Sadie could see red lines of desire flare up momentarily as he kissed her, and Sadie's stomach churned at the sight of the horrible man touching anyone from her town.

Cassie blinked in confusion as he pulled back, while Siphon removed both gloves and placed his hands in the prints on the lid of the box still in Cassie's arms. It popped open and to Sadie's horror, he drew out the red switch. A part of her had been hoping it was some other box, that it was all a trick.

"Now," he turned back to Sadie. "Since you know exactly what this does, I'll ask again. Where is the recording? And I hope for that man's sake that he was lying when he said it's already gone. Because that wound could really use a doctor. I'd hate to be here all day." His voice had calmed considerably, and he returned to his authoritative posture.

Siphon had the box, she thought, numbly. Jimmy was bleeding. And the recorder was still stuck against her rather trapped and vulnerable body. How had their plan gone so horribly wrong?

She went cold as her eyes locked on Jimmy's. He gave his head the barest shake, telling her not to crack. But she had nothing else to lose. If she handed it over, there was still the chance he might spare them, and the tape would be destroyed when Siphon burned her, anyway. Siphon truly held all the cards.

Jimmy swayed in his kneeling position, and she watched a bead of sweat drip down his forehead. No. She still had everything to lose. Troy's life in this cage with her. Jimmy's at her feet. Hetia's now, in Siphon's hand. Her whole town and everyone she loved. This place that had raised her, made her who she was. She glared at Cassie, the woman who had betrayed them. The woman now standing only a few feet from the cage.

A few feet from the cage. Cassie... had slowly positioned herself closer to the bars.

Sadie's mind reeled on a new possibility, the idea hitting her like a brick to the face. Could it be... was Cassie coming to get the recorder? She casually inched closer and Sadie became sure of it. Cassie was standing among Siphon and his guards as if she belonged there, as if she was part of them now, and she was a mere foot away from the bars.

But why would Sadie give up her only leverage to the person that had just betrayed them? Cassie could just take it and leave, issue demands from some place of safety. Sadie let herself see the binding lines flowing from the woman and noticed that none of her family was here. They were probably hiding somewhere in the woods. Cassie could just join them.

But that recording was even more damning than Sadie could ever have imagined. It really could stop the war. And she couldn't throw away that chance. Cassie had done a terrible thing in giving up the box, and yet Sadie could see she had done it to save Jimmy, who she clearly cared for. She had been so brave, running out in front of the gun. Throwing herself at the feet of a madman like that. Yes. Sadie was going to do what she should always have done with the people around her. She was going to give this woman the benefit of the doubt.

Sadie didn't dare let her gaze stray to the wood nymph as she opened her mouth to speak. Not wanting to make any further demands that might set him off again, Sadie looked at Jimmy, tears still streaming down her face, and answered Siphon's question. "The sheriff put it in place. Ask him."

It was the truth and so the hag would read no lie from her. Siphon looked to him and back to her before relaxing back on his heels. And then he barked a laugh. "Oh, Sadie. Thank you," he said, turning to face Sheriff Bray as two of the guards began to search him.

Sadie caught Cassie's eye. The woman looked back at her with an unreadable expression. As quickly as she could, Sadie removed the recorder from her shirt and held it at her side against the bars. Cassie took one more casual step closer, her gaze fixed on the back of

Siphon's head. Their eyes connected briefly as Sadie released the tiny black box into the other woman's grip.

Cassie moved away from the bars as slowly as she'd approached them, and Sadie waited to see if she'd just made a terrible mistake. But Cassie kept moving away. When the nearest guard faced Siphon again, she'd stepped up right next to him, cleverly making herself seem somehow on their side.

She had always had a way of doing that; seeming like *she*, in particular, belonged in whatever space she was in. Right now, she was in the Siphon's guard group, and they didn't look twice at her. When Siphon looked back at Sadie in outrage, she saw Cassie in the distance as she took a few steps back from the guards at the perimeter and darted behind the nearest tree.

She'd done it. Left with the recorder. Sadie might have just made exactly the right choice. She almost could have laughed. Her hope was short-lived, however, when she realized just how bad things were looking right about now. But at least with the recorder safe, they finally did have some leverage, which gave her confidence.

The sheriff was shaking his head in refusal, saying decisively that he would tell them nothing. Siphon pulled back out his weapon, and she knew now that he wouldn't pause before using it. Realizing she truly had nothing to lose by trying, she decided to switch tactics.

"Siphon," Sadie bit out. "I know you're going to kill us. First the people I love and then me. But you want the whole truth," Cassie was running full pace down main street. Sadie could see her tiny form in the distance over Siphon's head. Sadie would just have to hope she was far enough away that she could play this card now. "The recorder was on me. The sheriff put it on me. And that's where it was up until five minutes ago." Sadie looked at the hag and the man gave some unde-tectable signal that caused Siphon to whip back to face her.

"And now? Where did it go five minutes ago?" he asked, the vein reappearing in his forehead.

In the distance, Sadie could see the tiny figure of Cassie breaking the window of the corner store. What the hell was she doing? But then she understood. The nymph was headed for the payphone. Who would she call? Did she know anyone else with a recorder who could get it down on the other end? It's not like the things were that common. In fact, this one was the only such device in town and it had previously belonged to the theater department of the high school.

"Well, let's see." Sadie tapped her chin, stalling as much as she dared. "I gave it to someone nearby, and then that person left."

Siphon frowned and looked around frantically. "The girl. Where is she?" he said to his guards. They spent only a second scanning in confusion before he barked, "Find her."

Siphon, clearly having lost interest in Sadie at this new development, ordered exactly one guard to stay behind as he himself joined in the search. She watched in surprise and relief as the dangerous congressman stormed off, his cloak whipping behind him. Did he really think of them as that helpless? Or was he all too aware that he had a killer army just outside of town? Either way, Sadie thought he was drastically underestimating people who had nothing left to lose.

No. She looked down at Jimmy, whose eyes had stayed fixated on her. He was underestimating people who still had everything to lose. There was a commotion as the armed guards and Siphon pushed their way through the crowd and ran off in different directions.

It took all of a minute after their departure for people to react.

Sadie saw Jimmy's dad punch the remaining guard with all he had and a minute later, the town doctor was at Jimmy's side. He had his usual bag with him and he wasted no time in administering emergency aid. Her mother appeared with the keys to the cage. "I've got you, baby. God you were so brave. It's okay. We're going to get you out now." She fumbled with the lock, her hands shaking, before the door swung free. Her mom pulled her into a hug, mumbling something about, "Put my daughter in a cage."

"You aren't supposed to be here. You have to leave before they come back," Sadie mumbled, her eyes locked on Jimmy over her mom's shoulder.

"Oh, sugarbug," she said, putting a gloved hand on the side of her face. "I think we should stick together now. After all, that man has nothing else he wants from you."

Sadie didn't press the point as she wiggled from her mother's grip and pushed through the gathering crowd to kneel at Jimmy's head. He was so pale. "I'm here," she whispered. He tried to say something, but the effort looked like a strain and she stopped him. She bent to kiss his forehead and felt the familiar spark, but he hardly reacted.

"Doctor?" she cried, wanting information.

"He's lost a lot of blood," was all he said.

Sadie wanted to cover her ears against the squishy sounds of his work, but she couldn't stand to miss a moment of what was happening. When Jimmy looked back up at her a minute later, his eyes looked glazed. She panicked. "Jimmy. James Baker, don't you dare leave me," she croaked. She rocked forward to press her lips to his, and then rocked back on her heels and looked again into his eyes. They were closed, and the doctor swore quietly under his breath.

Sadie remembered the day last summer, when they'd been trying to open the succubus box. Jimmy's words from nowhere appeared like a flash in her mind. "Don't pull, push." That was just what she wanted. She wanted to push life into him. She'd learned how to suck it out, she should be able to push it in. Gabriel's information scroll hadn't mentioned anything like that, but she'd long since learned that she couldn't trust that document.

She had to try. Still attempting to bite back her sobs, she bent again and did to Jimmy what she'd once done to the succubus box. As she pressed her lips to his, she felt it, the feeling of her own life force flowing outward in the tiniest trickle.

With the box, she'd always had to feed right beforehand. Apparently, pushing life into something wasn't as easy as sucking it out. Luckily, she'd been preparing for days for this, without even realizing it. These past few weeks, she had taken on three lovers who were as insatiable as she was, and the power of feeding off them had left her with such a constant high that she had stopped noticing it.

She pushed harder, and found she had plenty to give. It flowed from her in a steady stream, but one that didn't easily part from her body. With the skin contact she could feel his broken body, the hole in him, the slow pounding of his heart. She felt the beating increase as she pushed. It pulsed loudly in her consciousness, and she thought she could hear the whoosh of blood in his veins as it carried oxygen to his brain.

Time seemed to pass slowly as she held on, willing him to stay conscious. Jimmy's lips twitched against hers right as the doctor said, "I've stopped the bleeding, but without a transfusion he's going to be in trouble of brain damage. That's if he makes it through the next few minutes. I'm sorry."

Sadie ignored him. She pulled off her gloves and put her hands on either side of Jimmy's face, gazing at his upside-down features. "I can heal him." Her voice was soft but certain.

Troy crouched at her side. "Sadie," he whispered tenderly as he swept her hair behind her ear. "I think your contact might weaken him further. You have to let go."

"No. I can heal him," she repeated. Someone in the crowd sobbed quietly. They needed to stop crying. There was still hope. She needed to stop crying. Sadie collected herself, slowly focusing her thoughts the way she had during the memory dives, and kissed him again.

This time there was no mistaking her impact. Jimmy's heart skipped in surprise and she felt a strong pulse from the blood pumping through his veins. She had so much life pulsing through her. She just had to use it. When Jimmy's eyes briefly opened as she pulled back, Troy's next protest died in his throat.

"It's like the box," Sadie said, her voice almost steady now. "We can take life. But we can give it too."

Troy made a tiny gasping sound in her ear. Then everyone was quiet for several long minutes.

Sadie kept her hands on either side of Jimmy's face as she stared down at him, frozen in concentration. She didn't kiss him again. She didn't move. She had only one task, and she poured everything she had into it.

The contact felt nothing like feeding. Sadie understood now that when she fed from someone, it wasn't something she took from them – a transfer. It was something they built together. It grew out of desire. But this was something she was giving. It was life. The feeling was intimate and pleasurable in a non-sexual way. She felt *alive*. And she'd never been happier to be what she was.

It was hard to know how much time passed, but eventually his heart began to beat on its own and Sadie sat back on her heels. A murmur passed around her and, for the first time, she looked up.

The crowd around them was small, much smaller than she'd thought. The square was empty except for the people who couldn't leave her or Jimmy. As she looked around at them, teary-eyed, they shifted and Cassie reappeared. She plopped down next to Sadie, her gaze locked on Jimmy.

"What are you doing here?" Mr. Baker, Jimmy's father, asked. "You are supposed to be fleeing with the tape. It's our only leverage."

"I'm sorry," Cassie said. "But it can no longer be used as leverage." A series of worried sounds passed around them. "It's being broadcast on radios across the country as we speak." She turned to Sadie. "You were right, that man is going to do what he's going to do to us. Let's just hope his army has some portable radios."

Sadie recalled a distant memory of music playing as she walked through Siphon's army on the East Coast. They did have radios. But even if the men were listening to them and got the news, would this army care? After all, they had split off from the nymphs when they'd moved west. The nymph-heavy army was somewhere back east.

Sadie looked back down at Jimmy. "It's out of our hands now," she said. "But I think you did the right thing." She cast Cassie a weak smile.

"You too," the woman replied.

Sadie turned her attention back to stare at the face still cupped between her hands. She wasn't letting go until she was sure he would be fine. Patricia sat down on Sadie's other side and rubbed her back as they waited for Jimmy to stabilize. An hour passed like that, while the people that remained sat vigil around them. Eventually, Cassie reached to check his stomach. "It's healed."

Sadie released a little hiccupping sob. She was exhausted with the effort, and tentatively relaxed before forcing herself to release her hold on Jimmy's face. He was going to be okay. The immediate threat had passed.

As Sadie's brain began to clear of dread, she pictured what might be happening beyond their little circle in the muddy grass. Jimmy's mother wasn't with them. She was likely still hiding with his younger sisters somewhere. Had Siphon and the guards given up searching the town? Was the army about to descend on them, making all her work to save one person count for nothing?

She looked down at Jimmy's sleeping form. No. Even one more hour with him was worth everything. And she'd stay right here, until the end.

Her head shot up at the movement in the distance, and everyone else turned to look as well. Siphon was returning. He strolled casually across the green. "I should have known you'd come back here," he said with a smile as he reached their gathering.

Cassie cast Sadie a fearful look. Sadie looked down at her clenched hand and saw the bulge in her pocket. Hetia's face flashed in her mind and Sadie's thoughts sharpened with intention. *Enough.* She hastily took back the recorder, snaking her hand into Cassie's pocket, and discreetly shoved it up her sleeve. *Here goes nothing.* She'd tried pleading and blackmail. Time for tactic three.

As Siphon walked up to the gathering with a little grin on his now-calm face, Sadie stepped within a few feet of him. His eyes twinkled at the look of rage she was sure coated her features.

"Look, Siphon. Jimmy is dying." Her recent fear added plenty of emotion to her words. "You've already taken him. I don't give a shit what else you do at this point. I know exactly where the recording is. And we've evaded you so far. Maybe it's time you take us seriously. Put down your weapon and we can talk about an exchange. The recorder for the button."

He froze, considering. None of his earlier rage returned at this. To drive her words home, she added, "You'll probably still win this war without that bomb. But you will definitely lose it if that tape gets out." Since the tape was out, Sadie very much hoped those words were true.

She stared at him with cold calm until he responded. "Alright, Ms. Hall." He pulled out the gun and set it a few feet away. "Bring me the recorder and you may have the detonator." Siphon fished out the device and held it out. "You've done well. I hadn't anticipated this town to be this much trouble." He smiled. Sadie looked at the device and then for one long breath, she stared at the gun on the ground.

Nothing to lose.

She pulled the tape from its hiding place and held it in front of her. This was hardly a smart choice, but stalling for time was all they had left. She resisted looking around to see if any of the armed guards had returned.

Very slowly, they each extended their arms to accept the other's offering. Siphon's eyes burned into hers, and she swallowed as she waited to see if he had some other weapon stashed. If he did, she was sure the people gathered behind her were ready to rush him. He was outnumbered here, and the second the detonator was in her hand, she would have a lot less to fear.

Her fingers closed on the base of the switch as his found the recorder. It was then that she noticed that the safety key had been lifted. Siphon was holding the now-armed button from the top, and with her grip on the base as leverage, he twisted. Sadie blinked, not comprehending what had just happened so quickly. So easily.

A wicked gleam appeared in his eyes as she froze in horror. "That's a little thank you for ruining my day."

"What have you done?" Sadie breathed.

He plied the recorder from her limp grip and looked south. "Hmm. I thought we might be able to see it from here."

Sadie was ice. Her limbs prickling with the shock. She didn't turn to look. "No," she whispered. "We won't be able to see it from here." She heard herself speak as if from far away.

Siphon smiled over at her, apparently thinking her words were irrelevant. And they were. After all, they couldn't undo what had just happened.

"We moved it," she said, mumbling more irrelevant words.

Only these ones were of more interest to him. "What do you mean *moved it*?"

"Amadi dug it up." Her lips were numb and the words slightly slurred. "Moved it."

Several emotions swept over his face in rapid succession. He seemed to settle on a tenuous belief that she might be telling the truth. He stepped forward so that he was looking down his nose at her.

"Moved it where?" The words were slow, deliberate, and filled with threat.

Sadie didn't answer. Her stomach was in a knot as she tried to hold off the emotion threatening to consume her. Hetia's rare smile – her piercing gray eyes – swam through her thoughts like a dream.

When Siphon spoke again it was in a shout, and the fear in his voice was a mirror of her own. "Moved it where?"

Chapter 25

In the Eye of the Hurricane

"Stay here," Amadi told Hetia. She narrowed her eyes and opened her mouth to protest, but he held up a hand. "The threat of you outside is greater. It will be less likely in their eyes that you'll bring down a building that you're inside. Though I know you're perfectly capable of such a thing." He put a hand to his daughter's cheek.

Gabriel stepped back to give them some privacy, but he looked around impatiently. The grounds outside the mansion were quiet now, though he didn't trust they would stay that way for much longer. After all, he'd only taken out the guards. If a servant happened to peer out the front windows and see the large truck now parked there, they would certainly have questions.

Amadi appeared at his side only a moment later though, and Gabriel glanced back at Hetia as the man added to her, "Oh. And maybe don't produce any earthquakes under the bomb."

Hetia gave a small quirk of a smile and leaned casually against the truck, while Amadi placed a hand on Gabriel's shoulder. "After you." They exchanged a quick look and a nod, before facing the front entrance of the historical Siphon family home.

Gabriel led the way inside. The front door clicked shut behind them, and Amadi stayed in the entrance as he continued down the hallway and into the ground floor ballroom. It was packed full of the Coalition leadership. The top human feeder generals and politicians were there. Unsurprisingly, few nymphs had been invited, though many of them were currently off actually fighting the war these people were waging.

Gabriel schooled his emotions as he entered the room, putting away the animosity in his thoughts. His gaze landed on Mia sitting on the upper landing, her long legs bare and crossed. She smiled down at him and he looked away. Remembering her now would only make this moment harder.

Amadi couldn't just stroll into this crowd. He would be killed on sight. He needed Gabriel to make the threat and set the scene. It meant blowing his cover, but ah well, he'd grown tired of this game anyway.

When Amadi had taken him from his lonely life and given him purpose for the first time, he'd thought everything was going to change for him. But years of working toward attracting Siphon's attention and then living under his thumb had been taxing. It was time to build a life for himself somewhere. Something real. Assuming he survived the next few minutes, that was.

The room was quietly listening to the proposal of President Maddox. The silver-haired woman was peering down her nose at the crowd around her as she said, "It may take years to establish this, but I think that with enough pressure we can ensure—"

Gabriel cleared his throat. "Pardon me, President," he said. His heart pounded as everyone turned to look at him.

"Excuse me?" Maddox said, looking thoroughly affronted at the interruption.

A man made to pull Gabriel back with a hand to his arm, but jerked the hand back when he realized he was a succubus. He had chosen not to wear a shirt under his leather vest for this, feeling safer with his skin exposed. Of course, his faded blue jeans and black leather vest left him seriously underdressed in comparison to the showing around him. Though he still noted the flashes of lust thrown his way as he stalked forward to claim the center of the room. God, he was looking forward to being away from these people. He was tired of sleeping with women and men he secretly loathed. Gabriel let himself feel the emotion now, seeing no need to hold back any longer.

He grinned. "I apologize for the interruption, but I have rather urgent news." Gabriel scanned the suddenly alert faces. "There is a bomb out front. One capable of leveling a city." He had to wait for the uproar of initial gasps to quiet before he could add. "And if anyone leaves this room or attacks the man coming in to negotiate, Hypatia Pierce, the powerful earthquake nymph, will level this whole building."

The looks of surprise were utterly satisfying. Gabriel had been around for many of the preparations for this meeting. Everyone here was a heavily vetted and trusted ally. Security was minimal because no one thought The United could have known about it. "Besides," Ms. Siphon had said to him last night, "they're thoroughly occupied on the battlefield. We have no need to fear them messing with us here." They'd been *so* confident.

Gabriel waited as the crowd sputtered and the generals threatened. He just stood there, his fingers casually tucked into his jean pockets, until they fell silent. When it seemed they'd all accepted the situation, he whistled.

A woman near the door screamed and jumped back as a middle-aged Black man wearing a welcoming smile and glasses taped to the sides of his face strolled past her. Though he might look like a quirky professor, Andre Amadi was their fiercest enemy, and the screamer wasn't the only one who recoiled at his sudden presence.

Gabriel couldn't help but grin at the sight of him gliding confidently into the room. The years of living such a lonely life felt completely justified just to get to witness this moment. Amadi came to stand at his side, and Gabriel shrunk back out of the limelight.

"I wish I could say I was sorry to interrupt, but it would be a lie." Amadi's voice was loud and strong as it filled the room. "In fact, I've never been happier to call a halt to a gathering. Well, except for perhaps my seventh birthday party when all the guests got diarrhea." He chuckled. Gabriel smiled. He was the only one.

The lines of light which flowed between him and Amadi were a thin mixture of green and blue. Gabriel avoided looking up at Mia. She could see the lines too and would know his recruitment by the man wasn't recent. He'd been a spy from the beginning, and everything he'd ever said to her had been a lie. Well… almost everything.

"You see," Amadi continued, "some of you are about to operate under false pretenses. And the others under false morals." The room was a sea of frowns at this declaration. "The bomb now cracking the asphalt outside wasn't made by me to threaten you. It was constructed at the direction of Derek Siphon. He placed it in Arlington with the intention of staging an attack against nymphs. When a fake group of humans took credit for the attack, the blame would fall at my feet, as intended."

"Lies," a man said, getting to his feet. "You can place your threats and demands, but you can't stand there and tell us this nonsense."

Gabriel was glad to see the man wore a general's uniform, decorated to indicate he was a nymph. At least that would be one person who would turn if he could be convinced of the truth. It had long been an open question, how many people would actually abandon the Coalition cause if they had different information? Today, that question would finally be answered.

Gabriel's gaze darted back up to Mia, but she was gone from her perch.

"What proof can you offer us of these claims against my husband?" a middle-aged blond woman said, still seated casually in a lounge chair and holding a martini glass.

"I can't offer any proof as it's all been destroyed, I'm sure. All I can offer is a very large bomb," Amadi said. He wore no trace of a smile now.

"You think to threaten us into believing you?" another general asked, also a nymph.

"No. I'm threatening you into taking a long enough pause to ask some pertinent questions. I'm sure there are people in the room that can vet for lies. How about we ask Ms. Siphon what she knows?" Amadi inclined his head to her as if politely passing the conversation to a dinner guest.

"Go ahead," Mia spat, appearing in all her glory on the ground floor. She sauntered forward, her hips rolling in their usual way, but her hands were clenched into fists at her side. "My mother would never be involved in bombing a city of innocent people and lying about it. How dare you? Go ahead. Let's question her." She looked to an old woman sitting by the fire, confirming Gabriel's long-held suspicion that she was a particularly powerful hag, the kind with the special ability to tell truth from lies.

If Ms. Siphon was displeased by this development, it barely showed, but as Gabriel continued to observe her carefully, he saw the smallest bead of sweat drip from her hairline. She knew something. By the claims in Vivianne Siphon's diary, Gabriel suspected she was the only person apart from Derek who knew everything. This might actually work.

"Mia. I allowed you to stay in this meeting on the condition you didn't speak," her mother said, getting to her feet then. "This man is trying to terrorize us. We will under no condition be cooperating with any of his ridiculous nonsense."

At this outright rejection of the proposal, the governor of Maryland frowned, cocking his head as he looked at her. "The man does have a bomb. If all he is demanding is an interrogation over an absurd claim, that hardly seems like an unmeetable request."

The man was a human feeder, and he had just called the claim absurd. Clearly, it wouldn't be just the nymphs that thought this action was too far. Committing such an act and blaming the large-scale violence on humans, did certainly undermine the moral high ground of The Coalition. Perhaps there was hope.

Gabriel's heart pounded as several more people jumped in to support the demand. Katherine Siphon, now visibly sweating, tried to look casual as she begrudgingly agreed. She walked slowly over to the old woman and sat down across from her. The whole room fell utterly silent.

The hag had strong green lines toward the Siphon family, and she clearly seemed confident that her questions weren't going to do harm. Asking bluntly and directly, the old woman prodded the powerful succubus as if playing along with a silly game. When it became clear Ms. Siphon was choosing her words carefully – scanning the exits as if looking for an escape – and the elder hag began to frown, Mia's face paled.

Gabriel barely noticed the interrogation. He had eyes only for the young blond woman as she went from looking angry, to afraid, to utterly distraught. Finally, tears appeared in her beautiful eyes. Gabriel could never have imagined her crying. She was always so cool and collected, like him. But as she realized what her parents had been up to, she turned and fled the hall.

He followed, casting one backward glance at Amadi for permission. The man nodded, and Gabriel stepped out of the hall in pursuit of the only woman he'd ever felt any love for. His guilt over his feelings faded as he leapt with joy at her strong reaction to this news. There was still hope for them. He hadn't let himself believe there would be, but as he ran full-on after the clinking sound of her heels, he saw the thick black love line grow strong. Gabriel caught up to her at the end of the hall.

"Mia."

"I don't want to talk to you," she said, slowing to a walk in her heels.

He stayed silent at her side as she led the way through several hall-ways and pulled open the nursery. It was dark and quiet in the little room as they crossed to the crib in the corner. Mia scooped up her son, and the little toddler began to cry over being woken. "Shh," she said, still half-sobbing herself. "It's okay. Mama's here."

Gabriel tried to help her pack a bag, but she still wouldn't look at him. Everything he touched, she jerked from his hand. It wasn't until she led the way out a side door and into the gardens that he spoke again. "Where will you go?"

She didn't answer. Though a moment later she suddenly handed him the babe and bent over to throw up. "Fuck," she said, as she stood back up. Her son cried louder, and she reached to take him back.

They stepped out of the hedges and Gabriel could see Hetia and the truck in the distance. Mia paused for a second to stare at it with an expression of shock, and then she turned her back on the house and left the only home she'd ever known.

They walked to the edge of the property, the house becoming

small at their backs. Gabriel looked back at the sounds of voices. There were people trickling out of the house. Some of the guests were leaving, splintering the feeder-nymph alliance. Amadi had won. Which meant... he had no more need of him.

Gabriel caught back up to walk next to Mia. "I'd like to come with you. If you'll let me."

She didn't speak until they'd reached the edge of the estate. They were just inside the large black gate when her shoulders slumped. Mia rested her forehead against the bars as her tears landed in her son's hair. She kissed his forehead.

A spike of envy went through Gabriel. He hadn't touched a child since his succubus skin had developed, despite the fact it was the only platonic touch he would ever be able to feel again. He longed for the intimacy of that kind of touch – something he'd never had much of even before his Becoming.

"I'd like that," Mia said, still not looking at him.

"Mia Siphon?" They turned at the throaty rasp of a voice. "Is everything alright?" It was the storm nymph in her father's employ. He was out patrolling the perimeter as expected. Gabriel wasn't quite sure if they could trust the man, but he had always had a kind face.

"Yes, thank you Alvin," Mia said, giving him a soft smile that was also a new expression on her. Alvin's gaze closed on something over their shoulder.

"Gabriel," Amadi called from behind him, and Alvin stepped back in confusion as he saw who it was. The man was strolling toward them with Hetia at his side. "If you three want a ride, I've arranged one back to town."

Gabriel smiled and went to shake his hand, but at the last minute switched to a hug. Amadi pulled him close. "Thank you, sir. It's been an honor," Gabriel said, and his gaze fixed on the tiny figure of the truck in the distance. He froze as his brain registered a flashing light coming from the back of the truck bed.

He released Amadi, frowning at the vehicle, and everyone turned to follow his gaze. The flashing suddenly doubled in speed, and there was only a second before Amadi reacted in a rush. Stepping forward, he extended his hands, and a sharp gust of wind swirled in front of them.

"No," Gabriel whispered in denial as he watched the storm nymph prepare to contain the blast. Hetia dropped to the ground next to her father and put a palm to the earth. A moment later the truck began to sink as if in quicksand, while the air moved in a loop around the mansion, bomb, and well-tended gardens, picking up leaves and furniture as it gained traction. The few people who were getting into their cars hit the gas in a hurry.

Amadi looked to Alvin. "It's a bomb," he said, his voice surprisingly calm under the circumstances. Gabriel had put an arm around Mia, but they were both rooted in place. Amadi held out a hand to the other storm nymph, the one that had long since been on the opposing side. Alvin's face was a heavy frown, but he looked to Mia and whatever he saw in her expression had an effect, because he stepped forward and clasped Amadi's palm.

It seemed to happen in slow motion. The terrain surrounding the mansion in the distance turned to a blur of destruction as the storm nymphs created a whirlpool in a circle around the soon-to-detonate bomb. Their windstorm became so devastating that it uprooted every tree and car in its path. Some of the departing guests got swept up in it, but the storm nymphs didn't hold back in accomplishing the vital task.

It was mere seconds after establishing the cyclone around the mansion, that the bomb went off – the sound of the blast hitting their ears as Mia and Gabriel pivoted into a crouch over the child in her arms; a foolish gesture of protection.

When Gabriel realized they were still alive, he craned his neck to look over his shoulder. The explosion had morphed in a mess of heat and light, which the storm nymphs had drawn upward. Hetia was still crouched with her hand to the ground, but the effects of her handywork weren't visible through the tornado the men had made as they redirected the blast. They sent the spiral of light to the heavens and it stretched up and out of sight as it morphed into a very symmetrical cylinder which resembled no tornado Gabriel had ever seen. It was an unnatural beast, terrible and beautiful all at once.

The blast spun into a giant pillar of destruction in the place in which the Siphon estate had stood for hundreds of years, and Gabriel and Mia got back to their feet to stare at it. As scraps of wind whipped around them, Mia fell to her knees, tears streaming down her face. Gabriel dropped to her side and wrapped his arm back around her, taking his eyes off the cylinder of light to look down at the woman who'd just lost her home. Her family.

Amadi and Alvin shouted with effort and Hetia was panting nearby, but Gabriel had eyes only for Mia Siphon, the daughter of his enemy. The woman he hadn't been able to stay away from these past months.

"Hang on!" Hetia shouted. Out of the corner of his eye, Gabriel saw the ground under the unnatural tornado began to shift, and a minute later the earth had swallowed what was left of the blast.

The woman in his arms was sobbing, and he tightened his grip around her. Everything she'd known was gone. Gabriel couldn't help but picture her pretty bedroom where they'd fucked – no, where they'd made love, the night before. It was all gone now. Everything… changed.

"I've got you. I'm right here," Gabriel said, stroking her soft hair.

As devastated as he felt for her suffering, Gabriel soothed her with half his mind on the future. Because this new life they were about to step into was full of possibility. And though her world was now finished, he secretly hoped they could find her a new one, and that he could be a part of it.

Gabriel turned to look up at Amadi, grand and beautiful in his triumph. The man had finally relaxed his posture, the storm dissipating around them, and he turned to smile down at Gabriel before facing his daughter.

"You're right," Amadi told Hetia, pulling off the broken glasses that he'd spent years taping to his face. "I should really get contacts."

Chapter 26

From the Ruins

Sadie slumped to her knees. After she'd become mostly catatonic, Siphon had given up on her in a huff. She barely registered his booming voice at her back as he addressed the remaining crowd. "I suggest you get the children out of town, because this place will be ash by morning," he said, and spat at their feet.

She tilted her head at the sound of a motor and saw a sleek black car pull up next to the green. Siphon repocketed the pistol and turned to stride toward his ride. Someone put a hand on her shoulder. They were saying something, but their voice sounded far away. She watched Siphon's coat billow behind him as he left her there, defeated and grieving.

She couldn't let him get away. A foreign rage built in her until she couldn't see anything but the steady plod of his boots as he trod across the muddy grass. Sadie launched herself to her feet, screeching as she lunged forward. She would put one of her bare hands on his face and suck the life from him. She would gouge out his eyes and tear out his hair.

Arms wrapped around her from behind before she'd taken even a few steps, but Siphon turned at her screech. He looked her up and down, smiled, and then turned his back on her once again.

Siphon's driver got out of the vehicle. The man was wearing a tuxedo and looked vaguely as if he was taking the congressman to one of his fancy fundraisers, not back to the battlefield. Sadie pictured him sipping brandy in a comfortable tent as he directed the troops from afar to destroy her town. She struggled against Troy's hold as he whispered soothing words in her ear. He had a hand over her mouth and was desperately trying to keep her from drawing more attention.

Which was the only reason that no scream of surprise came out of her when the driver pulled out a gun and shot Siphon in both knees. Siphon crumpled in a howl as the man pushed him over and removed the pistol from his pocket. A second later, two of the armed guards that had arrived with Siphon earlier got out of the back of the car and hauled him inside.

And then as if nothing unusual had just happened, the driver climbed back behind the wheel and drove away. Troy's grip went slack around her and they pivoted in stunned silence to watch the car leave.

Sadie was too shocked to register relief. Siphon was down, being carried back to a potentially fractured army. The war might have just ended, and her town might actually survive the night. They stood there frozen until the dust from the road had settled on their departure, and then someone shouted at them from the other side of the lawn.

It was Ina, standing in the doorway of the bar. It took Sadie's brain a long, slow minute to catch up to what had occurred in such a brief period of time. But as she watched Cassie, Troy, and Mr. Baker carefully lift Jimmy and carry him toward Ina, her feet followed as if of their own accord.

The bar on the edge of the town green was packed full of many of the people who'd been on the lawn earlier. They must have been huddling inside this past hour. Worried faces greeted them as they entered smelling of blood and mud. Sadie jostled into the crowd and plopped down in one corner, her gaze fixed on Jimmy's sleeping face.

"We knocked out another one of the guards," someone said in the distance. "We've been waiting for the others to return. Though it seemed two of them just switched sides."

"Michael Birch has a gun and is currently hunting down the fifth one," a woman said, Sadie recognized her voice, but couldn't place her. It didn't matter.

"All the houses were empty, the rest of town has fled for the woods," their mailman added. Empty, Sadie thought. Empty houses. Empty. Empty. Empty.

"But we're not ready to leave. The news has been blaring updates on every channel. Fighting has stopped in the confusion. So far no one in charge has been reachable."

"Probably debating if the tape is real."

The chatter blended together around her and Sadie leaned against Troy's shoulder as he pulled her into him. She was too stiff to relax, but she let herself be repositioned as she stared, wide-eyed, at the buttons on someone's skirt. Patricia sat down on her other side and began stroking her hair. It felt nice to be held by them. She should stay here a while.

Her mother put a hot cup in her hand, but she didn't drink, and eventually it went cold.

The television grew louder as the "breaking news" music blared. The bar fell silent and Sadie decided a nap sounded good. Now was the right time to sleep. She sunk lower until she lay across Troy's lap and closed her eyes.

"Terrible tragedy," an old man was saying. "The entire estate was gone in a flash. So many lives." Sadie wished she could close her ears too. She didn't want to hear it. A few people gasped around her as the newscaster described the explosion of the bomb.

"But in the midst of such a tragic event," the newscaster continued, not sounding like they thought the event tragic at all, "came a welcome story of hope, as two men from opposite sides of this war worked together to contain the blast. Tell me, how did you manage this incredible feat?"

"If we hadn't had a minute of warning it wouldn't have been possible," Amadi said. "But together we were able to divert the initial blast until it could be contained." Sadie's eyes shot open and the dim wooden floor swam in her vision. "The challenge was redirecting the initial pressure in a way which didn't cause it to build to something we couldn't hold," he continued. She pushed herself up from Troy's lap as Patricia gave out a tiny sob next to her. Sadie's eyes fixed on the little screen over the bar.

There were two men standing in front of what appeared to be an unnaturally round and very deep crater. The elder white guy she didn't know, but Amadi's smiling face filled half the screen. He looked strange without his glasses, but he also looked very much alive. The screen got nearer and Sadie realized she was walking toward it.

He finished his explanation of having contained the blast and the camera panned over to some governor as the newscaster asked, "And tell me about the events which occurred inside. You'd mentioned something about this war standing on false pretenses." But Sadie barely heard the question. The camera had caught a blur of a woman as it had panned away from Amadi's side.

Someone let out a loud sobbing sound, and as a hand began to rub her back, Sadie realized it was her.

"She's alive. They're alive," Patricia croaked.

"Who are they?" Mr. Baker asked.

Sadie didn't hear anything else, she cried herself through her happiness until strong hands led her to go lie down. Someone placed her on the large wooden table next to Jimmy, and after the initial sobbing was done racking her body, she rested her head on his arm.

Which was where she remained until several hours later when the announcement came of Siphon's arrest. The news panned from there to Tucker Stone, leader of the nymph army, declaring he planned to retaliate with all his force against any of the Coalition armies that didn't immediately disband. The newscaster declared the war over. The bar erupted in noise.

Jimmy woke with the sound, blinking open his sleepy brown eyes and fixing them on her. "What's happening?" he rasped.

"Nothing," she said. "You're safe, and—" She kissed his cheek. "Everything's going to be okay. Rest." And with that, Sadie sunk deeper into the curve of his shoulder and let her thoroughly exhausted body collapse into sleep.

~

SOMEONE WAS STROKING HER HAIR. Why was it so bright? Her eyelids were on fire. Like Siphon's cage. Sadie's eyes shot open in a panic, her heart racing, and she found Hetia's head resting on the pillow in front of her. They were in her old bedroom and light was streaming in through the thin white curtains.

"It's okay," Hetia whispered. "You're safe."

"Mwhy's my head hurt?" Sadie managed. She felt as if she could barely speak. She wanted to reach for Hetia and taste her lips. She wanted to be sure she was really here and okay, but she couldn't seem to move.

"You've been out for over a day. You haven't fed, and apparently you drained yourself saving Jimmy."

Hetia leaned in and kissed her. Sadie's senses were dull and the force of her hunger was slow to wake up. But as it did, she found herself tugging on the desire between them, and Hetia pulled back in surprise. "Sorry. I didn't mean to do that," Sadie said.

"I was worried about what harm a hungry succubus could cause. After all, you could suck the life right out of me. But Jimmy and Troy assured me that the harm is usually in the aftereffects." Hetia accompanied this with a wicked smile. "But I'm prepared to suffer those."

Sadie managed a half-smile in reply. "You're not at risk of a life suck," she whispered. "I've learned a lot in the past few days." She had at that. She'd learned she could give life just like she could take it. She'd also learned that people in general were good, and she should trust them more often.

Sadie managed to lift her hand enough to run a thumb over Hetia's lower lip. "Though I am very, very drained right now, and we might need to work hard to restore my energy." Hetia's mouth closed over the smile on Sadie's lips. "I mean, anything you can do to help..." she added when the woman pulled away enough to pull back the covers and scoot in closer.

"You can flirt with me later, succubus. Just shut up and kiss me."

Jimmy walked in and jumped back when he spotted them. "Sorry," he said, through the half-closed door.

"It's okay," Sadie croaked.

Hetia readjusted on the bed, clearing her throat in a not-to-subtle sound of frustration, but she said, "Come in, Jimmy." Patricia and Troy trailed in after and the three of them made themselves comfortable. Jimmy sat at Sadie's head and Troy put a hand on her foot, while Patricia climbed up on the bed and smiled down at her.

"It's really over?" Sadie asked, her voice cracking from more than just lack of use.

"Well, actually..." Hetia said, and they all looked at her. "We do still need to fix that fence. The wolves got another chicken last night."

"Yeah," Jimmy said. "And this was a light year at market for the Halls. We'll need to get the fields prepped if we're going to make up for it next year. And my parents are equally happy to have me back, so there'll be plenty of work to do."

"Plus, as soon as my dad can sell his house, he's promised to move to town," Troy said. "He's going to need help moving and setting up shop. He's a shoe cobbler. Apparently, there's not one in town. He might have his work cut out for him. Could probably use a hand."

If she'd had any more energy left for crying, she might have burst into tears. But instead, Sadie relaxed into the soft mattress and looked around at her family. For it seemed she was truly home now, and they weren't going anywhere.

Chapter 27

The Little Things

Six months later.

"Sadie? Do you have my eyeliner? I can't find it anywh—" Patricia stopped in the doorway and Sadie froze with guilt.

"I swear I put it back," she said, but Patricia's attention had shifted to the sleek red dress that Sadie had been trying on.

"No," her friend said. "That dress is my favorite and you can't wear it today. Or ever."

"But... it's so shiny," Sadie said, petting her waist.

Patricia rested her hands over her increasingly pregnant belly and sighed. "Look. I may not be able to *wear* most of my clothes right now, but that dress is off-limits."

"Not even if I promise to keep it clean?" Sadie whined.

"Your promises are nothing." Patricia waved a hand dismissively in the air. "First of all, you can't wear that dress with your dirty boots, which I know is precisely what you'll have on your feet since you never seem to wear anything else. Second of all, you *will* get it muddy, or you'll spill something on it. And I don't even want to know about the stain you left on my white dress. What was I thinking letting you leave in that? Off. Take it off."

Sadie carefully removed the soft fabric and put it on the hanger, making a show of treating it delicately just to prove she could.

"I found it," Troy said from the hallway. "It just fell behind the toilet. We really need to clean that bathroom." He stopped in the doorway and held out the mascara. He was dressed as nicely as Patricia, and Sadie paused to admire him. Troy seemed to appreciate her fully naked garb just as much, and they exchanged a good long stare.

But his attention never stayed too long on her these days. He looked to Patricia and his smile went from playful to loving. Sadie watched the blue light of family flowing between everyone in the room, including separate strands directed at the growing baby housed in the bulge under Patricia's dress. It pulsed strong and thick as Troy moved forward and wrapped his arms around Patricia's tummy.

Sadie pulled back on her threadbare blue summer dress and left to give them a moment alone in what was technically their bedroom now that Sadie had moved most of her stuff into the side house.

Continuing down the hall, she ran full force into Jimmy at the top of the stairs. "Sorry," he said. "I was just coming to get you."

"Is the ride here?" she asked, moving closer so they were almost pressed together.

"Not yet. Are they ready?" Jimmy seemed to be trying to resist putting his arms around her. With Amadi and Mae in the small house and everything going on, they hadn't had a moment alone together in days.

"Maybe. But we're not," she said, and cast him a wicked grin before pulling him backward into the bathroom.

They exited ten minutes later, red and sweaty, to find Hetia tapping her foot. "You couldn't do that in the woods like civilized people? Some of us need to pee." She pushed past them in a hurry while they exchanged guilty looks.

"Take this out to the truck, dear," her mother said, not stopping to look at her as she bustled by. Jimmy disappeared along with her mom as Sadie took the basket of baby shower gifts. There were twice as many as there had been that morning.

"Where's your mother?" her dad said, coming out of the bedroom a few seconds later.

"Just missed her." Sadie looked down at the basket. "Dad, did Mom go shopping again?"

"Let her be. This is her first grandkid. Just take the basket to the truck, please."

Sadie shrugged and then did as he asked. The truck was dragging a beautifully decorated open-air wagon, full of lush pillows and brilliant spring flowers that had only just bloomed. Amadi and Mae appeared first, then Hetia, followed by Sadie's parents. They mulled around the front entrance of the house until Patricia and Troy finally arrived.

They looked radiant framed in the doorway, and everyone paused to acknowledge them. Troy gave Patricia a hand up into the wagon, and only once she was seated was the spell broken enough for the rest of them to hop up.

Though it was still May, the sun was shining as if it were summer. Sadie leaned back and closed her eyes as they drove one farm over to pick up Jimmy's parents and sisters. At the tiny gasp from Patricia, though, Sadie and Troy both sat bolt upright. Hetia had moved just as fast and they were all looking at the woman for any sign of distress.

Patricia's mouth was open and her eyes watery as she stared at something in the distance. Sadie frowned and turned to check out the front of Jimmy's place. The crowd was a little bigger than she'd expected. There were nine people where she'd expected five. One of them had one leg and two canes. Patricia's grandmother and her pilot boyfriend had made it after all. And as they got closer, Sadie had no doubt that the other woman was also related to Patricia.

"Is that—" Troy got out.

"Mom," Patricia said.

"That's your mother? I thought you weren't speaking," Sadie gasped.

"We weren't," she breathed.

Sadie's mom leaned forward and put a hand on Patricia's knee. "Now that the war is over, your mother has forgiven your grandmother for getting you involved. I've been giving her updates about you. She says she wants to be around to see her grandkids grow up."

Patricia let out a half-sob, and Troy and Hetia jumped out in a hurry to help her down. Tears pricked Sadie's eyes as she watched

Patricia rush forward and hug her mother. After ten long minutes of introductions, they scooted over to make room for all the new guests.

The wagon led them straight to the river, and it seemed half the town had turned out for the celebration. Sadie had never heard of such a large baby shower, but after the long, dark winter it seemed no one wanted to waste an opportunity to socialize. Or maybe it was just that they hadn't been gathered together since the day Siphon had come to town. Whatever the reason, everyone seemed determined to erase that memory and replace it with a new one.

Sadie and Troy offered their arms and the two of them escorted Patricia to the riverside. Marisa Canopy was sitting between her twin and Cassie Ash in the place of honor. Their families had elaborately decorated the seating with interwoven spring flowers, and Sadie had to admit that wood nymphs really knew how to throw a party. Marisa waved Patricia over, excitedly making room on the loveseat.

The women were both about five months pregnant, and their bellies had popped in nearly the same week. It had led to some fast bonding between them and they took each other's hands as Patricia made herself comfortable. Sadie had released her friend's hand reluctantly and moved back to look at them.

"Marisa, this is my mother. She snuck in last night, apparently," Patricia said, beaming. Sadie moved around to stroke Patricia's hair and Troy followed her. After a long round of introductions, complete with laughter and tears, Patricia's mom politely and forcefully nudged Sadie out of the way and took her place at her daughter's back.

Sadie pouted, but stepped aside. When she saw the same expression on Troy's face, she shook herself. What was she doing? This wasn't about her. She smiled with genuine joy at the sight of Patricia's mom kissing her daughter's head and then stepped back to watch as Cassie assisted in weaving flowers through Patricia's braid. They stood out beautifully against her dark hair and Sadie paused to appreciate her radiance. Then she took Troy's hand to lead him away so the guests could get in with their gifts.

This was her baby too, after all. They'd agreed to that much. So as she saw it, if she didn't get to hover then neither did Troy. "Come on. We'll come back later."

They'd only managed a few steps when someone called her name. "Can I borrow you?" Mae asked. Troy squeezed her hand and dropped off while Sadie pulled up next to the concerned-looking succubus who had once changed the course of her life.

"How did you sleep? Was the house comfortable enough?" Sadie asked.

"Very comfortable," Mae sighed. "Not that we got much sleep. After all, that was the first time we'd seen each other since right after the war ended." A group of young men moved to hover nearby, all sporting red lines of interest directed at one or the other of them. Sadie and Mae exchanged an exasperated look and Mae nodded for them to continue walking. Sadie followed her to a more private space, getting increasingly nervous to see Mae agitated.

"I'll get to the point," Mae said unnecessarily as Sadie expected nothing less of her. "The ongoing work Dee and Hetia have been doing, well, it just isn't full-time work anymore. I know you've asked Hetia to spend more time at home and—" She adjusted the folds of her skirt. "I've asked Dee to move in with me."

"Oh. But that's great! You haven't lived together in years, right?"

"No. No, we haven't." Mae smoothed the wrinkle from her sweater. "And the problem is, my wife and kids are in Texas, and he's unsure how to tell Hetia that he won't be settling nearby. And that he's semi-retiring."

"I understand," Sadie said without hesitation, understanding her exasperation now. Hetia could be a lot when it came to things like this.

"Good. Because he's going to get her now," Mae nodded.

Sadie tracked her gaze to the two people at the buffet table. Even from here, Sadie could see the strong blue line of family connecting them. But Amadi wasn't the only one Hetia shared that color with anymore. Sadie had almost cried last week when she'd woken up one morning to find a thin blue line connecting her to Patricia's stomach. Hetia had been the last of all of them to show such a connection, but its appearance seemed to complete something inside Sadie.

"I've been thinking more about your idea to write an information scroll for new succubi," Mae said. "I've begun to jot down some notes." Sadie's gut leapt in excitement. She'd felt very passionate about this idea and had been hoping Mae would agree to help. "We can work on it more when you all come to visit. I have some friends we could even interview," Mae added, opening her arm to wrap around Amadi as he appeared at their side.

Hetia held up a plate of food and Sadie smiled at her as she accepted a slice of cheese. Sadie watched Mae and Amadi exchange a nervous look.

"I'm glad you're all here," Sadie said, clearing her throat nervously. "Amadi, I was... uh, really hoping Hetia could be here more when the baby comes. Any idea when things are going to relax?" Why did her voice sound robotic? Hetia didn't seem to notice as she looked up at her father figure.

"Yes, actually." Amadi squared his shoulders, standing up straighter in a way that looked unnaturally stiff. "The last holdouts have all but disbanded. I'll always keep my ear to the ground, but I was thinking it might be time to settle down a bit." Sadie could have laughed. For Amadi being the leader of a major underground network for decades and Sadie having played an essential role as a spy, their conversation could not have sounded more staged. How had they won the war again?

They wore identical expressions as they looked at Hetia with raised brows.

"Oh," the woman said, then turned to Mae. "I saved the last of the oysters." Hetia held out a second plate to her father's lover. The woman blinked back at her in surprise. "I know they're your favorite and they were going fast."

"Thank you," Mae said, accepting the plate.

"So how long will you two stay before going back to Texas?" Hetia asked. Sadie did laugh then, and then blushed when they all looked at her.

The older couple visibly relaxed. Then Mae began to tell Hetia all her plans and Amadi caught Sadie's eye. He seemed to have something to say, and they moved away from the two women, though the man's eyes glistened with tears as he looked back at them.

"I have something for you," he whispered, turning his attention on Sadie as if by force. "Mia Siphon survived the explosion. She's currently staying out of the limelight, but she asked me to deliver this. Or rather, Gabriel made the request."

Sadie took the letter with her name scribbled in elegant cursive across the front. "Gabriel?"

Amadi watched her as comprehension slowly dawned. "Gabriel and Mia were on our side?"

He shook his head. "Mia was not, though she's made substantial growth these past few months. But Gabriel has been my most trusted plant. We'd been working for years to get him into Siphon's inner circle. Everything we knew about the army movement came from him."

Sadie's mind raced as she processed this information. She hadn't realized how much she'd been carrying around a little hole of sadness that her succubus guide during her Becoming had been her enemy. "And he was the one who sent someone to me to feed from when I was captive in the estate," she said, comprehension dawning.

Amadi nodded. "And Gabriel told me he vetted you while you were spying and you did well under his questioning. He'd planned to assist you more, but decided you would be mostly fine on your own."

Sadie remembered the way Gabriel had questioned her after they'd slept together. She'd worried he'd been sent by Siphon to test her, but he'd actually been watching out for her all along. She smiled up at Amadi, relief settling over her at this welcome news.

Amadi patted her back as he added, "Gabriel was also the reason we were able to bring the bomb to that gathering. No one but Siphon's most trusted people knew about that event. I doubt Troy would even have been invited if you'd still been in Siphon's corner. Sorry I couldn't tell you about the man that had played an important role in your life, but it was essential no one knew but me. Though I must confess, our secret might have been what pulled you into all this."

Sadie raised her brows.

"Last summer I got a message from a nymph who had just stolen an important box from the Siphon attic. Jon was a housecleaner who had come across something valuable, only he wouldn't say what. I arranged for him to deliver it to Gabriel, who was to bring it to me. Since we didn't want anyone to see us meet, we planned the meeting to happen when he came to this coast to help a young succubus through her Becoming. The meeting would take place at a little river near the woman's house, in a town I had no reason to go to."

"What happened?" Sadie asked. She hadn't forgotten about the mystery of the ocean nymph, and as she listened, the woman's distraught face flashed in her mind.

"The man was killed, but not before he could pass off the burden of the box and delivery to his wife. Unfortunately, she came to deliver the box herself. We can't know for sure how she found out where Gabriel was going to meet me, but since his original train tickets were stolen from his room, we suspect the woman made use of them. Gabriel and I both had a map of the river near your place marking precisely where we'd meet. This, combined with the tickets, likely led her to draw her own conclusions.

"Tragically, she didn't know that Gabriel's trip west was booked for him to arrive several weeks before our meeting so he could assist in your Becoming."

Amadi sighed. "She had my full name, so clearly her husband had entrusted her to give it only to me. Perhaps Jon thought Gabriel had betrayed them, and that was how he'd gotten caught. But in the end, it just led to his wife's death in her desperate attempt to fulfill his dying mission. We never even had her name."

"Leah," Sadie said. "Siphon called her Leah."

"Well, I'm sorry the box landed in your lap. So many things would have worked out differently if Jon had just trusted Gabriel."

Sadie smiled, and looked around. "I think things worked out alright."

He patted her on the back.

"You'll come visit when the baby's born?"

"Wouldn't miss it," Amadi said.

Sadie hugged her father-in-law goodbye and wandered toward the nearest bonfire. Troy was shirtless and bent over, lighting the base, while people watched in excitement. The flames were roaring when he finally stepped back. Noticing her, Troy wrapped an arm around her waist as people moved in to enjoy the warmth.

They both turned as the south-end baker said, "I tell you. We're never going to hear an end to this hateful talk. Not 'till folk come together and stop spreading these rumors."

Sadie's fourth grade teacher sighed. She'd recently come out as a feeder. All these years, they'd had an excitement feeder in town and none of them had known it. "I think it's going to take more than that. People will always gossip."

Hetia appeared at Sadie's other side and she found another arm around her waist. A few people batted an eye in their direction, but the town had more or less gotten used to them.

"It's the segregation of the species," a man from across the fire chimed in. "If people knew each other better, none of this would have happened."

"It's true, there are too many human-only or nymph-only towns," a woman said. "And far too few feeders mixed in."

Sadie looked up to smile at Jimmy as he appeared directly across from her. His features glowed in the firelight and she took in the hard angles of his bearded face. The face she couldn't wait to spend the rest of her life with.

Sadie didn't agree that the problem was segregation of the species. After all, the feeder Coalition had worked hard to intentionally spread discord. But she figured if she was going to live in this town, maybe she should participate in the banter around her. "Did you hear about the town down south that's mostly fire nymphs and excitement feeders? I've heard they have an epic circus." Sadie's heart pounded as everyone looked at her, though it was only a single breath before the next person spoke.

"Yeah. I hear people are traveling from all over to see it," someone said.

"It's a new world," another added.

"Yeah. A new world," Sadie said, nodding along.

And she for one, couldn't wait to live in it.

~

You have finished The Carnal Fever Trilogy!

If you'd like to receive an exclusive bonus epilogue as well as updates regarding new releases, sign up for my newsletter at www.rileykade.com or scan the QR code.

If you enjoyed this book, please consider leaving me a review or rating. I truly appreciate it!

Acknowledgments

Thank you to all my beta readers for their feedback and for talking about my characters as if they're real. You helped bring them to life. Thank you to my editor, Julie Mianecki, my interior designer Joe Donley, and my cover designer E-book Launch for putting up with all my requests.

About the Author

Riley Kade is a fantasy romance writer from the pacific northwest. She loves writing high-tension story arcs with big payoffs.